SAM IN THE MORNING

Books by Sid Chaplin

SID CHAPLIN

SAM

IN THE

MORNING

Foreword by Alan Plater

SCORPION PUBLISHING LTD

PUBLISHER'S ACKNOWLEDGEMENTS

We are most grateful to the following for their assistance
in re-publishing Sid Chaplin's work:
Rene Chaplin, *The Guardian*, Bloodaxe Books Ltd and John Boothe.
Stan Barstow and Melvyn Bragg who gladly gave their time
and contributions.
Michael Chaplin for linking together all the missing pieces
throughout.
Finally, Alan Plater whose fine obituary of Sid Chaplin in
The Guardian indirectly initiated the re-publication and
subsequently helped us in many ways.

SAM IN THE MORNING
© Rene Chaplin 1989
Foreword © Alan Plater 1988

First published in 1965 by Eyre & Spottiswoode Ltd
This edition first published in 1989 by
SCORPION PUBLISHING LTD
Victoria House, Buckhurst Hill, Essex IG9 5ES

ISBN 0 905906 75 6

Editorial Director: Leonard Harrow
Publisher/Art Director: Colin Larkin
House Editor: John Orley
House Designer: Andrew Nash
Production and Editorial Assistants: Susan Pipe,
Doreen Channing and Kay Larkin
Typeset in Linotype Plantin Roman 10pt on 11.5
Covers printed by Allan Cramp and Co Ltd
Printed and bound in England by Biddles Ltd

FOREWORD

There are a few people in my life who represent more than father-figures. They are rocks you can strike any time and get living water, trees under whose mighty branches you can shelter – and the fruit and blossom are constantly there, elemental beings whose voice you can hear at any time. This is not an explanation but a statement – how it happens is a mystery – but once met they become part of your psyche. There is no need to call up their ghosts. They live on in you.

That is the opening paragraph of an essay about Jack Elliott of Birtly, written by Sid Chaplin – one North-East legend celebrating another. It is also a very astute, if unintentional, self-portrait. Sid was more than a father-figure to dozens of people, and especially to writers. We could strike him at any time and find living water. He was always there when a writer was battling with the words and in trouble.

An example. When Walter Greenwood died, the *New Statesman* asked me to write his obituary. It is the dual nature of such assignments that the invitation is an honour and the copy is required by tomorrow at the latest. It was the first time I had written a public obituary but I was game to take it in my professional stride. I knew *Love on the Dole* and the dark tales of its attempted suppression, had read the marvellous Greenwood autobiography and knew my way around the reference books; but pretty soon I was in trouble. I couldn't hear the essential heartbeat of the man. But I knew what to do. I telephoned Sid and we talked about the man and his work for maybe fifteen minutes. Then I wrote the words, not easily, but passing well.

The tale has a sad but proper sequel. When Sid died, *The Guardian* asked me to write his obituary. It was difficult because suddenly I was on my own and fatherless; but I stole a few words from the Jack Elliott paragraph and found shelter in the living language.

All writers feed off each other. The sad and lovely Jean Rhys described literature as a great lake, fed by huge rivers like Tolstoy and tiny trickles like herself but, she insisted, you must not even think of feeding the lake until you had drunk deeply of its water. We are all readers before we are writers – an idea I first met in a story by J. D. Salinger – and I have a theory that the best writers are also the best readers. Beyond that, we, all of us, in our apprentice years, discover authors who sing with a cadence that echoes some tune within ourselves. I moved into my twenties resolved to be some sort of writer, carrying the usual O and A level intellectual knapsack – Jane Austen, Thomas Hardy and the man from Stratford who terrifies us all – but with a nagging anxiety that all the modern books I read seemed to be about totally alien worlds, light years away from the Jarrow of my birth and childhood, the Hull of adolescence, the Tyneside of student days. The soul was ablaze with righteous literary zeal but looking at the business objectively it seemed clear that nobody could become a writer without a thorough working knowledge of Chelsea, Kensington, the Home Counties, the South Seas and quotations from the French. On that basis, I wouldn't even come under orders.

Sid came to the rescue, along with D. H. Lawrence, George Orwell, Robert Tressell, Jack Common and Gwyn Thomas – another writer whose richness has been too long forgotten. There were others and at this distance the chronology is blurred, but what I recall with total clarity is the recognition, at last, of a familiar universe. There were even characters who talked football and ate chips, and they walked the same streets that I walked. It was no instant Damascus Road transformation. The light shone in my eyes for some time before I grasped its true significance: a slower burn than Oliver Hardy's. And Sid's light shone more brightly than the others because he was writing about the North-East. He spoke to my formative condition and, ye bugs, I understood his accent.

Reviewers, literary trend-spotters and Guardians of the Higher Thought-Flow always have difficulty with writers like Sid. The term 'regional novelist' tumbles out, at best patronisingly, at worst as a perjorative. The critical sloppiness of this approach has many mansions. Shakespeare was a mere regional writer and London is, in itself, a region composed of small parishes, and none the worse for it. A London cabby once said to me: 'Cor – I hate London.' Asked where he lived he replied: 'Tottenham.'

Besides, nothing is more parochial, provincial and petty than the average university; yet campus novels have become a genre, bestriding the world as they line up to receive their glittering prizes. So it goes – to quote Kurt Vonnegut, a well-respected regional writer from Indianapolis.

The problem is simply stated, and has its roots in the class and caste system peculiar to the English intellectual climate. The critical consensus that informs us, on a daily, weekly and monthly basis, what we should be thinking, still prefers to deal with Metropolitan/Oxbridge subjects in a M/O manner, ideally by comparing the work on offer with other M/O artefacts. Confront these people with an unfamiliar reality – like Sid's great continuing theme of the imposed urbanisation of village dwellers by the dictates of the industrial revolution and its consequences – and they flounder and flap, reaching desperately for the claret and the standard paragraph marked Regional Novelist. To be sure, this is a prejudiced view, but I never believe anyone who lays claim to objectivity, and this is an appropriate time to temper justice with score-settling, in the sure and certain knowledge that Sid was too kindly to do it on his own behalf.

During the summer of 1988 I worked in Australia, enjoying their balmy winter and the company of good, vigorous writers battling to free themselves from the more corrosive brands of English and American imperialism. In Melbourne, I met a talented, laconic writer/performer called John Clarke who reported that when he was growing up in New Zealand during the 1960s, he was powerfully impressed by imported television plays and series: notably *The Wednesday Play* when it dealt with non-metropolitan themes, and by *Z Cars*. He identified in the Northern working class a people colonised, oppressed and disenfranchised, and found common cause therein. Travel, it says on the wrapper, broadens the mind. It is even more heartening when it strengthens the inherited passion and prejudice. The North, historically and culturally, has had a raw deal, and it will require more than wall-to-wall theme parks and fast-food joints to ease the pain.

Writers have been disenfranchised too. We should, as Gough Whitlam advised, maintain the rage.

Above all, we must fight for the dignity and integrity of the individual. Once upon a time in a radio interview, Sid said: 'When you walk through the streets of Birmingham at night, and see those huge glass canyons, glowing like dying television screens, it would be a gift from God to hear a baby cry.' If you put an arm-lock on and force me into a critic's posture, I would say the absolute core of Sid's writing is implicit in that quote: the battle for survival of the human spirit in our post-industrial urban society. It's a seam that runs through *The Day of the Sardine*, *The Watchers and the Watched* and *Sam in the Morning*.

That is my last word about the novel. Prefaces telling readers what to think and how to feel deserve to be skipped. Instead, let me quote Sid, writing about the great Northumbrian engraver, Thomas Bewick: 'Seeing straight, he can teach us to think straight as well. Here is art that is apt, and still needed.'

Here is a story-teller who sees straight and writes straight. Here is an artist, in an age that worships glass canyons, whose wisdom, scholarship and compassion are needed more than ever.

Alan Plater
November 1988

ONE

Walking under the canopy I charged with an elbow at the swinging doors. One hand was occupied with a briefcase, the other hand, arm and a lot of shoulder, with a heavy suitcase. The door snapped shut like a trap as I emerged at the other side, inside UK House, the world's greatest vested interest in any kind of filth you care to mention; catchers of the wealth in outfalls, salvagers of sewage, inheritors of rich lode in ashpits and WC's, by appointment or otherwise rag and bone men to the nation. It was late September 1970 and London was clean at last; the sky was a well of clear air with men glancing casually up from the bottom; and I was in search of the gold at the end of the drains.

The door snapped shut on my past. It trapped not me but my past. Shapeless overcoat, suit from the hook, cheap shirt, stained tie, down-at-heels shoes were all so much camouflage. The shapeless black overcoat was a cloak for a new man and a gleaming, razor-sharp mind. I knew my way; I had been there before; I knew it was made for me. So I walked confidently over a carpet which met my feet halfway. The shop to the left beamed at me with teeth of chocolate boxes and jars of expensive sweets; curtained enquiry office to the right winked decorously and murmured of anything but the human product which is basic to any bordello. I veered to miss a good round table about half the size of a cricket pitch and bearing a vase of late red roses where batsmen would say hello in passing. Two strolling commissionaires saw me and didn't see me; their snake-tongue eyes flickered and rejected in the space of a heartbeat. I was not Very Important People they mistakenly assumed from my very cheap clothes, and an ancient suitcase not even new when we had been introduced ten years before, prior to taking off on a school holiday together.

Let them ignore me. They had ignored me six weeks before when I arrived for interview, for the job I was now picking up as my right. The appointment wasn't until three, but I had arrived on the night train. I shared a sleeper with a middle-aged man who talked in his sleep, in another language, with a lisp.

All night long he mumbled in this language, a sort of Russian of the soul. In the morning he stumbled out without washing or shaving, precisely five minutes after the train had docked. He looked like a spy for our side. Two hours after I had been deserted I had a long wash to freshen up and a very quick shave just to hone the senses. Then I left the train and went to the most expensive hotel you will find within twenty miles of any major station and had a leisurely breakfast with *The Times* to keep me company; reading the city and industrial notes to see if there was anything about UK. All it said was that UK's were steady. I was steady too. That was six weeks ago, but on my first morning, as indeed now, I remembered everything that happened. I took a taxi to Charing Cross Road. I dismissed it at Zwemmers. I went inside and bought a very expensive facsimile copy of Blake's 'Marriage of Heaven and Hell'. I looked into every bookshop on the way down with the feeling that I would find the secret which would give meaning to my life. I didn't; forewarned is forearmed, and that's why I bought the Blake. It was in my pocket. I didn't understand it; I don't understand it now; but I'd a feeling that the secret was there; right on the first page, perhaps in the lines, perhaps in the picture of the young woman helping another young woman up into the tree. My boss at Percy Main, Mr Snorry, was a dedicated reader and when I returned with the trophy was delighted to see the form in which the poem had been first produced. 'Look,' he said. 'Look at that penultimate (nudging me), ah, ah, ah verse:

> *"Now the sneaking serpent walks*
> *In mild humility*
> *And the just man rages in the wilds*
> *Where lions roam."*

D'ye see it? Your position exactly.' Just like Snorry not to say which of the two I was.

To return to the day of the interview – I'd had a good breakfast, so instead of lunching I went into a place off St Martin's and ordered some good fresh sandwiches made of cream cheese with chives, a beer to keep up appearances, and a Gaelic coffee. After which I went to a barber's shop behind the Empire, Leicester Square, and had myself a treat: a real shop shave. The barber did me proud. I was amused at the man in the next seat; he had his nostrils and ears snipped free of hair while a girl was working on his finger-nails. I like a barber-shop shave that leaves your cheek and chin like a baby's bottom. I went out like a lion; I crossed the river on the Hungerford footbridge and worked my way downstream so as to see UK House leaping up like a bloody great rock crystal from the Embankment; I stared until I imagined I could see the relief of the dustman with his saint's halo of a miniature sewage ring all around him, instead of just around his head, and the legend: Waste Not, Want Not. Standing there I knew it was mine; I knew what the Lord Jesus Christ felt like when the devil took him up on to the pinnacle, only there wasn't a struggle to resist and decline. It was my destiny; I was proud of it; I couldn't wait to take.

I had a notebook full of answers to all the questions they were likely to ask me. I threw it into the crystal-clear Thames and watched it float uninterruptedly, excepting when a fish of some kind came up and flicked the open page with his nose.

You can either make an interview or you can't. They never ask the questions you are prepared to answer; on the other hand they may be tired of the correct answers. Give the first answer that comes into your mind; and don't care; that was Snorry's advice. Which I took, remembering not to care whether I won the job or not, which is the important thing to remember.

'Whatever you do, don't care,' said Mr Snorry. 'You know you'll pick, whatever happens. Not to care is the mark of the new aristocracy – which is you and me among others.'

He meant the educated Jonahs of the working classes. Both of us pretended that I was one.

So I didn't care, and I won; and so I returned to UK House with confidence as well as a job in my pocket. Would I have walked a little less confidently had I known how little a fish I was? I doubt it. Would I have walked in confidence had I known that life was about people? I think not. Even the knowledge that I was spied upon as I entered would not have disturbed me one little bit. I was a rock crystal like the building itself, but in instant growth; the moment I entered the place I filled it.

The spy was Patrick Wills. Later he told me about it. Having seen my letter of acceptance on the circular file he'd a rough idea of when I'd arrive, so he'd wandered down for some mints. He really wanted mints at the time, he explained, as he was trying to cut down on his pipe-smoking.

'Oh, yes,' I murmured – this was after I'd lost my poise.

'I was depressed because I was cutting down on smoking at a time when I desperately needed compensation,' he explained. 'I was depressed that you'd got the job, I was depressed for myself, I was depressed at the thought of the bloody-awful taste of tobacco and mint when I lit up again –' He shrugged and stared intently at me with goggly eyes full of that revolting blend of hatred and respect, and continued: 'Then in you came. I knew you instantly. and the depression was nothing – nothing.' He paused. He squeezed his belly – there was a bit of the ham actor in him. 'At the sight of you something like a boa-constrictor took hold of my guts.'

'Professional jealousy?' I murmured.

'Quite. I watched you and hated you and hoped you'd prove as pathetic as your clothes,' he continued. 'I followed you to the lifts. I remember how you lowered your suitcase to the floor and looked at your hand. I stopped and put a ten bob note into my wallet, enjoying my moment of hate. You stepped into the lift and smiled as you asked for the fifth floor – it was the lame lift boy –'

'So it was,' I said.

'You were looking out as he pulled the mesh. Your face was sallow, tired, broad and self-indulgent about the mouth –'

'And *you* were clean-shaven, impeccably-dressed and wore your wrist watch with a leather strap,' I said. He looked at me, surprised. 'You saw me?' I nodded. I saw he didn't like it. I was, I am, his daily doom.

Indeed, I saw everything that afternoon. Like Napoleon, years before exile, I saw faces and never forgot them, nor the names the foolish fairies had attached. Only one face ever defeated my memory. But I saw it then.

I saw the lame lift boy – I was very much the good general at that period – fingers against the panel of a box almost as big as the office I'd occupied up North; I saw the title of the mystery magazine that lay covers upward on the seat; I saw the Cambridge blue of the carpet in the lift; but most distinctly I saw the thick sole on one of the lift boy's shoes; his grey hair, large nose, and sullen disposition. He was a challenge I accepted.

I noticed that he always said 'Floor Five' going up, 'Floor Four,' 'Floor Six', 'Floor Seven,' and so on to the Holy of Holies at the fifteenth. Going down he would say: 'Fifth floor, fourth floor, third floor, second floor, first floor – ground.' It was in mitigation of the Chinese torture of his up and down all the deadlong day. I slipped a copy of *The River of Stars* by Edgar Wallace out of my pocket and left it on the seat. 'Floor Five,' said the lame lift boy.

'What's your name?' I asked.

'Jones,' he said. I waited, head lifted slightly, as he opened the lift doors. He stared irritably back. But I won. 'Herbert,' he completed grudgingly. Three weeks and a third thriller later he thanked me sincerely. He told me I was known as the Bookie. That was a start.

Stepping out of the lift and trying to orientate myself I was touched to be recognised by one soul at least. A big fellow, until you looked closely, then you saw that it was breadth and big head which produced an illusion of three inches more in height than he actually had. Not a common illusion. Only a very few broad people possess it. Mostly power-types, like me. But he was nowhere near being a human dynamo. He had one of those craggy crucified faces, eyes and bushy eyebrows acting as cross piece, nose for rough timber standard, straight hair ending in a natural cowlick which would come over his brow for a scroll at the merest shake of his head. A man who could have been strong. A man who had not even stopped trying. A simple case of abdication. Instead of power he had contentment. I guessed that he had the treasure because he didn't ask much; there would always be a little left over in the way of food and pleasure, because this was the life that pleased him. An epicure with stoic tendencies.

He said: 'You won't remember me. I was the chap that put you in the waiting room when you came up for interview. Name's Charlie Squires.'

I was surprised I hadn't noticed him. Perhaps there had been a measure of tension inside me on the day of the interview. But I recognised his tone and manner. He was engaged elsewhere. We had a couple of men at the plant, one had a small-holding, the other a couple of trades at his fingertips. The plant was their bread and butter. It so happened that both were very good workmen, but they were passive, they were outside the stream. Squires gave me the same impression. Only he wasn't so passive. He was a spectator and mostly enjoying it. I liked him and he knew it. As for his liking me – he was prepared to give me my head, study form, make a bid. In his own time. He was that detached.

'Come along to my office,' he said. 'You'll be wanting to see the Deputy Controller.' As we turned I glanced down and saw his footwear.

'I do remember you,' I said. 'Man with the canary suedes.'

'I know,' he said. 'It's past the time for canary suedes – for any kind or colour.' He glanced ruefully at them.

'I'm a rum customer too.'

'That's clever, by God,' he said. He didn't bother to explain why he considered the remark clever and I congratulated myself on my judgement of a minute or two before. 'Let me take your case,' he said as we walked along a distinguished-looking corridor, over a wallflower coloured carpet – they were different on each of the fifteen floors. He took it without wincing. 'Heavy,' he said. 'You could have left it downstairs, you know.'

'You never know the hour or the minute when you'll need to consult your Chamber's Encyclopedia,' I remarked.

'It can't be the full set!'

Actually, I told him, it contained three shirts, a pair of brown brogues which I'd almost worn with my charcoal business suit, just for the joy, a miniature tape-recorder radio combination, a piece of cannel coal of peculiar shape, shaving kit (one electric, one manual and a cut-throat), and a mint copy of 'Brand's Antiquities'. And one or two other things, including, most especially, a leather skull-cap one of my great-grandfathers used to wear when he worked in a coal-mine, complete with the stains like rust around the three inch cut where the stone went through on its way to grey matter.

He laughed and I laughed, and I liked the combination of his craggy face and busy eyebrows and my middling big nose and deep-set eyes. His eyes were blue. Mine were blue or green, according to the weather. He danced ahead, throwing the case from one hand to the other. 'You can leave it in my room, Mr Rowlands, yours isn't quite ready yet, general services let me down badly, still waiting to install the internal phone.'

I said that it didn't matter.

'I daresay it doesn't to you. But I like to be on top of my job. After Simpson left – he was the man before – there was an awful lot of cannibalism. I had to get you a new filing cabinet – by the way, we've a very good central registry clerk. I had to have a new lock fitted to one of the drawers in your desk; Simpson lost his keys once and forced it, the day he came to work without his dentures –'

'Filed under everything but dentals,' I said.

'Under "lost", would you believe it! He spent an entire morning going through his personal filing cabinet. Then I snaffled a better bookcase, since you're a shade more important than Harry.'

'At least twice a month I have waking nightmares in which I'm only a thought in the mind of the universe,' I said, and felt the corridor suddenly shift a little and return to normal.

'Do you, now? It's more rarely in my case. Then as suddenly life is real, life is earnest, and you lose it – do you?' I nearly said 'never' then remembered that the subject was sacred, so only grunted. 'You'll be seeing the DC first?'

'Man named Walker Johnson,' I said, like a good scholar.

'A fine administrator, a most interesting man,' said Squires. 'Awfully impressive Army career. Rose from private to major. Cyprus, Africa, other place.'

'He didn't seem the military type,' I said, making myself comfortable in Squire's office. It wasn't hard. The office was like all the provincial offices I'd known; dirty blotting pad covered with calculations, beermats for coffee cups, several dirty wire trays, odd ashtrays, folders stacked on the cupboard top and in a couple of free corners, as well as enfilading the blotter on the desk. If you squinted you could see them move, squirting fine dust as do cuttle fish their ink.

'He hated the military,' said Squires. 'Can well understand. Loves books, records, mountains.' Making a Charlie Chaplin pivot he returned to my side and whispered confidentially: 'And a very wise man. Takes an interest. Studies the personality. Talks to you for hours – probing. Driven at least a couple of typists to the point of suicide. Terribly clever.'

'I'm looking forward to a session.'

'Be warned. Don't. He's death. A born bore. When he's really serious he's as fetching as a very ancient family vault. Do smoke.'

'No thank you,' I said. 'I smoke cigars – in the evening, take after my father.'

'Is *he* in this racket?'

Taking a deep breath I lied in his teeth. 'He's a roadsweeper by choice. He's been dustman, sewer attendant, lavatory man – anything that allows him time to think. He's a philosopher and anarchist.'

'My father was a Bishop,' said Squires and looked at the two telephones. One was ivory and the other scarlet and one of the two was purring sweetly. The kind I'd used had a noise that made you hit the ceiling. Not that the noise is the cause. After three months at UK House I was back to where I started from, internally hitting the ceiling at every purr of the two-headed pussycat. If we are thoughts in the mind of the universe it may be possible to secretly change the thought; take on another identity. This is treason. There may come a day when the universe will accuse of unlawful identity from the other end of a telephone wire. 'That'll be R. Walker Johnson,' said Squires disinterestedly, finally picking up the ivory internal one. 'Yes, Squires speaking. Yes, Mr Rowlands is here. Will do. Right, sir.' He coloured when my head jerked incredulously. Carefully replacing the telephone he said: 'I've survived ten reorganisations plus a denationalisation and a renationalisation followed by the usual bits and pieces. I am neutral, safe, respectful. So I see them come, I watch them go.'

'Not to worry,' I said.

'It's force of habit, doesn't mean a thing, they never think of me,' he said fretfully to himself. 'I've a nice little sideline, few quid a week, review books: the Dracula of the literary pages – compensation. Would you like coffee?' I nodded and he whipped away out. I calculated his weight at sixteen stone and guessed him a bachelor. Never saw a Bishop's palace in his life. So he didn't believe my father was a roadsweeper. Sometimes I hardly believed it myself. I was a great one for changing Dads as you change a library book. Sometimes he was changed several times daily. But he was never revealed for what he really was, a branch bank manager, respected by his subordinates and hated by his son. Squires returned, a little breathless. 'R. Walker Johnson's girl's gone for coffee.' He hesitated. 'I say, I've seen your personal file. I thought your father was something in a bank?'

'He's a roadsweeper,' I said. 'At the moment.'

'And mine's a curate,' said Squires, laughing. He thought he had me taped, and he was approximately correct.

'What does the "R" stand for?' I asked. My eyes were fixed on the girl with the tray.

'It doesn't stand for anything. It stands before the Walker Johnson singing "Holy, Holy, Holy", that's all,' said Squires. 'It's not in his personal file. He won't volunteer. He flushes darkly and walks away. Hasn't even told his personal assistant, has he ever told you, Cathie?'

She set down the tray, smiled at me, turned to Squires. 'Told me what, Charlie?'

'We were talking about the initial "R",' said Squires.

'Not "reckless", anyway,' she said. I liked her voice.

'This is the new man, Mr Rowlands. This is our Cathie,' he introduced. I took her hand. It was like touching your own hand, in one of the moments when you're trying to prove that hand belongs to body and body to self. Quite extraordinary. At first glance she wasn't even pretty. She was very clean. You saw skin before cosmetics. Looking as though she'd just stepped out of the bath – or the sea – a split second before. 'I'm very pleased to meet you,' I announced very pompously. Her answer was an impartial smile. I'd forgotten for once that my hands were very large: made for a navvy. I saw that she was rubbing her right hand; the one I'd clasped, and looked guiltily down at mine.

'The next time you're pleased I'll keep out of your way,' she said, smiling to take out the sting; and departed.

'A mystery woman,' said Squires, following my eyes. I asked why without words. 'Hard to say,' he said. 'Keeps herself to herself. Are you married?'

I smiled. 'Not at the moment. Women like me; but owing to a traumatic experience at the age of six I'm practically impotent.'

'The reverse, I'd guess,' said Squires, scoring an outer.

'What's her name?'

'Cavendish,' he said, a little enviously, thinking of what I was thinking and knowing what I knew; that a mutual attraction had come into being.

'My father smokes Cavendish,' I said dreamily, and he laughed, as I intended. It's pleasant to know someone who cottons on quickly; it is a great feeder of vanity and a joy. I was regaining confidence; a king once more. I felt I couldn't go wrong. I decided to play to the limit. My one worry had been that I wouldn't find a mirror like my old boss, Mr Snorry; now here he was; once again in the very place, in the very body I'd guessed he'd be in. It takes a little wit to review books; and resilience too when the books are novels. I decided to play. There was nothing to lose. Snorry had drummed it into me: 'Nobody dies of starvation today. Nobody wanders the streets, homeless, unless they choose. Cradle to grave, spotless all the way, unless there's a war. And they're out of fashion. So don't care, boy, don't care, be your own master.' Which I was, which I would be. A long time ago my grandfather had sat on the knee of Prince Kropotkin. It came out not as a boast but as a casual aside to my Uncle James one day.

The telephone went off like a contented pussycat and Charlie restrained himself visibly from snatching it up. When he did it was to say: 'Yes. Yes, sir. Yes.' and 'Immediately.' Catching my eye he clipped off the second 'sir'.

He stood up: 'He's ready for you. I'll take you along.'

'You don't stand in awe of him?' I asked, refusing to budge.

'Well, no. It's only that I'm a natural flunkey, that's the way I was brought up: my father not being able to afford proper servants, financially or morally; being a Red Bishop he picked on the family to fill the menial positions.' He drew in cigarette smoke. 'I was the butler. It's harmless and pleases any amount of people – deprived people. Shall we go?'

'When I've finished my coffee,' I said, leisurely sipping.

'Of course,' said Squires, stubbing his cigarette. 'Finish your coffee.'

'I'll tell him the coffee arrived as he rang.'

'For God's sake, no; don't start him off. He's against coffee. he's against cigars. They make him physically sick. He used to be addicted, and they're the worst sort.'

'Quite a collection of prejudices,' I murmured . He laughed and continued: 'And ball pens. Never sign a memo with a ball pen. He hates them. He says the ball pen was invented for Attila the Hun and Calvin and the Chief Inquisitor – ideal for death warrants.'

'All that and phallic too,' I said, and he laughed.

'You're a rum bugger.' I looked pleased at the compliment and leapt to my feet. The rabbit was off. We set off on our pilgrimage to the hater of cigars, coffee and ball pens. 'You'll find R.W.J. a very interesting study,' said Squires. 'His hobby at the moment by the way – and be warned – is A Club.'

'A Club?' I mimicked complete with the capitals.

'Oh, a kind of self-improvement society,' he said. 'Indeed, that's what they used to call it, SIC, self-improvement society, debates, discussions, reports about books, music – he's a demon for music.'

'Oh Lord, I thought all that was done with,' I said. 'The kind of thing that lingers on in old people's clubs – senior citizens. Never mind, I'll join.'

We paused outside a door. '*Only* if he asks you, don't mention it first,' urged Squires. He was a lover of peace, I could see. But he liked to stir up a little once in a while.

'Promise,' I said. 'I'll not give you away, Mr Squires.'

'Call me Charlie,' he said, leading me into the last league of corridor, a posh end where carpet, paint, fittings and even floor polish changed imperceptibly. You couldn't precisely see where the vulgar left off and the refined and sumptuous began, but you felt it and smelled it. It was like stepping into another world. The only definite note was struck by the pictures: the pen and wash drawings of squeezers, suckers, riddlers and muffling machines came to an end and were followed by oil paintings of our kind of plant, including a blatantly romantic one of Percy Main, where I had worked, seen from the opposite bank of the river. For a moment I was back among the pipes and tanks and boilers, walking the spider ramp to the slim little tower with Mr Snorry my foster-father. Then I was back with another good friend, I was sure, Miss Cavendish. She smiled and said: 'He's waiting.' There was another desk behind another door. It was empty. That must be the entrance to the Controller's office. 'You'll meet Mrs Arcot later,' said Charlie, seeing my glance.

'She'll be annoyed. She likes to inspect new boys,' said Miss Cavendish.

'You'll meet her,' said Charlie.

'Come what may you'll meet her,' said Miss Cavendish, laughing, picking up an insistent telephone. 'Mr R. Walker Johnson's in conference. Can I take a message? No, not to be disturbed.' Putting her hand over the mouth piece. 'See how important you are! Go in – have fun.' Mirth bubbled. I had an idea she liked me.

Charlie went first, knocking, poking his head into the room beyond to be received with a murmur, taking me through, sheepdog and sheep advancing together to meet a sort of gentleman farmer, whose chair revolved where he had left it, his arm outstretched. 'How nice to see you again!' I was not so sure. Words and clothes alike were part of a very old act. It was beginning to wear through. He wore a nice tweed suit and a red tie impeccably knotted old-style. His hand was small, cool, dry. A woman's hand. More than ever I felt a sheep rounded up from the fells with a fluke in my stomach and maggots in my feet. 'Sit down, old chap.' He actually led me to the seat.

I made a careful survey during these preliminary operations. This was my immediate boss. His power to attract or repel was important. My immediate impression was neutral. Like me he was a dark-visaged man. But he was the kind with a blue chin. He needed a beard, a real one, desperately. You could see how carefully he had shaved that morning. But the gunpowder blue was still there, shiny, a little revolting. Yet he had presence. He was well over six feet, which gave him an advantage over me, his shoulders were broad, he had a strong fleshy nose and face erosion lines to match. But something was wrong. There were the girlish hands. Egg-smooth. But it wasn't the hands. What gave him away was his expression as he took his seat and settled back in a well-rehearsed move. The eyes were brown and actively afraid – it could only be of me. Because I was new but expected, known but a possible imponderable. Behind the eyes was a fearful little thing which worried about death twenty years from now, and about a tiger-quality in life which was lovely when you were with it, but terrible when some day you had to take it. He had been waiting for that day. This might be it. I put the scales away. I had nothing to fear from him, and he had nothing to fear from me. His death was inside. I felt sorry for him.

'I'll push off, sir,' said Charlie.

'Must you?' said the deputy, in a tone that said 'Good!' 'You're looking after Rowlands?'

'Few odds and ends, we're looking after them.'

'Push on, old chap. A welcome is more than words, eh? Little services make a chap feel at home.'

'Right!' said Charlie, retreating backwards. Would he trip? No, he made it, disappearing with a grimace. 'Grand chap. Harmless, but far from helpless.'

'Should think he takes care of himself.' I was mimicking the Army-style prose.

Walking back to his revolving chair R.W.J. wagged a finger, 'You're perceptive!' He pushed over a cigar box. 'I don't smoke them,' I told him earnestly. If this was a test I would give it a build-up.

'Nor me,' said R.W.J.

'I smoke a *strong* cigar.' He wriggled uneasily.

'That's something I don't have around.' I told him not to worry, I was an evening smoker. He relaxed.

I said: 'Sometimes through the day when I feel like it.' He squirmed. I pulled out the box, looked in it, pushed it back.

'Do have one if you –' I'd a feeling the unspoken word was 'must'.

'I'll remember the invitation,' I grinned. He laced his fingers.

'Now,' I leaned forward brightly, expectantly. 'Squires: Call on him for anything material. He's a tower of strength. You'll meet the other chaps later. There's Holinshed. Nice chap, Jack. A little weak – well, that's unfair. A little lost in a world he didn't make.'

'Is it finished?' I meant the world. He stared at me.

'Ah – yes – I see. Continuous creation, humanly speaking.' I didn't bother to tell him I meant different. 'Let's say he doesn't believe he made it.' He leaned back triumphantly, having polished off me and Holinshed in one slick phrase. 'Then there's Wills – Pat Wills. Tries too hard. A good chap, ambition-wise always like the miler at the tape, mouth open, all in, all out. See?' I nodded gravely. 'The chief's busy. Told me he'd slip along. He's like that. Charming man. Wanders round and talks to people.'

'I promise to make him welcome.' He didn't laugh. The sense of humour was atrophied or something. I was beginning to feel bored. My hand was playing with the box of slim cigars in my jacket pocket. My eyes wandered. Charlie's office looked into a well at the bottom of which was a little garden with seats. R. Walker Johnson's office looked out on the great river, only I couldn't see it, just the buildings at the other side, glasshouses through which, with a little patience and a pair of binoculars, you could see the human ants. I wanted to walk to the window and look down on the river. I love rivers. They are impersonal. They never boast, or complain and now they are almost always beautiful. If we have done nothing else we have made a land of rivers fit for an Isaac Walton to return and explore.

He was asking if I had rooms. I said I had indeed. Where, he wanted to know. I considered. Not having any I had to invent. The whole shoot. 'Fulham Road.' He shuddered. 'With my brother. He's a painter.' He brightened. 'Is he good?' I told him without a doubt.

'I envy him. Indeed, I envy you. I like –' He laughed. 'Correction. I adore art. I daresay that sounds silly – Yellow Book and all that. But I mean it. To make the paint go where you will it – that's a triumph, and a tangible triumph. Something we're not allowed in business. The concrete!' I waited, watched, listened. 'I come of a long line of agricultural engineers – father, grandfather, great-grandfather. Norfolk. I didn't have the knack. But I like tools, I like to see a job of work well done. Creation's the thing – continuous creation.'

'You ought to sit amongst it,' I said. 'Paintings drying all over the house. Stacks of frames. Sticky paint. A jungle full of traps. We were glad when he got out –'

'Treasure him,' said Walker Johnson. 'Treasure him, lad. We're the second-raters.'

'I don't agree,' I said. 'Playing round with paint and canvas is one thing. Working with men and materials is another. We're the generals who make the world go round. We paint pictures, but they can't be seen.'

Walker Johnson sighed. 'But can't be seen. That's the crux of it. What's to show? *Our* pictures don't enchant the eye or stir the heart.' I was getting tired. There were times he almost turned my stomach. It had to be finished. Asking for coffee would be just too obvious.

Fiddling round with a ball pen was out of the question for the simple reason that I didn't have one. I stooped to the floor and pulled a hair in my right nostril. Halfway back I was sneezing fit to bring the house down. The Deputy Controller paled and pulled out a drawer. I found myself looking, between sneezes, into a little plastic box. I said I was allergic to cough sweets. He said they were for hay fever. I said I thought mine was a cold. He said to take one anyway. I said I'd tried them once before and had come out in a sore red rash around my nose and mouth. I pulled out the cigars. 'The only cure,' I told him. He shivered visibly. He winced at the smell. So I really worked on the thing, blowing out smoke. The Deputy Controller stood up whilst I worked furiously. All I needed was a cow-catcher and a shining brass funnel. I worked all the way to the door, and he followed, distastefully saying he'd introduce me to the rest of the staff.

Later Charlie told me that the cigar had possibly saved me from the favourite culmination of all first interviews, the one that began with a narrowing of the eyes and a lowering of the head to bring his nose into line with the customer, and ended with: 'Be happy. Be industrious! Remember, I'll not always be here; I'll be moving on; consider: You may be the man to succeed me.'

And that was a joke. He didn't know it. But I did. It was all going to come true in the end. I was going to be industrious as well as happy. He would move on and I would move up.

TWO

Sometimes I think back to the very beginning. Sitting in the office which belonged to R. Walker Johnson, and in which I shall always feel a lodger if not an interloper, I look through the door. It has accidentally been left open by my secretary, or perhaps she has gone out to get something, or perhaps I have left it open myself. But it is never by accident that I find myself looking through that open door. There is where she used to sit and I try to visualise her. I mean, I try to see her. But the mind won't remember what it's best to forget. The first day I ever saw her she was wearing a severe brown dress. I can see that. When she turned there were odd little tendrils, or curls, errant behind the ears. I can see those curls. She had blue to purple eyes; she was not born to the purple but there were times when she wore it in her eyes. I remember blue, I remember purple. I see her neck and the way she held her head. But I cannot put the parts together. And I haven't a photograph.

What have I belonging to her, or marked by her? She gave me books. They were never inscribed. She sent me notes of one or two lines, mostly in pencil, I used to find them on my desk. Signed 'C'. They went straight to the point – a meeting place, a time, a reminder. Messages but never writings. I have leafed through the six or seven notes – mostly on quarto sheets of typing paper – and she resisted even writing 'love' between the message and her initial. She had such a sense of the temporal that she gave it every aid and comfort. We rarely had a meal at the same place twice; never met in a room that was our own, or sat holding hands listening to a record. Not for Cathie the supreme indignity of having to whisper or listen to the words: '*our* song'.

I used to worry about arrangements. It's all very well having an affair, but an affair demands a convenient point of contact, a meeting place. It's the most difficult part of the business. It was even more difficult for me. With my remarkable talent for involvement I had not only found a room but a family as well. A foster-mother and a mistress. So that room was out; especially since the girl was only next door. I need not have worried.

The insidious conspiracy with the temporal nature of things looked after that. There was no familiar picnic spot, no cluster of trees where our caravan had rested, no friendly little hotel to which we were glad to return. All roads and lines ran south and west; sometimes we had to pass by a place we had visited before. She always insisted on driving and would go miles out of *her* way, not *our* way, to avoid a place where we had made love only once. So they are all vague. The lovely lost places. Sometimes I remember them only when a journey takes me unknowingly along the road; suddenly an inn sign becomes a pang. Sometimes we camped. She knew a place in town where tents could be hired on demand. She was a good woodsman. She loved trees and loved to make love under the trees. Perhaps I can remember her face if I take her under the trees.

It was one Sunday. It was Springtime, not long before she left me, if she can be said to have left me. I remember that morning particularly well because I hadn't thought up a story to tell the other girl and the landlady, who was curious about movements; knowing like the good woman she was that all life can be reduced to movements. Fortune was with me. The telephone rang. It was a wrong number and I had the wit to murmur inconsequential things until the caller had replaced his telephone. I told them it was Snorry's nephew passing through town and wanting to see the sights with me. I was casual in planting the idea that poor Joe was a bore but that I had to put up with him. Afterwards I felt guilty at using Snorry's name, especially at that time, even if only as the uncle of a man visiting town. But you learn to live with these little pains.

Going down on the bus she told me that she must go up into East Anglia in the afternoon as her mother was ill. I think this was the first time she had mentioned her; and I remarked that I'd always imagined her as a large, comfortable woman. 'She's not,' said Cathie. 'She's thin and has red hands. She complains a lot. She complained because I said I was staying in town this weekend. She said . . .' She was silent, then smiled. 'I'm beginning to sound like her, to myself, I mean. Let's not talk about her.'

We got off the bus at random, a place selected on the spur of the moment because there seemed to be a path striking up the hill. There was a thin sun. Rich green sprigs of hawthorn burst like shrapnel in the hedges, a month earlier than at home in the North. The first thing I did when we had dismounted was to pick a sprig to chew. 'Cigars are only a substitute for hawthorn leaves with you,' she said. That might be true. We climbed to the top of the hill, passing a comfortable little chalk quarry on the way. Surrounded with bushy hawthorn it was almost a cavern. She noticed me looking at it, and openly laughed. It was too early for her to even think of it. We walked along the ridge and saw a pattern of ploughed fields on the other side of the bowl; ploughed fields and seagulls. A tractor was ploughing and seemed a mechanical fly as it clung to the steep edge and puffed blue smoke into the air. We could see the smoke against the brown swathes of earth. She knew where she was going, but that was because she had studied her map. Knowing her ways I knew that she had never before been within miles of the place. We descended through an avenue of holly trees and crossed a wooden bridge into the back of a village. We stopped to watch fish facing up-stream, sharing the water world with a treasure of tin cans and one boot with a waving tongue. The church bells were ringing. 'Hawthorn's powerful against evil,' she suddenly said. 'Let's go to church.'

You can judge her power over me by the fact that we went. We made up a congregation of eleven. The Vicar was a fat little man with sparse hair streaked over his head and a button nose. I think he was slightly mad. I have looked up his text. It was: 'And when he thus had spoken, he cried with a loud voice, Lazarus, come forth. And he that was dead came forth, bound hand and foot with grave-clothes: and his face was bound about with a napkin. Jesus saith unto them, Loose him, and let him go.' The preacher said all sorts of things in a flat whining voice, but I lost interest after the text. The thought that troubled me was that I had never seen anyone dead. I amused myself making out the things carved out on the tomb beside us. They were spear, scourges, ladder, pincers and hammer; for which I mentally substituted typewriter, telephone, lift, in-tray, out-tray and memo.

The Vicar shook hands with us. He looked as though he'd soon be ready for that napkin over his face himself. We walked on a long time in silence. Then she said: 'People don't rise from the dead today.' There seemed to be nothing to say in reply. I felt sad about the fact myself. It must have been good when everything was set out in order to learn by heart and believe; when all the acts were arranged. Now there is nothing, no Passion to share, but the acts are just as inevitable.

Under the lee of the other side of the hill we found another hollow ringed by a living stockade of tall leafless trees. Looking up you could see the buds getting ready to burst. They were big buds, eager and ready. Once upon a time people knew their trees and the kind of life they carried inside. I don't mean the birds. There were rooks dancing among the buds and she said that there must be a house nearby.

After eating lunch we lay on our raincoats and watched those rooks. Some were busy fetching and carrying the furniture which had blown away in the winter. One or two philosophers were searching the air-currents and rose and fell to the thrust of invisible spouts and breakers; at the end of each kind of thrust, or near the end, they screamed. Perhaps another rook on the tree was recording. Their wings were like satin in the sun; her lips were like silk to my fingers. It was about then that I forgot that uncomfortable (for me) little incident in the church. I had turned on the way out to find her swiftly turning from the altar and an act of obeisance.

Now I remember her face. It was a small square face, almost too small for the column of her neck, but the wide mouth ending in little lines of gravity gave the needed balance. That day the purple had spilled out from her eyes to the hollows below. I kissed them shut and roved from there to her lips. I remember bending over and being lovingly critical. The nose was cheeky but there was nobility in the flare of the nostrils, comedy in the freckles which summer would turn to the colour of her hair. She moved uneasily and I rejoined her. Her face is hard to remember because I knew it by touch better than sight, and touch was better than sight because there was a hint of the imperious in it, something I did not care to see. To close with her body was a way of escape as well as a means to delight. Hands can only see so much. Hands play Judas. So I cannot recall her face.

The point of the story came later, in the evening. After the expedition I saw her to Liverpool Street. We had to wait for a train. We wandered around. There was a camera-kiosk. I suggested that we might try it and exchange photographs. She shook her head. I was astonished. I remembered Uncle James saying that country folk used to have a fear of having their photographs taken; they thought they might fall under the power of the photographer or perhaps of anyone who got hold of their picture. There was that kind of fear in her face. Hoping to persuade her by example I sat in the place myself and showed her how it worked. She turned away. Feeling dashed I gave her the six small prints of a bewildered man. A shade of her fear had found its way on to my face. She graciously put them in her handbag, but I suspected her of murder the moment the train moved out. I could see her working on the little squares, hands concealed in her handbag. Later she would lean out of the window and let the train's slipstream take them away. That is why I haven't a photograph to help me to put the parts of her together.

Remembering the other is easier. One of the advantages of the executive ladder is that the higher you go the more you can delegate and the more time you have for your own devices. Mine is observation. It trained very well. She is its only failure, unless there's something else that mislaid the representation, for the sake of my health. I was a day-dreamer first, but that gave way, and I filled the gap with a game of reconstruction. I attempt to reconstruct the bit of past which counts. Perhaps there is only another kind of dreaming, but it's something to occupy one's self with, resting between rungs. I ask questions. I interrogate. I supplement my memory.

And I find talkers. Wills, for instance. Wills is always very willing to talk past, present or future. He has nothing to fear so he talks frankly, and often quite accurately, so far as I can judge, when he forgets that he's a liar. When I'm doubtful I can cross-check with Holinshed, or whoever happens to be available. It's a matter of elementary engineering.

On the day of my arrival these two were together. They were in Holinshed's office. Wills told me afterwards that Holinshed was worried. I was the new boss, after all. He told Wills: 'There'll be the usual Royal procession around, you know Walker Johnson's style, introducing the staff. I wouldn't want us to be caught on a bad footing.'

'Oh, very well,' said Wills. 'Only, I've seen him. I thought you'd be interested.'

'Look,' said Holinshed. 'Look, I've been working hard, re-drafting an instruction. You know what his writing's like – drunken fly with inky legs. R.W.J. wants it on his desk by five – to take home, so help me. Anyway, I know what you're going to say: he's a clot.'

'He is,' said Wills. 'I saw him in the foyer. A triangular sort of person. Shapeless overcoat, shapeless suit, dirty shoes.'

'You're a malicious bastard.'

'I'll admit he beat me to the gravy. You too.'

'I said you were malicious,' said Holinshed, flushing. 'Anyway, he'll learn. He'll find a good tailor, get lean through squash or tennis –'

'His sort never does – he'd crumple any suit and soil the cleanest linen. Straight out of the buffing tank, and that's his strength, that's why Walker Johnson picked him. I believe they brainwashed R.W.J. in Korea. He's a romantic communist at heart, goes into an orgasm every time he comes across a real working class boy.'

'There's no such thing surely? Anyway, I still believe in R.W.J.'

'Wait till he knocks you back again,' said Wills.

'I'll depend on my record. All you have to do is keep your nose clean. They rarely pass you over twice. The Chief Controller plays fair –'

'He plays a useful game of chess.'

'Walker Johnson's a fair-dealing man.'

'So he's told you that time can wipe out obstacles, and that there's still a chance that you might sit in his chair. You know, the

CC might have a thrombosis, or he might wake up and join the Salvation Army . . . He said the same to me. No doubt he's said the same to the messenger boy.'

Holinshed told me later that he was shocked at Walker Johnson's duplicated duplicity; so shocked that even in recollection he forgot how breath-takingly accurate the observation had been. Anyway, to continue, all that he said at the time (hugging his pain to his bosom) was: 'One was aware that the line was a quote from his favourite play.'

'But one didn't happen to mention it, did one.'

'I'll bet you didn't utter either,' accused Holinshed.

'Of course not. That's our trouble – circumspect, too circumspect. We're too much in awe.'

'I don't know,' said Holinshed. 'Have you noticed how the threads all lead to R.W.J.'s side of the corridor. The Chief's in the cold. I'll swear he spends most of his time playing Patience.'

'The Chief goes around saying he's naturally indolent,' remarked Wills. 'There was the time Rampion came breezing along the corridor with his red beard blazing – you know, Rampion from Plant Design – and who should he bump into but the old man himself all trim below his bowler. "Were you looking for me, Rampion?" says he all merry-and-bright. "No, just going along to see the Big Boss himself!" roars Rampion, meaning R.W.J., of course.'

'That must have been before I came,' said Holinshed. 'Which reminds me: I've been here a long time.'

'That's a matter for congratulation, not bitterness,' said Wills.

'What did the Chief say, then?' asked Holinshed.

'He said: "Put in a good word for me!" ' said Wills. 'And I'm not being bitter. Just objective – hello!'

And that was where we came in, R. Walker Johnson leading the way. 'Now here we are; we've caught the two senior men in close harmony. Gentlemen, this is Mr Rowlands; Mr Rowlands meet Mr Wills and Mr Holinshed.' I knew Wills; I had known him from time immemorial. The spade-shaped head with the black smooth hair so like my own, but much too plastered, the moustache like a faint line of contempt for the world at large, the thick, overfed neck. The very good suit and the nice tie as foils for the self-indulgent body. And there was fair Holinshed, deliberately chosen by Wills for contrast. Tall and so slim as to be nearly frail I have seen him look like a young Lear, bowed down in his golden time. Black man and golden boy, that was Wills and Holinshed as I first saw them together. I could have taken to Holinshed. He was a good soul. It was a natural goodness that came shining out. He was physically fair. His moustache was golden like the whiskers of those Elizabethan adventurers. His skin had that translucent quality. He was quick, deft, boyish: too boyish. Slow in growing up. His mind was all right but he was, or seemed, retarded in his emotional being. I was his real counterpart. I could have helped him earlier. He could have helped me. But times were out of joint. It wasn't that Wills was visibly sullen, or Holinshed stiff and withdrawn, when we first met. They were too determinedly civilised for that. But their hostility was there. I quivered in the air. I decided to bring it out into the open.

Holinshed held out his hand and I approached only to ignore both it and him. Diving past him I stubbed my cigar in a convenient ash-tray.

'Must get rid of this,' I said. 'Cigars don't do for work.' After a natural hesitation on his part I shook hands with Holinshed. I turned to Wills. 'I know *you*.'

He was smiling. I reacted badly as he said: 'You're the first cigar smoker we've ever had.'

'I daresay there's room for improvement,' I quipped. 'I remember you. You were going into a room as I was coming out.' That was referring to the time they'd interviewed me for the job. I didn't like sneaky people. That routine detective act in the foyer had annoyed me; but still, I suppose, my remarks were inexcusable. 'But, however, that's life,' I said. 'No hard feelings.'

R.W.J. was making noises, which I ignored. I slapped Holinshed on the shoulder. 'I remember you as well.'

'I don't remember meeting you,' said Holinshed.

'Correct,' I said. 'Absolutely correct. We didn't meet. But we had words over the telephone when you were in Personnel. The buffing dispute. Who gets the extra shilling? Remember?' I could see from his face he had. I could also see that Wills was beginning to enjoy himself again.

He was the one who'd tell Holinshed I'd already managed to cook my goose. Gabbling disjointedly R. Walker Johnson carried me away to meet people in other departments. He thought I didn't know I'd cooked my goose. He was wrong two ways. It doesn't do to be faint, neutral, or shy. 'Always make your mark,' said Mr Snorry. I had. Actually I'd boobed. I should also have given them the hand-clasp that hurts, in addition to words that sting. But in the exuberance of my acting, as so often before I'd remembered my lines only to lose my bits of business.

What else happened that first afternoon? R. Walker Johnson took me along to my own office. It was an official launching. The slipway began in the small outer office and my secretary. I gathered her name was Miss Miffin. I shook hands and forced myself *not* to say that I was sure we would get on well together. You either get the balance or you don't, and it takes more than a platitude. I liked the look of her. I liked the look of my office. After R. Walker Johnson had left I buzzed her to see if I should like them together. I did. I told her to get me a dozen files at random. On second thoughts I put her to the test. We are the organisation's club of queer projects, the cooks who try to make old broths new, and the new as unspoilt as is humanly possible. I asked her to select the more interesting.

She was back within five minutes. I noticed she was cool and courteous, a little too cool. She was a large girl. She carried herself well. That meant there was mental balance in addition to the training, the discipline, to combat the tendency to put on weight. She was pleasant to have around, but only pleasant. There wasn't the slightest stirring of the carnal instinct as she walked to the connecting door. I was so pleased that I suddenly said: 'You can go home now, if you like.' Instead of putting on a show of conscientious protest she smiled and said thank you. She was on her way in five minutes flat, but called to say good night. She had a broad face and brown eyes set wide apart and as she smiled I saw a natural mother. She could mother me. The smile said she would.

On my mind was the business of rooms. I'd lied to R. Walker Johnson. I am negligent about personal things and hadn't bothered to make enquiries, or even write to one or two people. Anyway, I wanted to be on my own. I wanted everything to be clean and new. In a new job it always pays to start as you mean to end. I had to shake myself before packing up. After all, I wasn't nursing Mr Snorry any longer. I was my own master. A proper master must allow his mice to play. So at four fifteen, shortly after Miss Miffin had gone, I slipped along to see Wills, as the more noxious of the two. I told him cheerfully that I was tired and was going home. I didn't allow him time to warn me that the Chairman, or Deputy Chairman, or Chief Controller, or any other character, was a stickler for clocking on and clocking off at the precise times. I just told him.

That would give them something else to talk about. As a matter of fact I reconstructed all his thoughts and conversations, and a few of the others as well. Being able to do that is just as much a necessary skill, in top business, as being able to read handwriting upside down. You notice I didn't mention typescript? That's because a typewritten document comes easy once you've mastered handwriting. But this reconstruction of other people is important; putting the scraps together is fun; and when in doubt you can always use yourself as a model.

I knew exactly the impression I'd made on R.W.J., Wills and Holinshed. I wasn't so sure about Miss Cavendish. That was a different field. In that field I had to rely upon myself. In business you have to call in all your acquired selves. The one I had used was a mixture of Hermann Goering and Charlie Chaplin. The effect had been a mixture; amusement, bewilderment, and just a little fear. And perhaps a little mild contempt, which also is useful.

After I'd glanced at the files I went home. That's a laugh. The reality was that I left home. I loved that building from the moment I first walked into it. But I was worried about getting a place to lay my head. When you are as lonely as I am you must have a place to be attached to, no matter what so long as you can tack yourself to it like the big muscle of a rock limpet. I'd mentioned the Fulham Road to Walker Johnson, so I went there by Tube, thus proving how very much the liar is enslaved by his lies. It was cold and I didn't have gloves. The case was heavy. My hands both ached and froze. I walked about one hundred yards from the station and decided that I didn't like the look of the place; it was the main street of any industrial town, but planted in London. The streets leading away were if anything more unpleasant. There was an open door with a folded newspaper on the mat. It hurt. I walked back to the Tube, quailed at the sight of soulless people and trains, picked up a cab, and asked for the Dorchester. A man in uniform opened the door and took my case, but I lost my nerve, and said no, I wasn't a boarder, I was meeting a friend. He let me in by a hair's breadth. I lost myself in the corner of a very big seat but soon tired of the very odd looks. They came from a very odd lot. What I'd realised was that they wouldn't have a room, first for anyone like me, second for anyone like me walking in out of the blue. I was ashamed of my clothes. In more ways than one I felt like a visiting Russian.

In the end I called a porter and told him to find me a cab. He gave me an insulting glance in exchange for my case; but I had my revenge when he handed the case into the cab. 'Thank you,' I said heartily, slammed the door, and told the driver to take me to the Cumberland, the only hotel I remembered. It came very expensive, but it made a rock for the limpet in me. I gave the page five bob and explored the bit of rock I was going to join.

There was a writing table, a wardrobe, a bench for my case. There was an electric fire, which I turned on, and a private shower, which I used. I turned on the television to keep me company while I washed.

Coming out from the shower I saw my miserable trousers in a death agony over the bed. I was green about clothes but I knew then that I had to revise. As soon as I had re-dressed I went along to the men's department of a store in Piccadilly and blew thirty quid of the hundred I had in my wallet on a suit that seemed to pass muster. It was a week before I dared wear it to the office, but at least it gave me the opportunity to have the old ones cleaned and pressed. They sent the new suit to the Cumberland for me. I wandered off to see if the barber shop was still in Soho, not to use, but simply to assure myself I had at least one inanimate friend. Then I looked in bookshops, sat through a cartoon film show, had a meal, bought a thriller for the lame lift boy and myself, and went home.

It was only when I was in bed that I realised why I'd wandered. There had been a faint hope of meeting Miss Cavendish. In the end I'd settled for Miss Miffin, or even anybody. To say a word to, I mean. I conquered the loneliness by lying in bed and reading my thriller with the television turned on. At intervals I ignored one or the other. Then I closed the book, switched off the television, and went to sleep.

When I awoke it was dark and the telephone was ringing. I felt trapped. Who could know I was here? Certainly not my parents, or friends, or any of my colleagues. That was a most terrible nightmare. In the end I plucked up sufficient courage to take hold of it. A woman's voice from a long distance said I promised to ring, darling, I'm glad you're not out. I muttered something and she went gloriously on for five minutes or so, telling darling about the two boys and Millicent, and how bad the day had been, and something about a pony with an injured fetlock, and would darling not forget to pick up the new pair of dress gloves at Martins? It was just gossip. She must have been a scatter-brain, not establishing I was darling before starting her gossip. I suppose I should have told her at once, but I was sleepy and dazed. I was also lonely. The gossip did me good. There was only one thing to do: break the connection, which I did. The moment the line was empty I felt the loneliness sweep over me again; disassociation, or the fear of it, made me tremble.

Do you really exist? The question fluttered at my heart as I hopped out of bed, reaching to switch on the television before an answer was demanded.

After this I knew it was to be a hard, bad night. I had that bathed-in-moonlight sharpness of the mind which indicates that I'm not going to sleep. Going to bed would be a start on the treadmill which never stops. You know the one? With me it is like this: some little episodes from my life with Mr Snorry; an examination of certain dreams which seemed harmless when I had them first, and then take on a sinister quality in the cold glare of insomnia; a succession of faces – too dangerous, I shy off, and explore a smuggler's cave. The tunnel always comes back to the sea; then cuts to the kitchen of the first house I ever remember and through a cupboard into a priest's hiding hole, the journey's the thing, wriggling and squirming around the low, bad bends, with the small room, the raised bench and disarrayed blanket, the low table, coming as something in the nature of an anti-climax. I am not dreaming, or re-dreaming these fancies, experiences, or dreams. I am actually examining them. You have no idea of the arid quality of despair. And it always comes round to that girl's face in the room of the empty house, framed in the old newspapers, not so much her eyes as her mouth. You knew without telling that it was dry. Where is she now, and whose seed –?

So I knew it was useless to put the light out. I read the thriller three times and went to sleep just as light was breaking. I had two non-personal dreams. In the first I was the unlucky one in a cowboy story. A tall man fell off his big rangy horse and took aim between the legs. It was so quick. I could hardly believe I was dying; then the incredible happened: the bastard rode his horse over me. I awoke with the belly part of the belly band imprinted on my mind, so relieved that I didn't feel cheated when I heard the noise of the traffic and saw that it was seven. Back in bed I went out like a light and awoke with a start in a studio and on a studio couch, set on the platform. The other bed was in the far corner down below. After a long time the noise stopped and I got out of bed and lo – the girl was in my bed. She lay with one hand between her belly and her thigh, what they used to call the lisk, fast asleep and slightly perspiring. Then she wasn't there and I padded over to the sink and had myself another glass of water. It was ten past seven; and I knew I was lonely again. The only compensation was knowing that I wouldn't have to cook my own breakfast on a greasy gas-cooker, finding the bacon smoked and cigarette ash in the butter and hearing the noise of the others getting dressed.

I walked along to the Tube and got a train to Aldwych because it was raining. All the male faces were alike. Luther would have delighted in them. The train was too crowded for newspaper reading and was full of damp clothes; discomfort and lack of occupation (you couldn't even read a paper by the longfold method) meant a lot of restless eyes. There wasn't much to see and it's astonishing how repulsive plastic hats and macs can make a decent-looking lass. There wasn't a decent profile in sight, let alone a lovely dimpled knee. For me, I mean. You could see other characters taking little nibbling glances, or long devouring looks, according to their nature. Eventually I worked it out. There was a girl facing the next door down and I knew without being able to see that she'd crossed her legs to get that wonderful mixture of blanching and dimpling. Once again I was aware that I was lonely, so lonely that I had no mercy at all on male or female, old or young, but most especially the men, because they were so well-shaven.

Clean-shaven men make me feel a mess and there's nothing I can do about it. Shave at eight and by nine I'm itching. I'll swear the whiskers are growing again. I have unfortunate whiskers and an unfortunate chin; that's why I use a barber on very special occasions. But I never use after-shave lotion and the fact that Mr Snorry did was the very sternest test of our friendship. The odour of after-shave mounted in the carriage second after second until it was stronger by half than violet passionesque, lavender lush, embrace, swish, tender, the gallons of stuff the girls had used, or carried in their handbags. The men were clean-shaven; they were tall; they had clean haircuts; they carried umbrellas rolled up like folded sleeping bats; but the odour was after-shave and not good, honest musk. I hated them and it.

The Aldwych. My real-life father, the manager of a small bank, had raved of the comedies; Tom Walls, Ralph Lynn, Robertson Hare, in plays and times that were good for bank clerks, when they could kid themselves that they were in it, or could have been in it, running around the corridors of the country house, wearing pyjamas or plus-fours, or, cut, nothing at all. I know why he adored them: they made him feel special and at the heart of things, master of London's West End and at home in a long weekend world of cars, golf and dressing for dinner. Yet he had savvy enough to know it was only an illusion, right away at the back of his mind he knew that he was the cuckoo in the nest, one of the many yearning heads of the big, ugly, and ever-yearning bird.

This hardly differed from the reality then, thirty, forty years ago. People on the run. Compared to this, going to work in the North was a fiesta. On the run. There's fire down below and behind. The flames were licking their arses. Yet my pace and pulse quickened. I had to force myself to a saunter. It was no use saying that the moment was what counted; this immediate, rain-drenched now which you could explore in several dimensions. You had to concentrate on walking slow, like a man trying out a pair of artificial legs in a world organised to tip you arse over tail. They bumped into you and you knew that falling wouldn't help: they'd only walk straight over you. Walking was the first test. The second was trying not to be taken in. They were not a black and plastic tide. They were not bits of iron filings on a card following a magnet below. Each had a forest fire inside and could send a deadly spark to me. There was an old man with a beard and snotty nose; I remember vowing I'd sooner join him than join the hurrying herd. I would much sooner be sunk in apathy than join this pitiful lot. And of course I had failed in my intention. I actually ran up the steps at UK House. I remember realising I'd been caught; I remember stopping and saying 'No!' and turning, taking a deep breath, and walking back down those steps. I was concentrating so hard that I ran into Holinshed.

We each took a step back and stared at each other. The first thing I did was sniff for after-shave. It was there. A sort of sweetened pine. I hated that, and the smooth baby's bottom shine of his chin. Not a whisker. I wondered what sort of private life he had, if any, and decided it would be neat like his chin. I wondered about his wife, his parents, his children, if any, his passions, hobbies, sports, habits, dislikes, likes, favourite newspaper, and, strangely, did he like sponge trifle? Perhaps my lips were moving. 'What's the matter? Forgotten something?' he asked. I decided not to tell him I was off for a coffee. Taking a deep breath I gripped his arm and turned him round facing the road. His umbrella had lost its press-button and was hanging sadly open.

'It's just occurred to me that nobody takes the trouble to notice anything or anybody in Gehenna,' I said. 'D'you know there's the ghost of my grandmother up the road a little crying "Fresh mint and hard-boiled eggs tuppence each."?' He had very blue, bewildered eyes and a fresh, oval face even if his moustache was a prop and his ears stuck out a bit. I took pity on him. 'Listen, Jack,' I continued, as the work-hungry hordes divided around us and poured in three separate and distinct streams, up, down and a tributary-in-reverse into my beloved building. 'Listen, you're inches taller than me and you've a better brain. How often have you gone up these steps?'

'Never thought of it, old man,' replied Holinshed assuming the tone of a man dealing with imbeciles and seniles. I was beginning to feel nicely intoxicated and held him with my unwinking eye.

'First, material. Don't look! What are they made of, eh? cement, marble, granite? See. You don't know.'

'Does it matter?' said Holinshed, looking uneasily around him but never at the steps.

'Because it's part of your world,' I cried. 'As much an extension of your person as your neat little hands and twiddly little toes. How can you hope to understand people if you don't know the pavement you walk on? How can you possibly grasp the reach of mind if you're ignorant of matter?' The act was in full swing. My resonant voice and magnetic eye had mastered him because they had also mastered me; I was succeeding because I was battling as much with myself as this handsome, bewildered adversary. 'D'you know where this kind of thing takes you? You forget to count people when you forget to count steps; starting from here you'll end by slapping your big feet on their most tender sensibilities. You'll reduce flesh, blood and spirit into something like the oblivion of stone.'

'You've got a point there,' said Holinshed, looking wildly for an escape. Without as much as by-your-leave I snatched the vampire umbrella from his grasp and used it as a pointer. 'Aberdeen granite hauled from a hideout older than life, and almost as old as time itself. Never wears into a groove (I was exaggerating) if you walked up and down it for a million years. Truly the mother-rock.'

Switching the umbrella to my other hand I took his arm and led him up the steps. I'll swear he was so embarrassed he still didn't bother to count them. He was more aware of the one watcher, a long, lean commissionaire who rocked a little on his heels at the other side of the open door and looked out with a little smile of contempt. I discovered later that his name was Jim Clay; an ex-regimental sergeant-major of an old and respectable regiment who survived with half a dozen others in the mountains of Crete until the end of the last big war. He found his wife married again when he returned from the tomb and was apt to be cynical. He was six feet three inches in height and gave us a kindly look as we passed under his Gibraltar heights. Guessing rapidly, I said: 'Good morning, sar'-major.' Holinshed ignored the response. Still hanging onto Holinshed's arm I reminded him that he hadn't counted the steps. 'Count them yourself,' he said, and broke away.

He went for the left-hand lift as it moved out of sight then moved in an arc for the other. He was like a runaway, well-groomed bullock. I followed at my leisure and sidled up to him.

'Here's your umbrella,' I said, my voice exuding pity. He murmured a thank you and flushed like a girl. He took off his hat as he entered the lift, and I saw that his neck glistened with sweat; I made a mental note to get myself a bowler hat just for the gesture. We were wedged face to face but he avoided my eye so I gazed with manic intensity at his tie, which had a narrow little knot. He should have consoled himself with the thought that he was taller than me. Instead, he looked like a man on the verge of a bad dose of malaria.

'Floor two,' said the lift boy. People left. As soon as we were in motion again I shifted my gaze to his face. 'Floor three.' Ignoring the people around us, including some very pretty girls, I said: 'Aren't you interested?' He shook his head. 'It's nice to know one little thing that thousands ignore. Trivial, I know, but the knowledge that there's five steps to the foyer is something worth having. When you're lonely, unhappy, shunned by the world, you can say to yourself, "Well, at least I know there are five steps below that canopy."'

'Floor four,' said the lift boy, his big nose quivering. 'You're wrong there – about the steps. There's four.'

'Want a bet?'

'Take you on,' said the lift boy. 'I'm betting there's four flats between the pavement and floor level. Take me?'

'Take you for a shilling!' I told him. 'T'would be a shame to take your quid.' We were at floor five, but the lift boy had forgotten to name it. He was also smiling. Holinshed walked out but couldn't resist a look, not at me, but the lift boy. More accurately, at his smile.

'I'll pick it up this time tomorrow,' I told the lift boy, wondering if he were right.

'*I'll* pick the bob up tonight,' he said confidently. I rejoined Holinshed and remarked: 'That's part of the job. I've made his day. He won't mind the shilling.' I had deliberately made my voice oily and patronising. 'It's good for them. It's good for us. I noticed it once, during a budget period. Working against time and a pile-up of other work. I suddenly noticed I'd stopped seeing people and things . . .'

'This is where I meditate,' said Holinshed politely. We had reached his office door.

'Which I've never seen. Let's break two eggs with one stone.' I elbowed him through the door. Wills was approaching – one of those types who suffer from insomnia and turn it into a virtue. We both said good morning. I believe Wills answered; but not with the words in his heart. Holinshed gave him an abject look. I said, 'Come on, Jack,' as if I could hardly wait to get on with our talk. Who was to know that I was putting off the terrible moment of meeting people I'd have to lead, nurse, control; bully or praise, treat to the occasional smile and founder with the intermittent frown? I sat on the edge of the desk, prattling on whilst he got rid of some, but not all, of his bits and pieces.

'To continue: I realised that the best way to start would be to look for the odd things about people. I used to jot down odd sayings – there was a character, for instance, well-educated, who used to urge us all to implement, that is, get the thing done. Good, eh? There was another type whose eyes would flood with unbidden tears whenever he'd cause to run anyone down. Like Mistress Clark, in the song.' I took a deep breath and burst into song.

> *'There's Mary Smith, upon the stairs,*
>   *A wild an' rakish lass,*
> *Aw wunder where she gets her claes,*
>   *Aw's sure she hes ne brass,*
> *They say she's thick wi' Draper Jim, –*
>   *He's not up te the mark, –*
> *But mind aw shuddint menshun this,*
>   *Aw hope ye'll a' keep't dark!'*

'What in earth was that?'

'That,' I proudly remarked, 'was a song.'

'Oh . . .' he said.

'In my native language,' I continued. 'There's much more to it than that, but I'll spare you. Now, Mistress Clark didn't give a damn. But this type did. It wrung his withers to scandalise his pals. There were lots of little things of the sort. I discovered that some of the peculiarities belonged to me. You'll see them, if you're really observant. For instance, every senior man in the office wore a moustache.'

'Odd,' said Holinshed with a sigh, obviously wishing he could tell me to scram.

'It's the same here,' I rapidly continued. '*You* wear a moustache. So does Wills. All the chaps below thirty wear 'em, with one exception: me. Everywhere else you'll find it's beards, but here it's slit-trench moustaches. Why? I ask you why?'

'You tell me,' said Holinshed, fingering his own two by three-eighths of an inch.

'It's the environment,' I said. 'We're a big, solid organisation. You wouldn't think it, but we're big and safe. Did you ever know anybody get fired? Of course not. We're self-insured against loss of personnel. All inter-locked, swings and roundabouts, can't lose, can't even lose staff. Anywhere else they regard a moustache as something sinister. Here at UK the chaps can have a fling. They take it with a moustache. Symbol of built-in safety, whiskers betwixt the nose and the upper lip.'

'Very clever, very,' said Holinshed. His telephone purred. It was the internal. He picked it up, drummed with his fingers on the desk, said 'Yes, by all means, any time you like. Yes, come along.' Looking up at me, he shrugged. I guessed it was pal Patsy Wills ringing to see if the coast was clear. I was done anyway. 'You keep your eyes pinned,' I instructed in departing.

He nodded, looking sad and intense. He was still wearing his hat, forgotten in that drawn-out strip-tease act on entering, which had actually been calculated so as to offer me his back for audience. I decided not to tell him. Let the spectacle provide an opening gambit for friend Wills. 'Give me a tinkle if you need anything,' he suggested, worried at my thin little smile.

'I will,' I promised, with that little extra heartiness which means not-on-your Nelly. Should I need him he'd be all the more delighted; but the chances were that I wouldn't. I left him uneasy in his chair.

THREE

I'm so good I just have to be dilettante. Shying away from the serious for all sorts of trivial reasons; quick-witted, digesting paper quickly, I have time left on my hands. Being a born liar, devious, deceitful, and cunning to boot, I save the world a lot of trouble by working my defects out on myself. That's why I hate television: it's like watching countless versions of myself. Even the late night prestige shows are too simple for me. Two scenes and I'm with it to such a degree that I know the end they'll give and can only relieve the monotony by providing my own. When I say it's like watching myself I mean that I'm practically a fictitious character; and don't put on airs. You're the same. We're not serious about anything.

It was the smell of incense that stopped me becoming a Catholic; stopped me being a serious person in the only possible way. I can't stand it. It makes me gag. I'd spew over the priest at my first confession. But that's an act, and the simplest act is beyond me. Don't blame me for riding people; it's the only fun I get, apart from polishing off a difficult piece of paper work, and the odd day dream or two; the day dreams being a compensation for the dreams in the night, and in sleep, which I cannot control. And don't blame me if I entered my office feeling a little like Alexander the Great, slipping off that shapeless black overcoat which was really my banner, smoothing both hands over my slick black hair, literally preening myself for my little victory over Holinshed.

I didn't like my chair. It had bars across the back. The man before me had been a man with a lascivious mind and a Nonconformist rearing; the chair had been his sole concession to

43

the latter. I buzzed Miss Rosalie Miffin. 'This chair doesn't fit,' I said. 'I want a revolving chair with an adjustable back-rest. What's the drill? Do I just ask Squires?'

'You could,' she coolly replied. 'But he'd only ask you to put it in writing, because he'll have to make out a requisition and have it countersigned by Mr Walker Johnson.'

'Ah? Mr R. Walker Johnson?' I said indulgently. 'You know the drill. Type a memo, and I'll sign it. That's known as division of labour.'

'Only I get paid less than you.' I was glad to note her pertness.

'Never mind, I'll make your working life pleasant beyond measure.'

I hesitated, then leaned and said: 'And you can make *my* working life pleasant too. You see, I'd a fall last year. Doing a method study on a buffing plant – empty, of course – fell to the bottom. And didn't bounce. My back still gives me trouble . . .'

'Oh, I'm sorry . . .'

'Thank you. Mind you, they patched it up with aluminium wire. But it sometimes aches.' I noticed she hadn't made a note. Sackless, or she'd a first-rate memory. Her eyes shone – I'd given her the emotional jolt which every business woman needs per day, to keep her at her pitch. 'Now let's see, make a note of these: I'd like to see Messrs Holinshed, Wills, Henry, Osbourne, Swift at intervals of ten minutes, beginning at eleven.' She nodded. 'You're the organiser, fit them in at our convenience, tell them to be prepared for a quick run through on what's in hand at the moment.'

I rapped this out at a fair pace, noticing that she barely looked at her book and that the pencil moved smoothly, as if following an invisible magnetic line in the paper. On the other hand, she kept giving me little pecking looks of interest. 'What about post?' I asked. She said she was sorting it out. She was a large, not to say lush, girl. Her hair was purple and her eyes intelligent. Her eyes looked ready for laughter. I looked at my watch and found it was nearly nine-thirty. 'In future I'd like it on my desk by ten past nine.' She took it without flinching. Gratefully I applied the salve. 'What we're after is getting the work load flowing so that we've time to play around, do some thinking, even some picking of other brains.' The brown eyes were laughing. 'Shall I fetch it now?'

'Not to worry. At the moment we're organising. Slip out and get another notebook.' For a large girl she moved quickly. 'This may sound a bit ridiculous to you, but bear with me,' I told her. 'You'll have two books for dictation. Always bring them with you. One's for them, the other's for me. Private, personal, confidential. That's mine. And lock it up between shifts.'

'Of course.'

'I don't mind sharing my thoughts with you,' I said. She gave me a dubious look. 'I'd better explain. I'm building up a talk on middle management. I shall give it to the assembled students and staff of Staff College.'

'I'll enter it in the diary,' she offered, too quickly for my liking.

'They haven't asked; but they will,' I affably answered. 'And you can call me Mr Rowlands. I'll call you Miss Miffin.'

'My first name's Rosalie.'

'Charming! But we'll stick to surnames. Makes me secure, and you safe.' She was smiling. 'Do I sound pompous?' She shook her head. 'Always tell me when I'm pompous,' I continued. 'I'd rather we laughed together.' That stopped the incipient giggle. 'All right, kiddar – sorry, Miss Miffin, let's start.'

I looked into the polished surface of the desk to find inspiration. I found my face, which proved a sufficiently acceptable substitute. 'A spectre is haunting Europe, Russia, the United States; it is the spectre of the humdrum. All the powers of old Europe, modern Russia and a prodigiously wasteful United States of America, have entered into an unholy alliance to exorcise this spectre: Russian and Italian Popes; President and Prime Minister, IMB and FBI, British radicals, French Monarchists, Spanish milk-and-water fascists, industrialists, managers, scientists who are secure in administration, all these; and also the secret agencies who know only what is happening where and when their information cannot possibly be confirmed or contradicted . . .'

Looking steadily at her averted face I asked: 'How does that sound?'

Her look was as steady as mine. Full marks. 'I didn't understand a word, but I like it. Much more romantic than the stuff Mr Simpson used to put over.'

'That was an adaptation,' I said.

'I'm sorry, I thought it was your own,' she cheerfully remarked as she put her pencil through her shorthand.

'Hey,' I said in alarm. 'Don't scrap it, we might manage to work it in somehow. Put "stet" alongside and carry on. First, in brackets, "H-Bomb missiles absolutely essential to provide edge of despair necessary for millions who are sated with affluence."'

'That sounds reasonable,' she said. 'I'm sure I don't know what we'd do without the thing.'

'You gladden my heart,' I said. 'Continue as follows: But the spectre cannot be exorcised. Heaven in the sky was replaced by manna on earth. Now that there are bread and circuses for all, there is no heaven, hope, anticipation, nothing to be deluded by, to live and die for, to be possessed by . . . where is the goal for millions who need uplift as well as manna?'

How her pencil glided! I could already see the immaculate typescript of this imperishable nonsense. 'Communism, which began as a revolt against capitalism, ends as a more efficient way of working the system. Capitalist imperialism, which began as a necessary reaction to collectivism, is now as near collectivist as can be. Now it is only necessary to merge white with black to finish a revolution which began with a mighty effort to keep them apart.'

'The saviours who asked millions to die have failed more miserably than the saviour who died for uncounted millions.' I paused and she lifted an enquiring head. 'I'm stuck.'

'I should jolly well think so!'

'Can you give me a clue?'

'So far you don't believe in anything. Now you tell them you do. And tell them what it is.'

'There's the rub,' I murmured, tasting sour grapes that set my teeth on edge.

'It's time for coffee,' she suggested. 'Do you take milk and sugar?'

'I take tea with both,' I reprimanded. She rose, bubbling over with mirth and delight. At least I'd achieved that much.

She returned with the tea, and proceeded to leave me alone in that very large office.

'No, don't hurry away. Tell me some more,' I said.

She hesitated.

'Go on,' I urged.

'Well, it's copied, it's not your own; and it's copied from something very good . . .'

'You don't know what?'

'No, but it was something good and it must have had something new to offer and an ending just as good as the beginning. But yours . . .'

'What's going to be wrong with my version?' I probed.

'Well, I don't know, but I've been taking notes for speeches for a long time, not only here, and I think it's going to end up about decency and dignity and human beings are important . . .'

I got up and walked round the desk. 'Actually, you're wrong. I wasn't going to say that selfishness should become the prime virtue, because all of us are quite convinced in ourselves that it really is; but that selfishness or self-interest should be recognised, approved, and rewarded. Y'know, bring it out into the open. Let's have heroes of laziness – I mean, anyone who can manage to get away with it, I mean live without work, has to suffer, organise and use his brains . . .'

She was openly appalled. 'But you're wrong!'

'I'm not, you know. Laziness *was* a vice, now it's becoming a necessity, men have to be lazy to make room for the machines, but they'll have to work at being lazy. Same with courage, generals, soldiers, war – they're out of date. We can't afford to strike medals for bravery today, when the kind of thinking that was fine fifty years ago could result in killing not just one soldier in a trench a few yards away but millions of us. So we should be looking for cowards, encouraging people with survival values – Distinguished Cross for Cowardice, Medal for Unmilitary Conduct, Ribbon for Running Away, with Bar for running away at least three times . . .'

I was getting in my stride.

'We'd encourage strikes. Call up the shop stewards and say "Look here, it's a month since we had a decent strike; you're not doing the jobs you're paid for." There's a thought,' I continued thoughtfully, struck, as always, by my extemporaneous brilliance. 'We could ensure strikes – have at least twenty days in the year as a modest beginning. Ben Tillett Day, Cook's Day, Shop Steward

Monday, when everyone has a paid holiday, only they're bound to come in and then walk out again . . . How's that strike you?'

'I think you're a Communist!'

'Ah – you *think* I'm a Communist – I *think* I'm a real wolf, with real teeth – and I bite!'

'Terrible things,' she said primly. 'I'm sure I don't know what people would think if they knew.'

'That's not important. Did you get it all?' She glanced at her book aghast, then at me reproachfully.

'But I didn't know you wanted it taking down!' she wailed. 'Honestly I didn't!'

'It doesn't matter this time,' I said. 'It's all in my head. I'll dictate it some other time. Now you run away and look after the visitors. Who's first in?'

'I'll get Mr Holinshed – and I'm sorry about the dictation.'

'Not to worry. Get a looseleaf book and type down what I've already given you. Then bring the book into me.' I lowered my voice to a conspiratorial whisper. 'We'll keep it in the bottom left-hand drawer.' I laid two fingers over my lips: 'Top Secret.'

Purring, she departed. I tipped back my chair, murmuring something to the effect: 'She'll do.' Stretching too far, the chair slipped. I found myself on the floor, shaking with laughter. Recovering, I stood up, placed finger-tips on the polished surface of the desk, declaimed: 'A spectre is haunting Europe, Russia, the US; the spectre of a shadowy fly-by-night. The spectre strikes at will with deadly accuracy from the obscurity in which he has his chosen being and in which he will most probably die.'

That one I discarded as soon as born, with a single sharp command: 'Wipe.' I nodded gravely. The cameras began rolling again. Now I was the head of the world-wide secret service.

'Who is that spectre? Ladies and gentlemen, Martians, I have news for you. Over the past ten years a thousand picked men, the cream of our trained operatives have been scouring homes, factories, offices, schools, research establishments, universities, drydocks, hospitals, public conveniences. Their efforts at last have borne fruit. The Unknown is not, as you may have imagined, a young multi-millionaire with an IQ of 200; or some unlikely genius in a position of power and authority with the resources of an entire nation behind him; or an extra-sensory heading a vast conspiracy. No ladies and gentlemen, Martians, Moon-dwellers! This is the unimaginable!'

A record interplanetary audience, the largest in history, leaned tensely forward. In Peking the eternal Mao rapped: 'Is this being recorded?' without for a moment taking his eyes from the tri-dimensional screen. They were also watching on moon-stations as meteorites ripped through fabric of Selenite shelters and automatic puncture-repair outfits whipped, unheeded, into action. Rocket ships went into a second orbit in order that crew and passengers alike might not miss the most astonishing revelation in solar history.

'No, fellow-citizens, he is none of these. He is, in fact, a humble member of middle management who has earned the tolerant contempt of his colleagues and superiors, a quiet, industrious business man working conscientiously from nine to twelve every week-day. Can you think of a better camouflage than this – the suburban home and oblivious family, the innocently unaware neighbours, the daily eight-thirty train to town, the humdrum office . . .'

I paused expectantly, whilst cameras panned to the back of a familiar figure walking casually along the Embankment and approaching the entrance to UK House.

'There he goes. We have cameras waiting inside and in a moment, citizens of three worlds, you will see his face; the face of the author of chaos . . .'

What made me pause was an appearance at the door giving direct access to the corridor. The appearance was a face. The skin had that parchment quality and it was folded around extraordinary ice-blue eyes to form a smile. 'Am I interrupting?' asked my boss. It was the Chief Controller, Mr Small Summers.

'Nothing in the least important. Do come in,' I invited. A very good couple of lines, had not my voice cracked. He was only an inch taller than me; but he was thin and I was embarrassed. The inch seemed more like twelve.

'I can always pop in again,' he protested, revealing more of himself, including a very yellow woollen tie which gratefully hid the most poisonous part of itself under a nice blue waistcoat. 'I'll not sit, thank you. I like to sit when I'm drinking but not when I'm in action: it's the hyena blood . . . sorry to interrupt your lecture rehearsal, by the way.'

'Actually, it was an interplanetary video thing,' I explained. An important rule is never to allow anyone else to cover up for you; this follows never allowing yourself to conduct a cover-up operation.

'Ah, yes,' he said. 'Well, I hope it comes off. I want to forget television – that's video, isn't it? Only appeared on it once, turned to the compère, said: "Jolly good show," and he fainted. Well, practically, the thing was still alive.'

'You're safe enough this time,' I said.

Ignoring this, he continued: 'Sorry I didn't get in to see you yesterday, succession of meetings, I'm sure Walker Johnson . . .' He'd a trick of leaving sentences suspended which was actually better than a flowery compliment. His manner suggested that a gesture was sufficient between men of reasonably good intelligence. 'And you're suited?' He paused. 'Everything batches?' I was dying to look that one up in the dictionary, not believing it was even a crossword-type word. I was rather put out to discover it was, in fact, a proper word. 'By the way,' he continued vaguely. 'Have they really settled on the Moon and Mars?' I said no and he smiled gratefully.

I was about to go into details when he continued: 'You'll have met Squires. Good RSM lost . . .'

'He's looking well after me.'

But the Chief Controller had lost interest. Finger to mouth, he had gone into a trance. The eyes were frosted glass. I realised I was sitting against his standing; just for something to do I stood up. 'Sit down, sit down,' said the Chief Controller. 'I knew there was something. My wife asked me to call and get cheese biscuits, cocktail kind. But I can't remember the kind. I'm going home tonight. Always go home mid-week. Do you know any special kind of biscuit?'

'I wouldn't touch them,' I told him. 'The proper place for marrying cheese and biscuit is in the mouth. Before the event's a kind of bigamy.'

'That's very shrewd – no right – of you. But would you call a biscuit the groom?'

'Better the bread they *don't* make today.'

'Crusty bread. And beer as priest.' He was beaming.

'No, strong tea diluted with milk.'

'Depends on your taste,' he said. 'I was brought up on beer.'

'I wasn't.'

'No, of course,' he said. 'They tell me you like a joke.' It was a statement, not a question; so much so that I barely stopped myself from bowing.

'Life gets monotonous.'

'It does indeed,' he agreed. 'So why not look for – what do they call him – the fall guy, eh? A lovely phrase. Can you see him in his changing shape and – er – humours?'

Stung by his description – I can hardly call it a reproof – I said: 'He's the fall guy before he ever takes the fall. Look at Adam; the fall was a built-in characteristic.'

He was looking at me with some respect. I returned the look, with interest. His news-service was working well. '*How* many steps are there?'

'Five, sir,' I said, with the finality I always gave my sparing 'sirs'.

'Well, they've certainly proved steps to a widening of – er – life, eh?'

'I hope so,' I said modestly.

He chose to sit down, visibly struggling against the onset of yet another trance. 'Drop in when you feel it's absolutely necessary, keep up the good work. Without taking it . . .'

'I hope my idea of moderation coincides with yours, Controller,' I said. I was just about to tell him that he was in *my* office when he managed to re-orientate himself. 'I shall have to grow a moustache,' he roguishly remarked. He departed, a man after my own heart. The best I'd met of the ilk so far. And the first to return a volley.

FOUR

And if you think I scratched my own back after he'd gone, you're wrong. I'm not perverse, but I know when I'm knocked. Otherwise, why should I be saying so assiduously to myself: 'He was born like me, exists like me, hanging on by the very fingernails he will die as miserably as I will die.' See? But it didn't do me any good at all. He was a smooth operator and I respected him to the edge of a tiny, crawling fear which had nothing to do with status, power, increments, promotions. He couldn't hurt me. I was, after all, a bachelor, seeking freedom, anxious to be out and aching for a spell of unemployment and dying to sleep on the street. No, it had nothing to do with business. Damn and blast his eyes, he was simply the superior beast. And I so wanted to please him.

Henceforth he stayed with me. How long is it since they carried him out of his office – six months, six years? He's still with me. The mere mention of his name makes the provincial jump – good dog! The parchment skin and azure eyes are still clear in my memory, and sometimes, thinking of him, I look up, half expecting him to walk in and seat himself with the same easy grace, cross his legs and lean forward, as prelude to an easy interrogation, with the crooked smile I grew to fear and respect.

Of course, I tried the proper technique. When something humiliating happens you must regard the whole sequence as something in the nature of the rough cuts which a film director runs through at the end of the day's shooting. You run the thing through the machine time and time again until familiarity breeds contempt and you are able to see and judge it quite objectively, you know, making notes on the weak scenes and lines with a view to re-shooting. No, not with a view. With the certainty that you must re-shoot; same scene some other day not necessarily with the same actors. In this way you kill anything that might cripple you. That's the theory.

I interviewed the underlings. Wills was cool and made three attempts to pull the wool over my eyes. I allowed him to think he'd got away with it. Holinshed was so nervous and co-operative that my heart was warmed and chilled alternately. I remembered Wills saying he had troubles. He had guilt as well. Otherwise, why should his eyes mist so easily?

The lower ranks were uninteresting, with the exception of Osbourne. He was thin, spotty and casual; but I was shocked to find that he'd mastered my trick of reading upside down. I pretended to make a note then pushed the paper clear. He got the message. Thereafter he religiously kept his eyes clear of my desk, pretending great interest in the neighbouring office cubes. I had written: 'Do you steam Mummy's letters open as well?'

I went to lunch with Squires in the staff canteen, and didn't like the company around us. There were too many. Rampion came over and introduced himself as head of Technical. I said that this could be lived down. He laughed and waggled his beard. 'You'll be getting an examination paper from me. West Hartlepools study,' he said. 'God bless you,' I said. I judged him a rogue who didn't care about anything, even being caught – like the man who travelled all over the world, learning to build bridges, the hard way – for others.

'I hear the Chief was in to see you,' said Squires. I nodded and remarked that he seemed to be an informal old gentleman. 'Don't be taken in,' said Squires.

'Well, it's something,' I said. 'I'll bet R.W.J. sends, or rings and asks in a pleasantly-ugly way for your attendance.'

'R.W.J.'s the perfect example of the split mind,' said Squires. 'At home, mysticism and music. At work, the theology of self first, last, and bugger you Jack. You'll enjoy watching him playing musical chairs, selecting the appropriate moment to jump into the discussion.'

'Ah, but that's the game.'

'But not the serious part,' said Squires. 'The serious part is getting your expenses – you've got to work at it, you know. Watching the car racket: next time it's a Zephyr with a radio. And curtains; no stock material for him, no, Joe Soap brings a bloody great book to the master so's he can feel as well as see. Did you know that desks and carpets grow with the man; and did you know how difficult it is to see that it's done with the minimum?'

'I'm so glad he's so human.'

'All I'm saying is that the Chief reserves his energies for the important things.'

'Then one ought to be glad the others are distracted.'

'But it's blockage, can't you see?' cried Squires. He dug into his pockets. 'Talk about ancient Rome! We're as bad in our organised way. The booty of business . . . where is that dam'd thing – ah yes – your memo, sir.'

'My memo – so you got it?' I smiled.

'So you want a chair? Well, I'll admit the one you have's a bit rough. But the new chair won't give you half so much pleasure as dictating this scrap of paper.'

'Let me read it,' I said. He handed it over.

'Aluminium wire!' he said reproachfully, as I handed it back.

'I signed it but never really saw it,' I said. 'A beautiful piece of initiative on Miss Miffin's part.'

'That makes no odds,' he said. 'Whoever wrote it, and however beautifully, I still have to lick some uncompromising backside to get it for you – your little bit of booty.'

'Well, it's your job, you know.'

He grinned wickedly. 'I'll tell you a bedtime story. Happens a CO 1 – like yourself – was translated to the Siberia of a Deputy Area Controllership – isn't that much better than Centurion, or Legate?'

'It is. Go on,' I ordered.

'He was hardly out of the office before a CO 2 over the corridor – who was in for the job and the office anyway – was on my bones for the carpet. I pointed out that he might get the job. He replied that in that case he'd have to claim it back. In the end, for peace, I bribed a couple of handymen to operate the transfer –'

'With what?' I asked.

'The nature of the bribe's my business. What's important is that

54

I managed it. The CO 2 was happy and I was at peace – for a time. I'll give him good, he knew in his bones he wouldn't get the job.'

'But the carpet was his consolation prize.'

'And a chap as objective as you would never mind –' He was bursting to laugh. 'I mean, you haven't seen – seen the hole yet.'

'Let's have a walk down to my office,' I murmured. It was as he had said; I'd never have noticed the hole.

I didn't need to ask who it was; now I knew why Wills had smirked when he glanced at the carpet.

'Let's go for a pint,' I said. We had a drink at the local pub. He pretended to like whisky and lemonade. I gathered he lodged with a woman named Pennington, an undertaker's widow; so that paid for *my* round. I'd a feeling there was a coffin with something in it, but he wouldn't talk. He told me again his compensation was reviewing books; his pseudonym was Simon Sharp. The name of the newspaper made me whistle. 'Oh, it's not the money,' he said. 'I get a kick sorting the sheep from the goats. What's your compensation?'

'Separating the goats from the sheep,' I said. 'People, not authors.'

'There's more to it than that,' he said.

'There's history,' I replied. His Adam's apple went up and down and he never took his eyes away from my face, but I wasn't enlarging. Plenty of time for that later.

Back in the office I disregarded the paper about Hartlepools, copies to self, Chief Controller and Deputy Chief Controller, and thought of the day I'd make my pilgrimage to the Churchyard at Wallsend to hunt for tombstones. I found my paternal grandparents; devout Methodist minister, dedicated wife; saw, with a shudder, he'd died at sixty, she at sixty-two; mourned the child died in infancy; then had my flash of inspiration. Why should I be so respectable? Why shouldn't persons as well as political parties re-write history? Only, I would re-dream it. That was how it started. You can't change the future; it grinds out the way you never want it. But the past is like clay, soft, pliable, potent. You can make of it what you want.

The trouble is the present. You can do nothing about that, except kick it in the backside. But the other was richly rewarding.

Mind you, Snorry, the wise one, was never taken in. 'What didn't your ancestors do?' he'd say, as I pointed out the site of the famous gibbet, the stone where he spoke, the gaol where they kept him; or various relics of grave-stealers, illicit whisky manufacturers, stage-coach whips, Chartists with a cast in the eye but not in the heart, etc., etc. 'Sykes' Local Records?' He wasn't far off the mark.

I looked out at all the other office blocks. It was dusk and all the pretty squares of glass were alight and ablaze.

Each block was a ship streaming through time and leaving behind the spume of life's trivia: heading for that harbour where man's Flying Dutchman will come at last to rest, drop anchor, and accept extended shore leave and a free pardon from the ancient curse: Cursed is the ground, the sea, the air, for thy sake; in sorrow shalt thou rule them, ah! ah! all the days of thy life. Thorns and thistles, galleyslops, desks and duplicators, sick headaches and fear of customs shall they bring forth to thee. A pretty trick if the curse were changed: Cursed is the earth for thy sake; in idleness shalt thou eat of it all the days of thy life. All the masses and the classes being poured out like cards through a computer, flipped onto the appropriate conveyor, fed into the multitudinous seats of an amphitheatre as big as the world. Doors magnetically locked until the end of a show that may go on for ever.

I shivered and plunged into the paper about the Hartlepools. By four-thirty I'd gutted the thing. It was a pretty piece of work, all the figures added up, but I knew it wouldn't work. I knew the plant; the buffing tanks were the oldest in the North East and were known at the Area Office as Weary Willie and Tired Tim; the expected throughput was impossibly high. I scribbled a note to this effect and suggested new twin tanks at an estimated cost of £200,000.

The phone went miaow. Walker Johnson asked: 'Is that you, old chap?'

'I think so.' It was pretty near the truth. The work had skated me around the hole in the ice which is disassociation: at the back of my mind all the time had been the picture of that fleet going nowhere from nowhere.

'Feeling ill?'

'In fact, I never felt better.' There was a pause as he pulled on the reins and held his seat to work that one out.

'I rang you up about our little society – you've heard about it?' He went into an explanation and I went into a dream about Miss Cavendish. Returning too late I managed to snatch at the note of query.

'Hello – hello – I can't hear you. Something wrong with the line.'

'I said: "Can you make Friday evening?"'

Cuddling the phone I shouted: 'I'm still not getting you; can you give me strength seven?'

'You needn't shout; I can hear you all right at this end,' shouted R. Walker Johnson. I detected a note of saintly annoyance.

He was also beginning to sound a note of suspicion. I decided to help him on a little. 'I couldn't possibly stay all night.'

His outrage almost broke him a blood vessel, '*Not* all night – and listen, I can hear you – can hear you all right!' This was the one which pulled Cathie in high alarm into his office.

'That's funny,' I said, dropping my voice to a whisper. 'It must be my end – you were saying?' He babbled rapidly that now he wasn't getting me. Halfway through I interrupted him: 'Hang on, I'll try shaking the phone.' I held the thing away from me and heard him remark to Cathie: 'I'm beginning to think he's accident prone –'

In that instant I dropped the telephone bang onto the desk. Picking it up again, I said: 'How's that?'

'Can you hear me now?' asked R.W.J. He sounded like a man trapped in a traffic jam for a long time.

'Clear as a bell!'

'I'm glad the knocking worked – or was it gunpowder?'

'Flat of my hand,' I explained. 'As the peasant says in New York: "One cure for the fast woman and a stubborn telephone: the flat –"'

'Yes, yes,' said R.W.J., tiring. 'We meet at the Roman Ruin, a pub just around the corner, friendly little place. Holinshed's giving a paper on the *wonderful* new book by the woman who wrote that *tremendous* thing last year, y'know the one, about the man who had an affair with his mother.'

'That surely wasn't last year's book,' I said, pretending to be puzzled. 'You must mean Oedipus Rex – it's as old as the hills.'

'This was modern, not Greek,' said Walker Johnson shortly.

'And a novel not a play. Will you join us?' Desperation had driven him to utter something in the nature of a threat. Innocent words, terrible tone.

Holding the telephone away from me I murmured 'Or else?'

'I can't hear you again,' he shouted.

'Delighted!' I cried in a voice that shook the room.

'I'll call and pick you up on the night, then,' said R. Walker Johnson. He sounded an injured party. I hoped he was and would continue to be.

I returned to the paper. At the back of my mind I was roasting Walker Johnson. I decided to make him trouble. He needed some coming his way for his soul's sake. I was still deep in the Hartlepools project when Miss Miffin put her head round the door to say good night. My sallow, weary face must have pulled at her heart-strings.

'You shouldn't stay too long.'

'I'm enjoying myself.'

'That's the wrong kind of enjoyment,' she said. 'What was the racket?'

'I was having an all-in-wrestling match with Walker Johnson – over the telephone.'

'You look it,' she said. 'You get yourself home and eat a good dinner.'

It was the 'go home' that did it. Home is the place you hate only when you have it. I didn't have it. This was my home; the collection of cubes in the van of a mighty fleet. I put out the main light and switched on the desk lamp, enjoying the cosiness of darkness as I crossed the room. I should have been a caveman: Jules Verne type, deep down, in a cosy inner world, with a streamer of flaming gas for cooking and to keep me warm. In the old days, wandering in that land just south of the Cheviot, I'd often looked for the pipe through which I'd wriggle. I'd been convinced then, was still half-convinced, that it lay somewhere among the bents. In the utter silence with the sun at half-mast you could sometimes hear a noise in the lower register. If once I could only follow that noise . . . I rapidly sketched out the world which must lie below that old, healed volcano: forest of fungi; river of light; inland sea; island, shrouded in milky mist, home of John Carter's white apes, civilised now and natural allies; the outlet, falls of Zimmerman, whose stone hut and pathetic diary I'd found on the edge of the canyon; blue land, where limelight played on one bit of forest at a time, revealing faces of angels, or demons. And far in the distance and downwards the terraced descents of Diamond Hills and the single great tree hung with jewels which were fruit . . .

'You're staying all night?' It was Miss Cathie Cavendish. She had remembered me, then. I was pleased.

'What else is there to do?' I asked pathetically.

'The world's yours.' She'd a wide generous mouth. I glanced at the little sketch, slightly amazed at the coincidence. 'A bachelor boy with the world at his feet . . . you could have all sorts of adventures.'

'Where do you live?'

'Kew,' she said. I knew she was joking.

'You must take me to the gardens some time.'

'I'd be delighted.' I leapt to my feet and reached for my coat. 'But not tonight.' I hunched my shoulders and returned to my desk and that lonely pool of light.

'You've a date of your own?'

'What else is a date?' she asked.

'You've never known a date till you've dated me.'

Some girls have necks and others have a lump of flesh between the shoulders and the head. Hers was an excitingly moulded column with a delicious area of shadow I badly wanted to touch. I'd never seen gentian, but I imagined they'd be the colour of her eyes. Sloe-eyed and toffee-eyed women are often sluts; so are some of the women with gentian eyes, but one forgives *them*.

She pulled on her gloves, laughing. 'You're a brash young man.'

'I'm as young as you.'

'I suppose you are,' she said. The laughter had gone.

'Will you have a coffee with me, then, before you take your train to a wholly unsatisfactory date?'

'You are well?' she asked, ignoring the suggestion, and I was touched by her concern. 'R.W.J. didn't know what to think.'

'I hadn't the courage to turn him down.'

'I thought so,' she said. 'He's a pet; you shouldn't do it.'

We looked at each other, reluctant to part, I imagined, flattering myself for once. 'Well,' she said, leaving several sentences unspoken. 'Don't work too hard.'

Everyone so chummy. In quick order came Squires, Holinshed and Wills to say good night. 'Everyone so sociable,' I said to Wills, and ticked off the names of my callers.

'We're all very close,' he said. 'But none more than Miss Cavendish and Holinshed.' Then he left me shattered, like a maiden aunt who had just discovered she's illegitimate.

I went to my splendid bookcase and found a sweet little brochure on the MacArdle-Munster process, the one which annihilates the foam of any detergent. I hadn't known that MacArdle had been a works chemist and coarse fisherman who objected to casting a line over six feet of foam. He'd made the bullets, and Munster, a motor mechanic, had devised a method of firing them; all the complicated apparatus of the buffing tank. Munster had a lesser claim to fame: he'd bred a black rose and a purple sweet-pea. As I tried to read I saw Holinshed's hand on hers in a dark little coffee-shop. I decided to do Wills down for telling me with such expedition; not then knowing that he was at his usual game of compensating. I doubt if the knowledge would have made any difference. Emerging from the pit at seven-thirty or so I picked up the telephone. I was beginning to doubt my identity again.

'Switchboard?'

'Sir?'

'Your Grace,' I corrected. 'This is the Bishop of Sodom and the Blessed Isles.'

'Yes, your Grace?' She'd a sense of humour, then.

'I'm in retreat on the fifth floor. All my vicars, rectors, canons and curates have gone. I can endure no more, my child. Is the canteen open?'

'Satan himself went up and closed it.'

'Has he now? And me slaving over a hot desk all day.'

'You can have one with me,' she said. They always have a kettle on the boil; it's their substitute for a cradle . . . out of the kettle, endlessly boiling.

'As long as you don't mind condensed milk.'

I told her I loved nothing better, and she laughed.

'Where are you?' she asked. I told her. 'Well, you come down the backstairs. Come out of your corridor and turn left and left again on the landing, sort of double back into the other corridor. Walk to the end of that and you'll find the rear service lifts. Come down all the way into the basement, and don't forget to bring your overcoat and things 'cos it's a long walk back – then walk straight ahead from the bottom of the stairs –'

'I'm writing it down, wait till I catch up.'

'Sorry – but this place is a rabbit warren and you could get lost.'

'I'm ready again.'

'Quite simple from the bottom of the stairs. Walk straight in front of your nose, then take the first turning left . . . the switchboard's the first door on your right.'

'I hope I'm not keeping you . . . ?'

'Oh, lord no. I'm on until ten. There's always somebody on the switchboard. The computer room's on twenty-four hours, you know. Then there's His Nibs – '

'And who's His Nibs?'

'I shouldn't have said that.'

'Okay, I'll be seeing you, then,' I said.

'Okay.' Her voice was doubtful. She was wondering who and what I was. There were some funny types about. Slouch coats, popping eyes, limping walk, scarred faces . . . But who was His Nibs?

I also wondered, this being in the nature of young men and sometimes the aged, what kind of girl she was. Girl, not woman; that delighted laugh was indubitably girlish. The voice had just that right rough touch of suburban or Home Counties cockney. In a man's voice it irritated beyond measure. In a girl's voice it could be as kind on the ear as unblended whisky to the throat. Smoky voice, sultry girl, I dreamed, walking along the quiet corridor, leaving behind the single night light, the cavern's evening star. It gave me great comfort to be alone, or practically alone, in this great building. Nostalgia for an old dream swept over me. My roadsweeper-father had once stood in for the nightshift man at the pumping station down by the river, six till six, and my happiest memory, or invention, was of taking his supper down in the Autumnal dusk, can of hot tea in one hand, steak and kidney pudding basin wrapped up in a tea towel, in the other. It had been a pleasure walking past the last lighted pub, leaving behind the heart-breaking honky-tonk piano music, walking through canyon walls of cement factories and chemical works, emerging at last into the lost meadow stretching down to the river.

Down there the silver grey petroleum tanks squatted in their serried ranks, reflecting back in the blue glare of welders climbing high above the slips on the other side of the river. Working ships sounded off like Leviathan himself, great Leviathan, and sailed past like cities to the Commissioner's Quay. These were a delight; but the best ecstasy was to be greeted by the old man, impatient for his supper and a long, lingering cigar, and the talk that would go with it. We would sit on the bench outside and dispose of a world that included incoming tide and the tankers, cargo boats, colliers and luxury liners that it bore so softly and serenely. But it was best when it was cold, or raining. Then we would sit inside the pumphouse, in the bait-corner with its cracked mirror and old postcards and mountainous fire. Behind our backs the great motors would hum softly and powerfully. The three pumps made a different noise, continuous soughing and sucking like the river, but at intervals one of the three would clear its clack as easily and naturally as the old man cleared his throat. And in that place, carried away on the surge of power and function we were perfectly secure and happy, by God.

So it had been in my dream. Now I remember something that was almost reality. There was something of the same atmosphere about UK House. The deserted building slumbered like a beast. The nerve-edge feeling of tension that came of busy telephones, typewriters, and possessed people had gone. The invisible surge of power to lighting, teleprinters, dictaphones and duplicators had subsided. The building slumbered, its claws retracted. The surge of benevolence gave me a really physical feeling of pleasure. It was as if the beast's nervous system was extending out into invisible silken tendrils which stroked and soothed me.

I walked with a springy, confident step along deserted corridors and stairs, resisting the temptation to open office doors and violate their unprotected private parts. I must do nothing to alarm the building. There was a pact between us. That nothing went wrong confirmed me in the illusion. It was like being led; the corpuscle which is part of the body knows the way it takes even although it must pass through a maze without signposts.

'I'm here,' I said, and she spun round from the switchboard, battle-map of the building with its still dead ranks of little bulbs and snake-headed plugs. Turning down the mouthpiece –

'I kept wondering if you'd make it.'

'It was like coming on radar,' I said. I made a swift evaluation, but not so swift that she wasn't aware of it. I had been completely wrong in my extemporised telephone picture. I had expected a girl as full-bodied as the voice; not large but plump and comfortable at least; dark with merry sloe-eyes. The reality was compact, confident, neat; with just a hint of the sensual in the green eyes, of appetite in the upper lip. Hardly a beauty but well-found and interesting, as I saw when she stood up. There was an explosive promise in the body below the strict business suit. The line of shoulders and neck pleased me.

'If you'll watch the panel I'll make tea. Tell me if one of the little bulbs lights up – that means a call.' As she went down on one knee to put in the plug of an electric kettle the several movements presented flow-lines of still further interest. Opening the tea-caddy and without turning she challenged: 'Disappointed?' There was no coquetry in her voice, or in the fleeting glance she gave before returning to the caddy and the teapot. The question was factual, a little ironic, the implication was that we were on even terms. The tone you'd expect from a widow who has made up her mind never to marry again.

'No, delighted,' I said. 'And your reaction?'

'I decided you were sincerely lonely. Otherwise you wouldn't have been invited. It happens so often. Men I mean, a little bored, attracted by a telephone voice and sent by a whim.'

'Or a sense of adventure,' I added defensively. She was getting at me.

'That certain sense of adventure that's based on the assumption that somewhere there's a girl simply dying to be a wanton.'

'The mistake's in the timing, not the assumption,' I said.

One of the lights was flashing. 'You've a caller,' I said.

'Oh, dash!' she cried and came hurrying back. I worked out that the call was outgoing. I was surprised. So up there, above the basement, I had a Man Friday – or perhaps I would prove to be his. Much more likely. 'Pour a couple of cups,' she ordered hurriedly. I heard her voice change, the marked 'Sir', then the dialling. 'Your number, sir,' she said. There was something about her voice which confirmed my feeling that Crusoe-up-there wasn't an ordinary stay-late like myself. Anyway, there are rarely stay-lates in business these days.

She came to the table beside me. 'You're quite right, of course,' she said. 'Or partly right,' she corrected hastily, smiling. 'Courtship's a forgotten art . . . Now – where's the condensed milk – there it is!' Like all men I found myself awkwardly dispossessed by the woman's swift assumption of divine right in a simple domestic task. I had poured two cups and was standing with the teapot in my hand. 'Put it down, now,' she said. 'The trouble with condensed milk is that it makes such a mess around the holes, gives you a queer feeling to see it, but it's so much easier than looking after a supply of milk bottles, isn't it? I'm surprised they haven't invented a non-congealing condensed milk.'

She was trying to contain a naturally warm and open personality. It kept spilling out in little movements of the lips toward a smile. The lips never quite made it; but they wanted to. 'Now we'll take our cups down to where we can watch the switchboard. I wouldn't dream of asking your name – mine's Esther . . .'

I enjoyed listening to her. 'Esther – what's the rest?'

'You'd never believe me –'

'Try me.'

'I won't,' she said firmly. 'I'm down here and you're up there and we're never likely to meet again, but if I tell you – drink it up, it'll be getting cold – you'll run away and tell everybody. And I don't like being *that* kind of heroine – y'know, "A funny thing happened to me on the way home from work last night." No thank you – let's meet and part in mutual respect.'

'I'll not tell.'

She looked at me over the rim of her cup. 'Men always tell. They tell about important things –'

'A name is important?' She ignored the question.

'What's yours? No – let me guess. You're from upstairs so it must be something like – well, the Christian name must be distinguished – Robert, Robert Roly-Poly for Christian names, the Roly-Poly's being friends of the family and Sir Robert Roly-Poly your godfather, and –'

'It's Sam Rowlands,' I interjected.

'You'll never get on,' she said. 'Take my advice and change it by deed-poll to something more – more substantial. Sam will never do.' She examined me critically. 'You look a Charles to me, not a Charlie but a *proper* Charles. And Anthony for your second name, Charles Anthony Rowlands. Can't you hear it? Sir Charles Anthony Rowlands, that's the strength of a name, will it stand up to a title?'

'You're wrong there. There are plenty of Sir Sam's around.'

Snapping her fingers : 'But I'm sure they're comic turns. Now you're not – and stop making the place untidy. Sit down and be happy.' I sat down. 'Were you called after your father?'

Before I'd time to answer she turned and deftly removed a switchboard plug. 'Was that His Nibs?' I asked.

'That would be telling.'

'So there's no chance of getting to know who His Nibs is?' She shook her head. 'Somebody important, somebody male,' I mused. 'Somebody who stays working late and gets the most instant and courteous attention. Nothing less than a Board member?'

'Forget it,' she laughed. 'We were talking about the origins of Sam – having inherited a really deadly surname of my own I've an interest in names of any kind. They form character, you know.'

'Sam can't be anything else but a comedian,' I said, a little sadly.

'Or a very good actor,' she retorted.

'I can see the influence of Esther on you,' I said. 'Warmly helpful by nature. Hospitable. Service in the blood.'

Shaking her head – 'That's only one face. You haven't seen the other. Brooding, fatalistic, a sense of the temporal –'

'All flesh is grass,' I quoted, puzzled. 'All things pass away . . . don't tell me you're Miss Time.'

She smiled gravely at the pun, then placing her hands together in a praying gesture with the tips of the two forefingers pressed against her lips, said: 'You never told me how you were christened Sam. It's not a popular name – indeed you're the very first Sam I've met.' I took a deep breath and conjured up that poor old fantasy about the dustman father with anarchist leanings; the one based upon my great friend as well as uncle.

'Five sons, all Esses – Simon, Stanley, Sydney, Spencer and self.'

'The eldest?'

'I'm the youngest – that's why I'm Sam: all the posh Esses had been used.'

Closing her eyes – 'Your parents weren't so very adventurous. Let me see . . . there's Stephen with a "p" and Steven with a "v"; there's Simon, Simeon, Sean . . . there's royal Stuart as well as common Septimus. Then, of course, there's the one you'd like but could never deserve –' I raised my eyebrows. 'Solomon,' she laughed, and the eyebrows went sadly down. Throwing her head back she laughed freely, calmed down, then said: 'It's a pity your mother –'

I was angry. '*She* died when *I* was born,' I muttered, giving her a lie in her teeth.

She was so sorry I was almost sorry for the lie. I told her not to worry, that I'd managed to get over it.

'I wonder?' she asked of no one in particular. Her hands were well-kept but they belonged to a boy. She reminded me of a picture of a little boy in a very old silent picture which I never saw. Coogan was the name, wearing a sloppy cloth cap. Appealing but diabolically clever little urchin. 'I wonder?' she repeated.

Ignoring the comment, I continued: 'My old man's a queer 'un. We're all named with esses because her name began with an "S" – Susan. He thought the world of her; he thinks the world of all of us, and we all think the world of him – and go in mortal fear of him. He's an anarchist with a small "a" and a sense of tragedy.'

'My landlady's an anarchist.'

'He's a little man who wears thick glasses and smokes cigars. The easiest man to get along with, once you've got used to the idea that he's hard to impress.'

'Do you talk to other people like this?'

'I choose my people,' I said briefly. 'Sometimes I make mistakes, but mostly I don't.'

'Is that a compliment?'

'By definition.'

'Well, I like you,' she said firmly. 'Despite the faults of your class.'

'Working class?' I hopefully asked.

'Upstart class; the modern management class. Thinking the world's your oyster and never dreaming you're nicely inside it.'

'It so happens', I said, 'that I'm very much the reluctant management man.'

'Then why are you in it?'

'Can't stick the monotony of manual work.'

'That isn't enough . . .' She screwed up her face and pretended to shiver. 'You've got the pride of Satan. Can't abide being spoken to, let alone commanded; and there's a terrific compulsion in "getting on", isn't there?'

'I like to live well,' I said defiantly.

'Any bachelor can live well today,' she pronounced.

'All right, then, it's the competition. I've a jealous nature; want to be top and first all the time.'

'You're bitter about it, aren't you?'

'It's impossible to be left alone; that's what I want most. The other's just rooted in me. I despise it. And here I am – a No. 3 type.'

'That's a long way up for a young man.'

'What you don't want, you get . . . But I also get some fun along the way.'

'I should imagine you do, you poor boy,' she said.

Her compassion made me feel uncomfortable. 'I suppose I'd better be on my way . . . Aren't you going to tell me your name?'

'You've had my tea – my condensed milk. Let that suffice. Come again. I'm always on night duty, by choice.'

'And it suits His Nibs?'

She looked at me gravely. 'That's not *you* talking. It's the upstart – never content not to know . . .'

'I like information, I'm curious.'

'Well, this item won't do you any good.'

I'd evidently overstayed my welcome. 'I'd better be on my way. Good night.'

'Good night,' she said indifferently, turning to the switchboard and her handbag, like a lady searching for coppers for a beggar.

'I'll be back,' I threatened lightly.

She sniffed. 'I doubt it . . . By the way, you walk in the same direction, taking the left-hand turning for the steps up the foyer. But if you want to see a really up-and-coming young upstart, look in the door first right and right. Don't be afraid – no one'll notice you.'

I'd an idea she meant the new computer installation. To prove my hunch rather than take her hint I turned the wrong way. I passed the existing installation. There were lights but little activity. Just a barely audible hum. Through an open door I saw a grave girl dressed in a white smock, seated at a very ordinary metal desk. She was blonde and pretty but the jeweller's glass in her right eye gave her an odd sort of look. She was working away at a tiny pillbox with a pair of tweezers and looked up as I paused. The glass in her eye made a most peculiar thing of her smile. In the background a khaki-coloured rectangular box hummed, clicking like an insect at intervals. I liked the computer better than the girl.

Further down the corridor was another room, in darkness. I glanced sharply back. All clear. I stepped inside, flicking on the light switch. The new installation was reputed to be bigger and better; at the moment it didn't look it. I estimated the room was only three times the size of a VIP's office. There was a console with something that looked like a midget typewriter but wasn't. Facing it was something concealed below plastic sheets. The plastic sheets were peculiar. When you lifted some tiny suckers near the floor they slowly rose, like balloons. There was a kind of curtain cord. I tugged it and the plastic covers returned to their place to keep out the dust. I released the suckers again and found nothing very interesting; six extra-large things reaching to my chin. They looked like radiators and were about as thick as my thumb. Thin as they were, they were boxes, greyish-green in complexion and with tiny hinged doors at intervals. One door was open. Below the skull lay the brain. There was a kind of miniature conveyor, probably for tape and a succession of rollers about as big as the jewels in a wristwatch. Above and below were silver sheets embossed with the hieroglyphics of the new age, the nerve cells of the computer. I could feel hundreds of things like roots under my forefinger when I touched one of the plates. Somewhere else there'd be a printing machine to take instructions from hidden hairlike cryotrons.

I remembered the volatile young man with rimless spectacles and no face. 'It's not a brain – that's a modern superstition – but a calculating machine with a built-in checking system for error. It works like lightning. But it doesn't think. It only serves.'

Replacing the sheet over the face of death I walked out, automatically reaching out to switch off the light. I was still arguing with the telephonist. Also, without knowing it, with the computer. 'I'm doing the only thing I *can* do. If you're good at a thing it's a waste not to be good at it.'

I would see Miss Esther – or was it Mrs? – again. I'd win her friendship, discover that mysterious surname – it would probably turn out to be something silly. Comical and somehow pathetic, but entirely lacking in mystery. And I'd also find out about His Nibs. But that was unimportant and merely by the way.

FIVE

So my first day; my first full day. I remember with affection not so much the day as the blissful ignorance I brought to it. I have to admit that at the end of it I knew more than most could have gleaned in so short a period. But it was only superficial knowledge.

Now, after a year, and a magpie gleaning of facts and nuances, information and statements of anguish, I know so much more about *them*; so much less about myself – except when despite myself, they have enlarged me. Small Summers, I suppose could have told me even then that nothing counts but the threshing motions a man makes in his quiet sea of loneliness; he must splash to keep afloat. The sun in the sky, brazen as a round open furnace door, is the woman who greets him in Brighton; not wife, mother, mistress, but Terror. In his bath, in his club, he knew a moment's peace. The polished case was only the machine in which he lived; the Jaguar which made life tolerable. I also have a machine.

Last week, in one of those extraordinary moments of self-disclosure, Wills told me about his mother. He and his wife nursed her for two years through a series of strokes. 'But that was nothing,' he said. I looked at him with unashamed interest I always find so much more encouraging than careful neutrality. 'My father failed in business,' he continued. 'Nothing to do with his capacity. Had a little factory for making strip lighting and such like – do you know I worked with him?' He paused. 'Happiest days of my life. Feeling of absolute security. He knew his job, he knew people. But he couldn't raise money. A guilty feeling that you must live out of your own resources leapt out like a demon from a bottle every time he went the rounds. In the end he went bust; and she never forgave him. Or me, for that matter.'

'She' was his mother, who fought through five or six strokes because she had to live to see some symbol of her son's success. As a good chief I try to get around. The other week I called at their home.

He went out for some beer; the children were playing in the garden and we could hear their laughter. We'd been talking of the long Calvary of the old lady. Marie said: 'I often have to stop myself from telling the children to keep quiet, it's so difficult to realise she's gone.' She was a small, dark little thing. 'Often he'd only three or four hours sleep.'

What she didn't tell me was that Pat's mother died supremely happy. They had one holiday. Marie's sister came down and looked after the old lady, and the family went off each day; I know because he borrowed the money from Holinshed; a large sum because he wanted to hire a large car. Why not a shooting brake? My guess is that he drove up in the car and waved to the old lady, knowing she would see him in the large mirror that was hung at an angle in her bedroom. What he told her is his secret; but easy to visualise the scene before they set off on their first day's excursion. I can just imagine old Mrs Wills lying in bed and watching the family pile in the huge grey thing which the firm had given to their newly-promoted Chief Controller – you see, he had to be right at the top to be good enough for her. She went off quite peacefully at six o'clock in the evening one day during the holidays; Marie's sister said, incredulously, that she hadn't been any trouble at all.

It's just as well we don't always know this kind of thing, otherwise there'd be no progress, personal or otherwise. What I'm trying to say is that Wills went off that night to a sick, unreasonably yearning mother, a tired wife, fractious children. But I might have guessed.

Not that this was his only problem. More of this later, more of Cathie and Holinshed, more of R. Walker Johnson, who was sometimes mean as well as a bore. The most unlikely thing *he* could do was to sell all he possessed, abandon all he possessed, and take a vow of silence. He'd a lot to abandon. Later he took me up, or at least tried to take me up, and I saw his wife and his flat. Well, that flat had everything; a wonderful kitchen with a waste disposal unit, an electric cooker going right up to the ceiling (he liked cooking), an infra-red thing for instant grills, mixers; and a living room with racks and racks of books, long-players, hi-fi, colour television (which they used only sparingly, because there was so much else to use) and, believe it or not, a ship's radio receiver.

He put on that old record of Bach played straight and running, imperceptibly, into jazz, a lovely record; and never stopped talking. His wife's name was Katherine. No, it wasn't a coincidence. Occasionally he allowed himself a whim; on that kind of whim Miss Cavendish had also been selected. She was a very good personal assistant too. He often told me. He also told me how astonished he'd been to find Cathie and Holinshed in the coffee shop that evening of my first day. 'You know,' he said, 'there's something about a couple with a guilty secret. The things that can go on under your nose! I got out as quickly as I could, of course, I doubt if they knew I'd seen them.' I didn't tell him that it wouldn't have made any difference anyway. There was a peculiar expression on his wife's face when he told me. Contempt? I don't know. All I know is that she left him in the end; I shouldn't think there was another man. Just enormously tired. But he was a good man. A better man than me, a better man than all of us, not that that's saying much.

But this was long after and I'm giving the impression that the events of the day were over. You know how it is. Up and down. The previous evening I'd been deliberately and efficiently lonely; I might have gone down to see Simon D'Arcy (believe it or not, his father was a wherryman at South Shields, his brother was a wherryman, there'd been D'Arcys plying in boats on the Tyne for more than a century). But I hadn't gone. For two reasons. One was pride: you mustn't go running for companionship the moment you arrive. The other was self-knowledge: I knew I was in for a lonely spell and would be lonely whatever. But the second day was different. Two women (attractive by my lights) were interested in me. I'd also seen the computer and wanted to talk about it.

So I got on the Tube and rushed through outer space to Walham Green – I'd gone to Fulham the night before because it was practically parallel with the place – and merged into a nice sharp kind of night. I'd seen Simon the last time I was in London. He's an artist and I'm very fond of him; long ago I promoted him to be one of my brothers, all their names beginning (remember?) with 'S'. I admired him because he lived *his* fantasy; he'd even made it work for him. But then, in art this is easily accomplished.

There was this girl Sal; there the last time, still there, and framed in the door despite all his glib talk of a rota. He'd given me this yarn about casually introducing whips into the conversation and so getting rid of the girls, most of whom are very conventional – I'm quoting him. A month or so, he said, was sufficient . . . But here she was, wearing an apron, looking a bit mean, I thought. For a very specific reason I was rather put out.

'It's Sam – Sam Rowlands,' I explained. She didn't even say hello. But then, she teaches through the day, cooks in the evenings, works most nights.

I don't know about her teaching or bed-work but her cooking is splendid. We ate and Simon dismissed her, like a loving husband, I thought. 'Give us a chance to talk,' he said, but made no effort to say anything further. I could see he was worried about my intentions; maliciously I said nothing about them.

'I thought she'd have completed her service,' I remarked. He told me to keep my voice down. 'It's time she had a rest,' I continued. 'You work her like a beast of burden.'

'So what,' said Simon uneasily. 'She's a frustrated domestic animal. Once they used to pine for a career; now they eat their hearts out for cooking, cleaning, washing, etc.'

'You might as well be married,' I said. He was strangely silent. 'But I suppose you've noticed that there's no such thing as change of life; applies to everything from marriage to a revolution. After it's over, life goes on just the same as ever. Take these computers, for instance –'

'Look here –' he began.

'I introduced myself to a new one today, panels open and all the guts exposed; fascinating little conveyors for taped instructions, little veins of printed circuits –'

'Do you mind if I tell you something?' asked Simon. I ignored him, knowing full well what was coming: one more for the count.

73

'Do you know how they work? Pulses; on and off, couple of pulses, the ideal police state, one working and the other watching.'

He was standing thoughtfully with a plate in his hand. From his expression it was impossible to say whether he was interested or not. I continued quickly, just this side of manic intensity: 'I placed the palm of my hand on one of those circuits. There was no power; from where I was standing I could see the end of the cable, but I'll swear the bloody thing talked to me. And it moved, I felt those printed lines move against my skin like bluebell roots.'

He dropped the dish. It broke in half. We both looked at it; but I never stopped talking. 'And you know what I saw? I saw a multitude of people on a sightseeing tour of the computers; sleek, well-fed and absolutely idle. But the funny thing was this; there were no guides; each part spoke up for itself, gently, smoothly and without a trace of self-consciousness or condescension.'

'Remarkable,' said Simon, briefly. 'But I'm not interested. I've been trying to tell you, you can't stay.'

'But I'm not wanting to stay,' I said, smarting all the same. It would have been nice to have been invited. He actually smiled. 'I knew how things would be. It was obvious the last time I was here you were in deep.' The smile faded. Sal came in and picked up the two halves of the plate.

'Well, I'll be on my way,' I said. I walked back into that big room I remembered so well from last time; the one with the two beds, shivered, and picked up my old, weary overcoat. Throwing it over my shoulder with a flourish I turned to find the two children watching me.

I walked with them to the door. I suppose I could have carried it off magnificently. I could have said: 'So I sleepwalk? Thousands do. Nobody knows. Why? Because there are generally walls between rooms.'

Or: 'So you're about to get respectably married, or are indeed married, and there's no room for an old pal! Don't let it bother you, my children. I have reserves . . . reserves indeed.'

But I said nothing until I was out on the pavement. They looked so mournful I ran back and hugged the pair of them. 'It's all right, it's all right,' I said. 'I've a lovely room at a smashing hotel, television, radio, my own shower . . .' I marched away, waving cheery good nights. I was so upset that I forgot my main cause for worry; I hadn't a book. I'd cased the joint with a threadneedle eye and hadn't found one. Artists never read books.

I got on a bus which went through Chelsea, hoping to find a cinema that would suit my taste; skipping from one side to the other of the upper deck in case I missed one. I considered a dance hall. At the top of the steps I saw my face in the porthole mirror. Until then I'd thought of getting off at the next stop and walking back. I imagined a gum-chewing girl looking me up and down with the steely-eyed compassion that the very young reserve for the aged; and changed my mind. A railwayman, going on or coming off duty, watched me return to my seat. His mouth was open. I said: 'Excuse, please. All right for Dagenham?' He told me how wrong I was. I gave him half-a-crown and beat a retreat.

I went walking. It wasn't a bad night, but the environment was bad. The place was a desert of tarmac and pavement; the buildings had high, unclimbable walls around them. I crossed a railway bridge, walked past what looked like a school, mournful in the distance, and came at last to a cemetery. It was nearly as big as the City of London; beautifully laid out with tree-lined walks and arterial and sub-arterial pedestrian ways. It was a badly built-up area, but not so monotonous as most. There were broken pillars, angels, old rugged crosses, and lots of doors that didn't open built into walls that would never be built. I stopped and stared at one, a curio if you like, indicating influence as well as opulence: it was softly illuminated by a street lamp. I've been back since, but couldn't find it – a lady expiring in black-veined marble, while her pekingese, with its forepaws on the bier, tried in vain to bring back the lady from the grave. The bier was actually a four-poster, but the legs had been deliberately shortened to allow the little pet to view its mistress. The inscription was in shadow. I craned to see it, trying various approaches and posture, wishing I could pull the bars apart. All I could see was 'beloved'. I fell into a reverie, wondering if I'd ever be beloved enough to get a monument. I decided to buy my set-piece long before death set in; my image would stand on a computer block with several of the panels removed and with a power cable snaking into its guts. The motto would be: 'In the midst of life we are in death.' When I came to myself again I'd company. They were a tall thin man wearing a burberry, and a pale freckled boy, wearing spectacles and large ears.

'Something wrong?' asked the thin man.

'I'm not sure yet,' I said shortly, looking at my watch.

'Expecting something to happen?'

'Any time now.'

'What's it all about?'

'It'll be better for you if you move on,' I said, toying with several ideas and deciding that a contemporary Burke and Hare was out. Suddenly, as if struck by a sudden suspicion, I added, 'You're nothing to do with the Press, are you?'

The man inched away, pulling at the boy's hand. 'Come on, Frederick we don't want to get mixed up in any trouble.'

'That's right, son,' I said kindly.

'Is there going to be some shooting or something?'

'Not if I can help it,' I said.

'Come on, Frederick!'

'I wanta stay, Dad.' Pulling at my overcoat. 'What's it all about, Mister? Are you a copper?'

'Shsh! Keep your voice down,' I said, staring intently over the desert of monuments. 'Did you see that light?'

'By those trees?' asked the boy helpfully.

'Two flashes, that means they've backed the van up against the wall.'

'Who has?' asked the thin man. I took a deep breath –

'You'll find out soon enough. I'm Special Branch. I'm going in after them. I want you two to stay here and pass the word to my pals – they'll be arriving any minute. In a police car.'

'I'm not staying unless you tell me what it's all about,' said the thin man, his voice breaking.

I pretended to hesitate, then said, decisively: 'All right, then. Ever heard of illegal burial? No. Ever tried to lose a body, then? I thought not. But if you want to lose a body you couldn't pick a better spot than this, thirty acres, a dozen burials per day.' I lowered my voice. 'Especially if you've got the grave-diggers in your pocket.'

'Swamp me!' said the boy.

'We're going home. Come on. It's getting late,' said the father.

'You've a citizen's duty,' I said, sternly. 'You can do a good job for your country simply by staying here.'

'I don't want any trouble. I've a wife and family –'

He stopped as he caught Frederick's look. 'All right, Mister, we'll stay.'

'Inspector Smittle's the name,' I said. 'Don't talk, move away from this light, lie low . . . that's better.' I walked away with an easy air of command around me.

'How many, Mister?' shouted the boy. I held a finger to my lips. He ran up to me, breathless, 'How many have they done?'

I held up four fingers.

'Swamp me!' he swore, and I felt a little ashamed. Frederick was not fair game. Now the fat Alderman was. He'd been to view the plant and Snorry asked me to drive him back to town – our town. On the way we passed the truncated windmill. 'Built by the great Smeaton,' I rattled off. 'Dome removed in 1940, sails in 1926, in use as a coffee grinder during its last five years of active life.'

The Alderman did a double take then craned for a look.

'Coffee!' says he.

'A dead calm was a calamity for the coffee-addicts,' I concluded. He went out of my life and split the Freemen right up the middle at their annual dinner; six or seven could remember the smell of roasting when they were boys, or so they said. The information almost made the City Guide Book.

The thin man and his son were still lurking in the shadows as I turned the corner. Actually, if it had been my habit to carry a pistol I'd have worked my way round the place and fired four or five shots into the air, simply to please the boy. Just like life. It's my experience that more opportunities are spoiled through lack of the essential properties than mere will.

I needed something to read. I went to Piccadilly and bought an American comic called 'Monster', knowing I was surrounded by them, poor devils, looking for the great city tits to suck, not even suspecting she's barren.

Here is my reconstruction of the scene taking place at Wills' home as I left Piccadilly. As a piece of automatic writing it's probably as good as anything Wills would produce; and he was in it.

77

As he closed the door behind him he saw his mother's eyes open; it was as if one act triggered the other. Yet he had closed the door gently. He decided that it was a mind like a clock and not the click of the door which had awakened her.

'It's me, Mother.' He sat by the bed. 'How are you feeling?'

Ignoring his question – 'Have you been a good boy?' He nodded. He watched, fascinated, as her lips worked. 'Made progress – they think well of you – must keep working. Still a long way to go – your father –'

He carefully wiped her lips. The mouth was awry to the left. 'Your father . . .' she said, her right eye blinking furiously, as it always did during their evening conversations. 'Your father – greatly respected – gone too soon.'

'I'll make up for him some day, Mother.'

'You,' she said, staring intently. 'You – you.'

'Yes, Mother. But it takes time.'

'Without me, Patrick. Oh, Patrick.' A tear squeezed out of each closed eye. They moved slowly. They were small tears. As he watched they became a little dampness, then the skin became dry and brittle again. 'You'll get better, Mother; you'll be out of bed soon – you'll be in the garden in the Spring.'

'No more Spring,' she said. 'No more –'

'I'll switch the wireless on for you,' said Pat.

'No, I'm sleepy. Put my arm under the bed-clothes.' The arm seemed heavier tonight. He had to nerve himself to take hold of it, but that was easy compared to the kiss. 'Good night, Mother.'

Her lips were dry and brittle. 'Patrick?'

'Yes, Mother.'

'Tell her – tell her – no medicine.' There was always a scene when Marie came with the glass, prepared downstairs, so that it could be taken quickly. 'She bullies me.'

'I'm sure she doesn't, Mother. Marie's only doing what's best . . .'

'She – looks at me. Her eyes – burden.'

'It's imagination, Mother. You know it is.'

'No medicine, none tonight. Patrick?'

He shook his head hopelessly. Once again the lips writhed in the struggle to articulate. 'Short time – but come between mother and son.' He stood up. 'She has – Patrick?'

'I'll turn the light down. You'll sleep better,' he said, ignoring her accusation.

'No, son – the light please.'

'You're going to sleep. You must learn –' He sighed as he switched off the light, then went quickly out, shutting the door on the unintelligible sounds.

'Must she take that medicine?' he demanded of Marie.

'For obvious reasons.'

'She goes on and on about it.'

'You'd better talk to the Doctor.'

'I'm not in to talk to the Doctor – you know perfectly well he doesn't come till eleven.'

'Then you'd better phone the office tomorrow, tell them you'll be late,' she said, tight-lipped.

'Oh, I'm sorry, Marie,' he said, turning away. 'It's only that she puts me on the rack.'

'She'll hang on to you until the end – and after,' said Marie.

'She's self-willed.'

'Completely selfish,' she said dryly. 'No gratitude –'

'I know how she feels – father dying so soon.'

'Now she's being cheated again,' said Marie. He turned away, knowing it was useless to protest that some day he would really be someone. 'Know when you're lucky,' she continued. 'You've done very well for yourself. *You* can't go bankrupt.'

'Ask the Doctor if he'll come in on Saturday morning.'

'I will,' she said, and took the medicine upstairs. He went into the garden so as not to listen to the muffled sounds from above. Marie sometimes lost her temper. They lived on the edge of a little triangle of country; there was a lane with a couple of gas lamps illuminating the trees. About that time there would be foliage, but it would give him no comfort. All he could see was the lineament of death.

So much for reconstruction. Now for some fancy. Bedtime stories and dreams:

How do they dream? The Chief Controller flat on his back like a hopeful woman? Holinshed rigid on his right side, away from his wife; Wills with knees drawn up in pre-natal condition, away from the wife who can forgive him everything but his mother; Walker Johnson on his belly with one arm thrown over his succulent wife; Charlie Squires diagonally across the double bed hopefully provided by Mrs Pennington, his landlady, and as hopefully eyed by Dorothy, her daughter. Cathie's posture changed but I remember the way in which she slept once with the sheets thrown off and her arms outstretched as if being gently crucified.

I can be more explicit about myself. Under the date, the 26th of October, are two entries. 'The march against the Bomb was really a demonstration of unreadiness for death.' I should explain that I never marched, not wanting to be an historical fool: my father once told me of his shame when he discovered how he had been hoodwinked over Spain. The second entry might pass for a poem: 'My poems are pistol shots fired point blank at the shadow over my shoulder. At least the blue pocks of powder burn will remind him that I took good aim.' These things must be written down, otherwise there will always be a feeling of loss deeper than the feeling of loss twenty years later when one sees not only what was written, but its worth.

My posture in going to sleep: head high on at least two pillows and stretched full-length but trying to improve by extending feet and toes like a skin-diver in motion; left hand between thighs holding the thumb of the right hand to keep it from straying. Tense to begin with but gradually relaxing unless I'm in one of those awful 'dry' periods prior to vertigo. So much for postures. Now for the dreams I was able to collect – other dreams. I got the Chief Controller's through Mrs Arcot. Middle-aged, divorced, bereft, she had glimpsed me in the corridor with Holinshed. I had evidently intrigued her. Carrying some paper from Small Summers to me she lingered. Startlingly she said: 'I dreamed about you last night.'

'I hope it was pleasant,' I laughed. She flushed and I saw that below the overlay of cosmetics and cynicism was a very lonely soul. 'Oh, quite,' she said, and left it at that. Only in a dream would she be unfaithful to Small Summers, whom she worshipped. She was one of those who start with a heart-shaped face, but not the bone. With age the soft flesh had dried and stretched leaving only the eyes, large pekingese eyes which looked for affection or something better even when she snapped. I told her I had dreamed during the night.

'That makes three of us,' she said.

'The third being your chief?'

She nodded. 'Tell me?' I asked. She hesitated. 'Oh, he was in Crete again,' she said at last. 'He was there in the war with the Germans.' She would say no more, but later, after his illness, she told it to me in detail. It was a recurring dream. He would be on the beach again with salt on his lips and the breakers crashing behind, white sands rising to the cliffs in front. There was a winding path up the cliffs at the least difficult point. In his dream he was not with his men. He was alone and confident of what he would find. There was nothing to fear. In a hollow over the cliffs there was a low cottage with olive trees around it. In their shade was a plain wooden table with food. Waiting outside the cottage was a woman wearing a red blouse and holding a goatskin of wine. She would wave at him and he would start running, waving as he ran. I have altered one detail. Small Summers told Mrs Arcot that he saw a man holding the goatskin of wine and wearing a red jacket, but I'm sure he lied. Mrs Arcot knew it was a woman too. Perhaps she sometimes hoped that she was the woman. But I know it was a woman and a beautiful woman. The good dreams always have a woman.

A pity Mrs Arcot never made it, either in dream or in reality. I have met his wife. She is a grey angular woman who probably brought him money. Mrs Arcot told me that Small Summers was a wasted man. His father had been a parson's son who'd got into synthetic textiles and made a fortune. The works had been in the country and the old man had been a success, even in failing to win a difficult Labour seat. He'd become magistrate, chairman of the local hospital board, President of the Red Cross and a power in the land, not because of his wealth, but because he was immensely competent. A man born to rule. I said that he sounded quite a pleasant type, and why should he bother Small Summers? Because, she said, Small Summers could never be sure of how much of his own success he owed to his father. She hesitated, then plunged: 'Even his wife . . .' I don't think it was that. I think his father was masterful. His own will had been atrophied. But it only goes to show.

In *his* dream Wills was once again in the foyer of UK House. His dream was short and poignant. He was coming out of the shop in the foyer of UK House when two men walked through the doors and towards the lift. One was me, easy and self-assured, and the other was his father, brisk, smiling and as falsely confident as he had been in life. As is usual Wills was aware in his dream that something was wrong, but vaguely, so that when he awoke he felt a terrible sense of loss because his father was dead. In the dream his father looked at him. There was no recognition in his father's look. He heard the lift attendant say: 'Going down, Sir?' and even more distinctly, his father's reply (as he looked without recognition over his shoulder): 'No, up, right up to the top.'

Wills said that he then realised that his father and myself were equally his enemies. He did not need to tell me that he awoke to tears, the kind which never reach the eyes.

What we never realise in this kind of dream is that others also get the hammer. Mine, for instance, was much more refined. I was in my native Borough Library, where the shelves were full of beasts' heads instead of books. They were neatly cut off at the neck and were alive; there were card indexes and all the usual equipment, including girl assistants; like books again, the heads were arranged by species. I was poring over the rodents – house and field mice, moles, voles and shrews, etc. – when I looked up to find the Chief Controller. 'Fancy meeting you here,' said Small Summers, 'and how very fortunate.' He was carrying the panting head of a dog-fox under one arm. I felt trapped.

'As a matter of fact I'm getting a water-rat out,' I told him.

'Small enough to go into your pocket!'

Walker Johnson passed quickly by with a couple of hares: sure sign of the bestophile. He was holding them by the long ears. Their large, liquid eyes and twitching whiskers expressed extreme disgust. 'You should try the giraffe – immense, sir,' he called over his shoulder.

'Thanks, I've found what I want,' said the Controller; and led me to it. It was a donkey.

'I do wish they'd keep their mouths shut,' he said. 'Disgusting the way they loll.'

Then the Thing rolled its large white eyeballs and brayed.

I find in my notes the following:

'Don't want to dissect this one. Very uncomfortable dream. Could be that the Unconscious likes a joke, and it ran like one; only the laugh was on us – me?'

After writing this I went back to bed and slept like a log. Had it not been for the chambermaid with the tea I'd have overslept. As it was, I had to skip the correspondence columns of *The Times*. It was a stark lonely breakfast. I got a taxi to UK House. It was one of those many mornings when you can't get to work quickly enough.

Only the other day my good friend Wills told me that he always comes to work with a sense of impending doom. He says that for this reason he welcomes a legitimate worry. A real worry is not half the burden of that indefinable guilt that hangs over his life. Every time the telephone rings – and ours are gentle creatures – he says to himself: 'This is it!'

We are very much alike, although I disagree with him. Mere words can never bring doom. But I do have the feeling that at any moment work and time together may bring the consummation of a prophecy; a descent of angels; deliverance. Doom and splendour, but both are probably delusions.

SIX

R. Walker Johnson called me to his office to discuss my paper on the Hartlepools project. It was obvious that he didn't like my little essay. I waited patiently whilst he took apart the case I'd made and held up for inspection most of my arguments and some he'd invented himself and read into the text. He also hinted that I was trying to show off my local knowledge. So far as Percy Main and Hartlepools are concerned they are separate continents with an ocean between them which I wouldn't care to sound. But I held my peace.

Taking the first possible pause I skipped through the original paper from upstairs, pointed out the three appearances of that hyena phrase 'it would appear', obviously inserted for purposes of alibi or full retreat. I left the Deputy Controller looking thoughtful. In the outer office I paused to watch Cathie's hands brushing softly over the keys of her electric typewriter. Then I looked at her neck. Aware that Mrs Arcot was watching me I switched to the hands again. Esther had paws, boyish hands. Cathie's were good competent hands for work, but they also had beauty to the fingertips. I was looking over her shoulder. Mrs Arcot glanced up from her work. She smiled the pussy-cat smile of the well-disposed who knows all and wishes for the best. It might have been a different smile had she been ten years younger. Cathie stopped typing. I walked between the two women and looked Cathie square in the face, feeling my lip might tremble at any moment. She smiled. 'Well, Mr Rowlands?' she asked.

Obviously I couldn't ask her about Holinshed with Mrs Arcot sitting there. I found I had absolutely nothing to say. I dredged and out came: 'Do you know there are still hundreds of horse-troughs in the City of London – they're filled with clean water every day?'

Her smile was on the verge of laughter. Mirth bubbled and I wanted to take her away and hug her. 'I don't believe it,' she said.

'We must go and count them some day,' I said. She resumed her typing and I made my departure. The other lady was on the verge of laughter as well.

'Goodbye, workhorse,' said Mrs Arcot. Even the kindest of women must flick a paw. Late in the afternoon I left my door open. I thought it might encourage Cathie to look in and say something on her way home. So I began to recognise the sound of her passing. She was a tall girl, taller than me when she was wearing high-heels, and she walked with long, confident strides which never slackened as she passed my openly inviting door. I told myself that any woman was a perfumed and padded cell and got on with my work. Miss Miffin came in to say good night. After she had gone I strolled down the corridor. Mrs Arcot was tidying up. With my eyes anywhere but where they wanted to stray – why should Cathie's desk and shrouded machine excite me so? – I asked for a stamp. Mrs Arcot said she was out of them, and added: 'You should have asked Miss Cavendish – she does a lot of letter writing.' 'Ah, yes,' I murmured.

She looked me up and down for wounds. 'Lots of them. But never in office hours; she only brings them in to post – but never through the office out-tray.' I took the suggestion of a highly private correspondence without flinching. Dreamily putting on her coat she continued: 'I've seen her stamp them. Dozens. Then into her handbag.'

'She's probably the president of some international correspondence society,' I said. 'Data on the ringing of bats or the incidence of purple orchids.'

'Whatever it is,' she said, pausing at the door, 'she writes an awful lot. So do you, I hear. The two of you ought to get together.' I wasn't surprised. News travels quickly.

'Swamp me,' I said in mock alarm and wondered where little Frederick was today, and what he thought of it all. We went up the corridor together. If her face was a little bit battered her figure was good, and she was neatly dressed. She kept giving me little nibbling glances, but I wasn't taking invitations. Life at the moment was full enough, without taking on a divorced lady. But the bruised eyes stayed with me.

The evening was young. The notes for a new 'manifesto' were lying fallow at the moment, but I had a new thing on packaging.

I opened the drawer and took out the book and the fat, expensive fountain pen. It gave me a cosy feeling, as always, to read over what I'd dictated in that immensely long thirty minutes before lunch. It was the last section I liked.

'Today a wide range of processed, manufactured and natural materials are packaged for more effective distribution, via semi-automatic vending. The articles range from the relatively small to medium sized objects: from vegetables to nuts and bolts; from groceries to solid fuel.

'Larger articles, such as aircraft, cars, battleships, are already packaged but only for storage. Real distribution awaits the perfection of an instantaneous and efficient method of transport; i.e. breakdown, despatch and assembly at a distance of the constituent parts of bulky machines or straightforward delivery of packaged goods.

'The present suggestion relates to the packaging and distribution of human beings. It is suggested that present methods are highly inefficient, particularly when considerable distances are involved. Since the human element is the most random, there is a need for more organisation of the basis of packaging. Packaging would eliminate latecomers (no waiting for unpacked persons) and enable more effective use to be made of the available storage space.

'A prototype sleeper train should be put into operation. In effect it would be a fast goods train, which would be as clean at the end of the journey as at the beginning. Stewards and restaurant staff would, of course, be eliminated. Passengers would arrive and buy a numbered storage space, and a stamped number on their wrist instead of a ticket. They would then enter the train at the end nearest to the barrier and disrobe in the packaging chamber. The function of this chamber will be to package both the passenger and his clothes and put the former "to sleep", after which he would be conveyed automatically to his registered place – a sensing device would ensure that he was placed in the correct receptacle, or rack.

'Discharge at the destination would be equally automatic.

'The advantages are self-evident, as are the military applications. All institutions dealing with large numbers of personnel will find that the new system has obvious advantages.

' "Free" or wasteful transport will be a privilege bought at a high price. Needless to say, the system can be extended. Packaged humans could be transferred from one form of transport to another and door-to-door delivery is not unthinkable. Delivery of children over long distances would prove a boon to anxious parents, as well as to police, warders of prisons and mental institutions, and schoolmasters.

'As for the economics –'

There the dictation had ended, as it generally did, on the verge of the practical. I sighed and scribbled at the end. 'Good idea for science-fiction story; only possible if universal delivery by pipeline could be perfected. By definition, packaging and distribution of human beings demands a new method of transport. Will not dovetail into old. New wine into old bottles will not go.' I turned the pages idly, back to the graveyard of 'Notes on a New Manifesto' and the scribbled posthumous note: 'Nothing can be done until the managers take over. Leave it to Super-Marx, AD 2290 – who wants to be a voice in a wilderness?'

I picked up the telephone and announced myself to Esther. 'It's Sam – remember me?' I asked.

'Barely,' said Esther without taking pause.

'Never mind; you didn't forget,' I replied with a hurt little laugh.

'Well?' she said coldly.

'Can I come down and see you again – about seven-thirty?' I counted five then broke the silence with: 'Let us consider hospitality. Does it pick and choose?'

'You'd better come and find out for yourself,' she grudgingly invited.

This gave me a straight hour for exploration before the cleaners arrived. I wasn't bothered about meeting really top and over-conscientious executives working late; a confrontation might even be interesting. But what I was after (next in priority to the

Bluebeard complex) was to orientate myself, like the dog which circles before lying down to die.

I'd already consulted a guide to the building; an offprint from some architectural journal which had never been touched since it reached our library. It was worth getting out for one item alone. We are the country's major pipe manufacturers (for obvious reasons) and the main columns, said the offprint, were steel tubes manufactured by the Client. I wonder, was it to save money? Or had a little romance gone into the decision to dress the building on those hollow tubes on which our business depends? I was almost sorry to find no mention of a link with the lavatory system; every great beast should have an intestine, but this one could have been unique. The business building is a bird of passage, and it's only right that its bones should be hollow – although the offprint suggested that ours was the only native example, apart from bridges and other engineering structures.

Apart from the tubes there is nothing unusual about the building – excepting the feeling we have for each other. Item: three storey podium: not the platform on which the conductor of an orchestra stands, but delightfully like, supporting as it does the 15-storey tower in which I and so many work and have a little of our being. Item: the podium contains entrance hall, exhibition area, boardroom, cinema and canteen. Item: basement and sub-basement. Item: rear basement approach with roof overhang for car parking. Item: four service lifts to the fourteenth floor, capable of clearing the building in 30 minutes flat – not bad for 2,400 population.

It's nice to know. That green glow I'd observed at night wasn't flood-lighting but fluorescent lights behind glass spandrels giving an effect of floating trays. Nobody decided when to switch on the corridor strip lights: photo-electric cells took the initiative. Central heating was complicated or simple, according to your outlook. But those suspended tubes in the ceiling gave me a kick. It was also exciting to know that aluminium acoustic absorption strips were looking after my voice, footsteps, rub of my clothes, even my breathing.

It was only an illusion that the beast was asleep. True, the stairs were in darkness but pilot lights burned on each landing. Sewerage and water pumps simply waited the command to ease into life. All that I could not see, copper bus bars and sheathed cable for electricity; pneumatic tube ring circuit with 33 stations, 2,200-strong telephone system and teleprinters, only awaited the touch of a single mind. The whole vast system was on call. I thought it whispered as I walked. I imagined that photo-electrical eyes might report as well as activate; that the slave clocks on each landing might register more than a pulse of time. There was nothing malignant about the watching and recording: the building observed me like a dozing dog who lifts an ear as you approach one door, an eyelid as you open another. It was interested; it wanted to know, perhaps to assist beyond the call of duty.

The most important floor maintained a blazing independence. All the lights were on. Going up the stairs, looking up, I saw a bright glow.

I felt like Quatermain in the heart of the mountain and approaching the temple of Isis; the simple explanation that someone was working late never occurred to me. But the lights were in contrast to the general atmosphere of the place. Despite the carpets and despite the furnishings – the entire landing was one huge lounge, or club-room, with deep easy chairs facing away from the lifts and with a huge round table in the centre littered with newspapers and periodicals – there was a feeling of absolute deadness (but not death, not the feel of a morgue or vault) about the place.

On the wall I faced was a painting of a military looking gentleman and a mass of equipment, including a primitive buffing tank. It looked circa 1950 to me. I liked the painting. It was a take-off of Nolan's Kelly series. After the lapse of time it was just right; in some ways Ned Kelly is nearer to us than say the men who built the first satellites. I was delighted to have my guess confirmed by a typewritten slip: 'Henry Norman Prinkstone, Founder of UK Enterprises, Strawberry Hill Plant 1950.' It had taken twenty years to build that first clumsy plant and master the outfalls. Now he was missing. He was always mentioned in the brochures and textbooks and now I remembered how skilfully, without ever inserting the 'late', they managed to insinuate that he was dead and gone. Lost in some take-over blizzard? I vaguely remember Snorry talking about a seven-day financial wonder. Now we were as good as a Trust. The managers ran the show and ploughed back all but a reasonable fraction of the immense profits – 'Assets are our asset,' said Mr Francis, our current Chairman, in a memorable staff speech. All had applauded, excepting lean, hungry Mr Crumple, the Chief Accountant. Snorry, who knew all, had always said that Crumple was the last of the Mohicans but that his days were numbered.

Then I heard the sound of one of the lifts. It is a shocking noise to break a total silence, rather like a prolonged high note on a tuning fork. After coming to earth again I dodged into the toilet next door to the lift in motion. It was only when I was in that it occurred to me that the interloper might very well be taken short. By then it was too late. It was Jones, the lift boy, limping hard under the burden of a tremendous bouquet wrapped in cellophane. I know because I timed the arrival of the lift and tracked his footsteps before I looked out.

I went into one of the toilets and sat in darkness until his return. It was easy. He came back whistling. It was interesting to hear that whistle diminish as the tuning fork of the lift took over again. I switched on the light and made myself free of the other amenity. There was a glass thing to protect the cuffs of your trousers; a mirror ran the length of the stalls to enable you to study your face; there was another vertical mirror beside the door to help you to check buttons or zips. Needless to say there were individual mirrors (with mermaids) to each wash-basin. There were also individual ash-trays. I was about to leave when I remembered the lavatories. I checked. Each had an ash-tray beside the toilet roll and a mirror on the door; there was also a tiny bookcase packed with midget editions of funny stories and cartoons. I wouldn't have been surprised to find a silver cigar box in each. That is certainly something I must put right some day.

I switched off the lights and walked quickly round the left-hand corridor, from which Jones had emerged. I memorised all the names on the doors and coupled them with the paintings, all originals, all non-figurative. By their size and the Italian look of the signatures they were in the £2–300 range. They also looked professional, unlike most English non-figuratives. I glanced in the odd one or two offices – astonishing how a man may make his personality felt with a nick-nack or two. On the evidence of their office nick-nacks the executives on the left-hand side of the Chairman didn't have much personality. I was wondering about the bouquet. There was no noise to indicate a reception, although booze enough to run one, judging by the several cabinets I'd seen. A green door at the end of the corridor gave me the clue. It said 'Private' and possessed a bellpush. It looked like a door strayed from a mews flat.

The offprint in my pocket told all. The bare details said that on top of the tower was a penthouse. This constituted a 16th storey. I was on the 15th floor. I hunted through the text. A sentence I had missed explained that the penthouse was used as a four-bedroom suite for executives staying overnight. So an executive was staying overnight – and entertaining. That would account for telephone calls after hours – and Esther's attendance at the switchboard. I got out quickly.

On the way to the right-hand corridor I decided that the occupant would be full-time – probably Mr Francis. There would also be a covered garden with dwarf palms and ferns, a large pool with water lilies from the Amazon, and a couple of small leopards with languorous and utterly deceitful eyes. The view would be as splendid as the one I'd briefly glimpsed as I went at an easy lope through the lounge club-room, but no one would ever notice it. Old men look inwards. I was satisfied that the penthouse dweller would be old and his visitor extremely young; on balance I was prepared to settle for a charming granddaughter who'd be stricken at the sight of me.

The right-hand corridor was much more opulent than the left, even in the quality of the lighting; it was like walking into the ray from a crystal prism. Office doors changed from red, to red with a greenish tinge, from black to black with a reddish-tinge, or glow, to silver, copper and something that looked like gold but which was more accurately canary in colour. Later I realised that the double-take was planned by Mr Francis. Canary suited him, anyway. I made a little reconnaissance in the vicinity and thumbed my nose at Mr A. W. E. Croat, PPS to Chairman (not parliamentary private but private and personal) and Miss R. W. Plumb, PA, and decided

I must really have something done with my name. Esther was right about that. An extra name has power. Try S. Pumpkin Rowlands, or S. Pool Rowlands, or even S. Mann Rowlands. All better than plain Samuel.

I opened the door marked Chairman and found another door inside. It was insulated like a midwife in the Cairngorms, but to keep out vulgar noises and keep in those secrets which travel a sight quicker by other routes. I must confess I hesitated as my hand grasped the ultimate handle and felt the great thing move away from me; so must Flinders Petrie have felt on entering great Pharaoh's tomb. I expected something to happen; and so it happened. The lights were on, I switched them off. Out of the darkness came a moan. I rapidly shut it off and decided that it must have been my imagination. I don't believe in the dramatic in real life. I dismissed murder gangs with a grimace and decided something entirely natural had happened in there. I looked at my watch. Seven-fifteen. Whatever it was the cleaners would find it. They would welcome a change. But there had been a shade of fear in arriving at this decision. I was mocked; and it was this rather than any good intention which helped me to open the two doors again. I said: 'Hello?'

A voice from somewhere below me said: 'God dammit, hell and damnation, switch on the light and get me out of this.'

I found and pressed a whole battery of switches. On came concealed lighting, a couple of desk lamps, and music and pistol shots from some concealed source, probably a television set. I turned the latter off. Behind the desk was a narrow tweed-encased backside, and swearing; it was as if one of Sutherland's odd tree trunks had come to life and speech. It was telling me to pull it out. As far as I could see it had been locked in the act of looking into the bottom left-hand drawer, the very one I use myself for the private and confidential stuff. It occurred to me that Mr Francis had been looking for some papers when the mysterious malady had struck him, not down but rigid.

The moment I took hold of those shoulders I realised that it couldn't be Mr Francis; certainly not the Mr Francis they called Roly-Poly in the Northern Region. This one was all skin and agonised bones. Further, he wouldn't come straight. I managed to pull him away from the desk and up against the nearest wall. All the time he was swearing like a trooper. In the end I left him on his side and stood up to get my breath.

'What's the trouble?' I asked.

'Effin' lumbago, effin' fool!' he shouted. I got hold of his legs and gave a tentative pull, and he screamed as some unimaginable pain struck.

'You'd better lie still while I get hold of a doctor,' I advised, moving to the telephone. He sounded decidedly negative about that line of action.

'Then what are we gong to do, Mr Crumple?' I asked, sitting on the edge of the desk.

'You know me?' The query was moderately sharp, considering his current preoccupations.

'I've seen your picture,' I said. I've nothing against accountants but I believe in keeping them in their place; this was the first time I'd seen one where he belonged. 'And believe me, Mr Crumple, you need a doctor.'

'You do as you're told.' I kept my hand on the telephone. 'I know what's wrong. Time's the only cure. Ah-Ah . . .'

I decided to give him a bit of my rack. 'You can't be left here,' I said, amused at the way his eyes followed mine around the Chairman's room.

He caught on. The sweat was streaming down his face when it wasn't standing out in big, fat beads. 'No – no,' he agreed. 'Listen, can you get me over to my office – just over the other side – Ah . . . I've some pills.'

'I'll slip over and get them.'

'No, no, you'll never find them. Best – take me. Better there . . .'

I couldn't resist it. 'You want to be in the big chair?'

The noise he made would have done credit to a bull in a slaughterhouse. He said quite a lot, but all I managed to catch was the tailpiece – 'Bloody young fool.'

I put on my haughty young Laird's expression.

'You want to be left alone?' I said in the role of Alan Breck.

He groaned. 'I'm sorry – if you *knew* the torment – didn't mean to be offensive – apologise –' He paused. On his face was the look of a man tied to the rails of a main railway line, waiting and listening for that express which stops for no man. His eyes were blank. The listening was internal. I was almost sorry for the bastard. The express passed by on the other track. He relaxed.

'Please help me to my office.'

'Very well, but no more nonsense,' I said. By his look I knew he was promising himself my guts for garters. Out of his mind with pain he'd forgotten who was the master. Leading an ape in hell is one thing; dragging one with a knot in his middle is another. I thought I was never going to get him over. I was a wet rag by the time I got him into his chair.

'Bottom drawer,' he said, when he was able. Like Francis, like me, he kept his confidential stuff in that magical left-hand bottom drawer. It was a patent medicine; just what I'd expected. That kind also read their horoscopes in the daily papers. I shook out a handful of pills. 'There's water on the desk,' he ordered the peasant. Biding my time I poured out a glass. I looked at my watch. It was quarter to eight. I decided to polish him off in ten minutes sharp. He had something to wait for. I had nothing. I tried his chair. I leaned back and nursed a Spatzer-Muller pistol in my lap, watching him with narrowed, mocking eyes. He didn't like it. I saw him press his lips. Shortly afterwards he closed his eyes and started listening again. 'I think it's going away,' he said childishly.

'Then I will, if you don't mind,' I said. I pocketed my pistol and walked over to the door. He followed me with his eyes. 'How did you know?' he asked.

I'd already decided to tell him the truth twisted a little. I said: 'I was working late. Leaving my office I heard one of the lifts go up; I still don't know why. So I came up to find out, thought it might be a break-in, found you – I'd looked in two or three offices before I found you.'

I could see the old fox didn't believe me, but I knew he couldn't fault my story. He'd have a job to tell me one that I couldn't fault. 'What department?' he asked.

'Special Projects.'

'Oh, that lot,' he said ungraciously. His lips weren't thin, but he had a trick of sneeringly twisting and compressing them. 'Under Small Summers, eh?' I nodded. 'And working late. You must be new?'

'I'm in lodgings,' I said.

'So was I when I first came here – that's a long time ago.' His tone was almost warm. 'What were you working on? One of your Projects.'

'One of my own, as a matter of fact,' I said, as pleasantly as possible. I could see he was recovering. He was well enough to try to get the upper hand. 'On packaging and distribution. A few ideas I wanted to get into shape.'

'Well, it has nothing to do with me; and I don't suppose anyone minds the electricity you consume,' he said. I thought he was having another attack, but it turned out that he was attempting a smile. 'I'll be obliged if you say nothing about this – what's your name?' I told him. 'Rowlands, much obliged. Don't like to broadcast a weakness, can't stand people asking after my health. Sentiment, slop, or a talking point – me, my weakness . . .' Which one? I silently asked.

Aloud I said: 'No, I won't.' He looked at me with naked doubt. There was nothing he could do; indeed there was nothing much I could do, if I'd been so disposed. 'Shall I look after the other room?'

Ignoring my question he said: 'Small Summers, eh? Must have a chat with you sometime. Where d'ye come from?' I told him, mentioning Snorry. 'I know him. Retired now, isn't he?' I said it was thrombosis. 'Yes, so I hear. Strange man. Rigid to the point of principle – without having any, I mean.'

'It was force of habit,' I said. 'At least, that's what he used to pretend.' I could see he wanted to say something caustic. The disadvantage stopped his mouth. 'If you don't mind, I'll go now. You're sure there's nothing I can do?'

'I'll look after it. Found the figures. Shut the bloody drawer with my foot. Taking no chances.' He raised himself experimentally to his feet, drew a deep breath, waited, wiped his face with the back of his hand like a labouring man, then concluded: 'You can go now.'

I turned. He cleared his throat. 'And Rowlands – when I send for you drop everything, do you hear?' I nodded and left.

I didn't need to wait around the corner to verify his swift dart into the Chairman's office, or time the swift simple motions of closing a drawer and switching off some lights. Later in the evening he'd remember the one little thing which had most disturbed him. I hadn't called him 'Sir'. I never would, either.

The next conversation went like a house on fire.

'You're late,' said Esther.

'I met a man who was locked in.'

'You'd have the skeleton key, of course.'

'I wouldn't dare pull the wool over your eyes.'

'You just try.'

'I'm looking for a place of my own.'

'In trouble where you are?'

'My brother's having a love affair and I'm just in the way,' I said, and added the grain of truth: 'In fact I'm staying at the Cumberland.'

'You should have stayed with your brother and done her a good turn.' I said nothing. 'Anyway, you've more money than sense. Hotels!'

'I can't stand filth and discomfort.'

'What do you expect me to do?'

'I thought there might be a couple of rooms at your place. You look the kind of girl who'd be willing to help.'

'I might be a little tired of helping.'

'That had occurred to me. I thought you might make an exception.'

'Your kind always does,' she said, knitting violently. 'All right. Come over on Saturday and be viewed.'

'Be viewed – come again?'

'By the landlady. I told you, she's an anarchist –'

'So's my old man.'

'So's my landlady,' she said with a look of utter disbelief. 'She's also a Tartar of the first order. She'll view you; then you'll accept, without sight.'

'That sounds as if you think I'll pass muster,' I said, pleased at the slip.

'I think you stand a good chance,' she said. 'It's a good place, if you can make it. But you have to be one of the comrades. She says she's in it for pleasure, not purgatory.'

'Them's exactly my sentiments,' I said.

'How are you settling in?'

'Fine, they think I'm a madman.' And I told her suitable portions of the tale, particularly omitting the bits about the 15th floor. She was a good listener. Halfway through I'd a sudden thought: that she was probably the granddaughter of His Nibs in the Penthouse. The thought grew. She started talking about R. Walker Johnson on the telephone; how he couldn't bear to wait one time, and couldn't care less at others.

When I came to, as it were, she was fumbling with her purse. I asked her to explain the laughter. 'That look,' she said. 'Straight through me. Makes me feel like a sheet of glass. Do you often go off like that?'

I couldn't tell her that she'd triggered it off. 'Day-dreaming', I said, 'is an art.'

'Don't be huffed.'

'I'm not. I'm only thinking of an answer. Do you know that early man dreamed two thirds of the day – and dreamed twice as much – and remembered what he dreamt, because it was so important?'

'That wasn't day-dreaming,' she said. The purse was ignored; she'd stopped looking for the penny.

'Day-dreaming is an art, I'll admit. But very useful. Do you know what any dream is – a letter to yourself.'

'And you drop off at any time you feel inclined – '

'I do.'

'That sounds like the Altar,' she laughed, then dropped her eyes.

To change the subject I said: 'By the way, you didn't tell me that His Nibs had a Mrs Nibs.' She looked at me blankly. I told her I'd seen friend Herbert, the lame lift boy, carrying a bouquet. She shrugged and went to put the kettle on.

'Don't worry,' I said. 'I'll sort it out myself.'

'You've no other choice,' she said. 'I wouldn't dream of spoiling your fun.' She returned to her usual seat. 'This is the only job I know, and I stick to the rules. Otherwise, you'd only be disappointed. If I told you the truth about the Penthouse, I mean.'

To change the subject again I asked the address. It was Malachi Terrace, 'not far from Primrose Hill' and with a delightful choice of Sabbath Church or Zoo. Her landlady was Miss Surtees. Known as Meg to her friends. I said she sounded like a witch, and she said she was, of the better class.

'While we're on names –' I said, leaving the answer to her.

She hesitated; it was one of those well-used hesitations. 'It's Death. Actually it's spelled D apostrophe e, a, t, h; D'Eath. Some of us pronounce it Deeth. The vulgar relative says Dearth. Ugh . . .' The shudder wasn't for the vulgar relatives. I was sincerely delighted; even a little envious, and showed it.

'You can't say it hasn't dignity as well as mystery,' I said. 'Now that I know, it's the only name you could possibly have.'

She said 'Thank you,' and, as usual with me when I happen to be sincerely generous, my eyes became moist. But she didn't like that, or the quotation. I murmured those lines of Vaughan: 'Dear Beauteous Death! The jewel of the just . . .'

'Get off with you,' she said. 'I know the end – Shining nowhere but in the dark.'

'That's good too,' I said.

'You could be very good fun,' she said. 'If you come to Malachi Terrace – should you pass inspection – it might prove very interesting to have you around the house.'

I raised my eyebrows and nodded agreement. I was thinking what any man might think after a statement of that kind. Her eyes clouded. 'I like friendships that stay objective and equal,' she said. 'Not the kind of thing you're thinking about.' The look that went with this was in keeping with her name. I nodded agreement and tried to look sorry for what had been, after all, only a look. But I was not convinced.

SEVEN

Esther's geography was at odds with the facts, which was what I might have expected – Londoners always minimize the distance between themselves and a park. I should have taken a taxi. Instead I went by bus and wandered to the top of Primrose Hill, found the view greatly overrated (squat Manhattan with odd squiggly little bits here and there), then set off to find Malachi Terrace, dead-reckoning. It took the better part of sixty minutes to find the place. Had I been on an objective journey of exploration the street might have delighted me. In a steady Saturday drizzle the line of red brick and bow windows gave me the Willies. Each house had bay windows up and down, and steps to a basement pit. Some had rotting vegetation, some had rockeries, one had a boot-scraper, all had empty milk bottles. No. 22 had a yellow lion with a crack in his haunches. The curtains were good and the windows clean. Paintwork in good condition, always a good sign. Like the bell-pull, door-knob, knocker and letter box were high-yellow brass.

The lady who appeared was as well-mustered as the house, age between 50 and 60, small, plump, dark, raven-haired and sloe-eyed; wearing a dress, which like face and body, managed to convey maturity without suggesting antiquity. Before I'd time to explain myself she cut me short: 'Ah, it's Esther's Samuel, is it?' and turned about, saying, 'Follow me.' She wasn't wearing carpet slippers; a kind of ballet shoe suited her pretty little feet too well for that.

'Sit down, Sam,' she said, at the same time taking a seat herself and presenting a very neat pair of knees; dimples and delicate flush would have done credit to a girl. 'Do smoke, if you wish.' I lit a cigar. 'You will notice,' said Miss Surtees. 'You will notice that I've taken a chair and given you a seat; *you* sink miserably, I sit erect. I flaunt my legs, *you* cannot but notice them. I have taken care of my legs. Before I became a business woman I was a chorus girl; my legs were my pittance, then my fortune. I sacrificed. I abjured the frying pan for fresh fruit. Do you think my sacrifice was in vain?'

'They're lovely legs,' I said as she obliged by re-crossing and renewing the flow of blood.

'Do you read books?' I tried not to look too startled. 'You do, of course. Then you will like to have them around you.' Her hand picked up an invisible duster. 'Then you must promise to dust them at least once a month.' I counted three, no, four, rings; at the end of the interview I was still not quite sure of the count. She used her hands a lot and kept her body still. 'The mania for collecting – books put away are books without value,' she continued. 'Hence my rule about dusting. Dusting enables the sensible reader to take stock. Why dust a book you will never read again, if, indeed, you ever managed to read it once?' She paused. 'What's your opinion?'

'It seems a sensible idea.'

'Not of dusting books. Of me, your opinion of me!' she flashed.

'I read one book at a time.'

'Good,' she said. 'You're reading me. All right, then, make it provisional.'

'Esther was right,' I evaded. 'You're a bit of a Tartar.'

'I'm selfish, self-centred and sensible,' she said. 'I've studied audiences over the footlights and my fellow-human beings in the wings. So I know. I know that man must have a master. You come from the North?' I nodded. 'I played the Grand, Byker. Sinister outside, lovely within. That's not a simile for men and women. Do you have a philosophy?'

'I have nothing,' I said, staring her straight in the eye. 'So we're marrers, we match up.'

'You're not telling the truth.'

'All right, I worship all sorts of gods. Take too long to tell.'

'You don't worship. You tinker.'

'All right. I'm an anarchist.'

'Superstition!' she cried. 'I knew a real anarchist. Juan and his

Performing Ducks. Marched on parade like a regiment. He shouted orders. Wife played trumpet. Also carried cash. She ruled him, he ruled ducks. And he wanted to kill off all the Kings and Queens and Presidents and Judges and Bishops, little knowing that they helped to keep him safe and sound in his own identity.'

'Who wants that kind of identity?'

'What it amounts to doesn't matter. What does matter is that we're becoming more and more alike and more and more a mob. We need hills and mountains, suns and moons. We need tall trees. We need to know where we are, man-marks as well as landmarks. You need a boss just as much as you need to be a boss. Anarchist! I'll bet you want to be a boss. Everybody wants to be a boss – do you ever dream of being boss?'

That was a shrewd hit, although I didn't know it then. My very first dream after moving into Malachi Terrace was one of a series; I'm absolutely certain of that. I'd been at the game a long time. What I mean is that I slipped into Small Summers's office with the ease of long practice and made my way to the position I wanted without stopping to think. With my back to his desk I took hold of the arms of his chair and slowly revolved until my feet were on the wall and my upside-down face was looking along the great plain of his desk. It was difficult to keep steady. I had just succeeded when Small Summers walked in and shattered my balance with one smooth little chuckle. My wrists turned to water but I couldn't come right-side-up and there was a confused and hilarious period when the two of us floated out of control on a kind of free-fall, ironical term for that ultimate state of helplessness. We were trying to steer ourselves to that coveted chair. Small Summers said: 'You'll never make it with your clothes on.'

I gritted between my teeth: 'I'll show you, buster,' meanwhile busily revolving but somehow managing to arrive sitting. I folded my arms and smiled. Small Summers ruefully alighted on the desk, no bigger than a lead soldier. He began to dwindle, or rather, I began to recede. 'Well, I'm still in the chair,' I remarked, watching the little white matchstick face and the arm raised in blessing. That was a letter if you like. To myself, I mean.

'I *am* a boss,' I told her, several hours before the dream.

She laughed. 'But you'd like to be a bigger boss. I'm telling you.

Status is wonderful. Status and power are good for the soul. Much better than sex, although, indeed, they make sex much better.'

'That's interesting,' I told her, and meant every word.

'I know from experience. Nonentities are hopeless in bed. I know, I used to be one. Then I became a Principal Boy. Seven times in a row. I loved it. Being first, and best and boss.'

'The most wonderful thing in the world has nothing to do with power or status,' I stated.

'Don't bring me love.'

'A deep rich belly laugh?' I suggested.

'Applause runs it a pretty close second,' she said, giving a little, which I liked. 'But good company and a laugh are never arranged. All you need to lift the roof is to be good at what you're doing. Applause can be planned.'

'I'll still stick to the laugh.'

'But applause runs it a pretty close second, eh?'

'I can't deny my own nature.'

'Here, take this,' she said, throwing something. What I caught was a latch key. She busied herself at a cupboard. 'The one's that do the damage always deny their nature – Lenin, f'instance, total abstainer, faithful husband, a saint in private and a fiend in public. Help yourself to water – should you need it.'

'Here's to living,' she said, raising her glass.

'And here's to dreaming,' I toasted, without the gesture. She didn't know how well she'd scored; I make it a rule never to drink before my evening meal; not out of righteousness but because my metabolism's wrong. By the third drink I saw an old theatre bill move: creep's a better word. Feeling mildly uncomfortable, I walked over to the thing. All I could make out was that it was the Vaudeville Tonight! Tonight! Holding my hand she read out the bill:

'Amy Mullican, Jones and Robinson, Dillon's Dogs, Hess and Lisbon, The Gabrielles, Sandford and Lyons, Jimmy Figaro and Guitar, J. E. Camp, the Man who Never Smiles, Sullivan's Show Band,' taking a deep breath after running through these. 'And the Parker Precision Girls, me in the front and solo.'

'The date?'

'The year of the devil and Depression,' she sighed. 'I lost a boy friend and a bottom drawer full of shares.' She went to make coffee. We drank it. We'd finished half a bottle of whisky. Now she broached a second, and I remember the big handsome apprentice of Bristol whose master died and whose mistress called him into the cellar to broach a pipe of wine, instead of which it was the mistress that was broached.

In this case it was the apprentice who was in danger of broaching. Nothing happened to her; her eyes grew a little brighter, perhaps, or she would pause in the middle of a declamation about Upton Sinclair, Bernard Shaw, Barrie, and gaze raptly into my eyes. Feeling a little drunk I couldn't make up my mind whether she was seeing me, or seeing through me. It was about one-thirty, when I was beginning to feel the pangs, not having had much breakfast, that she opened her bag and took out a notebook from which she extracted a very yellow newspaper cutting. 'Note,' she said. 'Note, no spectacles. Now listen to this.'

She read the way an opera singer reads:

'SOCIALIST SONG AT BYKER GRAVESIDE.'

'That's a hell of a long time ago,' I said lightly, wanting to escape. She gave me a look. In the end I wanted to stay; she read like Dame Clara Butt singing 'Land of Hope and Glory', lifting the old, flat newspaper prose into a magic that was ninety per cent voice.

'The unusual spectacle of a Red Flag funeral was seen at Byker on Tuesday, when the interment took place of the late Mr John Surtees, who worked at Walker Colliery, but was well-known as a leading member of the British and International Socialist Labour Party and the Workers' International Industrial Union.

'The coffin was draped with the Red Flag and on this was placed bunches of roses and a wreath of crimson blooms. Six "comrades" wearing ribbons of red carried the coffin from his residence in Macklin Street to Heaton Station, where they were relieved by others until Heaton Cemetery was reached.

'There was no religious ceremony at the cemetery. First of all Mr George Flynn read a long eulogy, including the following: "For worship of the unknown he substituted duty, and for prayer, work, and the record of his life bears testimony to the purity of his heart. His end saw him in perfect tranquillity, with no misgivings or doubts, no trembling lest he should have missed the right path; he went undaunted into the great land of the departed."

'Mr James Weston said: "He fought the good fight of free enquiry both in this country and the USA, where he was known and loved by many thousands.

'"He was free from the forces and superstitions of belief.

'"No man was the keeper of his conscience.

'"His religion was of this world, the service of humanity his highest aspiration."

'Mr Alfred Owens said that Jack Surtees was loved the most by those who knew him best, and hated most by those who knew him least. In spite of adversity and the most cruel and vicious opposition he stood firm in proclaiming what he believed was in the best interests of the class to which he belonged.

'The coffin was lowered into the grave amid cries of "Poor Old Jack."

'The coffin, which had brass furnishings, bore the inscription: "John Surtees, died July 17th, 1930, aged 42 years." Surtees had lived at Byker four or five years, for the last two of which he had been ill and practically confined to his lodgings.'

'Your father?' I asked.

'Poor Old Jack who went to America to save the workers and was sent home, not to save his wife and two daughters, but to save more workers,' she said. 'Poor Old Jack who never kissed a child of his own and put hundreds more in hunger before he went down with TB and hunger himself. The Workers and their beautiful bunches of roses and their bouquets of crimson blooms kept their charity for his corpse.'

'Were you there?'

She shook her head. 'I read it in the paper. If I'd known, and if they'd given me time off at the candle factory, I'd have gone to spit on his grave.' We looked at each other, she with too much and I with too little to say.

'I'm not a dipso,' she suddenly said. 'Only it's so long since I heard a voice from home – the real twang. Have you ever been to Heaton Cemetery?' I said yes, I'd once been to look for the grave of a man who wrote songs, funnily enough one called 'Keep your feet still, Geordie hinny.'

'It's an age since I heard that one sung,' she said. 'That's Joe Wilson of the Comic Tyneside Almanack. I once did a programme of his songs and patter at the Empire, songs and recitations – would you believe it?'

'It's nearly all gone,' I said regretfully. 'The place is just like anywhere else.'

'Don't you believe it,' she said. 'Any place where you died two or three times can never be like anywhere else.'

I wondered if that was my trouble; never dying. I also wondered if she could take it. Taking the plunge I said: 'It's a pity they weren't together in Heaton cemetery; Joe could have sung to Jack and Jack could have poured his heart out to Joe.'

'He didn't have much of a life, I suppose,' she said, her eyes filling. 'Poor deluded bugger.' She had almost said bastard. 'You'd be better off.'

As I went out she said: 'Now you know why you're here.'

I took a number of buses back to Baker Street and went into the Classic to see a double programme of Tati. The second time round I was fine again; it wasn't the whisky so much as the woman on whom I was drunk. Then I went back to the Cumberland and got my case, together with myself, into a taxi, and went back to Malachi Terrace. The second time round there was also fine; the hill was looking like a ballast heap, and I knew I was going as near a home as I'd ever find in London Town. My room was L-shaped with a Georgian-type archway leading from the bed to the sitter. It overlooked ours and someone else's backstreet. Our backyard was all garden; I wouldn't have been surprised to see a pigeon ducket over the outhouse. I wish there had been, pigeons bring peace: we both needed that eternal, imbecile cooing. On consideration, not imbecile, just a little less than mindless.

I looked around when the room was livable, said: 'Poor Old Jack,' and went in search of Esther. We returned to the Classic and I saw 'Hulot's Holiday' and 'Mon Oncle' through again for the third time. We walked home and Esther made a soufflé on the gas cooker in the kitchen we shared. It was a good day. I awoke to thin sunshine and church bells and, for the millionth time, wished I could honestly go to church. Then I went to sleep again.

Esther awoke me at twelve and said we were invited out to dinner; we had beef and Yorkshire pudding with Meg Surtees. Her Yorkshire puddings were good. When I told her, she said: 'As good as Mother's?' That gave me a twist, and she knew it. In the afternoon we left Meg to doze and went to Hampstead. Esther liked walking. By evening we'd agreed to share housekeeping, that's to say, combustibles and cooking. I'd a feeling I was getting as in-deep as pal Simon; I thought with an ache of Cathie, who was tied up with Holinshed. I knew I could break it, if I wished, but that is a bad way to embark upon a relationship.

Esther's bedroom, I noticed, had a door instead of an arch. The trouble with the man-woman relationship is that you always want to take it to the ultimate. The following day I went along to Cathie's office and asked for a stamp. She opened her bag, took out her purse, extracted a book. I expected her to pull off a stamp. Instead, she handed me the whole book. She smiled. Her skin seemed transparent. I took a stamp and left. Mrs Arcot was smiling as well. Cathie had resumed typing but I turned and found her looking at me, as if her hands and eyes belonged to separate persons.

At three the following day, or it may have been the day after, Mr Small Summers rang me, asking apologetically if I minded going along to his office – if I'd the time to spare and wasn't busy with something else – 'I'd have slipped along but everything's to hand here.' He didn't need to tell me; I'd been mentally tracking its course; I'd already heard that the Controller had flown North on Friday afternoon and had been closeted with Mick Rampion for half an hour before leaving.

I told Miss Miffin where I was going and said I was sure he wanted to see me about the Hartlepools project. 'Oh, I'm sure it is,' she said. 'I lunched with Cathie and Mrs Arcot today and they said R.W.J. had been in with the Chief Controller all morning.'

'What's the trouble?'

'R.W.J. thinks it should go through as it is. Cathie Cavendish said he was as cheerful as could be –'

I said: 'Bless you, my child,' sent her away, rang Rampion, got a load of nonsense about vintage cars and wine-making, and several valuable nuances, then went along the corridor, prepared for battle. I wasn't worried about arguments. I knew the scheme inside out. My need was for strength and staying power. No one would blame *me* if the project went haywire because of bad evaluation. I was small fry. But precisely because of this I was prepared to battle. It might be that there were nuances I couldn't know about and my resistance would get me into bad odour. I had to risk that. Going along the corridor I closed my mind to all these fears and concentrated on what I knew and felt; especially the I-ness of it. Cathie wasn't in the outer office. 'Taking dictation,' said Mrs Arcot, following my eyes. It's useless to dissemble with women.

'Tell her I passed by,' I said, and knocked at the CC's door.

No nonsense there. A warm welcome, told to sit down, given the freedom of a box of cigars – my own expensive brand. I lit up. After the cigar was away he said: 'I'll tell you what I know, and what we've decided. I've been up to Hartlepools. Went through the place with a small tooth-comb – production, manpower, management, equipment, views on equipment; costs, proceeds, profits. As you know, they've had one good month this year. Otherwise, they've broken even . . .'

He paused, but I resisted the temptation he offered. After all, he wasn't on a soap box.

'We've good men there. It's not the men – they're doing well on obsolete plant.' His eyes clouded. 'I like the spot. It's quiet, happy, you can almost hear the hum of contentment. They've never had trouble before.' I nodded agreement and wondered if he'd been long enough there to put his finger on the one man who counted. He had. 'Do you know a man named Charlton?'

'Charlie Charlton. Best branch official in the country. Gets drunk on a glass of lemonade. Writes and delivers dialect poetry at every annual dinner he can manage.'

'He has instinct,' said Small Summers. 'He knew what I was there for. He knows that a reconstruction will put them right . . . It's a pity they didn't have their slice of the investment a little sooner.'

He had to say 'Yes?' twice before I'd speak. 'You'd get the money back in five years.'

'We could close the place, switch production to Sunderland and Newcastle and never bat a financial eyelid,' he said.

'But you'd lose an investment in men,' I said, noting the

reference to closing the place.

'There'd be work elsewhere in the region,' said Small Summers, a little impatiently.

'I'm not interested in regions, Controller,' I said. 'I'm interested in a plant that's still self-supporting and could earn money. All that's needed is a little bit of the cash they've earned over and over again . . .'

'Policy's against spending money at the moment.'

'You're not interested in justice, even when it won't cost you a penny?'

'It'll tie money for a year or so,' said Small Summers. 'Listen, Sam, I appreciate the point you're making; I also like people.'

I dug my toes in. 'They're spending a million on the new headquarters. How's that for consistent policy?'

'I'll not argue that point,' said the Controller, laughing. 'The new buildings are for us. We can see its advantages. Also a bigger basement's needed for the computer spread-over.'

'And we need space for a middle-aged prestige spread-over,' I pressed, not smiling back.

'The trouble here is that I know what they'll take. You don't.'

'I'm just laying the foundations, Controller.'

He sat on the edge of the desk and laid a finger along his bottom lip. 'More than people, then?'

'No more. Only, there's more to it than sentiment. You met Charlton?'

He was quick on the uptake. 'I didn't like his eyes.'

'The union's very sensitive about employment – and their Government's in power.'

'Charlton hasn't the push.'

'You're wrong, Controller. He was the brains behind the last effort. It was quite something. This time he's on an easy wicket. We're not a truly private concern, we're a public utility.' I rose. 'Ask the Board if they'd like to be nationalised again.'

'Nonsense!' he said. 'And sit down.' He saw I didn't like his 'nonsense'. 'All right, then, it isn't nonsense. We were nationalised once. We can be nationalised again. Tell me how it could stem from Charlton?'

'I know that Charlton's pulled his weight to make the unit go. He played with us on a cut-back of industrial manpower at the smaller plants, including and especially Hartlepools. He scraped in with ten votes at the last election. He's going to be an angry man when you tell him he risked his neck for nothing. That's what you read in his eyes. Not badness. Just the mood of a good man who feels he's been fooled.'

'What's the score on Charlton – I mean, what can he do?'

'He'll fight you. He'll swing the Union. He'll bring a deputation to UK House, then he'll march over to the Board of Trade and lay level hell. He'll picket the Prime Minister – you watch, the deputation'll be arranged for Thursday morning so that he can spend the afternoon or evening in the House, with time for a bit of bird-watching outside No. 10. He'll have hired cars waiting to follow the Prime Minister to Chequers on Friday.'

'You curdle my imagination,' he said.

'Then there's television,' I continued. 'Some of those men have had a dose of the dole. They don't like it. Oh – and the closure would come about Christmas. That'll certainly help to sell it. I mean, *their* case.'

'Have you been talking to Charlton?' asked Small Summers.

'Just to myself,' I said. I knew I'd won him. Now I was wondering abut R. Walker Johnson. He was pretty much in the same case as my old friend Charlton; only, with less to lose. He picked up the telephone. 'Can you ask Mr Walker Johnson to put his head in here?' he asked.

We talked over the chances of Charlton's campaign until we lost the point about its chances of success or failure and saw only an embarrassment that wasn't worth a saving of £200,000, a saving that wasn't, in the long run, a legitimate saving. I was watching R. Walker Johnson. He was short with me, to begin with. Then that died. Half-jokingly I described the march of the six hundred Hartlepools men along the Embankment, their pathetic little banner ('Down with R. Walker Johnson'?), their dignified march up the stairs, the problems of reception (teas, food, medical, political – Ministers being called and calling back, invasion of the cameras, etc., etc.). The Chief Controller laughed, knowing that things are never so bad as the anticipation of them; but R. Walker Johnson stiffened. I knew then he was a doomsday-man; one who believes there is terror at hand and specifically, terror for himself, a terror worse than earthquake, flood or hurricane all together. Out of his sense of private doom he capitulated. I had won the first round.

I knew then that my line was right for me. As for policy, I couldn't know. Nobody ever knows what's right and what's wrong. You can only throw a kind of penny in the air.

At that moment I was feeling my pessimistic peak; to follow your own hunch is one thing but to see the others falling in behind is quite another. There are several flavours to that kind of triumph. Walker Johnson and I were leaving the room when the Chief Controller said, 'Oh – by the way, Rowlands . . .' I turned and knew it was something bad. When it is something bad you can never guess it. Walker Johnson went out. Small Summers asked me to sit down. 'You knew Snorry, didn't you?' he asked. The past tense told me all. I nodded. The grief of it was squeezing all my guts. 'Perhaps you've heard?'

'He's been ill –' I was about to add 'a long time' but couldn't. Not because there was a danger of tears, simply because there was no air to breathe and no means of saying the words. I was dead myself and hardly listened to his explanation. So Charlton had told him. So Charlton had gone to the funeral. Snorry's nephew had been asking for me. 'It appeared he thought a good deal of you,' said Small Summers. I said yes and thanked him for telling me. Then I went to my room and sat remembering the good times we had had together. There was no light in my room and Miss Miffin told me later that she thought I'd gone home. I suppose I was trying to follow Snorry to where he had gone. The mind works strangely. I needed Cathie but I knew that I couldn't wait for her. Because Snorry was dead, Esther would have to do. This may sound like calculation. It was – it is. It is the way most of us manage to overcome the bad blows and continue to survive.

EIGHT

The upshot of our conference was that Small Summers decided to
re-hash the paper from my point of view and present it personally
to the Board. At the same time another conference, of a kind, took
place.

It amounted to this:

Nettled by the fact that I hadn't consulted with anyone on the
Hartlepools project, more specifically himself, Wills complained to
Holinshed. I suppose he flayed me for my sins; I imagine
Holinshed listened with a mounting sense of impatience; in the end
he burst out: 'Don't tell me ad nauseam; tell Rowlands.'

'You're ticking me off?' asked Wills incredulously.

'I'm asking for peace, a little bit of peace,' said Holinshed.

'You're not interested?'

'I'm sick of your endless complaining,' said Holinshed.

Wills marched out. There must have been desolation as well as
anger; the kind of desolation we all feel when we see ourselves as
others sometimes see us. For a time, I imagine, he felt crushed and
wounded. This did not last. Desolation gave way to anger and then
to cold and clever calculation. He went downstairs and out of the
building, perversely determined to act out his role. My
reconstruction is based on my own feelings and experience as well
as upon hints culled from both Holinshed and Wills.

He rang Holinshed's home number, heard Holinshed's wife
repeat name and exchange number in a voice which never failed to
stir him (he told me this *in another context*), then said the dozen
words he'd composed on the way to the kiosk: 'Did you know that

your husband was having an affair, Mrs Holinshed?'

Or, 'Mrs Holinshed – is that Mrs Holinshed? Did you know your husband was having an affair with another woman?'

He would then hang up, quickly, so as to cut off the sound of her breath being drawn in, and the first stammered question.

But at that time, of course, I only knew about the quarrel. I dismissed it as a trivial affair, discovered I was too excited about the Hartlepools business to do any work, re-read my private correspondence. There was a letter from my mother saying that my father was being murdered by sciatica (only she didn't say 'murdered'); that sister Julie had been highly commended at school for a painting of her pony; that Major Carstairs had presented her with one of his famous black tulip bulbs; and was I comfortable?

There was also a letter from my black-sheep Uncle James, the one who speaks to an audience of three in the Bigg Market every Sunday.

> Dear Sam, [it ran] You'll be glad to know that I'm once again in steady work – and where would you think? On the pier! When you think of all the times we wandered along that pier and peeped into the workings of that big crane it makes you wonder if there isn't a powerful destiny working for the good men. So here I am watching the ships go by and sometimes hanging out a line for a buckshee fish – there are times thanks to *your* outfit when you can see bloody great hordes of them being chased by a bloody big fish.
>
> I spend most of my time in the storehouse which you may remember, it's in that little ravine about five hundred yards away from the haven; I am also the messenger boy and am kept fairly busy, as they have a clip-on telephone system, and it is always ringing like hell, mostly for more tea. So I'm getting the constitution of a race-horse (have you noticed that big girls get more like race-horses and little girls like whippets?), but I don't mind, I like the work. Unfortunately, we don't get so many ships as in the old days, they're all big 'uns now and few and far between, but it still shakes my soul to hear them pass through a sea-fret bellowing like Leviathan Himself, although most times I cannot hear them for the Pier

Master, a man named Horrocks, ex-Merchant Navy skipper with a good line in duty-free baccy and booze.

Never got the ship he wanted, retired before his time, so is ready for anarchism, we really get down to it, God Bless Godwin, so much so that often when the telephone rings he picks it up himself and tells them to bloodywell wait. He sometimes takes the can (of tea) himself, having wasted so much of my time.

You will be glad to hear that I still get along to the Bigg Market and my gang of Old Faithfuls; you'll doubtless laugh but I feel that the Time is Always Ripe; that the bottom is dropping out of the old-style unions and the Parliamentary wangle; and that one day the people (there are no longer workers, but then none of our Founders were workers) will come to their senses and see the big sell-out for what it is worth.

The Fabians started the sell-out when they organised the mess of pottage; for what is food, what are gadgets, compared to the freedom of men who live without Law? What they didn't know was that they were only delaying the day; it's bound to come; everything gets bigger and bigger, unions, industries, etc., and one day they'll drop like ripe plums into the hands of the people.

You should read a book by the last of our prophets, a man named Chardin who was only nominally a member of the Order of Jesuits; his book is naturally full of errors, but he is right on one thing; man is growing all over the earth like vegetation. The question is on the point of growth. He's covering the face of the globe all right; but rank like a jungle; quantity and no quality; the forest is full of brush and vines instead of tall Redwoods.

It's all right you laughing, but the evidence is all against you. One day you'll find out that it's anarchism or bust; death or glory; and that your muddled old uncle was right all the time.

Believing in the wicked nature of man as I do, I couldn't see it. Man has murder in his heart. The Communist military in Russia and China are clear-sighted men, and they believe that the big fight will really come and the blood really flow when all the world's united under Communism. Which is inevitable. We're all alike in a taste for murder.

The redwoods grow in every generation, but there's always an axe and electric saw ready and men fighting to pick them up.

If you can't be a redwood you can always be an axeman.

Waiting for a Tube I copied out the following 'for disposal': fine standards of Illomba Marori Obeche and other Mahogany. French Gaboon, fir, beech, oak and Finnish plywood. Kiln-dried American oak, steamed Yugo-Slav beech shorts, French beech and Japanese oak squared. The story of man is the felling of human trees; old, unique or rare; all are felled and up for auction. My Uncle James thinks that the timber's not wasted; that the nobility build themselves a floating palace which endures through the ages. Falls not in vain the tree.

The truth is that he can't pass a rubbish dump or a saleroom where he can yearn over the odd, the wrecked and the useless. His house is full of three-legged chairs, ancient umbrellas pile in a corner, one with a sailmaker's needle stuck into its hood for when he finds time to repair (which he never will), mildewed books, mostly Sunday school prizes to bodies since rotted away, wheelbarrow, scooter and tricycle wheels, battered hall-stands, timber, chipped pinto pots, not to mention those half-baked or fossilised anarchist ideas, which I take like his tea-wine. Sitting here in my acoustically perfect, centrally-heated, scientifically-lighted, airconditioned, womb-perfect office, I remember my last visit from pretty little Whalton to the house, not by the river he loved, but lost in six square miles of council housing estate. His fat little housekeeper got out the bottle and he never stopped talking until at last she handed me the tumbler; I remembered the red moonface of the innocent child set on the big body of a man, and the blue eyes watching me take the poison to my lips. At the last moment I made the wrong decision; instead of rolling it round my mouth, swallowing, and saying a long, drawn-out 'Ah!', thus saving a lie, I let the whole lot go. It was like cold sour piss; his doctrine, at least, is warmer, and has a nice tart bite to it.

We are all children. Thursday evening came the meeting of the famous society. Squires called for me and we went for a wash; I took off my jacket and religiously rolled up my sleeves; soaping, washing off, douching myself, getting into my ears, nostrils and the corners of my eyes, and then, and then only, picking up my towel. I found Charlie watching me. 'Combat boredom with a clean face,' I grinned.

'You seem in fine fettle,' he suggested.

'I pulled off the Hartlepools thing.'

'Don't kid yourself. R.W.J. doesn't like the place and he's just biding his time. You know Crumple's cutting down on all the frivolous expenditure? At the moment unit profit and loss accounts are his favourite weekend reading.'

My sensitive ear had only picked up the reference to Walker Johnson's dislike for the Hartlepools' plant. I asked why. 'Walker Johnson was acting secretary for the region when they opened the last extension. The ceremony was on the first floor with the VIP's standing on a floor of perforated plate. Sneaking down for a spare bottle of champagne, he discovered a dozen characters lying on their backs and craning their necks for a view of luscious silken thighs.'

'That wouldn't influence him, surely.'

'He'd just been married and he took an instant dislike to vicarious sharing.' He paused. 'Because of that he'll fight you to a standstill; if he doesn't get total closure he'll settle for care and maintenance, which means closing down sooner or later.'

'Thanks for the tip,' I said. With or without, I knew that Walker Johnson would go down in flames on this one. We joined the others and walked over in a bunch smack against a tide of home-goers. 'I have a surprise,' said Walker Johnson. 'See you in the pub.' He disappeared. Holinshed was already in the upper room, sitting on the perimeter of a big round table surrounded by scribbled notes and a copy of the book he'd been selected to review: 'The Lost Skyscraper'.

Squires took the orders; bitters for all excepting me. I asked for a double whisky and a bottle of lemonade. They looked at me. 'It's a drink,' I said.

'And you shall have it,' said Charlie, rubbing his hands. He was in his element here. 'Can I get you another?' he asked Holinshed, who wretchedly nodded.

Walker Johnson arrived with a bound, sedately followed by a plump, pale young man wearing a double-breasted suit of ancient cut and a modern shirt. He'd been double-shaved but still carried the shadow which, I should imagine, constitutes a very private anguish. 'A friend from the Soviet Embassy,' he announced, gesturing like the oldest ham, 'Ivan Sergei Koniev.'

'Field Marshal, man sentenced Beria to death,' I said. 'Any relation?' The guest gave me a look of quiet hatred. 'That's a long time ago,' I managed to conclude.

'Mr Koniev's an expert of economic affairs, a management man like ourselves,' cried R.W.J. 'I vote we postpone the discussion arranged for tonight.'

'Not at all, gentlemen,' said the Russian. 'I'm rather interested in literature myself.'

'I don't mind,' said Holinshed. I didn't say anything; I was wondering where Koniev's interests lay, and whether it was in our line of business. In the only reference to Prinkstoneism ever made by a Russian at an international conference, three points were made: (a) only capitalism needed to organise a full-scale operation on waste, (b) all the essential elements of the Prinkstone installations had been perfected by a man named Andrei Zoshchenko in 1863, then forgotten, (c) in the Soviets all waste was eliminated at source. The entire delegation had stalked out amidst laughter.

I didn't like the look of Koniev. This had nothing to do with his being a Russian and looking slightly alien. He had that unclean detachment you often find in American missile men – 'Yea, sure, I'll press the button; why not?' Having lived through so many push-button years I have grown to dislike detachment.

'I don't mind a bit,' repeated Holinshed.

We all looked at the man from the Embassy. 'I dislike extemporization,' said he. 'I should enjoy listening to our friend.'

'We might draw you out,' suggested R.W.J. coyly.

'Possibly,' said Koniev coldly.

'Ah – a drink, what's it to be – vodka?'

'Tell me,' said Koniev, 'what would you drink in Moscow?'

'Vodka, of course.'

'Then I will drink whisky in London. I have worked out the "kick" as you call it; the equivalent of one vodka is – let me see – a double treble whisky.'

R. Walker Johnson blenched slightly but went downstairs and returned with a tooth glass and half a bottle of whisky. The Russian watched contemptuously as I poured my double whisky into a half glass and topped it with lemonade. I wondered which he was – permanent staff or trade mission; how many plant he'd be good for; how much he'd cough up. Fitting up Moscow would be fun; furthermore it would be easy to wangle a couple of new buffing tanks for Hartlepools on the side.

I was about to drink when Charlie Squires nudged me – 'Not yet.'

R. Walker Johnson coughed and said: 'All set, Jack?'

Holinshed coughed, glanced hatefully at his notes, and said he was.

R. Walker Johnson stood up and the rest, including a couple of our up-and-coming juniors and two or three lads from Technical Branch, followed suit as he boomed: 'The Speaker of the evening.' Koniev knocked off his double treble, looked around, smiled slightly as his eye lit on the half bottle at his side. Holinshed smiled nervously and played with his glass; pulling a finger round the rim as if he expected to draw forth music. We all sat down. He coughed and said: 'I've had a list of characters stencilled.' He held them like a pack of playing cards ready to deal out.

'Just a moment, Jack,' said R.W.J. Glancing at Koniev he said: 'There's method in our English formality. First, gentlemen, may I introduce our honoured Soviet guest, Ivan Sergei Koniev . . .' He paused to allow the congregation to murmur 'good evening' or any other nonsense that happened to spring to mind, 'And our new member, Mr Sam Rowlands, whom most of you already know . . .' The murmur for me was about as warm as a Siberian Autumn. I stood up and bowed to each in turn; Koniev, his second glass in hand and ready for gullet, returned the compliment.

'A toast to our great common forefather,' I said. He raised his glass expectantly. 'To Moses who led his people out of the Wilderness.' He paled around the nostrils but drank with the rest. 'Now I will make a toast,' he said, smiling slightly.

I noticed poor Walker Johnson looking poignantly at the half bottle, as was, of whisky which must have cost him at least a couple of quid; trying not to forecast the full evening's score.

Koniev raised his glass: 'To the English Semite D'Israeli who led an alien race into a paradise of money-changers.'

'Now that we've had our little fun perhaps we can start the proceedings,' said R. Walker Johnson. I doubt whether he'd ever heard of Soviet anti-semitism. Holinshed passed out a list of characters a mile long. 'I'm afraid I'll have to stick to my notes.'

'Oh, my God,' muttered Wills.

'What's also needed, of course,' said Holinshed miserably – only Wills could guess that he'd been up half the night and that he was desperately trying to keep his balance on the crunching pack-ice of his marriage – 'is a biographical note on each of those many persons plus a table of forbidden relationships as long as the one in church porches . . .' I noticed he was sweating as if the reference had triggered off his own feelings of guilt about what is, after all, the most commonplace and almost conventional of all illicit activities.

'The windowless skyscraper hurling on to a mysterious destination may be intended as a symbol of the closed world we live in. Its architectural detail and function are – one imagines – irrelevant; what matters one feels, to Mrs Bloodshot, are the people who inhabit its different levels.'

'Nonsense,' said Koniev, re-filling his glass.

'I agree,' said Wills.

'You,' said Koniev to Wills, 'don't know with what you are agreeing. The architecture and function are all-important if we are to understand the people.'

'A point of disagreement we can discuss later,' said R.W.J.

'Er – one can only select a few of the more important characters and attempt a rough outline,' continued Holinshed. 'First, Mr Ludovic, the Manager, who never sleeps – and for that matter never seems to eat –'

'Breakfast well,' boomed the fat-faced Russian. 'Lunch with discretion. Give your enemy your dinner.'

'Quite,' said Holinshed. 'When Ludovic isn't locked in his enormous study, where he wrestles to the death with accounts that never come right, he's wandering about the upper levels, or storeys, asking questions about modern accounting methods. He's daily expecting the arrival of the External Auditor (the only external character in the book) who has powers of summary justice. There's no hope of putting the books right but there is of cooking them; and sentence may be suspended if the job's cleverly done . . .

'The guests and staff – the rest of the staff – have their own personal nightmare: that the air-conditioning apparatus may break down. The Chief Steward, Mr Spain, devotes the whole of his spare time to developing a portable oxygen machine. He's Mr Ludovic's wife's stepson. Mrs Ludovic is much older than her husband and an extraordinary virile woman – in the course of the book she has seven or eight very active affairs . . .' He faltered.

'You musn't forget that the stepson turns out to be the Auditor's natural son,' said Walker Johnson.

'Thanks, it's frightfully complicated. I was about to say that one of the affairs is with Sampson, Master of the Lifts and her own half-brother; and it's *his* wife with whom Spain is passionately and hopelessly in love; there's a wonderful scene where he succeeds in building a portable oxygen machine and goes to her –'

'Walking on air?' burbled Charlie Squires. I laughed out loud and Squires, who apparently hadn't realised the richness of his wit, joined in, slapping his knee. To my astonishment the others maintained silence, by their look, under extreme difficulty.

Squires stopped laughing, approximately. 'I'm sorry,' he said.

'I should jollywell think so,' said R.W.J. Charlie rolled sixpence along the table which the chairman caught and placed in his waistcoat pocket, then entered in a small black book. I hadn't seen anything so childishly adult since my Grammar School days; I'd a sudden strange thought that it was well worth inventing, and that I might very well have done it.

'Then there is Ruff,' continued Holinshed, quietly sweating. 'He's the Wine Steward who refuses to accept the fact of the closed world and goes on living as though he could walk out any time he likes; which he cannot, but it doesn't matter since he won't. He is extremely logical and, unlike most Wine Stewards, refuses to say good morning, good afternoon, good evening, or even how are you? because in certain circumstances they may not be meant.

'Then there are Ruff's three sons, Mark, Edwin, Ralph, not to mention his wife Millicent and his mistress, Amelia. A delightful side-plot depicts the scoring-off, pushing, conniving, and manoeuvring that goes on among the sons to secure the inheritance which, in any case, goes to Percival, Spain's natural son by Ruff's one daughter Sylvia.'

'I don't believe it!' said Squires.

'It's told uncommonly well,' said Holinshed timidly.

'I mean that name – Sylvia; the prettiest name in English song.'

'It will be very popular with our young people,' said Koniev.

'The insight is terrific,' said R.W.J. winging me, in four simple words, right back to boyhood and a collection of tattered old magazines which my Uncle James treasured with his Godwin, Bakunin, Tolstoi.

'Simple copulation and a little half-hearted incest,' said Koniev with contempt. 'No homosexuality, no lesbianism, not even a touch of heterosexual.'

I was about to tell him about the heterosexual when the youngest lad from Technical burst forth: 'It may be a side issue, but I think she cheated there. Tremendous feeling of anti-climax. It's not like Mrs Bloodshot. I mean, you're never given any indication that Ruff has the faintest feeling of affection for Squint – that's Sylvia's son,' he explained, to my slight relief.

'I disagree,' said R.W.J. 'Remember the tremendous beatings – they couldn't have been bettered by Gorki. Incidentally the business of Sylvia hanging a coin from Squint's little cap when he's a baby so that he'll develop a squint like old Ruff – that's a straight lift from Thomas Hardy's notebooks.'

'It's what she makes of it that counts,' said Wills. Holinshed gave forth a little laugh. 'Referring to the criticism from our Russian friend,' he said. 'Overtly and indirectly he'll discover all the perversions, plus cannibalism. Remember Bartlett's complex (he's the Chief Engineer) about the breeding pens and kitchen fields and gardens? He feels that if ever they fail there'll be an outbreak of cannibalism. He's wrong of course. I think one of the book's greatest achievements is the oblique – one might almost say, *creeping* – way in which one discovers why the plump ones disappear.'

'Can we move on?' asked Wills.

'Before we do I'd like to re-order,' I said.

'One of our rules is no re-ordering until the address is complete,' said R.W.J. 'Excepting, of course, in the case of honoured guests.'

Koniev stood up and held out his half bottle. 'Replenish your courage, friend,' he told me. I'd a feeling he was living in a private world far from Bloodshot or the Soviets or us. I gave him my thanks. 'Give thanks to Mr Walker Johnson,' he grinned. There was now a little pink in the office-pallor.

'How about the minor characters?' I asked.

'Oh, plenty,' said Holinshed. 'There are engineers, decorators, cleaners, cooks, towel-changers, page boys and girls. Most important, there are the scene-shifters who talk about the 'cast' and seem to be rehearsing and timing some big operation which involves everyone in the sky-scraper – by the way, there *is* a sky and they're responsible for it. The scene-shifters become more proficient at their job; not just faster but more skilful. In the end the guests don't notice them and one has the impression that they could remove the floor and the girders and get away with it.'

'How is it resolved?' asked Koniev.

'Well,' said Holinshed, 'in the end the Chief Auditor arrives. They're all up for judgement.'

'How is it resolved?' thundered Koniev. 'How do they become mortal again, ordinary people with a pain in their guts and anguish in their hearts?'

'It isn't resolved,' said Holinshed. 'The Chief Auditor looks at the books, talks to the people, wishes them happiness, and walks out . . . I think the runaway skyscraper's hell . . .' He had gone rather green in the face.

'It's a parable of insulation. They're insulated in themselves, not the skyscraper,' said R. Walker Johnson defiantly.

'Pig-shit,' said Koniev coldly.

'I beg your pardon.'

'I apologise. Pig-swill. People are *not* insulated. They care. Else why do we do our jobs – we martyrs of middle management?'

'There isn't a good manager in the book,' said R. Walker Johnson thoughtfully.

'Of course not. Your Mrs Bloodshot is in the skyscraper but

doesn't understand its nature. Notice everything is provided? These people are the rentiers, the middle-men, the investors, or those who live on the surplus – the academics – and take it as their right. If the woman understood – but she doesn't.'

He poured himself more whisky and stretched out a pudgy hand in my general direction. 'Come, my good tormented friend. You know what it is all about. Come beside me, where we can share the whisky.' I took him at his word. Wills' eyes were popping. 'Now,' said Koniev. 'Tell me, my good young friend who knows all about anti-semitism, what is the problem?'

I wracked my brains. 'To do a good job and remember why,' I managed at last.

Koniev placed an arm around my shoulder. 'That is a very good and simple answer, my friend. But it is not sufficient. What we need is food for everyone and a few gadgets, eh? But most important a little leisure time so that people can be free of labour. Surplus time, that is the goal!'

'The Empire is not in red on the map. It is the ticking of a watch and the tearing away of sheets on the calendar. That is the new imperialism. We waste our time!'

'I think I'm going to be sick,' said Holinshed suddenly.

Wills took hold of him. 'I'll take you out.' Eyes starting, Holinshed shook him off and made blindly for the door.

'The speaker is done; we can re-order,' said Koniev cheerfully.

'I don't understand,' said R. Walker Johnson. 'He didn't have much to drink.'

'And he is a manager?' said Koniev, smiling.

'We'll not talk about it,' said R.W.J., looking worriedly towards the door. He turned to Koniev. 'It's odd – the way you talk our language; management language, I mean.'

'Not politics, but management, that is the task,' said Koniev.

'Not the withering away of the State?' I asked.

'We have taken a closer look at that problem than you would ever dream,' said Koniev. 'Please don't – what is it – badger, bait me. When production is tenfold what it is today in the Russian lands – then ask me that question.'

'And we've taken a closer look at *that* problem,' I said.

'I think I'd better take a closer look at Holinshed,' said Charlie

Squires. Wills went out with him. Half an hour later they returned without Holinshed. He had gone home. I was still busy baiting Koniev and he seemed to be thriving on it. I wondered idly if Holinshed had been sick because of the paper, the subject, or the reception we'd given them.

'Is he better?' asked Koniev.

'Just a little tummy trouble,' said Wills.

'He has trouble, that man,' said Koniev, and turned to R. Walker Johnson. 'This time I'll buy the whisky: a full bottle and we'll all share it.' He grinned. 'And a bottle of the child's drink.' We drank until all but Charlie Squires had crept away. I fancy the discussion was a little over their heads. When closing time arrived the Russian refused to be taken home and walked away like a Guardsman. We watched him.

'He's a bloody sight more complicated than that book,' said Charlie.

'He has trouble, that man,' I mimicked.

'He carries it better than the other one,' parried Charlie and I involuntarily looked over my shoulder for that he-man writer in whom death was stronger than life.

'It *is* pig-shit,' said Charlie, mournfully.

'I don't know about his economics but I reckon he's a literary critic of the first water,' I said absently.

'I praised it in my review,' said Charlie.

'We all have a lie on our consciences that we didn't know was a lie at the time we uttered it,' I said.

'In fact, several,' I added.

'The point is, the moment you open a book with intent to judge you wreck the balance of your critical faculty,' said Charlie.

'Take hold,' I said. 'The critic corrected himself. He said it was swill, pig-swill.'

'I don't see the difference,' said Charlie gloomily.

'You try telling a pig to keep off, it's only his swill,' I told him. I left him meditating on the platform of a bus. As for myself, I went for a walk to clear my head and empty my bladder. It was a long way between public lavatories. By the time I reached London Bridge I was successfully resisting any temptation to run every time another blockhouse hove in sight.

If I'd known the Holinshed-Cavendish thing was in process of breaking up I mightn't have been so melancholy. I was trying to make up my mind about Esther. Mr Snorry, black-bullet eyes twinkling over spotted bow-tie, used to be fond of saying that when they opened their legs it was as much for the lover that would come out as the one that would go in. That's clever, but not very helpful. I tried that one; but it didn't work. It never does when things not only go wrong but are manifestly seen to go wrong.

As you may guess that was the night I went into Esther's bed, not uninvited, and without ever thinking of Snorry. I couldn't bide my time, I went, I awoke in grief. It seemed to me that Cathie had just looked at me with reproachful eyes. I crept out of the strange bed, drank coffee, and walked out on to Primrose Hill. There was a little mist and an iron atmosphere which the sun did nothing to soften. All the great buildings along the Thames were well and truly rooted in London clay; the count-down had been abandoned, as planned. After some searching I found something that looked like the summit of UK House. I couldn't be sure but I could swear that tawny shapes paced backwards and forwards there. I imagined they were under a latticed dome called a Climatron, with three or four micro-climates co-existent and flourishing: say Amazon, India, Java and – just for the hell of it – an Everest complete with a Sherpa or two.

Dismissing the thought that man was a Climatron in himself (her good-morning lips had been cracked and dry) I decided to have one of the things myself, one day. I would find peace among the giant ferns, maybe.

And what matters again is that man can always make the other kind of climate. The devil invented work as the most imaginably seductive climate: I hear that right until the end old man Rockefeller worked seven days a week and never had time to really go sailing in his big, luxurious yacht.

He wasn't crazy.

As evidence:

Here I was going gladly to work, almost sorry it was Friday, riding, walking, riding with a terrific sense of anticipation that almost broke my heart. It was good to see the other half-dead faces, the lips too numb with the misery of work to make a proper smile, and know that I was above all this. It was good to smell the familiar odour of the polish the cleaners used; pick up the telephone and draw in the perfume of the antiseptic they sprayed into it weekly. It was good to smell wood of desk and floor, sniff plastic, typewriter ribbon, rubber, pencil shavings, office girl and purely office girl, better still to pick up the scent of fear. All these were the spoor of home, lair, holt, form, burrow, den or belly. Belly is best. Smell, touch, taste floated me like a man-child in the belly of business; not unsighted like the embryo, but seeing as well as smelling and touching all.

I was at home. I was on top of my work. Telephone calls, conferences, queries, papers, thrust and parry of decision, never seemed to harass me. The House took the fatigue along with my works.

The House gave. It knew every moment at source, sensed every thought, and, having guided the act into being, purred its approval. The tiny plans in the brochure were insufficient. I had to know. So the House gave me time to know, I had the liberty and in time I was to know stationery, stores, duplicating, accounts, computer, library, minute but quietly positive public relations with its tapes, photo-library, film unit, radio and television monitoring rooms; boiler houses as well as board-room, the despatch rooms as well as the close-packed cells containing experts, specialists, engineers, technologists, economists, all endlessly reading, deciding, accepting, rejecting, sometimes idling away their time like firemen, sometimes creating work to provide justification, sometimes, more rarely, casually waiting for a count-down inaudible to all but themselves and then unleashing, in a three-line minute or a quarto memo, all the potential of our great organisation.

We all served the company, not for love but for cash: there were some who put cash first and some who put the work of the company (not just the company) first in their personal order of priority. I was above all these. I used to watch the computer programmer, inscribing the tablets, which others would reduce to the size of a pin-head, with as intense a degree of interest as I watched the window-cleaners on their transporters race along the exterior of the building. They thought they worked for the company which paid them. But I knew better. It was the House, the building, they served. It was their Unknown God. But I alone was in the secret. I'm not saying the House was God, or supernatural, or an idol in which I lived and worshipped.

It was simply that the House knew its business, and I knew mine. We both sprang from the earth and we were both highly complex and efficiently functioning things. What was important was this; we both knew where we came from. Same stock, different branches. That afternoon, I remember, I went out and bought a Christmas Rose for my office; we both took pleasure in it.

Wills keeps telling me he can never decide when he is most uneasy, at or away from work. Well, I'll admit that some of the mystique has gone. But I'm never uneasy here. It's when I'm away that I suffer. *Me* and the building can play around with the ten million Leningrad order and enjoy ourselves; in fact, I've even managed to learn a little Russian during the busiest working days of my life. But outside, confronted with one naked human being with a lost smile and dry lips, I'm helpless.

It's all right with the House and me so long as things operate within our mutual terms of reference. Then we work beautifully together in harness. But just slip over the border –

One evening a long time after this halcyon period I waited for Esther on the 15th floor. It was fine while I was waiting. Then she arrived. She did as she was told. I had my way. But the House went dead. And so did I; from the moment she entered the room at the end of the corridor where I'd first met Mr Crumple the life I shared with the House drained out of me.

NINE

Sometimes I look at the scraps of conversation, queries, guesses scribbled in between bits of my dreary New Manifesto, a New Idea of Packaging, and other fragments of my personal fantasy. The clearest outline is of the famous meeting of the Society; that's because it was scribbled in that crystal-clear state which follows a walked-off booze-up. I distinctly remember writing it down while waiting for Esther. She arrived just as I was dealing (in writing) with Koniev, who hated and loved me so dearly because we were continental twins, he with his heart on the left, me with mine on the right; otherwise alike. The note on Koniev was written in the pool of light from her dressing table lamp; occasionally, I would look up and see her reading, naked, in bed. A pretty domestic scene. But did it help to make the record straight as well as memorable? I look at the notes and say to myself: Be Warned, My Friend – This May be a Fiction.

For some of my notes are vague. Several times I've written of R. Walker Johnson: 'Complains of his face growing old.' I may have walked into his office, he may have said: 'My face is getting old, Sam,' running his hands over the tired flesh from ear to chin. If he did, I don't remember. So – be warned, I tell myself. Was I speaking of myself when I wrote: 'His face grows tired every day between three and four. One day tired at two. A very black day?' I don't know. All I can say is that I've convinced myself it was R. Walker Johnson who had doubts about me, doubts about my line on the Hartlepools project, and no doubts at all about an ageing face.

Last summer I went down into Kent to see Small Summers. He was dragging a leg but was otherwise fine and fit, and we sat talking in the garden of his converted oasthouse until the sun went down. Swallows slid along invisible lines of delight as he told me of the long luxury cruise his wife had been able to take, and how grateful he was to Mr Francis for the generous severance sum which had made this possible.

'It was a nice reward for my last fling,' he said. 'You gave me another shot, you know. It was as much for you as for myself.'

I stammered my thanks.

'Don't bother,' he said. 'It was fun. True, it nearly killed me. But I'd do the same again. I'd forgotten what it was like to take a ride.'

Facing a great open field of ripe corn which flowed towards the brow of the Weald and was bounded by the Pilgrim Way he told me the story of his revised paper.

He took it first to Mr Francis. 'I thought you'd like to see it, Chairman, before I sent it up to Crumple.' He told me that Mr Francis, who managed to be both bald and shaggy, ran briskly through it. We agreed he must have laughed up his sleeve at the size of the matter considering that even at that moment in time he'd an inkling of the Sahara Scheme. And that wasn't all. Whilst Koniev was playing around with the small fry and picking up the kind of information which is valueless to us but pure gold to the Russians, his superior was meeting the Chairman to work out the first tentative outline of the Leningrad order. Each would mean a 24-hour-day for all our components plants; together, they would stretch all we had to the limit.

Francis kept a straight face. He possibly saw an opportunity for fun, *his* kind of fun: I refuse to believe that he couldn't live with Crumple. He simply loved stirring the pot.

'You haven't made up your mind,' he told Small Summers.

'I'm sorry if I haven't made myself clear. I'm for expansion at Hartlepools on two counts. One, that we'll clear the investment, two, that there's a political hazard in closure.'

'Old Charlton, eh?' said Francis. 'There's just a hint of hedging in this. Only a hint. Make it stronger.'

'I can tell Crumple you'll back it?'

'You'll do no such thing,' said Francis. 'It can come up as a Board paper – open issue. We'll discuss on merit.'

There was a disconcerted silence. 'I think we should do all we can to keep Hartlepools afloat,' said Small Summers.

'So do I,' said Francis heartily. 'But not at that price, and certainly not off my own bat. I think the market for fats and fertilisers is on the up and up. There are other factors . . .'

'The political?'

'Oh, that's there right enough. But on politics the golden rule is to let the chips fall where they may. No, I was thinking – say the Sahara irrigation scheme came up?'

'There wouldn't be ships enough . . .'

'If the Sahara thing broke – but it won't,' said Mr Francis decisively. 'No, we'll have to take it on its merits.'

'May I tell Crumple you're *almost* inclined to favour it?'

'You may not. Have you read your Ecclesiastes?'

'A long time ago,' said Small Summers, wishing he'd never gone to the trouble of bringing the paper to the Chairman.

'My old man was a chicken farmer,' explained Francis. 'He used to read the lessons in the village church. The clue's in what you've just said. Time. Chapter 3, verse 5, the following verses are useful too.' The interview was at an end but Small Summers lingered, hoping, he told me, for some little comfort. Francis glanced impatiently at him, then asked: 'What d'ye think of the new painting?'

'It's interesting,' said Small Summers.

'It's bloody awful,' said Francis. 'Cost me five hundred to find that I'd fallen for a reputation. Pictures are like problems, you've got to live with them before you can even begin to evaluate them.' As the Chief Controller was leaving he called: 'I can lend you a Bible.'

'Thank you, I've one of my own,' lied Small Summers. He was in no mood for borrowing from the Chairman.

'Ring the wife up, then get her to look it up – and tell Crumple it's entirely up to him.'

Back in his own office Small Summers asked Mrs Arcot to ring up the library for a Bible. The library reported their copy out on loan. 'They've just one Bible?' asked the Chief Controller. 'They didn't happen to mention who had it?'

'They weren't very helpful. Said they'd no idea when it would be back.'

'I'm not surprised,' said the Chief Controller, refusing Mrs Arcot's offer to borrow a copy from the City Library on her own ticket. Before lunch, however, he had regretted his refusal. He went to St Martin's, looked left and right before entering, then went swiftly inside. The few worshippers looked up in surprise as he went to the lectern and turned over the pages.

Verse five read: 'A time to cast away stones, and a time to gather stones together; a time to embrace, and a time to refrain from embracing.' He had a sudden, horrific vision of an entwined Francis and Crumple. The following verses significantly read: 'A time to rend, and a time to sew; a time to keep silence, and a time to speak; a time to love, and a time to hate; a time of war, and a time of peace.' Sighing, the Chief Controller closed the Bible. 'All that to tell me he's biding his time,' he murmured. The following day he revised the paper and took it to Crumple.

Crumple read the paper and removed his spectacles. The Chief Controller waited in silent hatred for him to tap the paper, which he did. 'If we were at full stretch I'd be inclined to agree with this thing,' he said, emphasising 'thing'. 'But as you know, we're not. What did the Chairman say?'

'He said it was entirely up to you.'

'I don't know what's happening to him these days,' said Crumple irritably.

'He didn't like the cost.'

'Well, that's a nice change.'

'We'll get our money back.'

'In five years,' said Crumple. 'But it won't be the money we put into it.' He was pulling hairs from his left ear. 'How's that youngster shaping, the new one, what's his name?' The Chief Controller knew the question of the name was simply a smoke-screen.

'Rowlands. Very well. Do you know him?'

'Heard of him, heard of him, ear to the ground,' said Mr Crumple. 'Rampion mentioned him the other day, and that's a sure sign the man's making a mark.' Once again he tapped the paper.

'Had he anything to do with this?'

'I always consult my staff,' said Small Summers, warily.

'It's an unusually thorough piece of work, that's all,' murmured Crumple, and the Chief Controller rapidly translated: 'His ideas, your writing.'

'Thank you,' said Small Summers. He took off his spectacles, leaned over the desk, tapped the paper and said: 'Do you want to consider this?'

'Put it up, put it up, we'll see,' said Crumple, showing his false teeth. 'At the moment I'm neither for or against. Back it with all you have. We'll see.'

Small Summers sighed and replaced his spectacles. 'I thought we might save a little time.'

'And cheat the Board of its lovely prerogative?' said Crumple, showing his teeth again, but not in a smile.

The Chief Controller told his Deputy the position. 'It's a pity we took it up,' said R. Walker Johnson. 'Now there's no way of not burning our fingers.'

'Oh, I don't know,' said Small Summers cheerfully, disregarding an all-too familiar tightness in his chest. 'We'll pull through. The waves and the winds may play for us. You've read Ecclesiastes, of course?'

'A long time ago,' said R. Walker Johnson, mystified.

'See Ecclesiastes Chapter three, verses five, six and seven. They're still very relevant.' He paused a moment. 'You don't happen to know if they're on a long-playing record?' he asked, as an idea struck him.

'I'll find out,' said R. Walker Johnson, never suspecting that this was the beginning of a quest which would take him out of UK House and to the far ends of the mind, if not the earth.

As R.W.J. was going he mentioned Crumple's interest in me. And that was the beginning of another quest. As soon as R.W.J. reached his own office he asked Cathie to get Holinshed; subsequently he sent for Wills. We all tend to resent a nepotism that doesn't work for us as well; the consensus of opinion (and feeling) was that Crumple was behind me for some mysterious reason or other. Since we both hailed from the North it was easy to put two and two together and coax into being a family or friendly relationship; to the Londoner, Staffordshire and Northumberland are much of a muchness, a hinterland which was only civilised yesterday. Watch their eyes shine when you tell them how Grandad took part in the reivers' raid on Burslem.

As far as R. Walker Johnson was concerned I'm sure the quest for my non-existent relationship with Crumple was nothing more than a relaxation. He was rising fifty and one bit of his conversation with the Chief Controller kept coming back to mind. He had said, at one point, 'With all respect, Controller, I don't think you'll be able to push this one through.'

'Well, then, let's try, shall we?' suggested Small Summers.

But R.W.J. was at the point where he couldn't summon energy for lost causes. His old, tired face was troubling him. The weight of his cheeks and chin dragged down on his eyes and his forehead pulled to the centre of strain above his nose. He had a pronounced feeling of futility.

As he told me a little later: 'The trouble with management is lack of a faith. Doing a good job isn't enough.'

'You might have a point there,' I cautiously told him.

'I'm sure I have. What's needed is a philosophy that extends from office to home and all the way back again. We need God; oh God, how we need a Lord God in our lives.'

'Not MRA? New pattern,' I suggested.

'As long as it takes all and goes the limit,' he said. 'As long as it leads to a goal – not just more for more all the time.'

And all the time he was telling me about God he was stacking the timber for my martyrdom. I knew about it, of course. That sort of thing doesn't come through on the grapevine; although Miss Miffin, my Rosalie, threw out her hints. What told me were looks, silences, missing papers, little slights of commission and omission, and all the other spoor you must learn to read when you're in business. Sitting in the shadow of the oasthouse Small Summers told me of how even he had been conscious of the animus; I asked how and he replied with a grin: 'Twigs break like thunder.'

After a time he added: 'They enjoyed talking about you. There were endless little meetings, a sort of standing jury, to discuss your sins, your frivolity, even your flair for breathing. You were the goat. They really had it in for you.'

'I found out,' I said, and told him about our famous pub crawl, and the ugly scene in the select room: for the moment I'm reserving that story.

'Of course, it wasn't you,' said Small Summers thoughtfully. 'It was a Rowlands they'd invented, almost on the spur of the moment. But you helped them, didn't you?'

His judgement was just: I did indeed. Against all the rules of the text-book I lived to myself, dishing out the work, being generally fair, cheerful, and completely detached. I never asked advice; and the cardinal, conventional rule is that you must ask for advice, even when it isn't needed. I didn't spurn their help out of arrogance. I considered them as so much surplus baggage, and so they were – then. Now that we're really in business each of them is holding down twice the volume of work. And I find time to ask for advice, not for use but for fun. But then, I wasn't at full stretch; and I didn't know that in holding away from them I was providing free time for a perpetual hymn of hate.

But to follow the fate of my Hartlepools project:

A week or so after the non-committal interview with Mr Francis and Mr Crumple the paper was presented to the assembled Board. R. Walker Johnson actually found Small Summers a long-playing record in which Albert Finney read extracts from Ecclesiastes, including the appropriate verses from Chapter three; rather sadly he decided against using it. Only a boardroom packed with men like Francis would have taken the point.

Prior to this, R.W.J. had played it over several times; the thick, earthy voice was just right for the ancient words of wisdom. He went out and bought a 'Bible of the World', some of the later Huxleys, my Uncle James's Chardin, and generally added fuel to his fire. And the record was never used. I wish it had been. Too late Small Summers thought of a really useful gimmick. 'What I should have done was to get someone to make a tape of Charlton fulminating about the thing,' said Small Summers, very regretfully.

It was early November. The late afternoon mists which have replaced the old London fogs were rolling up-river when Small Summers presented his paper to the Board. He had mastered his brief. Long before he had finished speaking he knew that his paper would be bowed out.

'Most interesting,' said Mr Francis, bland, affable and completely disinterested. 'Thank you for your presentation, Small Summers. As I see it –' He summarised the case in three or four succinct sentences. 'So there it is. It's perfectly correct, of course, that we'll get our money back. However, what Small Summers hasn't proved – if he'll forgive me – is that we really need to spend it. All he can show us is a political imponderable, dangerous but fairly remote. Any comments?'

'Argument falls down on necessity: do we need the plant, with or without the proposed extensions?' said Walker, the Chief Chemist. 'Answer is we don't.' Crumple nodded but held his peace. The Chairman glanced around for further comment.

'I must say, we've got a bit of a bogeyman argument here,' said T. C. Thomson, Head of Process. 'The Union, I mean. Give 'em the jobs, they'll fall into line.'

'If the Sahara business comes off we might be glad and willing to use this plant,' said Crumple, thoughtfully.

'That's a point,' said Fenwick Jones, the Chief Engineer.

'Quite,' continued Crumple. 'Anyone prepared to gamble on Sahara? Bearing in mind the history of the thing – how long is it now – five, six years?'

'There's a strong feeling in Whitehall that it's going through at last,' said Small Summers.

Crumple looked at his notes. 'There was a strong feeling on –' He reeled off several dates. 'In every case, the feeling faded. And let's face it; if the Sahara Project started tomorrow, Hartlepools' contribution'd be a drop in the bucket.'

'There's the political angle,' said the Chairman. 'Do we dismiss that as well?'

'Up in the air,' said Walker. 'Those days are over. Too many fingers burned – and I don't mean ours. Thomson's right. That one's a bogeyman.' He nodded in the direction of the Chairman. 'We'll leave the Chairman and his Ministerial friends to look after that angle.' Mr Francis was dreamily contemplating a yellow non-figurative painting from Yugo-Slavia; without taking his eyes from the twelve by eight feet canvas he said: 'In the normal course of things, yes. But I happen to know some of the union people up there. There's one in particular. A very clever man. Ministers are reasonable chaps, but they don't like to lose face.' He lost interest in the painting and addressed himself to Crumple. 'Crumple, you're definite about the Sahara. Like to be as definite about the politicians?'

'We've a good record,' said Crumple. 'I'd say we've a strong hand, if it came to a pinch.'

'You seem a little bit lukewarm.'

'Not at all,' said Crumple indignantly. 'We're in business to deal with waste; we provide the plant and, where we're asked, we do the processing. We're a big, progressive concern; but that doesn't say we've got a special obligation or something to perpetuate obsolete plant. Or are we frightened of shadows?'

Mr Francis was glancing alternately at the yellow picture and his pad. He was piling up wickets of four and crossing them over to make fives. Small Summers realised he was counting the secondary black and scarlet squiggles. 'Well, gentlemen, Crumple thinks we're dealing with shadows. I don't mind admitting I'm a little wary of those shadows, but I have to admit – they are shadows.' He gave a final glance at the canvas, made a final stroke, looked up. Small Summers told me, in the shadow of the oasthouse, that he was suddenly aware of the power of Mr Francis; or rather, of the source of his power. He knew more than all the rest and he knew how to use his knowledge.

'But I hope I'm not interrupting the flow – I've a feeling you were about to extend the discussion into – er – your own special field.' That pulled Mr Crumple up short.

'I've finished, Chairman,' he said at last. 'Perhaps you'd like to develop the theme.'

'Delighted,' said Mr Francis, and looked it. 'I take great notice of our financial men, appearances to the contrary, and it seems to me that we've stumbled on something – I'm saying "we" but the credit really goes to Mr Crumple. What applies to Hartlepools also applies to ten, fifteen, perhaps twenty other plants. If Hartlepools has to go down the drain, some others must necessarily follow.'

'We're moving from a case on its merits to general policy,' said Mr Crumple.

'Precisely,' said Mr Francis.

'I've just been glancing at my list,' said Fenwick Jones. 'At a rough count we've 23 plants just breaking even. That puts them roughly in line with Hartlepools.'

'Circumstances alter cases,' said Crumple fretfully. 'After all, we've had a good look at Hartlepools.'

'But this time we've policy to guide us – I take it we could make policy at this moment?' said Mr Francis.

'That's a lot of work, an awful lot of work.'

'I'm surprised,' said Walker. 'I thought we had a computer. Let's get something for the rent we pay. Let's set up a program.'

'We can't include imponderables,' said Small Summers maliciously. The hounds were baying and he couldn't resist the one small yelp.

'We can set up a program,' said Crumple. 'But I suggest that this is a policy decision. We ought to think round it a little.'

Silent Mr Ransome, who lived in distant Suffolk and had been glancing anxiously at the clock, made his first contribution: 'With all due respect, Chairman, I think we've made progress. I entirely agree with you. It's time we consolidated. So let's get material for thinking. Feed the others into the computer; we'll get round to a decision later. But we know all we need to know about Hartlepools and it's certain the place is ripe for closing.'

The Chairman was preparing to go off at a tangent again. He turned to Small Summers. 'You started this. What do you think?'

'Let's not rush,' said Small Summers. 'I suggest we put Hartlepools with the rest of the plants in hazard and await the result of the computer analysis.'

'Delaying tactics!' said Francis, grinning. 'Never mind, Controller, it was a good try. What do you say, Crumple?'

'I'll change sides,' said Crumple. 'Close Hartlepools and program the rest.'

'Ah!' exclaimed Mr Francis and withdrew into himself. Hunched in his chair he pondered, tapping his forehead with two fingers. The light glanced from his spectacles. 'I'm still not convinced,' he said. Small Summers observed that the fingers were crossed. 'Good arguments don't always end in good policy. I have a feeling . . .'

'Now you're raising the bogeymen, Chairman,' said Crumple

rudely. 'I make the strongest recommendation we go forward as stated.'

Mr Francis expanded. 'On your recommendation, eh? That's official?' He glanced meaningfully at John Wilson, the secretary, fat of face and fast of pen.

'I'll go on record,' said Crumple.

'On Mr Crumple's recommendation,' said Mr Francis, glancing at Wilson, who looked up and nodded. Catching the exchange Mr Crumple fell thoughtful. Mr Francis' shoulders straightened. His figure filled out. His personality expanded. He smiled, and produced a summary of the discussion in which the name of the Chief Financial Officer prominently figured. John Wilson was smiling. The meeting broke up.

Later, in the Gentlemens', Mr Francis said to Small Summers: 'A very good meeting.' He checked the several toilet doors with the heel of his shoe. All were empty. 'I'll bet you think I'm a devious bugger.'

'Yes,' said Small Summers.

'Never mind. You made a better effort than you realise. Want another text?'

'I shall have to buy a Bible,' said the Chief Controller.

'You should be ashamed to confess it,' said the Chairman. 'Now I wouldn't be without mine.'

As Small Summers told it to me, he left the office early that evening and bought a nice edition at his booksellers. 'Shall I wrap it up, Sir?' said the bookseller.

'No thanks,' said Small Summers, finger to lips. The verse from Isaiah read as follows: 'The wilderness and the solitary place shall be glad for them; and the desert shall rejoice, and blossom as the rose.' The Sahara scheme sprang immediately to his mind; he never thought for one moment that Russia might also be involved.

The bookseller was intrigued. 'I'm just verifying the text,' he explained to the man.

'An expensive sermon, Sir.'

'Far from it, my friend,' said Small Summers. 'Tell me, have you ever seen a desert rejoice?' In telling me the story he repeated the riposte. I believe he was as pleased with this as with the comfort the text had given him. The following day Francis' aide told him that the Chairman had dined with the Minister for Overseas Aid and Development. From that moment he was sure that our ship would come home.

Just about that time I was engaged in research. There were plenty of people I might have directly approached but I preferred to do the job crabwise: I like my little mysteries. The identity of the Penthouse Person was a game I wanted to prolong a little. Esther could have told me; Charlie Squires; even the lame lift boy who was so much indebted to me for paperback thrillers. But this would have constituted cheating.

Even in those early days I was picking up the scent of Henry Norman Prinkstone, our original founding father, the first to see wealth in waste and substance in sewage – on an organised basis. My friend Simon gave me an introduction to the librarian of a daily paper, and I spent a fascinating afternoon looking up the history of Prinkstone contained in an obituary and an envelope bulging with cuttings. There were a number of features telling the golden legend of Twaddell, the Glasgow tradesman who went around the tenements collecting the contents of chambers. The urine was sold by the barrel to market gardeners. Sometimes the customers cheated and diluted the stuff, so Twaddell devised the hydrometer which young Prinkstone was to use in his early days as an analytical chemist. So went the story. Prinkstone was fascinated not so much by the invention as the calling. And so began those early experiments in large-scale sewage utilisation which led to the concept of an industry based on *all* waste. The features concentrated on the 'King Sewer' aspect and were thick with phrases such as 'He realised that every sewer had a silver lining', or 'outfalls and effluents brought the smell of success', or 'where others saw filth, Prinkstone saw fats and fertilisers'.

One of the photographs was of Mr and Mrs Prinkstone outside Buckingham Palace – small man and large woman; the gates and the glimpse inside, top hat in hand, not so comical as they generally are in morning suits. A little man, with a large woman, gazing at him with a little pride and a lot of affection, not at the plush-lined case containing the CBE or whatever it was. The one thing I disliked about the representation was the parting in the middle of his hair. Middle partings are inept in my experience.

Back among the cuttings again and an era of take-over bids. A business page headline asked: 'Who's Buying Prinkstone's?' Headline a week later revealed: 'UK in Take-Over Bid'.

'And Prinkstones are a good buy,' said the cutting. 'Here is an embryo, rapidly growing industry complete with diversification: manufacturers of sewage extraction plant, producers of machines that range from a 2,000-ton buffing tank to a tiny extractor no bigger than the fist for effluents in liquid or smoke form, suppliers of fuel, fats and fertilisers and a thousand and one items of interest to virtually every industry. What more could the investor ask?'

The rest of the clippings raced home with a story that must have been as slow as death itself at the time. Exchange of letters between giants locked in distant combat; on my right Mr Henry Norman Prinkstone, on my left Mr Arthur Joseph Sullivan – and may the best man, in terms of money-muscle, cash-cutting, skull-duggery, human-swinery, together with wire-tapping and string-pulling, fall down and kill his contender; eyes may be gouged so long as the rules are religiously kept; pressure must be continuously maintained from the brainpan out to the bulging eyes. And press not to blind but to kill and keep alive.

There were appeals to Government to save a great basic industry in pawn, and Government went on trimming its collective fingernails. Rescue rockets went up in the air and life-lines were prepared by unnamed City Banks and City Merchants; but in the end it was the big soft battalions came squirming into the aid of Sullivan, no less. Like quiet black snails in the gloaming they came, item, an insurance company; item, a very wealthy trust; item, a very prosperous pensions fund. Victory was told in a last sad headline: 'Prinkstone Goes Down' and a reserved little statement, which ended: 'I intend to play chess in a quiet room far away from it all.' It was suggested that the founder had in fact been retained in an advisory capacity – 'Influential City sources suggest a figure of £20,000 per annum.' A sum which would top up an income from patent royalties amounting to more than a quarter of a million, said another source. And was there also included, I wondered, a snug sweet penthouse, complete with microclimate and personal switchboard operator? I sat and pondered on the role of the man in the clouds who had my own sweet Esther to activate the thin vibrating line of what might well prove to be a conductor of lightning. So many questions – so much pleasure. And more to come.

The victorious Mr Sullivan's file was still in being, which surprised me, for Mr Sullivan was dead. It had been saved from destruction because a man had once started to write a book, explained the librarian. It was twice as fat as Mr Prinkstone's file. The interesting bit was about his final day. En route for a luxury liner the volatile Arthur Joseph Sullivan had met doom on the Portsmouth Road in the unsubstantial shape of a whey-coloured morning mist which treacherously lay in ambush in a hollow. A workman homeward bound from nightshift had to pick mushrooms. He had found thirteen, precisely the number of coups pulled off by the financier. Putting the mushrooms into his carrier bag the cyclist disturbed the balance of his machine. The Bentley swerved directly into the path of a lorry bearing perambulators to a score of happy families. The Bentley and the road carried a harvest of fragments of red and steaming fruit. The mushroom gatherer fainted. The lorry driver shook his head and walked to the nearest telephone to inform the police of a death and his wife of a delay. Sullivan had been married three times; had lived in a wilderness called Sunningdale; had racked rents in his youth yet had been generous in his donations. He had founded a great golden trust fund which distributed a third of a million pounds per annum amongst three missionary societies – Anglican, Roman Catholic and Baptist. That would give him a fine choice of hells and purgatories, but it absolved him from the tenancy of the penthouse.

I remember Charlie calling me as I came to this definite dead-end. I had left the number with him. Darkness was falling and lights coming up as he told me over the telephone that I was invited to a celebration at Walham Green. He hadn't liked to ask when other people were around, he said. 'That's all right, Charlie,' I replied. 'Believe it or not I used to be like that myself.' Not mentioning that I was still. He didn't ask me what I was doing in a newspaper library. I was not pleased. I couldn't ask questions of Charlie or anyone else in UK House, but the rules allowed them to ask questions of me. One question might give me the clue I badly needed at the moment. I thanked the librarian and took myself off. I was feeling a little low. Sullivan was dead and Prinkstone had died before him. I was sad for both and sad for each kind of dying; which is only another way of saying that I was sad for my own mortality. The morbid fattens on itself. I walked up to the Guildhall to see Gog and Magog and passed dozens of girls on the way. Each walked enfolded in a mystery I could never have time to uncover. Lust is a giant that leaves the old city fathers, old Gog and Magog, stone cold.

Just for the hell of it and because I really needed comfort, I found a backstreet barber's and ordered hot towels. I lay back and curled my toes to convince myself that I was truly alive. In an hotel lounge I ordered a pot of tea and biscuits, and smiled at a dark-brown girl who smiled readily back. She was too sated or too indolent to follow up her advantage. I smiled at her a second time and she frowned. I saw the pretty flesh of her face melt to leave that kind of bone which is frightening even when it belongs to a rabbit. The grimace betrays the skull below. This was a better corrective than Snorry's dictum: 'They are built to conceive and not to fornicate.' The air of mystery, the unexpected boldness, the parlour talk, the catch of the breath, the fallen strand of hair that somehow breaks the heart a little, the softness of lip, cheek, chin, the glow of sweet eyes; these are the signposts to conception, labour, a sucking child, and an addition to that vast muck-heap of grief which not even a genius like Prinkstone can use.

When I am melancholy, I eat. After buying myself a bag of assorted nuts I went to a news theatre. It was the poorest printing of 'Way Out West' I'd ever seen, and I think I've seen them all; perhaps three old prints from out of my tremendous film-going past had been cannibalised to make up that magical sixty minutes. I stayed for the first reel again; the one in which Stanley and Oliver, having alighted from the coach, stand listening to the bar-room loafers singing a syncopated cowboy song. The mule taps a little dance; Stanley, born at Shields over the water from me, over the water, in which perhaps, he once saw his reflection and wondered what he was going to be – nudged Oliver, each smiled and the world melted in the meeting and mingling. In time they swayed, they tentatively shuffled, they – glory be – danced: keep Pavlova and all your airborne children so long as I can have the large man and the thin man moving in step and moving the bellows of the lungs as well as the bowels of compassion.

I was better after that. It's a mistake to take life too seriously.

The great sour world was alight and hurrying; Sullivan's mist had become a peppering drizzle; just right for walking. Behind the question: Is it Prinkstone? sprang another larger than Bovril, World's largest Bookmakers, twisting flames of barbecue hells, Billiards. The question said: What is Prinkstone?

Setting my face against the November spray I swung arms and legs and hummed a tune from Piccadilly to Knightsbridge; whistled till my throat was dry from Knightsbridge to Sloane Square.

In that wilderness which lies between the Square and the Green I entered a telephone kiosk and rang UK House. Spacing my words and using a refined Scottish accent I asked for Mr Prinkstone.

'We've no person of that name listed here,' said Esther.

'I'm very well aware of that,' I said rolling the two 'r's, 'I believe he's resident there.'

'We've no residents – have you the right number?' I said I was sure I had; and that Mr Prinkstone would be awfully annoyed if I didn't get through to him. At the same time I thought there must be a code. Awfully romantic; but it left me high and dry. For the benefit of the waiting couple (waiting for the abortionist, by the look of them) I took out my handkerchief and vigorously polished mouth and ear piece, then came out bowing and clicking my heels.

I watched them squeeze in. The man had a pimple in his cleft chin. As the girl reached for the telephone I opened the door slightly and said: 'Six cases reported today. They're flying them out to the Western Islands in old Viscounts.'

'Six cases of what?'

'Bubonic plague.'

'Clear out – bugger off,' said the youth with the spot.

'That makes a total of one hundred and twenty,' I said. 'And they all start on the chin.'

'What's the game, mate?'

'MOH for the Tower,' I said, and slammed the door. I looked back once and saw them talking about me, or the plague. The telephone was still in its cradle.

TEN

The company consisted of Mrs Pennington, an undertaker's widow; her daughter Dorothy Pennington, middle thirties at a guess; and my friend and myself. Both the women were angular, the daughter was quiet-voiced, and plain, excepting when she looked at my friend. The meal consisted of a good tomato soup, cheese cauliflower, apple dumpling with custard, and a warm, fine, strong atmosphere of affection. I could see that the widow was very fond of Squires, mostly because he was a man, but also because he happened to be her daughter's last chance, because the house was incomplete without a belonging and belonged man. Dorothy simply loved him. Her reasons were her own.

The apples, it appeared, were Bramley Seedlings, sent by a Mr Morris, a farmer-widower, whom Mrs Pennington had met when on holiday at Clacton in 1948. The apples were grown in an orchard which had once been a Roman cemetery. I liked the idea of a centurion's dust nourishing my after dinner sweet; I was also exalted at being invited to approve of my friend's choice.

'She's not an intellectual,' he defensively said. By this time we were sitting in his room. Contrary to the usual order, his books were piled up in all four corners and stacked on the table.

'The question is really quite simple,' I replied. 'Will she make you put in bookcases? Tidy you up? If so, don't marry.'

'I've been here three years,' he said.

'Well, that seems fairly conclusive. It's always difficult to judge, but here I see a couple of women with a real sense of proportion, that's rare. Don't bother why. They want to feed you and keep you comfortable. Best of all, not being an intellectual your wife-to-be won't set herself up as your rival. That's good too.' I was feeling expansive.

'You wouldn't put it at a higher level than that?' he asked.

'No,' I replied . 'That part of it's up to you. What you want in a wife is heart, not intellect. Otherwise you may as well resign yourself to dying alone and unmourned.' He asked me to repeat what I'd said. I did.

'How did you know that – about dying unmourned?' he asked in amazement. 'How did you guess the way I felt?'

'I have a sense of the temporal,' I said. 'Sooner or later and mostly sooner, every bachelor's room begins to resemble a coffin.'

I was amused and touched. Give and take, he was only ten years older than me. Yet here he was, amazed that I should know how loneliness, which is second-degree death, can drive a man out of his coffin bedroom in search of a woman. Woman is the common man's only weapon against extinction; and a wife is an endowment policy drawn for the day of mourning. The point is brittle. But it is also true.

They were both shy. Perhaps he'd touched her hand, or she the crown of his head in passing one evening, before placing his Horlicks on the table. 'I'm selfish and set in my ways,' he said. 'It'll be difficult thinking of two – three with the mother.'

This annoyed me. I'd an idea that I wanted to keep Charlie at my side; he was a cutter of corners, he knew people, he knew the game. I considered that he was wasted in his role of a glorified furniture man. 'You can't go wrong,' I said irritably.

'Everything can go wrong,' he said darkly.

'Nonsense,' I said. 'It's a million to one chance against that happening. They're good people. Are you trying to tell me it's an ambush?'

'No, but they might have an urge for a better house, a car to go with it and all the other odds and ends.' He sighed. 'Women don't plan – they *know*.'

'Three years is a long time to keep up an act,' I said. He wriggled like a fish on a hook, then glanced uneasily at me.

'She's not pushing me to marry – in spite . . .'

'Don't let me into your most intimate secrets,' I said hastily.

'What should I do – what would you do?'

'I'm not answering the last one,' I said. 'The first is easy. You're the pattern of the confirmed bachelor. Break it. And graciously take what your handmaidens offer.'

I left him in a decisive mood. The following morning he could hardly meet my eyes. I knew he'd lost his nerve. The man who could despatch a major novelist in one stinging line couldn't make up his mind. 'Never mind, Charlie,' I told him. 'Circumstances may help.'

'What do you mean?' he asked, rather sharply. The glance I gave him back was equally sharp – what *was* he up to? I must say I was in the position of pseudo-superior sapiens here. I'll bet her mother knew.

Anyway, his reaction was entirely healthy. Whatever the relationship, a man should take his time. In his dream of the sacred, good old Jung most willingly bowed his head – but kept a millimetre between his forehead and the dust. I remember my Uncle James reading out a bit from one of his anarchist classics where the man refused allegiance to any power material or spiritual because nothing must damp down his 'sun of consciousness'.

Old Charlie was groping for that one, and I wished him luck. All the same, I wanted him beside me when the die was cast. I'd an idea that marriage would do the trick. His gifts had lain fallow too long. Let them contribute to the sun of *my* consciousness.

I went home and out of sheer loneliness went into Esther's room to read Grimm's Fairy Tales (please do not confuse Hans Andersen with the Grimms; I am out of tune with the former). I was deep in the book and sitting at her dressing table when she came in from work. A dressing table is just the place for Grimm's tales: you and the book stationed among the crowded half-circle of pots, tubes and phials, keeping company with tiny teddy bears dating from God knows when; perpetually aware of their little glass eyes watching you, seemingly dumbfounded and dazzled at the enormity of your memories, plans and thoughts. If you think Grimm's out of date all you have to do is lean forward and see the backs of their little furry heads. They are alien, but not half so alien as the back of a human head; say your own. That also can be seen in a dressing table mirror, if you can raise the nerve.

I saw her arrive, tired, mouth a little discontented and said hello to her reflection and mine. I said a masculine 'Aya!' and returned to the truth of the two philologists. She came over and kissed the back of my neck. 'You rang tonight,' she accused.

'Me? I've been dining out with the present Miss Pennington and the future Mrs Squires.' I could have cut my tongue out, then decided she hadn't noticed.

'But you called from a kiosk on the way. I know your voice. I know your ways. Sneak! I don't mind you trying it out on other people – but not on me, my Sam!'

'Well, it doesn't matter,' I said. 'Friend or stranger, it's all the same. Loyal for ever. Not that I care. I'd rather find out for myself.'

'And that's another fairy tale.' She went to take off her coat.

'Come over here and I'll tell you a fairy tale,' I said.

'I'm not in the mood,' she said. But she came.

Taking her on my knee I said: 'There was once a poor provincial boy. His only possessions were his appetites . . .'

She raised her eyebrows: 'Tell me the bit I don't know.'

'One was worse than all the rest. So he dreamed of a princess who could bring him a treasure –'

'And who would never ask the fatal question,' she said, and slipped off my knee. Just as well; she'd frozen.

'Marriage is no longer *à la mode*.'

'Not that one; the other: do you love me?' I could hardly hear the question.

'That's below the belt.'

'Highly appropriate,' she murmured and went through to the kitchen. I followed, a little indignant at what I thought was laughter. I was wrong. She was crying. I touched her neck. 'You know I can't tell lies.'

'Just to yourself,' she said. 'You're too bloody high and mighty ever to be frail and human. Don't you know how much compensation there'd be in one plain, decent lie?'

'I do; but it's not in my nature.' I ran my kiss along the line of her neck. She shivered.

'Now you're stopping the conversation.'

'Anything to stop you crying.' And I meant it. I'd rather stand on a window-sill fifteen storeys up – and I've a horror of heights – than have to bear them crying.

Coming round and holding my face in her hands she murmured: 'Have you any idea what it's like to love one way – not to be loved in return?'

'No idea at all,' I lied. 'It will come, in time. One mustn't press. But I know what's good.'

'Any girl would do,' she replied. 'What do you live by, Sam?'

Nuzzling her I murmured: 'Twelve midnight and she wants to know what winds the clock and keeps the pendulum in its ways.'

'What *do* you live by? You're serious . . .'

I stopped. 'I don't know; that's God's honest truth. I wish I did. All I know is that I'm poor – the story's true – so I play it by ear.'

'But what about me?'

'In the words of the song: You are the one.' All the little teddy bears stayed still on the dressing table. It would be nice to say that the vow was made in all innocence, but that word would choke me. I was already contemplating ways and means of establishing a relationship with Cathie. I was almost certain that within days she would be in my arms. I knew it was coming. Here is another truth. I only told the lie because I cared deeply for Esther and I was caring for the future as well as that present. There's nothing to sex as such; but you're in deep when you care.

So we went to bed and later she slept. I watched her sleep for a time before I went back to my room. It was a change after watching myself. In an act of betrayal. But eventually I slept. When I awoke there was a hunger and thirst for Cathie, which I encouraged. Almost as soon as I arrived at the office I had to walk along and see her. I saw her and went away. I didn't know about the break, but I sensed that something was wrong. Those who travel through the purgatory of the unwanted are implacably alone. She was in that state. When the loved one is unapproachable you seek someone who will talk about her. I tried Miss Miffin. It was easy to get her to talk about herself and hell's own job getting her away from that most fascinating of all subjects.

'That's a pretty brooch you're wearing,' I said.

'It's copper,' she said. 'Hand-made.'

'Interesting.'

'But not to you,' she retorted, then changed her gambit. 'Do you notice anything different about me today?' This pulled me up short. I gave her the quick once-over and wished I'd been more cunning about the brooch. One day, when I've finished with computers, etc., I'm going to take a course in dresses, fabrics, colours, hair-style, cosmetics. The knowledge is just as essential, and it's no use kidding yourself that you see a woman as a person and not a construction of fabrics, and cosmetics, shoe leather and jewels. Clothes as much as flesh are part of the woman. A woman dresses like a flagship going into battle; and for the same reason; every bit of fabric is a message, but only if you can read it.

'Ah, yes,' I said. 'It's your hair – different tint. Very becoming.'

'It's been the same for a week now. Oh, and I thought you'd notice this time!'

'You've got new spectacles?'

'You're just guessing. Oh, you're simply hopeless, Mr Rowlands. It's a new two-piece.'

'I'm sorry,' I said. 'I don't have an eye for detail. All I know is that I like the total effect.'

'You're better than Arthur,' she said. He was the boy-friend. 'He's just as unobservant; but you do rise to the occasion.'

'That's what I've often thought myself.'

'Only you take such a long time,' she said.

'How do I rise to the occasion, Miss Miffin?'

'You're a good fibber, Mr Rowlands. You use the right words. I melted when you said "total effect".'

'I meant it.'

'I wish I could believe you – I'm sure I haven't a single point. I try to dress, but oh dear I'm just average, both face and figure.'

Careful now, Rowlands. 'You carry yourself well. Your eyes are good. You knock those juniors right out of the picture – who wants pipe-stem waists and whippet legs and cow-eyes?' By those very eyes the reaction was right. Indeed, I don't think I was lying. They were really hazel eyes and the eyelashes were natural. I examined her critically. 'You've very expressive eyes. Lively when you're lively, pensive when you're pensive. They give. They're deep.'

They were lively enough now. 'Deep, really deep, Mr Rowlands?'

'If you were a deaf-mute I'd know your moods in a shot.' I didn't tell her that this was true of all her kind. I didn't tell her that her strong points were really a transparent sincerity and an equable temperament. Instead, I remarked, 'Only one other girl around here comes anywhere near you, eye-wise.'

'I know,' she said, flipping over the pages of her notebook to hide that certain smile of knowledge. 'You mean Cathie Cavendish, don't you?'

'How did you guess?'

'I've always admired her eyes,' she said.

Treacherously, I remarked: 'She hasn't your complexion; it's good, but not good enough. Of course, you've a very good skin.'

'Now you're spreading it on like butter.'

'I'm being as objective as I can.'

Miss Miffin considered, then nodded. 'I think you're right. A good skin's a gift – and she's got freckles. Mind you, they suit – just a peppering. You should have seen her with the pinkness – she doesn't tan, of course – it goes nicely with her kind of freckles. Don't you think so?'

I agreed, and suggested she must have been abroad for the sun.

'She's a terrible traveller. Abroad every year. Always Italy. Takes the full four weeks.'

'Where does she live?'

'You *are* interested,' she accused.

'I like collecting people. She's in my collection – along with you.'

She laughed. 'There you go again. All right, I'll tell you. She lives out in Essex. You won't believe it – she's a farmer's daughter.'

'Where?'

'You must go to Liverpool Street and watch the trains.' She pondered a moment. 'I've one clue. She does *The Times* crossword in the double journey.'

The bit about the crossword was a disappointment. Life's too short. Her father would be a large man, slow-moving, observant, with some surprisingly penetrating views on life. The mother would be large and comfortably quiet. Cathie would be the youngest of seven, scattered all over the world.

'I can never make up my mind.'

I came out of my dream. 'What do you mean?'

149

'You can always tell. I mean, whether they're married or not. But you can't with Cathie. Sometimes she looks – sometimes not. She doesn't talk much about herself.'

'She doesn't wear a ring.'

'You *have* collected her.'

For that I gave her some priority typing, to be on my desk immediately after lunch. 'There's no hurry for this?' she asked.

'I'm accidentally having lunch with Miss Cavendish today.' she raised her eyebrows and flung her head, but I wasn't deceived. I knew that she was pleased. Then there was an upset. Pat Wills came in. Seeing my look, he murmured 'social'.

'Make yourself at home,' I said, resigning myself for once to the textbook. Miss Miffin heard our voices and came to the door. Laughing maliciously she returned to her typewriter. I could hear her singing.

'That's what I came to see you about.' He shifted uneasily. 'You must feel a bit lonely – in town on your own.'

'At times,' I said truthfully.

'The Society – the other evening – was a bit of a fiasco,' he said. 'I don't know about you – but I like a night on the town, just occasionally.' In a rush he continued. 'I thought Jack and you, Charlie Squires and myself, might make a foursome around the pubs. Tomorrow evening.'

It occurred to me that they were after drinking me under the table. I was on the point of refusing when he said: 'I've trouble at home. My mother . . .' Then he told me a little. Taken off my guard – and anxious to get up to the canteen – I said I was game and told him to enrol the others. He looked pleased until I demonstrated all too clearly that I wanted to go about my business. I was rewarded with a mean look; a sharp one detected as I was clearing my desk and he was moving to the door. For a second I felt a qualm about the pub-crawl. The typing next door had stopped. I went in to investigate and say my fond farewells. My handmaiden, Miss Miffin, looked up at me, startled. Her eyes were troubled.

'It's all right, I know all about Mr Holinshed's activities,' I said. All that I'd told Miss Miffin about her eyes came true in that exchange. They *were* deep; and I was touched by her concern. 'Ever heard of Beatrice's Dante?' I asked.

She nodded: 'There was a picture at school. The bridge. A girl crossing it.' I turned on my crooked smile. 'Well, I'm content to watch from a distance,' I said. 'There are occasions when the Formica top of a table is wider far than all the Russian steppes laid end to end.' I spoke confidently because I was oozing self-confidence inside. I believed it myself. But her eyes were still troubled when I left the room in search of a canteen and Cathie. I might have known I was in immediate danger.

I rushed thoughtless into the place, then held my breath. The place was full of food-smells, faces and dirty dishes; of clatter and the chatter of many voices. Babel was probably a staff canteen and the nearest thing to hell on earth. But I held on to my nerves and played the game, slinking along the line of wall to the serving hatches and never allowing my eyes to stray; picking up my food and walking out blind, shooting what I think they used to call veiled looks. All to no purpose. Her back was to me.

As I lowered my tray she lifted her head. Her hair was drawn back and electric, yet it was only brown hair. The line of her throat made me catch my breath; sometimes I think I was mostly in love with her neck. The eyes were dark and deep; for a moment they managed to be sad and amused and a little disturbed. The slight dusting of freckles accentuated the translucent glow of her skin. I suddenly realised that as a male, Holinshed was almost her counterpart. The light came through his skin in the same way, from within, he also was as physically wholesome. I felt for my sallowness; then it occurred to me that as a man of the night I could complement her daylight being.

'Can I join you?' I roughly asked. It sounded rude to me.

'Of course,' she said. 'Not to appear rude in getting up as you sit down – I was trying to make up my mind whether to take tea or coffee.'

'I'll have the same as you – tea.'

'Now you're trespassing on good nature.'

'Not at all. I'll have the same as you.'

'I'll take you at your word,' she laughed. I noticed that the laughter stopped short of her eyes. They remained grave, or subject to grief. And grief is sexually exciting. The easy flow of her rising, the healthy odour of her, constituted something approaching a total experience even for an old philanderer like me. It was difficult to resist watching her, so I watched. She had womanly legs, a little heavy at the ankles and richly heavy at the hips. She placed her feet out a little as she walked, naturally seeking security. I didn't need to measure my pulse-rate. She was something more than woman. I kept my eyes away from her as she returned, much as I would have liked to watch her bearing on the approach. I was feeling disturbed. There was an unyielding quality, I sensed, something which kept me, the man-me, about a millimetre at any rate from the floor in my momentary worship. Yet I realised my hands were too large and my finger nails uncut. I could feel lines on my face I'd never felt before. In total I felt like an unpressed suit in a shop-window with all the nice new ones. You could say she had succeeded in damping down my sun. But I still wanted to remain in her company.

I wanted to come conversationally to grips with her and went badly about it. She remarked that I didn't generally eat there. I said I didn't generally eat a lot during the day; that I liked to walk out and eat a sandwich and drink a cup of tea; I didn't explain that this wasn't escape, but an expression of the freedom I felt in the work and the building. To leave your work easily and return with grace is something you can only accomplish when you've managed to eliminate the ordinary idea of labour. I didn't tell her this. I was so eager to find the key to her that I forgot to give her the key to myself. So she never had it. She never knew I was on holiday all the time – and that she was part of the holiday. What I did say was something banal, about how did she use her spare time?

'I read, I sew, I think,' she said. 'I have a long journey home.'

'That takes up a lot of time.'

'Not too much. But it helps to eliminate distractions.' I couldn't help wondering where they went (she and Holinshed), how they met, how they indulged their relationship. She didn't tell me where she lived. Instead, she asked me how I spent my time.

'I like to find people – unexpectedly.'

'You talk to them?' I said that I did, but not in the orthodox ways, I hoped. I told her about the scene outside the telephone kiosk. She laughed. 'I couldn't do that. It's dangerous. You're a man, of course – but I'm still surprised. People are dangerous.'

'You don't like people?'

'I've a respect for them. I like gentle people. They're hard to find.' Her voice was low, amused, tolerant; but it had an undercurrent of pain.

'Would you say that I'm gentle?'

Elbows on the table, fingers supporting her cheek, she regarded me. 'No. You're too much a manager. But you need gentleness.'

I ate in silence, then pushed my plate aside.

'You're not hungry?' she asked.

'I need some gentleness,' I said. 'And some air. Will you walk with me?' I was rather proud of the way I put that question. She was amused.

We passed Holinshed and Wills. She walked quickly ahead; it was partly convenience, partly a momentary dismissal. She looked straight ahead; Wills stared; I offered him a genial, crooked smile; Holinshed continued eating, without tasting anything he put into his mouth. That made two of us without an appetite. It only occurs to me now that in real literature one must never mention this kind of thing; excepting for sexual congress, literary types seem to detest the important business of bodily feedback. At the moment for instance, I definitely feel the anguish of her absence more in the pit of my stomach than my mind. Walking with her in the world these physical reactions didn't matter so much – but later, alone with her, my whole body used to be disturbed, I mean belly as well as pulse and heart, but more so the belly. That day I was conscious most of her tallness. Out on the pavement I told her so. She said she was five feet ten inches. That made us equal. I said: 'That's odd – if it wasn't for your high heels we'd match.'

'Next time I'll wear sensible shoes,' she said.

'For me?'

'For ease in walking,' she said; and she laughed at my face. A car endangered our crossing. As we ran I took hold of her hand and triumphed in the texture of flesh and shape below the thin sheath of her glove. On the riverside pavement she disengaged. We walked, then stopped to look at the brimming waters, winter-yellow, surging down against the tide. She seemed to be enrapt. That annoyed me. It hurts me now that I didn't read the mood for what it really was.

'Are you – or have you been – married?'

'Almost, twice,' she calmly replied. 'Two attempts to escape.' She looked at me, and I trembled. I had to look away. 'You know about Jack Holinshed, of course?' I nodded, hardly daring, but forcing myself to look at her. 'But of course you won't know – we're finished . . .'

'I don't know whether to say I'm glad or sorry. A bit of both, I suppose,' I said. She resumed her contemplation of the river.

'Why do you go abroad?' I asked, pressing for a truth that might hurt. 'Was that the first time you were almost married?'

'Oh no, it's not so dramatic as that,' she said. 'You know East Anglia –'

'I'm afraid I don't.'

'It's old and cold, even when the sun shines. My father's a farmer. You might say that the salt of his religion has eaten into his bones. His God's old and cold, like the land. Italy's an escape. It's not the sun, but the sun in the people. So you see, there's no high tragedy in it. I'm just running to human warmth; the first man was part of it, but not now – not any longer . . .' She turned and laughed at the expression on my face. 'You're wondering why I'm being so frank? It's just that I'm spiking your guns.'

'Well, you haven't. You've only told me part –'

'All that you need to know,' she said. We took the road back. 'You know, I'd like to take the first plane out. I hate England.' I was surprised at the passion in her voice. 'I've been in the sun but it dazzles too much. The English soil below the tarmac made me; I get sick for the mist and the dampness. The place is one vast House of Usher, but a House that Poe could never describe. I tried to think of something to say. Too bad it was trite. 'Did you know that last year they pulled a couple of hundred fresh-run salmon out at Richmond?'

'What's the moral? – that life renews itself, even at Richmond? Salmon are only fish,' she said. 'Now stop trying to cure me.'

'As God's my judge, I must,' I said. I was shocked at my own conviction. I believe it shook her a little.

'You're a good actor,' she said. 'You're one of those who don't want to believe in God because they've cast themselves for the part. However, I don't want a god. I just want the sun.'

'You're a bigot and a bitch.'

'You mean I don't stand and stare when you play your little games. I know you, Mr Samuel Rowlands.' For the first time in years I hated my Christian name.

We were late. The foyer was empty. She walked rapidly ahead. I trotted at her heels, summing up. I had angered her. That meant I had cut through. 'Stop trotting after me,' she hissed. I lengthened my pace to match hers. We were in the lift. My friend Herbert was grinning. Going up, I asked him how he was for thrillers.

'A bad run, Mr Rowlands,' he said.

'As long as you don't switch to True Romances . . .' I said, very lightly. The lift decked. I didn't have to look at her face to know that it was blazing.

ELEVEN

I remember keeping my door open all that day for Cathie's passing. I heard her footsteps. She didn't even hesitate. Had she done so, I promise she'd have missed her train. I stayed on, alone.

Stayed on, alone with myself, to be precise. The man I looked at had nothing to be smug about; but then, I am never smug. My way with people is only sleight of hand. I never got through to my own people. They brought me into a comfortable semi-detached world and nurtured me, all oblivious to the twenty-minutes' grace between me and death by fire; living on without a thought that their little niche could ever be rocked, let alone left in ashes – house, furniture, care, me, them, but most especially me. They kept me apart from the world of Uncle James, the world they had escaped. But they had taken their emptiness with them. That was my judgement.

Contempt is a terrible thing. Below the forms and habits my mother and father are people. But I never had the courage or the patience or the imagination to penetrate the things they had around them; policies, place, promotion, the Building Society, their few shares – my father is a bank manager and as hot on a market tip as any Joe on a horse's nose; only my father knows the score. He never makes a lot of money, he only makes a little, but he rarely loses. My mother is anxious about the people living around them but without them in a country estate which has pillaged the country. She needs a daughter crazy about horses; as it is, she feels out of it. They are so insulated. What offends me most is that they don't seem to have any idea of death. With a belief in death there is at least some hope of a marginal nobility. They ignore the very reason for living; that we must live in order to die. I haven't much, but have that much. But that was no reason for disowning them. I was as bad as the types who 'looked down' on their parents for being poor. Mine are very poor. Behind their comfort there is absolute poverty.

I explore because I know that I must die – and whatever there is after the sudden blade of absolute finish it has nothing to do with exploration here. The ghost that walks through walls, floors and locked doors can only do so because it walks elsewhere. It is exploring something or some place which is alien to us. It is in my nature to explore; but a limited tenure makes me all the more determined to search this present world as hard as I can and so long as I am permitted.

So sitting at my desk after Cathie had gone I not only decided to go exploring again but comforted myself with the thought that this was one kind of exploration for which I wouldn't have to pay – that's self-confidence for you! I remembered the betrayal of the night before, still only willed and still awaiting consummation. I was in-deep and aching with it. My only cure was an exploration through the long intestine of Leviathan my lovely, my bringer of peace; to go on safari and hear invisible bearers chanting native songs audible to myself alone. The building and its business was terra firma; the floor was firm beneath my feet so long as I kept other flesh and spirit out of my mind. Every thought of Esther made me wince. To think of both girls together was to send the solid floor into a pitch and toss that could lead to vertigo, panic, extinction.

Yet it was terribly hard to keep Cathie out of mind. Going up the steps to the fifteenth floor I found myself wandering into a pleasing fantasy.

'Troubled, my dear . . .' she would state, rather than ask. 'Take off your shoes and I'll soothe you. There!'

'Oh, Cathie – and care for me?'

'And care for you always.'

All very pleasant until I remembered that Esther was involved. I seemed to see her face, intent and sad in our love . . . On the landing I found my forehead sticky with sweat. I went for ablutions in the VIP toilets. I washed my hands and face for a possible confrontation. Drying myself on a crisp individual towel I caught sight of my face in the mirror. It occurred to me that I looked a little haunted myself. 'Look, get sense,' I addressed myself. 'Get wise to her! Not a giver but a taker she is – and you with a life to live on the ever-present edge.'

What is there about a face that not only makes you catch your breath but traps your will – concentrates it like a burning glass?

Wild-eyed I answered myself: 'What has to be must be. Selah.'

Levitating along the rich thick pile of the carpet I considered the problem of what I would say to the blank then astonished face in the penthouse. It would be Prinkstone's face. It had to be. But there was a fear of the Minotaur, half bull, half man, ready to take a half-man like me at a bite. Worse than a blank face and anger would be the presentation of short thick horns. It seemed to me that I had been given time to compose the answer to a riddle which would save my life.

Only a matter of yards from the penthouse door the noise of people almost sent me scuttling. But it was too late. I was too far forward to retreat, too proud to melt into one of the offices. And the murmur of voices was pleasant. Frozen, I saw someone emerge. He was no sooner in the corridor than he was pointing at me, body as well as eyes. Recognition on my part was instant, thanks to the Company magazine. It was Mr Francis, our Chairman, bald, pink-faced, eyes and moustache on the alert.

'Who the hell are you?'

'What's that?' Where Francis was dressed for the street the other questioner was informally clothed in the manner of a householder seeing off a guest. A tortoise head with spectacles looked curiously from an aged woollen pullover. He had aged since the photographs were taken. But it was Prinkstone in the flesh.

'Good Lord! Don't tell me he's a burglar!' exclaimed Prinkstone.

'We'll soon find out,' said Mr Francis.

'My name's Rowlands,' I said. 'I work here.'

'Never heard of you,' said the Chairman.

'I don't expect you have,' I said cheekily.

'In any case you've no right to be rummaging around this part of the building,' said the Chairman.

He looked decidedly unfriendly. I walked into the light from the open door. I smelled the Minotaur still. 'Come on, what have you got to say for yourself?' said Mr Francis.

I blurted out the truth. It was a sight better than any lie, anyway. 'I knew there was somebody living in the penthouse and I wanted to know who,' I said. 'I thought it might be Mr Prinkstone. And it is.'

'He knows my name!' said Prinkstone, smiling.

'A very peculiar chap,' said Mr Francis. 'What's your Department?' I told him. 'The club of queer trades,' he explained to Prinkstone. 'And what's *your* name again?'

'Rowlands – Sam Rowlands,' I told him, disliking myself intensely for the schoolboy whine in my voice.

'Of course, I might have known – old Snorry's protégé.'

The recognition didn't excite or please me. What did please in retrospect – and does still – was *my* acceptance of immediate identification by a man I had never met. From then on I was able to keep my balance. 'Snorry's man, eh?' said Prinkstone. Casting an odd little glance at Francis, he added: 'In all these years he's the first to find his way.'

'I'm not surprised,' said Francis dryly. 'He seems to have done quite a lot of finding up North – at Percy Main.' His tone was a little warmer as he turned to me. 'Mr Snorry had a warm spot for you, young feller. Often talked about you. His spoken testimonials helped quite a lot. To get you here, I mean. And this is what you do . . .'

'How is Snorry?' asked Mr Prinkstone. 'Still collecting pornography and old saws?'

Something impelled me to say a non-committal: 'I should imagine so, sir.' Mr Francis gave me a glance in which I thought there was a shade of approval. For not throwing a shadow over the proceedings? For playing it by ear? I think it was a protective feeling for the founder which had made me evade the truth. It was all the same to me if Francis took it for subtlety. 'We must – we really must celebrate this one,' said Mr Prinkstone. 'Come back for a glass, Mike. You'll join us, young man?'

'I don't mind,' said the Chairman. Through the door was a tiny lift; the three of us stood together during the journey up; all the jolly sociability of a football match.

The woman of the Buckingham Palace picture was knitting. She had a peaceful, contented face which took on a trace of worry as we entered. 'This is Mrs Prinkstone, my wife – Mr Rowlands, my dear. One of Snorry's boys.'

She knew he was dead – Snorry, I mean.

'How long have you been with us, Mr Rowlands?' she asked, while her husband was getting drinks. Mr Francis had seated himself, nursing joy as well as a bowler. 'I hope you like brandy?' asked Prinkstone. He handed it over. 'Just a week or two,' I answered Mrs Prinkstone. 'Thank you,' I said to the founder.

'A thin cigar,' said Mr Francis to Prinkstone. How did he know? Because I'd worked for Snorry – but I *didn't* collect pornography. Not yet. A box was produced. They were the very expensive kind, but I made do.

'Now, how did you find us?'

'He's our kind, of course,' said Mrs Prinkstone.

'The bouquet,' I explained. 'I saw Herbert bring it. So I looked at the brochure.'

'But the barrier?' asked Mr Francis, with his head on one side. 'A place for work isn't a place for people – relationships – meetings?'

'I wanted to find out about the place . . .' I said, glancing around. The furniture was heavy and old; there were photographs, mostly of Henry Prinkstone; a superb model of a plant with Perspex walls so that you could see it working; seeing my interest the Chairman got up and pressed a button; green, red, and yellow lights began to flow; compressed air equipment, tiny turbines, the sweet little pistons of innumerable pumps began to suck; I was back again by the river with that substitute-father of mine once again. It was a nice little toy; using 'nice' in its truest sense. The Chairman was pleased with my personal pleasure. His hand moved to the button, hesitated, withdrew.

'Bump of curiosity,' said Mrs Prinkstone.

'But very well-developed,' said Mr Prinkstone. I felt like a character in Dickens; specifically from *A Tale of Two Cities*. But Prinkstone was happily engaged in his version of shoe-making. He took me over to the model and explained it. 'But of course, you know it all.' I nodded. The door to the bedroom was open and through the far wall of glass I could see a group of rectangular spaceships with all their rows of rectangular portholes alight. The brandy was very good.

'Well, sit down, boy,' said Prinkstone, 'tell us about Snorry – the wisest man in Northland who had not the gift of foresight.'

'He knew how to handle men,' I said.

'Knew?' he asked.

'You know he's retired, dear,' said Mrs Prinkstone.

'And writing a book – the book,' said Mr Francis, moving between me and the founder. One day I would tell him that a year before his sudden death, outside the Town Hall, Snorry had discovered his dreams again.

The last one of the tumble-down pub against the marble walls of heaven and his father, who had never touched a drop, sitting on a bench outside – holding an empty glass. The old man had been dead thirty years. Snorry had told me how disappointed he was on awakening at the absence of his mother, whom he adored. It had not occurred to me that Snorry of all men was being prepared; now I would never know whether he had suspected that this was the case.

'I'm sorry,' I said. 'I never drank a toast.'

'You can give it now,' said Mrs Prinkstone.

I raised my glass: 'To the founder and his wife who waste nor want in hospitality.' In the silence, as Mr Francis and I drank the toast, I seemed to hear a distant commotion of birds.

'What d'you think of him?' asked Prinkstone.

'Wait till I count this row.' Her lips moved. Very rapidly, and in time with the needles, she said: 'Single, self-centred, clever – clever and knows it.'

'There you are!' said Prinkstone with pride.

'Simple,' she said with fond contempt. 'He's like you when you were his age. If he were married he wouldn't have the time to squander.'

'Is that all?' asked Mr Francis, switching off the model and sitting down. I felt a little squashed and more than a little fearful; there was nothing extraordinary about the summing-up, but it was after all about me.

'Oh, arrogance, absolute confidence in your sort of thing,' she cheerfully said, 'apart from that, he's lost.'

'Is he the –' The question hung in the air.

'I'm lost at the moment,' I said.

'He's not your Black Knight,' she said, looking at Mr Francis, who laughed and looked into his bowler. 'You're not ruthless at all, are you?' she asked me directly.

'I'm a softie.'

'Wait until he's tasted blood,' said Mr Francis, and explained: 'Mr Prinkstone's looking for a ruthless sort of young man who will do all the things he – er . . .'

'Hadn't time for,' said Prinkstone. 'Hadn't the capacity for. To get control. To overcome the Sullivans.' There was no sadness, or sense of tragedy in his appreciation of himself.

But there was from our point of view.

'I'm in process of taking financial control,' explained Prinkstone confidently. Then I was sure it was a kind of madness. 'But of course that isn't enough. Even Sullivan found he had to have help.' He put his head to one side. 'You've an idea of being a top man?'

'Must walk first,' said Mr Francis, watching me. To see how much I was accepting?

'Francis likes you – took to you at once,' said Mr Prinkstone.

I looked at the Chairman. 'You barely knew I existed half an hour ago,' I protested. He shook his head, smiling. 'Also,' I continued, 'there's an ethical point to consider – loyalty.'

Mrs Prinkstone stopped knitting and stared at me in mild astonishment. 'Loyalty to what?'

'And a very good thing, too,' said Prinkstone. 'But he'll soon see that his real loyalty is to the idea of making much of waste – of extension, expansion, adventure, the race against hunger . . .'

'But that's what we're doing,' I cried.

'Not very well, I'm afraid,' said Prinkstone. I looked at Mr Francis – he, after all, was the head of the business. He shrugged.

'Francis agrees,' said Prinkstone. I looked at Mr Francis. His eyes were closed. 'All we need is a measure of rationalisation – a world-wide linking. Have you ever heard of Salmon Farms Ltd? Whale Herds Associated? Atlantic Underwater Incorporated? Submarine Trawlers?' I shook my head. 'All interlocked,' continued Mr Prinkstone. 'But that's not sufficient. They need to be under one supra-national head . . . it could, in time, be you.'

Looking over Mr Francis' shoulder I thought I saw a leopard in the solarium, moving like a flash, a yellow streak of lightning.

On the way down Mr Francis said: 'He's been like that a few years now. But don't be deceived. All those ideas are sound enough – the working ideas, I mean, not the nonsense about controlling it all. He's lost in the power part. But his ideas . . .' His voice was dreamy. 'Are always worth a second look.'

'About the linking up?'

'And you, and you,' said Mr Francis with a chuckle. He was very like Snorry in his manner. Which of course included his matter.

In the event, I wasn't surprised when he failed to ask me to keep my mouth closed; and took it for granted that I had other business in the building. Going down into the basement I sensed that the building was happy. It knew about the entanglement with Cathie. But there was Esther up Its sleeve. Now It had added Mr Prinkstone and Mr Francis, both of whom seemed to be taking me quite seriously.

'Are you quite well?' asked Esther after I'd sat a while.

'I'm fine, fine.'

'You were talking to yourself, not even moving your lips, aggravating,' she accused. 'I saw you.'

'I was smiling,' I said. 'I've just met the Prinkstones.'

'Are you satisfied?'

'They're not in the least bit sinister. A very hospitable pair.'

'They're both quite dotty,' she said.

'Napoleon on St Helena's topmost mount,' I said. 'Accompanied by his Josephine.'

'Don't romance,' she said. 'Prinkstone was a clever man and they did him down. Only he doesn't know it. And she's gone with him all the way. It's very sad, really.' She looked at me seriously. 'Don't let them lead you up the garden path, m'boy.'

'A garden path around the world and including each and every one of the seven seas,' I said. 'Give me a kiss.'

'I don't like being used by an ego.'

'I've nothing else to offer.'

'You're a liar,' she said. And she was right. What else I had I was throwing away. There was nothing I could do about *that*, but the weight in my stomach told me at least I could hurt Esther now and save her from what would be worse. Mrs Prinkstone wasn't so astute after all. She hadn't seen the big, self-indulgent streak of cowardice branded on my back. She hadn't seen the traitor who was led by his loins. But Esther had. All merry and bright I went out and had a meal, then a steam bath, then returned by way of a reminiscent walk along the Embankment to wait for Esther. By that kind of coincidence she found me at the very spot where I had fought with the monotonous flow of the water for Cathie.

I said nothing of that. We went home. We went to bed. In next to no time it was all over, like a dream, and I was back in my office. I didn't know it, but I was due to begin payment.

The day started well, or so I thought. My door was ajar and Cathie called. She stood with the flush of the country on her face and we talked of quite ordinary things. The conversation was going nicely until Jack Holinshed came along the corridor. Looking over her shoulder I saw him pause. Seeing my expression she turned. Nobody said anything until I took the responsibility. 'All set for tonight?' I cheerfully called out. His look told me the old story: I can't have, but that doesn't say that *you* must. Typical dog-in-the-manger. 'Yes, of course,' he muttered, and went on his way. I'd referred to the pub-crawl, and so to something he didn't know about at the time. Wills had conveniently forgotten to tell him. However, I don't think Holinshed had really heard the question. The words just went straight through the conscious skin to the lost, quivering entity below.

Wills' story is that he suggested the pub-crawl to Holinshed later that morning. He didn't specify membership.

'I could do with a night on the noggins,' said Holinshed.

'I thought we'd take Rowlands and Squires,' said Wills uneasily.

'You what!' said Holinshed. 'No thank you. I'm afraid Rowlands isn't the kind of company I like at the moment.'

Wills sat on the desk and winked. 'Listen, he's locked us out. We don't know what's happening. With a drink or two – who knows? We might even get to know about the tie-up with Crumple.'

'I don't like his face,' said Holinshed very stubbornly. He took a lot of persuading. I suspect it wasn't so much my face and –

personality – as trouble at home. There'd been a show-down about his affair with Cathie and a night on the town might be mistaken for back-sliding. In the end he persuaded Wills to have a word over the telephone with his wife – after he'd spoken to her. Wills was in an embarrassing position; he found himself even more embarrassed when Holinshed handed him the telephone.

'Hello, Joan, my pet,' he said.

'Hello,' she said. 'So you're in on this thing?' The ambiguous words shook him and brought back the vicious telephone call he'd made to her. He must have come out in a cold sweat. It was as if he'd stumbled on the edge of the pit. At that point he wasn't sorry for what he'd done to the Holinsheds, but he was sorry for himself. It was this that drove him to the inept retort: 'I'm stealing your husband for the evening.'

'You can't.'

'What's that?'

'Can't steal him,' she said. 'That's already been done – or didn't you know?'

'I didn't catch that – bad line,' he lied. 'Hello – there you are. It's the new man. It's high time we had a night on the town and got to know him.' She was talking against him – something about: 'This is the limit, friends, covering up.'

He wasn't sorry – that came later. But he was afraid of being found out. Ignoring her voice he continued. 'It's not often, you know. All work and play makes Jack – who's going? The new man and Squires as well. I'll see that he gets a meal before, put him on the train . . .'

Very deliberately she said: 'Don't cover up, Pat. Send him home.' He couldn't be sure of the last few words. Had she said – 'Send him home now?' The sight of Holinshed's innocent, anxious face decided him. 'That's a good girl. Next time I'll bring a bottle of champagne over for you.'

'Send him home, now,' she said. He hung up. 'That's fine,' he said.

'I wish you'd kept the line open,' said Holinshed. 'Things have been a bit rough lately.' I suppose he was imagining trouble; kitchen door stuffed with papers, curtains drawn, gas-cooker on; anything but what was to happen in due course.

'You worry too much,' said Wills. 'Manufacturing guilt; you can almost see it coming out on that busy little assembly line.'

'I don't manufacture the stuff,' said Holinshed.

'Don't tell me she knows . . .' cried Wills, all concern.

'She knows.'

'What's the situation?'

'I've called it off with Cathie.'

'What's to worry about then?'

'It's not so long ago,' said Holinshed.

'And now you're in chains, is that it?'

'She took it badly.' They sat in silence. 'If I give on this I'm done,' said Holinshed. 'After all, it's more or less work. Why should she take it this way?'

'Don't ask me; ask her,' said Wills, watching Holinshed's hand on the telephone. 'If you must.'

Holinshed withdrew his hand. 'I'll ring her later. Wills, what did she sound like?'

'A bit vague,' said Wills. 'A bit cool, if you must know . . . the line was bad, of course.' The devil was in him; now that the crisis was over he enjoyed having Holinshed on the hook. 'Women always dramatize this sort of thing,' he added. 'You either fall for it or you don't.'

He was confident that Holinshed would go. He would go because he couldn't face home, now that home was the place where he saw most clearly what he had been and what he now was. A woman's face is the perfect mirror.

I persuaded Cathie to go out to lunch with me that very day. We went early. For the first and last time I chose the place; a roof-top restaurant, one of the very tall ones, from which, it was claimed, you could see the Thames and far beyond. It was true about the Thames, and I vaguely remember seeing the great curve of the southern monorail. But I had little time to view. As I had planned I was on the attack from the beginning. I was convinced she had a secret; well, I was right there, but wildly out in the substance. I thought – I was convinced she had had a tragic love. A man she could not marry. A man who could not return her love. A lover who had been lost.

So, looking her straight between the eyes, I said: 'There's been a man in your life.'

'Oh!' she said, amused. Everyone knows how a great actress is lost in every woman. But I wasn't deceived. Lightly I continued, 'Out there, in the Italian holiday place that attracts you like a magnet – that's where you met him. I know, it was beside a fountain!'

'Go on!' she exclaimed delightedly.

'You know those fountains. The pride of the town. The great place for meetings. Spray between you and the sun and sometimes the kiss of something like rain. Then something went wrong with the works. The fountain was dead for weeks. Then word spreads that the fountain is mended. You know what they're like out there. After weeks of dryness and not a cool place in the town they just had to have a public ceremony.'

'So?'

'So the crowd gathered. About five, when it's not so hot. All the little balconies crowded. The Mayor, the Captain of Police, a thin, bent old lady, the Princess, leaning on her stick . . .'

'You're doing very well,' she said mockingly.

'And the Mayor made a speech. The crowd cheered. The great sprays of water reached up to the sky. The tree of life. A tree of water with fruit like diamonds. The kiss of the water. And the chap next to you – you know these Latins – feeling the kiss of the drops turned and looked at you in his need to kiss as well. Probably a waiter, aged about thirty, family of six or seven howling kids, but there was the fountain and all the others were kissing. He smiled and you smiled back. And you kissed. And that was the beginning of your long miserable martyrdom, your crucifixion, your life-long bloody abortion . . .'

She was smiling. 'It wasn't like that at all. Pepi was only twenty-two. He wasn't married. But we met beside a fountain. We kissed. And he was run over by a bus, nothing so romantic as crossing a street corner, oh, no, he was driving down to Padua in one of those silly little bubble cars.'

'That's a bad way to die,' I said.

'Ah, yes, any way of dying is a bad way to die. But living –' She stopped suddenly and glanced at me with a detachment which was in itself a kind of death. For me. With a chill I remembered

Prinkstone's words on Snorry: 'The wisest man in Northland who had not the gift of foresight!' The past, then, was unimportant. The malaise was part of her, rooted in heart and intestines. It was the malaise I would have to defeat before I could win her. The unfinished sentence, 'But living –', was not a question as I had thought, but a statement of fact.

She smiled. 'It's too deep for you, my dear.' She was laughing, patting a stray tendril of hair into position. How was it possible to tell the colour of her eyes? They changed every time I was with her. Today the colour was blue. Yesterday it had been purple, but today that regal colour had retreated to stain the hollows below her eyes – the hollows, most delicate and vulnerable part of a woman's body. I wanted to lean over and touch each in turn, trace each hollow with my finger, then kiss. But it would be no more than the touch of the breeze, or the kiss of rain, or salute of spray from a fountain. Oh, she would like it. But the pleasure would be quite impersonal, unrelated to the source, like the dog-bitch closing her eyes and thrusting her smooth head to any hand that stroked.

'What's wrong?' I cried.

She opened her handbag in a swift, defensive movement. It was her way of telling me to pay the bill. As I would, in the end. But it would be entirely my personal and private account. Hers had been presented and collected.

'Now don't be down in the dumps!'

'It's all right for you,' I muttered.

'I can't pretend to something I don't feel. Now can I?' We were walking back along that heart-breaking stretch of riverside between the Needle and the empty spars of the *Discovery*, symbols of an age when achievement and adventure were truly married. 'It's not that,' I said. 'It's simply – well, it's simply that I can't help thinking of the day when I'll walk along here alone. Without you.'

Her face hardened. 'You must learn to live with thoughts like that. If you will have them. I'm not your mother.' At my look she said: 'I'm sorry.'

'I never knew my mother,' I said.

'How many of us did, or do,' she said. 'But you're such a child. Nothing like a big bold baron of industry. That's what you are, aren't you?'

My spirits revived. It was all nonsense, of course, all guesswork, this feeling that she lived with death. She was just a girl. All girls were women. All women were subject. She *would* be mine. And why? Because no woman can resist a master of men. She would capitulate when the day came – when I ruled Leviathan.

'Hello there!' The voice was as cheerful but shocking as the trumpet sound of a car bearing down on dreaming pedestrians. It was Wills. Beside him was Holinshed, withdrawn, sullen, carrying the burden of his own loneliness.

'Mind if we join you?'

'We're just on our way back,' I said.

'Do join us,' invited Cathie with a malicious glance.

'So long as we're not intruding,' said Holinshed sourly.

'Never into marriage of true minds,' said Wills. His glance said, 'It's all right, chum. You're not a menace any longer. Not now that you're on your way up.'

'My, but you are presumptuous!' said Cathie.

'For intruding?' asked Wills.

She laughed, shaking her head. 'For thinking you might intrude into a marriage of true minds. What's true, Sam?'

Now she was baiting me. Her eyes dared me to answer. 'True?' The word shamed me. 'True's a word you can't weigh with one half of a scale.'

'That's very clever.'

'And very true,' said Holinshed.

'I presume you mean when it's the marriage of true minds that's in doubt?' said Wills, with his spade-shaped head on one side, the indubitable serpent in the garden.

'If the minds are in doubt then what's the scale?' asked Holinshed.

'Why, the heart!' said Cathie, and I looked down, because she had driven the word like a spear into my side. Through the cage of ribs it went, to the very heart.

'Hell!' burst out Holinshed and broke away from us. We watched him run. The ejaculation seemed impossible. But he had said it, although the word had been cut off as if by the turning of the little knob on a radio, the one that impatiently seeks other voices, other sounds.

We had all stopped. Holinshed was stumbling along the opposite pavement. He looked like a man in a desert all sun and heat, where the only water was poisoned, and would stay poisoned for ever.

I might have guessed there'd be trouble that night. I expected it. I looked for it in his face when we left the building several hours later. It looked smooth but healthy, and the moustache helped in the illusion of all's well. It's hard to imagine any man with a moustache in trouble. I was relieved. 'A full-scale dinner's a weary thing,' I said. 'Let's make do with a bowl of soup and sandwiches at a delicatessen.'

'Agreed,' said Wills. 'Let's make room for the real business of the evening.'

'Suits me,' said Holinshed. 'You go in and order. I want to ring my wife.' He joined us shortly, looking a little disturbed. 'Not in,' he said shortly. In answer to Wills' look.

'A shopping revenge with an evening at the pictures for good measure,' said Wills, laughing.

'I suppose that's it,' said Holinshed. But I noticed his appetite was poor. He ate as if it were his duty. We set out on the great adventure, God help us all. By eight o'clock we'd worked our way along the Strand and Fleet Street and a few side-lanes as well; every place seemed crowded with the worst kind of crowd; people like ourselves. Wills said he knew a place with a quiet plush room near Liverpool Street. We took a taxi. On the way over Charlie said he wasn't staying out too late.

'You sound married, sort of,' said Holinshed maliciously.

'The landlady's daughter,' quipped Wills. I thought it was an inspired guess but I could see by the mouth he was making in the uncertain light of the taxi that he knew it all.

'I've a few things to do,' said Charlie, betraying his love. There was an ugly note to our laughter. As if we knew and resented his being the luckiest man of us all. Certainly *he* knew his luck. He sat there nursing it, knowing that when at last he was rid of us he could go home to find her waiting for him.

I felt a sense of separation. All that evening he matched us drink for drink, but never really joined the company.

So there we were. They thought they knew what they were about; and I thought I had them taped. Drinking me under the table was just an idle dream.

I remember becoming a little alarmed at one point. By then we were sitting in that bare little room with the pock-marked face of the dartboard looking down on us. Generously I admired Holinshed's suit.

'Good, isn't it?' said Holinshed. 'Take you to my tailors.' He leaned over the table. 'He needs you and you, by God, need him.'

'By God I do,' I said, a little hurt.

'To change the subject,' said Wills, 'are businessmen members of the human race?'

'The Chinese used to write man as a tiger, head and stripes,' I said. 'That seems to prove it.'

'There's no mercy,' said Wills. 'Get onto a branch and flick your terrible paw.'

'It's not so crude as that,' said Squires.

'Crude enough when someone gives you a lift,' sneered Holinshed.

I bowed. 'That's what I mean. The tiger helps his kind. Top humans know each other. They're kind – to their own.'

'How would you define the relationship?' asked Wills.

'Large ability.' I said. 'Competence isn't enough.'

'What about nepotism?' asked Holinshed. With a shock of disappointment I realised how much he hated me. With Wills, who managed to hide it, that made two. When you're young in the game it's hard to accept something which has no other basis than that you happen to be there and breathing.

'I wouldn't know, I never had any,' I said.

'Listen to him,' said Wills with simulated kindness. 'As if he didn't know that he'd friends upstairs. It's all the talk . . .'

'I have friends everywhere,' I said with an air of mystery.

'And relatives,' said Holinshed.

'According to the rumour you're related to Crumple,' said Wills.

'You might say we're so alike we're practically related.'

'Have you met him?'

'More or less,' I said.

'To the point of nepotism, more or less,' said Holinshed. I saw he was really nastily drunk. The pieces were beginning to fall into place. Had it not been for the repetition of that naughty word nepotism, I might have been happy.

'I wish it were,' I said, grinning. 'Actually –' saying it tight-lipped, 'actually, so far as Crumple's help's concerned I wouldn't know whether to expect it from the hand or the boot.'

'I think you're – you're a c-conniving sort of a bastard,' said Holinshed aggressively.

'A good judgement,' I agreed. 'I gladly admit I'm a devious, cheating, conniving son of a gun and far from being an OK kind of type. I'm the superior type of organisation man: I let the organisation help me to lead a full and happy life.'

'And bugger the others, eh?' I noticed he never looked in my direction when he said anything to me. Instead, he would look at Wills, and Wills would look away.

'I try to be kind. I try not to show I'm superior in the manner of lesser public schoolboys who think, by God, the world owes them a position as well as a living.'

'Touché!' said Wills. 'I'll admit I'm St Pauls'. Jack went to Winchester –'

'And I went to Barnard Castle,' I said. 'I'll not say snap – you've probably never heard of the place –'

'You're hellish class-conscious, then.'

'Caste-conscious,' I corrected. 'And for purely practical reasons. When you know the castes you can walk right through them.'

'Over them,' said Holinshed. 'Over their bodies – our bodies. Planting big feet on our faces and screwing your heel down to get where you want . . .'

He was standing up wildly addressing anyone but me. I rose with dignity. 'Shall we settle this outside, like gentlemen?'

Holinshed looked at me for the first time. 'I'd like to push your face in,' he said; and did. The blow was just strong enough to reseat me. I decided that this was a necessity anyway.

'Silly blighter,' said Squires, and I was too busy trying to work out which of us he meant, to be really angry.

'Wants to go outside – don't you, son,' said Wills to Holinshed. 'Run-off, then a taxi to Victoria.'

'So you were the pugilist of the Fifth,' I said to Holinshed. Something was running on my face and I resisted the impulse to feel for blood or sweat. My nose was sore. He'd hit me with the back of his hand the way they do in the films.

'Not going home,' said Holinshed. Wills tugged at his arm. 'You bloodywell stop it. I should have pushed *you* in the face anyway.'

'Me?' asked Wills.

'Of course; you're a c-conniver as well, but watch out – he'll drown you in his sea-green incorruptible soul.'

Wills flushed but pursued the theme. 'Come on,' he said. 'Home and beauty.'

'Unhand me, you little black beetle,' said Holinshed proudly. I felt sorry for Wills, who was evidently conscious of the fact that his friend had hit him off in a couple of words. Holinshed wove to the door, and Wills followed, mainly, I think, to hide his face. After they'd gone my good friend Charlie looked at his watch. 'It's ten-thirty,' he said. 'It always ends like this.'

'Let's find this place,' I said. I was vaguely uneasy. I wanted out of the place before the warning lights flickered and the voice said 'Time, gentlemen, please.' The mob in the bar looked like bees on a honeycomb and twice as busy. Coming in I'd never noticed their shattered faces. There was a corridor and a left-hand door concealing a pit with steps which Edgar Wallace had often described. It may have been accidental or it may have been an irresistible desire to throw myself down and out but I stumbled on the top step and would have gone had it not been for Charlie.

When we arrived Holinshed was sitting against the far wall and Wills was bending over him. Wills turned a startled face, straightened out, said: 'Oh, to hell, I'm going home,' then walked past us, at speed. I noticed the change on the stairs. His footsteps went like an old man's going to bed for the last time. We squatted and had a look at Holinshed. He looked green. There was vomit all over his legs and he was gasping. I went into one of the toilets and took a roll of paper to clean him down. He'd made a mess of that very good suit; his own tailor wouldn't have recognised him.

'He brought me down here and punched me,' he managed to gasp.

'You asked for it,' I said. His story was this: they had arrived, he had said he wanted to be sick, Wills had said, guiding him against the wall, this'll help, and had driven home.

'Well, he tried to help you,' I said, remembering Wills bending over him.

'Did he hell,' he said. 'He was telling me he'd phoned my wife – told her, you know.'

I looked at Charlie. 'About his affair with Cathie Cavendish . . .' said Charlie.

Holinshed laughed weakly: 'We were going to shake you down,' he said.

'You'll not be the last to fail,' I told him.

We got him onto his feet. 'The bastard spoke to my wife on the phone,' he said. 'I must ring her, now.'

'You'll be home as soon as we can get you a taxi,' said Charlie. That was noble. I could see him estimating the time to Victoria and then home to Walham Green. The steps were too narrow for the two of us to help him up. I took on the job while Charlie went ahead. Halfway up we stopped for wind. 'I'm sorry,' said Holinshed. 'All this . . .' 'Not at all,' I told him, turning my head away from the reek of his breath. 'Will you do me a favour?' he asked. I told him anything within reason. He started climbing again and muttered, 'Don't tell her.'

That was the first intimation I'd inherited. There was a noise, a rumble, sweeping through the earth, shaking the cavern – an underground train. It went off like a depth charge under our feet then belted away for a rendezvous somewhere along the line that Cathie travelled.

Watching Holinshed climb I thought of the day I'd follow him into the place he occupied now.

TWELVE

We went looking for a telephone. We walked a long way. We took to alleys, dodged round corners, walked up wide roads, rummaged in quiet mews streets. But we couldn't find a kiosk. They were in hiding, or it was their night out, or some sinister Underground in the war against the telephone had stolen them all away, stashed them in cellars or dumped them in the Thames. Naturally we stumbled. We were weaving as well. In time to a monotonous chant of Holinshed's. It went like this:

> *'The stink of death*
> *Is yesterday's beer.*
> *The rumble of trains*
> *Under the jakes*
> *Is blossom in my brain.'*

Once he stopped to earnestly ask me: 'Are you natural? Or are you sad, like Jesus. Because it's very difficult . . .' His eyes filled with tears and he turned abruptly away and stumbled along the pavement like a man in his seventh day of desert thirst. God knows where we wandered. Sometimes, I vaguely remember, there was an impression of mist from the river and an idea of sinister Chinamen hiding in passages. The taxi eyed us suspiciously with its two great glowing lamps but consented to take us aboard; when he asked our destination I first thought of hell then changed my mind. It came out like 'Helborn' but he seemed to take it in good part. I told him to stop when we reached the *Daily Mirror* building. Our noses led us in the direction of a kiosk near the bridge. Once within sight of the thing the urgency collapsed. We congratulated each other on our cunning and paused to spit into the depths far down below. We thought it was a river until a bus came along and scattered the illusion.

The kiosk was empty. This should have meant it was out of order. It wasn't. In a matter of seconds I'd Holinshed's number. You could almost hear the emptiness of the house below the dialling note; the thick smothered concentration of a deserted house. Holinshed gave me the number of a woman two doors away. A man answered. Ice-cold, I said: 'May I speak to Gladys?' He said I could. I handed the phone to Holinshed. He waited. He said:

'Hello, Gladys old girl. Is Joan there? No. Listen, Gladys, I've been trying to ring her all night – no answer.'

'She isn't? But Gladys. Listen, will you do me a favour? Yes. Slip out, there's a darling, and see if there's a light.' He gave me a stiff grin and a crooked wink. It was a long wait. 'Hello . . . yes. I don't know where. And you don't – no, of course not.' He listened for a while. By now the sudden sweat was drying on him where he stood. 'Thanks, Gladys,' he said. 'Goodnight, God Bless You.' He hung up.

'Must get a taxi,' he said.

'Stay with me the night,' I invited.

'That's generous,' he said.

'Good God why?' I was honestly surprised, having forgotten that it had taken total stress to make him human, or to slough the veneer. Me also. We decided an answer wasn't necessary. A look did the job. Anybody seeing us flagging down a succession of taxis in business would have thought we were fine, in a world we had made ourselves. It was like that all the way to Victoria. Going into the half-moon approach he went quiet. The train moved out as we got him through the door. We waved. He leaned out of the window and waved back. His eyes were moist. Nothing to do with his wife, or with us. Something to do with the way we live in a temporal world. It was almost a lovers' parting.

I walked over to the Underground with Charlie. 'Come home with me. I've a bottle or two,' he said. 'We'll sit up talking.' Generous, considering he'd a girl waiting for him. He'd forgotten he was the only living one of us, but I hadn't.

'I'm taking a walk to see a girl.'

'You won't see her tonight.' There was no answer to that most embarrassing one. Fortunately the train was in a hurry. I returned to Aldwych. Now I was in what I'd heard with Holinshed on the steps of the jakes. Which was only right. The trains are a crude representation of those that travel in the brainbox, dozens of them running in opposing directions on what appear to be collision paths. Trick photography gives an illusion of safety; in reality there are dozens of wrecks a day.

Suddenly I wished Wills had stayed to the end, the poor starving bastard, and eaten of what little manna we had to share. The danger of being superior!

For now I know for certain that Wills went home and rang Holinshed's number. There was no reply. He picked at some supper. After a while his wife, Marie, came downstairs and sat at the table. She said nothing. That irritated him although he knew perfectly well a word would have irritated him as much or more. 'I was ringing Jack,' he said. 'We had a row. I left him with the others.'

'You really detest him, don't you?' she said.

'I wouldn't say that.' She didn't argue; but there was a watchful look he knew too well. They talked about his mother. 'How is she?'

'She's been terribly restless ever since you left this morning. She's had the pills but they're not taking. You'd better look in. She's always this way when you're out late.'

Wills went upstairs and answered questions more or less truthfully. Long after his mother was asleep he was still considering whether he dare disengage his hand from hers. He heard trains passing by. About one o'clock he called Holinshed. The connection was hardly through before the telephone was lifted.

'Joan?' asked Holinshed.

'It's Wills, Pat Wills.'

'Oh, I see,' said Holinshed.

'I rang to apologise.'

'That's all right. We make a place, then we put people in it. I was wrong.'

'Is everything all right?'

'Joan's gone, I think.'

'What d'you mean – you think?'

'She's not here.'

'Didn't she leave a note?'

'That sort of thing went out before the Bomb. She'd have too much to do, packing and so forth. When she makes up her mind –'

'I'm afraid I didn't help on the phone today.'

'You mean yesterday,' said Holinshed with a laugh.

'I'm most sincerely sorry,' said Wills.

'Don't worry,' said Holinshed. 'Good night.'

Wills was conscious of Marie, hands inside the sleeves of her dressing gown, watching him from the stairs. 'That was Jack Holinshed. It never rains but it pours. Apparently his wife's left him.'

'I'm not surprised,' she said. He had not told her of Holinshed's affair. She sat on the stairs and her face puckered in that old, hellish and familiar way. The tears came as he took hold of her. He realised she was crying for him, not for Holinshed. It occurred to him that Holinshed was lucky to be alone and abandoned in an empty house.

That was the night Charlie lay down on the bed and watched pictures moving slowly up and down while piles of books shimmied. Dorothy Pennington was waiting, as was the coffee she had with marvellous instinct thought to prepare. He sat up, swung his legs over the edge of the bed, felt for the ground with his feet. It squirmed horribly. He raised his stockinged feet a little from the floor and drank his coffee with closed eyes. He couldn't remember taking off his shoes. So she must.

'I wouldn't like to say how long it is since this happened to me.'

'Sloshed?' she said gravely.

'Not really. Just on the edge. Holinshed kept ringing his wife. I felt definitely out of it.' She sat beside him, so near he could sense her warmth. But she kept her distance. Later she helped him to undress himself. As she switched off the light and left him he was conscious of the enormous step they'd taken. After this there could be no doubt at all of their intentions, one to another. And she hadn't giggled, as he explained to me later, when she stated he was sloshed.

Holinshed sat up until three o'clock in the morning. He knew he wasn't going to work. After Wills rang he continued the sort of silent dialogue we have with ourselves during the night watches, in a woman-less house. The telephone didn't ring again. He wasn't surprised. At two-thirty, tired of the strain of waiting and talking to himself, he decided to eat. It was something to do. He put a slice of ham in the pan, placed an egg by its side, considered, doubled both portions.

It was the best breakfast he'd had for a long time.

As for me, I went in deeper with Esther. We walked along the Strand and up Charing Cross Road to Tottenham Court Road Station. There we took a taxi.

Leicester Square was looking more like New Orleans than ever, the part around Bourbon Street, only the hopeless wanderers didn't carry their glasses with them and the doors weren't nailed open – yet. 'In fifty years – less – this will be the only live part of town,' I said.

'What on earth are you talking about?'

'The computer revolution. Buildings becoming bonnets for electronic machines – the end of the little people: clerks, typists, book-keepers, ledger checkers. United Assurance used to employ four thousand five years ago – they're down to half the number; Gluck Oils have one for every five they employed a decade ago. It'll soon be the silent city. Last night up Holborn all you could hear was a grasshopper sound; we were surrounded by little monsters.'

'They're going to call ours Great Jupiter.'

'What do they call the old one?'

'Just "It".'

'Great Jupiter's good – I'll bet that was Francis' idea.'

'You like those complicated things – you'll be moving into them one day?'

'They're only superficially complicated. These are the great days of electronics. Like the days of Stephenson, Hedley, Hackworth, Trevethick – band of brothers, united in a big break-through which was only a major postponement. That's why I like the Great Jupiter business – great alibi, great side-issue . . .'

'What'll we do without work?'

'We'll learn to use our leisure,' I said with a mocking little laugh.

179

'We'll explore – some of us. The seven senses, maybe more as they're discovered. But most of us'll play, and pine for a job of work. There'll be all hell let loose.'

'Tell me a science fiction.'

'Our children's children, the clever lucky ones, will be wanderers. Like cowboys, reporters, printers a century ago. They'll be drifters – setting up, maintaining, repairing the machines. They'll have feuds with the others, the static ones . . .'

'They'll be bachelors?'

'Naturally.'

'As sad as us?'

'Much sadder – they'll be travelling people. Hail and farewell; hurried embraces, tears on the runway; a hand waving a tiny expendable paper handkerchief.'

She slipped her hand in mine. I said: 'You made the first pass.'

'Distinctly aware it's a *cul de sac*.'

'Anatomy isn't all.'

'One wouldn't think so.'

'It's the approach to a reality outside ourselves,' I said. 'A most rewarding reality.' That night I dreamed a dream. In it I slept with Cathie. Her brow was fever-hot, her body ice, there was something wrong. There was a noise and we rushed to the window. The old Bible Christian, her father, his cowman and tractor driver, his boy-of-all-work, and the goose-girl, had wrested an apple tree from the orchard. They bore it down to the door roots first and it was when the outspread branches raked the avenue of trees that I noticed the symbol. The whole of the orchard was in bloom but for the tree they'd uprooted. They swung. 'One!' said the father. Cathie clung to me. 'Two!' The old man glared at us in exultation. 'Three!' The door went bursting inwards. I regarded the lack of blossom on the battering ram as an ill-omen. Nothing to do with incest, or lack of fertility. The old man was on my side and that meant an inevitable failure.

Three letters in the post the following morning.

My Uncle James –
'Your world-wide organisation dedicated to the maximum utilisation of soil and strata, the undersea, and all the waste

therefrom, enrolling all men and women of goodwill and appealing only to their skill and knowledge, is just another substitute.

'Men need to engage the affections and the emotions, they need the drive of heart and souls, as well as the idea. You've been taken in by the old Wellsian dream of an elite – and I'll bet the man who sold it to you was a boy when Wells was a man –'

That was shrewd.

'There's no alternative to anarchism. What's against anarchism? Inertia. But what started the Russian Revolution – I mean the real engineering? The belief in inertia. They let Lenin through because they never believed it would work. They were right, but in the wrong way. Sorry, digression. What I intended to say was: any idea which is discounted is dangerous. Apathy, or indifference, of the ruling classes allows the thin edge of the wedge to enter.

'In my time the masses were bairns. Every decision they made was forced upon them – action and reaction. We're no longer bairns. We're not grown up. We're in between. Pimply, sulky, broody, but putting inches on.

'We're looking over our shoulders when we sigh for solidarity. Solidarity came out of the big work camps, from the blast, the mine, the yard. I've heard your great-grandad say that in the old days before a strike the pitmen would gather in a field behind the heap and spit one at a time on a big flat stone. Spit and forget – and you found yourself at the bottom of the coal shaft with your head and your boots torn off.

'That was the solidarity of the ignorant and the frightened.

'What we need now is the solidarity of the lone and the enlightened: the men who will walk out on their own.'

It was interesting; but it no longer touched me on the spot that counts. I remember liking the bit about the men who will walk out on their own. The rest was rationalisation: I often wondered how he managed to keep going after so many years and so much disappointment. Did he think I was the new Robert Owen?

Koniev's was brief.

> 'I enjoyed the discussion about the book – the silly book. A degenerated use of a degenerate form of literature, if that is possible. Your contribution impressed me. I hope this will not bore you. My department are interested in the work of your organisation and I have asked your Chairman (a) if I may tour some of your installations, (b) if you may be my guide. I hope you will accept. The idea is a week or two.'

The beginning of a real supra-national organisation, I said to myself. Sixteen plants in a fortnight. I knew the form. Smarting behind the eyeballs before lunch as the fine spray of diluted chemicals took effect; a certain sleepiness induced by a necessity to talk elementary shop, which is to think in one language and talk in another. At the constructional units (there'd be four or five) the engineers would spring to attention and come out with the uniform Big Think: 'Let's show him the foundry and explain the new non-stick sand; the Sanderson blister-eliminator; then there's the plate-shop. They're great on pre-fabrication in Russia and those magnetic cranes of ours'll give him something to think about.' Explanations shouted direct into the Soviet lughole and most of them lost on the way; cups of sticky tea in close little shop-cabins complete with the usual boring (and bored) recapitulation of all that had been seen. Above all, the visitor needs a little tolerance.

When I'm boss, the visitor will step out of his car and into a works capsule. This will be transparent from the inside, opaque from the outside, and will move on a rail to all the most interesting and spectacular points in the works. The visitor will have his personal TV camera at his command; a touch of the button will bring close work zooming in for undisturbed and concentrated study. Tour completed, the capsule will be transformed into a lift and rise several hundred feet above the works to a comfortable lounge and dining room without a telephone. Latter the most important innovation. There the site engineer would join the visitor for lunch – and for a carefree chat.

Going on safari is child's play compared to a tour of several industrial establishments, largely because of lack of imagination.

The third letter was from my mother.

'My dear boy, we're still waiting for a letter. I know you are not a letter-writer, but please let us have something now and again, as your father keeps saying that you don't care. Of course you do. Have you found a permanent place to stay, and how do you find your staff? Have you made any friends? What made it worse was that your Uncle James rang up and said you'd written to him; your father brooded a lot about that; he didn't say anything but I know his moods. Sarah passed her ballet finals last week. I bought a new kind of cacti in Robsons. A girl rang up practically every night the first week you were away. She wouldn't give her name. I hope there is nothing wrong. I haven't told your father so please don't mention it. She seemed quite cheerful, which set my mind at rest, and do save some of your salary, you will need something for a rainy day or when you get married.

'Life is rather hectic at the moment. We had two bridge parties last week. Sunday was fine so we made the most of it and drove up to Alnmouth for a round of golf. Who do you think we met? Mr Snorry's nephew, he was executor you know and he says there are some books. I said he could bring them over and leave them but he seemed to think it would be better if you rang him the next time you are home, you know all about this legal red tape. Well dear that seems to be all I have to say. Take care of yourself. Your loving mother.'

I made a note to ring Joe Snorry. The bequest had been by word of mouth. Full marks for Joe. Apart from the pornography there was virtually everything that Jeremy Bentham had ever written and some handsome editions of Blake, Burns and – strangely, but not so strangely when you considered Snorry's complicated mind – a beautiful limited edition of Browning's shorter poems. And first editions of Robinson Crusoe, all of Bewick, rare items of early trade union history, a couple of dozen unpublished letters of Walt Whitman, written to Snorry's grandfather, and preserved in a folder that looked like a slim volume. He'd offered the maps to me as well; but maps are terrible time-wasters: I prefer to make my own. Joe Snorry would get the books to me; it would be some time before I gathered strength to visit mother and father, the cacti and the card-table, tried once again to get through to whatever was inside the case-hardened skin of my sweet little sister. Father would be delighted to know that I'd found a stockbroker and was siphoning off fifty quid a month, but not for a rainy day, simply because spending all my salary was beyond my very considerable spending capacity.

Mother hadn't mentioned any cocktail parties – yes, they still have them! Odd when you think of my great-grandfather coming all the way from Norfolk in a coal brig and lying strapped in a bunk, his pockets full of silver won in a backsliding game of cards with the skipper, listening to his father and mother and all the other tourists (blacklegs although they didn't know it) singing hymns in the hold or the scuppers or whatever they called the bowels of a ship in those days. That was during the storm. He kept the money but never played again. Subtle graduations of revolution: *his* father was a Wesleyan Methodist; Joseph, my ancestor, became a Primitive Methodist.

Mother's letter brought all this back from the repository of family relics kept in the memory of Uncle James. At lunch time I slipped out and bought a second-hand copy of the Methodist Hymn Book. The verse that Joseph Rowlands had loved because it had struck him to the heart at the height of the storm was:

> *When I tread the verge of Jordan,*
> *Bid my anxious fears subside;*
> *Death of Deaths, and Hell's destruction,*
> *Lead me safe on Jordan's side.*

Dutifully I read the whole of the hymn; my choice was the first verse, in its context as great as anything in any hymn book ever written:

> *Guide me, O Thou great Jehovah,*
> *Pilgrim through this barren land;*
> *I am weak but Thou art mighty;*
> *Hold me with Thy powerful hand.*

Every respect to the Lord; note the capitals for 'Thou' and 'Thy'. Second line my motto; still looking for the powerful hand, not knowing it was ready to scoop me up at the crucial moment. The chorus hurt: 'Bread of heaven! Feed me now and evermore.' Uncle James, who had heard it blasted rather than sung in the chapels of his boyhood, had sung it again for me; each line of the chorus is repeated; to paraphrase, you can sing that again, sevenfold in these Godless times.

Before going out I'd talked on the telephone to Holinshed; conversed with Wills; answered a memo from the Chairman's office asking me if I would be kind enough to accompany Ivan Sergei Koniev on a tour of plants (see below). The tour wasn't to be so bad as I'd expected; one constructional, and one of the larger processing units. And, joy of joys, a full week to do it in. This meant some free time if Koniev would play – and I was pretty certain he would. Holinshed told me his wife had left him; he had checked with his mother-in-law, who choked back a sob, then said that Joan and the children had gone into hiding and would contact him later. He was going to see a Doctor about his state of depression. ('I feel the world is going to end; perhaps it has.') Wills gave me some hints on how to play the streamlined Iago and manage to come out feeling both sorry and satisfied. Waste of a wonderful talent, I told him, according to the text book – a kick in the arsehole followed in sharp order by a pat on the back.

Thinking of Holinshed's condition I remembered that great-grandfather Joseph had reneged on his Primitive Methodism, becoming, at 71, a Christian Scientist. Uncle James said this was because he'd once had some warts wished away by a man who took a ha'penny for his pains. According to Uncle James, the Christian Scientists never quite knew what to make of my great-grandfather Joseph: to the end he was capable of shouting out a loud and triumphant 'Amen!' in the midst of their dreary lectures. His prostate and the betrayal of Ramsay MacDonald and his faith-healing killed him.

One of the plants we visited was Percy Main. We stayed there three days, and did it the royal way, which is the workman's way. We sat and smoked at various points of the plant and by the end of the second day were abandoned by the executives and taken up by the workers.

I have the taint. My favourite cure of all the ills is to tell myself that I no longer exist; excepting in the memories of my parents, Uncle James, and one or two schoolfellows who vaguely remember a Sam Rowlands who fell into the river and failed to get hold of the piece of timber they held out to save him.

In real life, I think, I made it. But it was good to imagine that I hadn't, and find something approaching peace through the simple statement: Sam Rowlands was drowned at the age of ten. Sadness, disappointment, anguish, despair, can no longer afflict him. Sometimes the trick almost works.

I had to see to my guest. We were both booked in at the Royal Station, which I used to view from a distance with pretended contempt. Now I was in it I enjoyed the atmosphere, even if it was at times a bit oppressive. I had to look after my guest. We had rooms next to each other, and we got to know each other very well. At the end of the second day we went drinking with the foreman and three men from No. 3 buffing plant. The foreman was a Scotsman and took great exception to my alternately drinking whisky and lemonade; at one point he walked out of the bar. I went after him.

'Man, it's blasphemy,' he said. 'I canna' stand it.'

'Just science,' I said. Anything to keep him on an even keel. 'The sugar and whisky combine. You get higher faster.'

'I don't believe it,' he said.

'Also, in the early stages the raw whisky makes me as sick as a pig. I love it, I love the stuff, but my body won't take it. The lemonade eases the way.'

'Well, I'll be buggered!'

We returned arm-in-arm and great friends. I kept on with the lemonade. I needed to. Guilt was eating away at my guts, and even a sense of anticipated exaltation couldn't overcome that relentless gnawing. I was on edge. Newcastle is still a small town. Someone would see me and carry the news to my parents. Understand, I wanted to see them; my only trouble was that I lacked the strength. I was suffering from a bad dose of inertia. I couldn't even summon the energy to go and see Uncle James. He'd blab it out the first time he saw them. For the same reason I didn't approach Joe Snorry about the books. But the guilt was only partly about avoiding my parents.

I had definitely burned down the bridge. There was no retreat. What happened was that I asked the assistant manager at the plant for the use of an office and a telephone. 'Thompson's over at Hartlepools,' he said. 'I'll show you.' He left me alone in a tight little office. What I mean is that the owner of this office had a magpie-mind. The office was full of furniture – filing cabinets, bookcases (without books), a small table and on top of all this a massive great desk with a roller top. He must have been a short man; he had one of those old-type executive chairs on castors and it was way down. My chin was just a little above the level of the desk. I asked for UK House. The girl said she'd call me back. I replaced the phone and sat in that low-down chair; humming like a tuning fork inside. The man I was sure had a persecution mania; the basic idea of the furniture was a barricade. All he needed for total security was an automatic rifle resting on the roll-top. I lined up on the door. Perfect. The telephone was a long time in ringing and when it did I snatched it up, like a gunman caught with his gunbelt off and his trousers down. I asked for Cathie. Her voice was small and perfect. I could see the pattern of sounds in my mind. She seemed surprised and pleased and asked if I wanted R.W.J. I said no, I wanted her. Wildly. She caught on. There was a silence of ten seconds, which is a long time on the telephone, before she brightly asked was I enjoying the trip – and home? I said no. I called up all my wickedness and said: 'I told you I wanted you. I want you to think about this . . .' 'Now don't be foolish,' she warned, but the voice meant more than the words. 'I rang you to tell you this. Cathie, I love you.' I looked up to see the head of a stranger in the doorway and nicely in the sights of my imaginary gun. Its eyes and mouth goggled. I put my hand over the mouthpiece. 'Go away,' I said. He went. I returned to the telephone. 'Sorry, an interruption,' I said. 'Did you hear what I said just now?'

'Sam, I knew before you said it.' She sounded distressed. 'I can't say anything now, and I don't want to say anything . . .'

'That doesn't matter,' I said. 'I don't expect you to say "me too". I don't expect anything. But I thought I had to tell you.'

'No,' she said.

'For the sake of the record,' I continued. It makes me wince now when I think of it. 'Put it in the file. Look at it. I'll talk to you when I get back.' I didn't say good afternoon. At least I had sense enough to avoid that anti-climax. I placed the telephone on its stand as gently as you return a trout to the water.

And that was how I burned my bridge. It left me with a private guilt and grief, and a sense of exaltation. Later I thought the assistant manager gave me some odd glances. The kind you'd expect from a man who has spoken to a man who has overheard you making an avowal of love over a borrowed office telephone. I didn't mind. I'd enough trouble with my own reactions.

We went to a big flash club with the men from the plant, and I paid two guineas each for membership for the whole party; all on the firm. It was big and lush but the prices were almost normal. Place stuck with mirrors and great revolving multi-coloured lights. But full of open people. We danced the latest dance with a bunch of girls who were jolly and almost maternal.

Mac said: 'Best bloody night since Hogmanay in Cowdenbeath last year.'

One of the workers, a thin little man, fell asleep over the table. Whisky and big pints of Scotch ale had given him the fix. Mac was still high and happy when we put them on the taxi.

'Workers are the same everywhere, eh?' asked Koniev. Instead of walking back to the hotel we went on the pedestrian way down to the old High Level and looked down river at the double dose of lights, the real lights and their wet, splendid reflection.

'We do the thinking for them, you mean?'

He laughed softly: 'I mean they do the living for us . . . why are you guilty, my friend?'

Alarmed, I discovered that my mouth was out of control. The best I could do was to offer a secondary guilt. 'The parents, Comrade, the mother and father.'

'A separation?'

'No, just that apart from an accident of birth I'm in no way related to them.'

'You are lucky,' he said with decision. 'I never knew my parents. Worse, I know nothing of them. So I wonder. *You* can dismiss the questions. You *know*.'

'I suppose so,' I muttered.

He looked at me and laughed: 'You would manage a better relationship if you could, but it is not possible. We have a good rule. Managers must not attempt to manage relationships.'

My other uncle – Andrew Rowlands – was a union organiser in Yorkshire. He was a part-time member of the Electricity Board and his spark had died. Not that the seat on the Board had anything to do with it. 'You organise for one thing, God gives you something else,' I said, thinking of this.

He grunted contempt: 'Some things are not possible, Sam. Take them or leave them. But do not ask them to be something else. We have learned that this is one thing not possible in one generation after the old. You must take care that you are a man of your own and your own son's time.'

Later, after he had watched me being sick in the bedroom sink he said: 'I think I like your recovery system. I believe we will take a dozen, maybe two dozen plants.' Seeing my stare he explained apologetically. 'All the steel goes to new cities. Would take too long to buy blueprints, eh?'

People always spring this sort of thing on me when I'm high-low. Anyway, I consoled myself, he's not the sort to be pushed.

While we were inspecting the constructional plant the news broke about Hartlepools closing. According to the papers it was the end of the world; when you've been hit twice you always see a straw dancing in the gutter (or let's say a drinking straw) as a sure sign of the end. The front pages came out big and black. One even mentioned Prinkstone. The reports pointed the finger at other plants in the region; all, I knew, were on the secret danger list.

The situation brought joy to our dinner party with the Chairman. I discovered that Mr Francis was a mimic. I kept off wine, which I consider greatly overrated, and piss on all your wine-bibbers. Francis was in great form and frankly in form, telling us how he'd made it his duty to keep Mr Crumple informed. When the senior member of Hartlepools sent up the first written question, Mr Francis had it neatly typed in red from the Agency tape and sent over by hand.

'You must meet Miss Plumb,' said Francis. 'Absolutely fearless – but then, of course, she's working for me. That, combined with a natural bitchiness, makes for quite a woman.'

Miss Plumb had placed the typescript on Mr Crumple's desk. She watched him reach for it, then read.

'What's this?' he testily asked. ' "The Minister says naturally Her Majesty's Government is watching the outcome with concern, but has no jurisdiction over the affairs of a private company" . . . None of their business, event or outcome.'

'Of course not,' said Miss Plumb.

'None of their business,' said Crumple. She lingered still, and he snarled. 'What are you waiting for?'

'Nothing,' said Miss Plumb, smiling maliciously, as Francis had foreseen. 'Nothing at all.' At the same time she managed to convey the impression she was closely observing – and recording – his every reaction.

The Hartlepools branch secretary was interviewed several times on television. In the most telling, Charlton was seen seated against a tremendous blown-up picture of Prinkstone pushing the button which started the very first buffing tank. As the interview was ending Charlton turned toward the picture and said: 'There's the man they should bring back to settle this lot.' Worse from Crumple's point of view was the way in which the interviewer picked up the cue, when he said: 'The man who put a new face on Britain and the faceless men – that would be quite a battle!'

At nine-thirty the following morning Crumple picked up his telephone to hear Francis say: 'I see we're now the faceless men.'

'Bilge!' said Crumple.

'You've seen the *Express*?' asked Francis, after a suitable interval.

'I only read *The Times*,' said Crumple, a lump of lead settling low in his belly. As a young man he had been written about by Mr John Gordon. Francis was silent. 'What do they say?' asked Crumple at last.

'Not "they" at all. The next Premier. Talks of a National Recovery Board – the – er – new brand of nationalisation.'

'They're making a mountain out of a molehill.'

'That's their profession,' chuckled Francis. 'It seems that you reverse the process – not very successfully.'

'Chairman, we'll ride this storm –'

'If the teacup's big enough to contain it,' said Francis, chillingly.

Francis rang again the following day. 'That you, Crumple?' he asked in an unnecessarily conspiratorial whisper.

'I said so when I lifted the phone.'

'Sorry, I didn't hear,' remarked Francis.

'Had you something to say?'

'I was wondering if you'd like to attend a little tea-party?'

'Tea-party?' asked Crumple with a sinking heart.

'A pack of very disgruntled Northern MP's are rapidly heading in this direction.'

'My desk's full and I've people waiting to see me –'

'I'd like you beside me when the assault starts,' said Francis regretfully.

'Had it been tomorrow afternoon I'd have pitched in,' said Crumple. 'I'll be clear by then. Why can't they be civilised and give us fair warning?'

'It so happens they *are* civilised,' said Francis. He waited a while, then said: 'See you at four in the afternoon tomorrow, then.' Then hung up.

For some unknown reason Crumple aroused the ire of the most pugnacious of the MP's. Mr Francis had introduced him as 'Our Mr Costs and Profits'. Later, he had cunningly turned and asked 'our financial expert, our accountant,' for a considered opinion. Crumple resented this. He also disliked the bull-dog manner of the MP, whose constituency was forty miles or more away from Hartlepools. But most of all he resented the stone-walling tactics adopted by Francis; all the more since they had originated in his own lack of judgement.

'I'm not a politician,' he irritably remarked after the MP's had departed. 'Anyway,' he added mysteriously, 'you didn't make out so badly as a politician yourself.'

Francis commented: 'He gave me a sharp look after this one, but 'evidently decided not to press it.'

'But this man is a colleague,' protested Koniev.

'This man is also an obstacle,' said Francis quietly. He pointed his cigar at my friend. 'But I'll promise you one thing. Any minute now you're going to duck a bit and dodge a little but the upshot will be an order for a dozen or so plants. You'll get them. I'll see to that. Even if I have to sell a million gallons of vodka a year for ten years to get my money back, you'll get them. But that wouldn't do for Crumple. Roubles or nothing with that gentleman.'

To end the story as I heard it through Rampion, who heard it from his chief, who heard it from Marshall, who was on the field of battle, Crumple quickly was put out of his misery so far as the remark of his being a politician was concerned.

Through a series of open doors the Chief Financial Officer overheard the deep, booming voice of the Chairman say: 'And, of course, he didn't make out badly at all – if you consider an inability to answer a straight question straight out, and a general shiftiness, as political virtues!' At the final laugh Crumple was fired with hatred and anger. Not a man lacking in courage he stepped over the corridor and through the Chairman's open door.

'Did I hear my name?' he demanded of the two. The other man was Marshall, who looked after Personnel. Crumple looked at him and wondered. Marshall now – who had it been earlier that day? – who would it be the next time?

'Not guilty,' lied Francis expansively and with an open shocked face on him which infuriated and yet at the same time flattened the accountant. 'We were talking about the next plant manager at Heckmondwyke.'

'Heckmondwyke!' cried Crumple as if to deny there was such a place, or plant.

'Heckmondwyke, wasn't it, Marshall?' said Francis, then quickly added. 'And say you *had* heard your name mentioned – you must have remarkably good hearing.'

Crumple exploded into ripe red anger. 'I'm treated like a pet bloody buffoon around here,' he shouted. 'Maybe I am the butt, but by God there's going to be a change, I'll see that you treat me decently.'

He stalked out. Afterwards, I imagine, he dwelled on the scene.

Marshall had been patently embarrassed. He might have been embarrassed because Crumple's name *had* been mentioned; on the other hand it could have been caused by his own unlikely outburst. To step into a man's office and bawl and shout like that! The first thing you learned in business was that dislike, even hatred, were part of your lot; and that people, being people, were bound to talk about you behind your back. If they didn't it was a sure sign that you were slipping.

He considered the doors. Francis had a mania for keeping doors shut. Why for once had Francis' office been open to the corridor? At the precise moment when his door had been open as well. How had that happened? Miss Cummings had been in for dictation. He'd needed a file from the registry along the corridor and had sent her for it. She had gone, leaving his door open. She had never done this before. How long had she been with him? Getting on for five years, the most reliable of women. He began to watch the girl. Miss Cummings soon became conscious of this. 'He gives me such strange looks,' she told Mrs Arcot. 'Not at his age,' said Mrs Arcot. 'Oh, it's not that,' she hastily said. Mrs Arcot looked at her. 'Oh, no, it can't be!' exclaimed Miss Cummings, who was 36 and a vestal virgin dedicated to the glory of UK House. 'No, he's suspicious of me,' she continued. 'He must think I've stolen something. Or told tales,' she concluded. Mrs Arcot confided in Mr Marshall's secretary, a woman who was given to long, cosy conversations with her chief. Mr Marshall promptly confided in Mr Francis. The information was quickly interpreted. He told us confidentially over the dinner table that at first he had felt the stirring of compassion in his bowels. 'Then my bowels consulted my mind,' he chuckled. 'My mind was quick to reply: "Let him go and advise one of those bloody great pension funds."'

'Surely you can manage him?' asked Koniev.

'I can manage him,' said Francis. 'I've managed him for a good many years. But one gets tired of faces. Equally, one gets tired of frittering away energy.' He drew on his cigar. 'But primarily it's his face. I just can't bear him around any longer.' He saw my stare. 'Call it pathological, if you like. Well, there's still an instinct for murder. This way he gets off with his life.' After a moment he concluded his judgement: 'But the corrosion's a strictly private affair.'

So ended a momentous dinner. For the first time in my life I felt fear for a given individual. I felt that hatred could really work. It was no longer a question of hatred as something existing outside one's self as something rather unpleasant but easily disregarded. Hatred could touch you. It could work. It could create corrosion. But then, I thought I was different. I dismissed these thoughts and returned to my private affairs.

I'd had a glimpse of Cathie before leaving the office for the dinner party. We flew down from Teesport on the three o'clock plane. A sane man would have gone straight home. I went into the office. I should add that the Chairman's invitation had reached us at Newcastle; and that his own car awaited us at the airport. It was a big, handsome car driven by a thin man who was not inclined to talk; he said good afternoon after deciding not to ask for proof of identity, asked would we like the radio on, and kept viewing us in a little mirror in case we began to strip away the fittings. After dropping Koniev, he took me into the basement car park, neatly bringing the vehicle to rest with the door exactly in line with the lift entrance.

I said: 'Very neat,' as he came round with my bag.

Casually he replied, 'I do it every morning.' His finger was already on the lift push-button. I went up with fear in my heart. There was no message from her among the papers on my desk. I discussed some minor points with Miss Miffin. The telephone rang twice. It was only the Chairman's PA checking up and Mrs Arcot to tell me that the Chief Controller would like to see me a.m. tomorrow. I suggested that I was ready and willing to come along now. There was a pause while she passed on the offer. It was rejected. In turn I rejected any idea of seeking out Cathie. There was nothing we could usefully say to each other in front of Mrs Arcot. The thought of seeing no in Cathie's face was unbearable. I could have gone home then. I tore off the Friday on my desk calendar and wandered restlessly around the office. There was nothing to do. There was nothing I could do, in the way either of work or private interests. I sat at the desk pretending to read a piece of paper and jumping every time footsteps passed. At a quarter to six, ten minutes after Miss Miffin had gone, she tapped on the connecting door. I called come in without looking up.

The idea that it was really her took time to unfold. I said hello and allowed the feeling of awaiting sentence to expand and take over from the delight. She said: 'It's still in the file.' I gave her the smile of the reprieved. 'That doesn't mean it's going to be yes,' she added quickly.

Humbly I replied that I quite understood. I was looking at her as if I'd been separated from her for at least a year, but my sense was not completely gone. I knew I must somehow manage to touch her. I walked round my grip and took down my raincoat. 'I'll walk down with you' I said.

'No,' she said. 'You mustn't. I wanted to tell you –'

Gracelessly abandoning the grip I took her arm and steered her out into the corridor. I gripped her just above the elbow and she shivered slightly. I only glanced once at her as we walked along the corridor to the lifts. She was looking straight ahead. I was sure she was biting hard on her teeth to maintain control. I still held her elbow. As we neared the lifts she murmured something and slipped her hand into mine. I thought she had capitulated. The hand was stone-cold and as smooth as ice. My heart was in my mouth. Then I realised she had passed me a piece of paper. She took her hand away and hurried ahead. I cried after her. She looked back with panic in her face. That stopped me running. She went down the stairs without looking back. I watched her figure appearing and disappearing as she went down the corkscrew of the stairs. When she was gone I looked at the note. All it said was 'Ring me at this number tomorrow. If you wish. C.' It was a London number.

Even then I wasn't sure I'd win. All the same I laid my plans. I went back for my case. I went home and changed and told Meg Surtees that I might be away for the weekend. She gave me a look. She has a good nose. After dinner with the Chairman, I turned down his offer to drop me off, taking a taxi instead. First I said goodbye to Koniev. He said: 'A very interesting evening. A most unusual man.' I nodded. 'A devious child,' he concluded, grasping my hand. I wasn't sure which of the three of us he meant. I had the taxi set me down at Baker Street Station. I had a slight headache from cigars and brandy. I went to a machine and got my carton of coffee at the second go; the first go gave soup. I looked in shop windows as I drank my coffee. Then I walked slowly home. The idea was to miss Esther. But she was awake and waiting for me. After all, I'd been away five nights. Fortunately, Meg Surtees had told her I was going away for the weekend. I had my story ready.

She accepted it without question, but this isn't to say that she believed it was true. Afterwards she clung to me. I was glad she didn't come down for breakfast the following morning. I re-packed my grip, said goodbye, and left. That was at ten. At ten-thirty my taxi deposited me in Hammersmith main street. I had a cup of coffee and looked at some second-hand books. I bought a mint copy of the abridged version of Spengler's *Decline of the West*. As one of the cruder kind of centurion I felt I owed it to him for so accurately foreseeing me. I read the introduction twice. My true father was born in 1912, two years before Joseph Rowlands, the Minister son of old Joseph of the hymn, was killed at Mons, five years before the introduction was printed. I skimmed over odd sentences in the early chapters and was relieved to find that there was no useful purpose in crying over spilt milk. The contemporary noble Roman emerged from his book, found a telephone kiosk and dialled Cathie's number.

It rang a long time. Later she told me of how she had sat holding herself in restraint until it had called ten times. In her panic she had miscounted. It was fourteen. I was there at the other end, and I know. At her voice my heart gave a kick like a rabbit going into the noose. Her voice sounded frightened. She said she hadn't really expected me to ring. I forgot my deliberate delaying of the call and told her in return that I had thought of nothing else since reading her note. She laughed to cover a catch of the breath. I asked could I call for her? She said no. I said not to be afraid. She said: 'I'm with friends.' That explained a guarded quality in what she had said. I arranged to meet her at the station and it was only natural that as I was saying the word 'station' I thought of her mention of 'friends' and of my grip, which I'd earlier deposited in the left luggage there. At that time I knew nothing of her resourcefulness.

She came into the station like a minor miracle. I was surprised everything didn't stop at her entry; people, clocks, trains. Like children newly-met we were a little awkward with each other. I suggested we might have a coffee. 'Let's not waste time,' she said.

I must have looked startled. She laughed. 'I've borrowed a boat,' she said. 'For the day. You can spare a day?' she asked anxiously.

'I can give you the weekend,' I brashly said. I thought she cooled at this. I told her I didn't know much about boats. 'You can learn,' she said. 'As long as you know the ropes,' I said. She laughed. 'I've my master's ticket,' she said confidently. She seemed excited at the thought of a day with a boat, not with me, but I decided I liked her to be excited about anything so long as she laughed like that. She seemed years younger than me. It was only when we were on the river that I discovered that it was cold and windy. It was a small boat and I sat on a side-seat and tried to keep warm. We went upstream for a while and I had thoughts of escaping the wind, which was driving in from the east, or of going ashore at cosy Kingston. To my alarm she took the craft around tightly like a London taxi and started to belt down river. It was not so much the wind which worried me as the thought that we might be going into the estuary. I had once been to Tilbury and had been appalled by the great waste of water. She laughed at my look then concentrated on navigation, for the river was crowded with craft, including sinuous nylon cargo 'sausages'. She only spoke once before we reached the Pool and this was to point out an innocent-looking bit of waterfront called Pickled Herring Street.

At last I shouted: 'Are we going down to the sea?'

'We could go to Whitstable and beat it down to Rochester,' she said. She was thinking aloud. 'No, I've a better idea.' The idea proved to be a canal. We passed through an area of warehouses and works. Sometimes there was a continuous line of very tall buildings with few windows. They were as dead as mother-rock. I felt dwarfed. But at least we were protected from the wind. It was quiet. She reduced speed. 'Hungry?' she asked. I'd enough life to reply, 'And starved!' I felt very inferior. 'We'll eat soon,' she promised. Ten minutes later we approached a small wharf. We idled in. I jumped ashore, tied up, and helped her out. 'It's up here,' she said, pointing to an alley, almost a slit between two factories. But I was determined to have it out on *my* ground.

The neutral ground between the boat and the place she was taking me to. I kept hold of her wrist. 'Well?' she asked.

'Your decision,' I said. 'The filing cabinet. It's due to be opened.'

She turned her face away. 'It's too soon,' she said.

'What's the problem?' I asked. I had her other wrist. She looked me straight in the eye. 'You're ruthless, committed, single-minded,' she said. 'I'm single-minded too.'

'About what?'

'Let go my wrists,' she said. I released her. She turned in the direction of the alley. Darkness enveloped us. We were in the eye of the needle. 'You're in love with the business,' she said. 'In love with UK House.' It was presented as an accusation.

'I wouldn't say "in love",' I replied. 'I feel it's essential to be at home, you know, in your work.' I decided I had to be honest. 'But I'll admit I have a special sort of feeling for UK.'

'A feeling for something abstract,' she said.

'You're not abstract,' I said, and trapped her against one of the walls, I don't mean that I embraced her. I simply stopped her by moving in front and placing my hand against the wall. As she turned in surprise I completed the corral. She laughed uneasily.

'Don't be silly,' she said. She closed her eyes. I kissed each in turn. She had very long eyelashes. She said no, or something of the sort. It became a moan as I found her lips. They were tight and hard. I couldn't awaken them. I felt a fool. I was hurt and angry. 'Look,' she said. 'You're of this world. You belong to things. I want to belong to myself. You'll make me –'

I caught her lips. We came together, mouth to mouth. I caught her completely by surprise, and the lips came alive and she came closer to me, still saying no, it's hopeless. I took her shoulders. I left her lips and kissed all of her face. She held back her head and I kissed that beautiful neck. In the end she was weeping. I held her close and comforted her. I could easily afford to do so. She was mine. I thought nothing of her doubts; indeed, I thought they sprang from perverseness, or from mere delaying tactics.

'But there WILL be problems,' she said. I allowed her to have the last word.

The place she took me to was one of those cabins for canal-users which have sprung up all over the country. There was a clubroom with a worn carpet and assorted chairs, a big map of the canal system on the wall, and a kitchenette with an electric stove. A florin in the meter gave us all the power we needed. The place began to look tidy. 'What about food?' I asked.

'It's in the box under the seat on the boat,' she said.

'I didn't see you put it there.'

She was getting crockery from a cupboard. 'I stocked up this morning.' She saw my look. 'It was lucky having the boat,' she explained. Seeing I was still uncomprehending – 'I had to be completely alone with you. Really it needed a month. On the open sea. Across the Channel and roaming through the Continent.'

'You'll get to know me,' I promised, and went for the food. In the box was a nylon net bag with a roll, butter, cheese, some assorted tins. It had all been planned. We had a good meal. Afterwards we sat in front of the fire talking. She allowed me to kiss her, but drew away when I tried to go further. 'Someone might come,' she said. It was late afternoon. Dusk was falling. Seeing my expression, she laughed. 'Pleasure boats are always coming and going.' She saw my expression and said, sadly I thought: 'It's really our bodies that want to make love.'

'Better to wait, it's all the more rewarding in the end, you'll be glad some day,' I resentfully mimicked the advice column. She laughed. She had a good laugh. I didn't laugh with her, but I managed to smile. 'Poor child, he wants his woman-mother,' she crooned, drawing my head to her bosom. She began to shake with laughter again. 'If you could only have seen your face! The small boy refused his ice-cream money!' I took that as a fair comment. It was nice to be pillowed on her breast anyway. 'All I'm saying is that there must be time for courtship. Courtship isn't only adventure, it's getting the opportunity to know before you make a mistake.' I stirred uneasily. 'No, I'm not hinting at marriage. Like you I'm too bone-selfish to even consider it at the moment. All I want is to pleasure you and hope you'll pleasure me in return.'

'That was quite a long speech,' I said.

'You'll have more from me,' she said. I told her I didn't mind. Her voice was soothing even when her matter wasn't. I said: 'Anyway, what is it that makes you so bloody different from me?'

She pondered a long time. At last she said: 'There's a funny thing. I don't really want to tell you. I'm afraid you'll run.'

Snuggling in, I said: 'No fears of that.'

'Don't be rash.'

'Fire,' I instructed her. She went off without preliminaries. It was like a starter's gun, my saying that.

'I hate it all. I hate and despise everything about this super-streamlined world,' she said. 'I'm a reactionary, a counter-revolutionary, but I'm too lazy to do anything about it.'

'That's all right,' I said, lazily. 'I'm non-conforming as well.'

'Not really,' she said. 'It's all a great big piece of fabrication. All your little pranks are only a cover-up operation. I told you before, you love it. You're infatuated.'

'Now you're exaggerating,' I said.

'About you, perhaps. But not about myself.'

'There's nothing terribly wrong about being in disagreement. Even businessmen need a good shaking up now and then.'

'That's your trouble,' she said. 'You don't mind a good shaking up, so long as you can keep the status quo. You're just a harmless rabbit.'

'Well, what do you want to do?' I asked. I was definitely interested. I had all these thoughts myself.

'I can't make up my mind. I'd like to opt out. For a time, anyway. Make my little gesture. But, Sam . . .' Her voice trailed away.

'Come on, tell me,' I said.

'It's almost indecent exposure,' she said. I turned and looked up at her, laughing, about to say that I didn't mind. I saw the situation wasn't ripe for that sort of saying. I returned to my original position. 'Well, at least we're good friends,' I said. She stroked my hair.

'I suppose so,' she said.

'Don't doubt me,' I murmured.

'It's myself I doubt,' she said. 'My parents . . .' She collected herself. 'My parents are religious maniacs. That's the only description that fits. It's a little dirty hole-in-the-corner religion, a kind of Bible Christianity, and it ruined me. But I'm drawn to the Church, the true Church.' I couldn't help myself. 'No!' I said incredulously. 'There,' she said. 'I knew what you'd say.'

'Oh, it's like my flirtations with anarchism,' I said comfortably, trying to calm her. 'We all want something to believe in.'

'I want to be,' she said. 'I want to be part of something that's apart from the world. I want to be able to stand apart. I want to be something more than temporal.'

I understood that too. Or thought I did. 'I respect you for all you've said,' I told her.

'Do you? Do you really? But what if I act?'

'So long as you stay with me, I'll respect you,' I said.

'But I won't be able to stay for ever. It must come to an end.'

'Let's not think about that,' I told her.

'I mean death,' she said. I reached up to touch her cheek. She was crying. 'My precious dear,' I said. 'That's why there are men for women, and women for men. So that they needn't be lonely all the time.' I came away from her breasts and took hold of her, realising that I was to blame. It was I who had brought all this to the surface. Realising also that she was different. There was strength of will, or conviction, despite the tears. Something occurred to me. I muttered it. 'What was that?' she asked.

'I hate the smell of incense,' I said. 'It's not that it's associated with religion, faith, ritual. I'm pretty neutral about that. It's not my cup of tea, but I can bear it. But I do hate incense.'

Then she laughed again, and all was well. Going back she asked me to spend the night with her. Standing there at the wheel. I said: 'Are you sure?'

'Of course.'

'You mustn't rush it.'

'But I love you.' On balance I think these words, and the way she said them meant more than anything else that happened all the time I knew her. She took me to the building. Indeed, she took me to the door of her friend's flat. But I didn't go in. That didn't seem right. Assured that I knew the way I went back to the station and took my grip from the locker. It wasn't very far, but far enough. Venus was sharp above the horizon. I walked on air all the way back. But I also felt as I used to feel when I was a boy before an examination. I felt humbled as well. I went quietly up those stairs. Her door was open. The living room was in darkness. I put down my grip and went into the bedroom. The light was out. Through the window I saw the steady green glow of that wonderful planet. I found the bed and leaned over. I found her face. She was shivering again. I took hold of her; through the sheets, I mean. She was smooth as stone, firm as mother-rock, mother-naked. Then I began to tremble too. It was joy to join her and hold her face for the first kiss of our loving. She cried again, twice, but the weeping was different from that of the cabin by the canal.

THIRTEEN

The friends were fortunately away for a long weekend, and Cathie and I stayed together until Monday morning. It seemed odd to be travelling with her; to take charge, to sit beside her, to feel her possessive hand in the crook of my elbow. But it was also good. It was good to be conscious that she was so near me in the building, to be aware that she was equally aware of me. It was good to see her to her train in the evening, although I felt a pang when I remembered that Esther was there, in the building.

As soon as Cathie had left me I knew I was a bad case of conscience, so bad that I was unashamedly pleased to be out of the building. I knew I couldn't face Esther; I couldn't even tell her over the internal telephone. That seemed almost as bad as face-to-face; I walked around and eventually made my call from that historic box in Holborn; the one Holinshed had used. To my surprise she took the news quite calmly – at first. Hoping she'd be impressed I told her what a coward I felt. 'It doesn't matter,' she said. 'I knew you had someone else in mind. I knew from the beginning you'd ideas far above *my* station.'

I protested at this. I told her that she was a wonderful person. I meant it. But it was like interrupting a private conversation. A conversation she was having with herself. 'I knew a long time ago,' she continued. 'It's that girl Cathie, isn't it? I knew the way you sheered from speaking about her – you wouldn't even talk about the other girls in case her name was mentioned . . .'

'I'm sorry, Esther.'

'But I knew for sure on Saturday morning,' she said. 'When you didn't come in to say goodbye – I knew then it was over.' I breathed into the telephone, wondering what to say next; she seemed to be waiting as well. At last I said good night. She didn't reply. I knew she couldn't trust her voice. I placed the instrument tenderly back into its cradle; tenderly and slowly I put it to rest. It was the best I could do; that and suppress the terrible vain thought that she was tearing her heart out for me.

It was strange to hear, later that evening, the noise of her movements in the room next door. I fell asleep with her voice sounding off in my mind. 'It doesn't matter,' she had said. But it mattered a great deal to me. I was surprised that it mattered so much.

Corrosion had started some more of its secret work. That was on Monday. On Tuesday the Chairman came to my office to see me. 'Is he in?' he asked Miss Miffin. She nodded, gulped, and managed to say yes. 'Perhaps you'd ask him if he has a minute to spare?'

As she opened the door into my office I heard her protesting: 'But I'm sure he has, sir.'

Astonished, I heard his voice reply: 'Never mind. Ask him, make sure.' I could hardly believe my ears. Miss Miffin presented a startled face to me. 'It's the Chairman,' she said, and every letter was a capital.

'Oh, yes,' I carelessly said. But I was nettled. 'Tell him to come in.' He could have entered from the corridor without all this fuss. I told myself that I was not deceived for a moment by all this democratic crap, all done to get me at a disadvantage. I decided to be offhand. All the same, I removed my feet from the desk.

'Keep them there if it pleases you,' said Mr Francis.

'It does, and I will.' I looked at him down my nose. 'Sorry the place is in a mess.'

'It could be tidier.'

'I've a tidy mind, that's all, that says to hell with material tidiness. When I'm really working I organise the place. Otherwise the untidiness stands for a kind of comfort. Empty desk sign of a confirmed office dandy, the kind who gets in five minutes before time and creeps out half an hour late. Not that it does the firm any good . . .' To my horror I discovered that I was unable to stop talking. 'But you'll understand it's organised tidiness, I really have to work at it . . .'

'I'm afraid I'm a dandy,' said Francis mildly.

'You're in the slavery sector,' I rudely said. Let him stick his democratic wanderings! I noticed he was standing. 'Won't you take a chair?'

'I will, I always do, I was just testing your reaction to *my* need.' Devil. That one made me squirm. He knew then that I was put out. All they want is that feeling of slipping easily from one saddle to another. Trick riders of business. Snorry tried similar tricks in our first six months together. The Chairman was talking again. 'Chaps standing in bars. Could never understand. Like to rest my backside. Always tired there, not the legs. I'm not going to apologise to *you*, by the way, for dropping in like this. This way I get a tough nut at a disadvantage. Must keep in touch – in practice – easy to lose – what do they call it – human engineering – Ah! Ah! Ah! – I call it man-handling, effortless garrotting.'

I resisted an impulse to cheer. I like a good act. Here's a man who tells you when he's dissimulating and is after anything but what he actually articulates. You take it as a joke, if you're dim. If clever, watch out!

'You come from Tyneside?'

'Born and bred at Percy Main.' That was essentially true. I didn't want to tell him – or anyone else – about pretty little Whalton, horse-riding, cocktail parties, problem parents. 'On the same ground as the plant. Saw them build it when I was a boy.'

'Kiddar's luck, eh? I was born at Hebburn, over the water. We've a lot in common. Got my chemical engineering qualifications at King's – Newcastle now.'

'I read English.'

'I helped to build the plant.' It was almost competitive.

'I know,' I said.

'They remember me?' he asked.

'As Roly-Poly, Mr Francis.'

He smiled fleetingly – and was it fondly? 'I lived at Tynemouth, in a house with a monkey puzzle tree in the garden. Something I'd always wanted. I liked my monkey puzzle tree. I like Tynemouth. A perfect setting for the tree. Grey but brand-new every day; a change from work and Percy Main.'

'Give me Percy Main.'

'A hotch-potch,' said Francis, wrinkling his nose.

'It's changed a lot since your day. They levelled the old houses and built a multi-level town beside the river. All the riverside's been grassed and there are lookout platforms. And a yachting club.'

'A good one? I used to sail myself.'

'Some of them look like windjammers.'

'And you worked with Snorry?' asked Francis. 'That would be quite an education. Snorry was the last of the cards –'

'You're not bad yourself,' I said sincerely.

He ignored this. Indeed, I thought it annoyed him. 'Why did you cover up his death the other night?'

'For several reasons,' I said. 'They happened to knit. I liked Snorry. I didn't want to confuse Mr Prinkstone. But I was still sore about Mr Snorry. He was a good man.'

'Goodness is the last thing I'd connect with Snorry,' said Francis.

'It was there, below the indolence.'

'And the self-indulgence,' chuckled Francis. 'He was idle, more idle than your present chief. And me, for that matter.'

'It was always fun working with him.'

'Oh, my God, you've got something there,' he said. 'I've been around with him. Could make the most innocent trip into a bacchanalia – never bought a woman in his life. They came with every breeze. They were waiting for him round every corner. I remember, we were at a conference . . .'

'Well?' I had to ask to bring him out of his reverie.

'We were at this conference and something had gone wrong with the booking. So Snorry and me shared a double room. Well, one night we turned in fairly early, but Snorry decided to have a bath. So off he went. I never heard him come back. Weeks later he told me how he'd walked into the bathroom and found a lady in the bath and not so many soapsuds either. "Hello," says he. "Hello," says she. It so happened they'd exchanged a word or two in the bar. "Mind if I wash my hands and face?" asked Snorry. "Not at all," says she. He bolted the door and washed in the hand-basin. "Let me wash your back," says he. "You're a gentleman," says she. So he did, and one thing led to another and in the end she told him that the key to the room was in her dressing gown.'

He sighed heavily. 'Snorry wasn't only a card. He was a man who rose to the occasion. Business or pleasure, but pleasure in particular. You're right, he was a good companion. Do you know, every time he was down we had a night on the town? Theatre, dinner, sometimes a club. But it could have been a walk through the park – I'd still have enjoyed it.' He looked at me. 'Company counts a lot in work. You've often wondered why I put up with Prinkstone. Well, he's mad. Or halfway there. But he's dam' good company. Then Crumple. He's the reverse. Crumple's no company at all. Yet I have to spend hours with the man.'

'Snorry never told me about you,' I said. 'I mean, about being friendly, meeting in Town.'

'And Snorry wouldn't tell you how often he talked about you down here,' he said. 'Snorry had a great liking for you, my lad.' I nodded. 'Snorry thought you were the cat's whiskers. He didn't rub it in. I suppose he reckoned that a couple of casual mentions a trip would do the trick.' He paused, with his eyes full on my face. 'It did.' His eyes became merry. 'Of course, a couple of other things have helped. You match up to his description. You –' he stopped short. 'No, I won't tell you that one.'

Emotion may have made my thank you sound a little ungracious. If so, he didn't seem to notice. Without changing his tone he continued: 'I like your work on the Hartlepools paper. You used all the wrong arguments. You shouldn't have isolated the case. But then you're young. Can't be expected to see what comes to an old 'un almost as second nature. That if you close one, you've got to close a lot. That if you go and close down a lot of potential you may be caught with your pants down. But you were right.'

'Thank you,' I said, nettled.

'Oh, you must accept what I've said in the spirit . . . The gift is intuition. But you must support the gift with facts, figures, a case; the full case.'

'I'll remember that.' Again he disregarded the irony.

'I'm sure you will. But that brings me to the point. I'd like you to work with me.'

'That's very nice of you,' I said.

'It isn't nice. Anyone who could stick old Snorry – four years was it –'

'Five and a half.'

'Well, five and a half, then, I'd have been impressed by a year, deserves watching. Crumple rather favours you, too.'

'Thank you again.'

'What intrigues me is – why?' Francis shook his head.

'Now come off it, don't sit there with your round eyes. Crumple's the perfect egocentric. He's his own sun, moon and stars rolled into one. If he favours you, it's for some very strong personal reason. Anything on him?' I smiled deliberately.

'You won't tell me, I know. So let me guess. You didn't catch him with his secretary on his knee. He doesn't know what it's for. Or rifling a safe or something. He's too much the fanatic. The only man I know who'd cheerfully dock his own wages to keep the company in the black. So what is it?'

'I'm waiting for you to tell me, sir,' I said interestedly.

'I'm getting round to it – playing for time to think. Look – I'm only talking to you like this because I'd like you on my side. I – er, rather like your cut, as they used to say up North. But I'd like to start with a clear sheet. You tell me.'

'If there *was* anything I wouldn't tell you,' I said.

'I bet he's made a deal with you!' said the Chairman merrily. 'The crafty old devil – but you weren't fool enough to accept?'

'Top people don't make deals with little middle people.'

Francis sighed. 'So you're not going to tell. Well, let me tell you. Crumple's an old woman. What's the old woman's fault – think?'

'You tell me,' I said.

'Young devil,' said Francis. 'You've got the fault. I've got it also. But we don't need to snoop around. We sniff it out of the air –' He leaned forward. 'Crumple has a passion for unconsidered bits of information – goes through drawers to get it.'

He sat down and turned his eyes reflectively to the ceiling, basking in my admiration. 'Now he wouldn't want to interrogate you or read your private letters upside down. He's not sharp enough to realise that the young dogs are worth tapping. And you've got a fix on him . . . You found him playing around my desk?'

I raised my eyebrows.

'I don't need a word from you, me lad, I know. Whenever I want Crumple to know something, I put it on paper and forget to lock the drawer. Always works. Nice to watch him the following day, waiting for me to bring it up, waiting for an opportunity to utilise his criminal omniscience.'

Cupping his face in his hands as he leaned on the desk he went on: 'But there's more to it than that. You didn't only catch him – you caught him with his trousers down. You caught him with his hand in that drawer.'

'You should have been a writer of detective stories,' I said sincerely.

Francis stood up and beamed. 'I like you. Wise to keep your mouth shut until you know which way the wind's blowing –'

'It can blow any way it likes for me,' I said.

'You're not bothered?' asked Francis. '*You* don't agonise about prospects, do you? – pray for a rise – dream of chairs?'

'Now you want me to boast,' I said. 'But it so happens, you're right.'

'Of course I am,' said Francis. 'You don't care a rap one way or another. All you want is your own way.'

'Not that simple.'

Francis subsided. 'No it isn't – life's a bugger.' The oath rocked me a little, it was somehow out of character. 'It is,' said Francis, answering my question. 'But one has to use strong words to shift stubborn boys. Look, in the old days you built your own machines, designed your own factory, ordered your own stuff, said anything from hello to bugger you to the workers. Matterless whether they said hello or bugger you back, one way or another. You could tell whether they liked you or hated your guts. Either way, you were operating. Today it's all remote control. Everything at second or third remove.'

I watched and listened.

'Well, what do you think?'

'You've got to use your imagination.'

'Distant friends, workers and customers . . . eh?'

'No. Listen to the business saying hello to its servants.'

Pointing dramatically to himself, Francis said: 'Me listen for that crap!'

'It's no more crap than the stuff they write in the business magazines.'

'You know it's all a game, then?' I nodded. 'That it's playing with us?'

'Well, I wouldn't say playing,' I said. 'In the sense of toying. Playing a game – y'know, like chess, or Canasta.'

'Do you know what I think?' asked Francis. His voice was low and a little embarrassed. 'This stuff about the Garden of Eden – do you read the Bible – and Adam and Eve getting the boot out of it? Well, I think we're looking for the system, we're building Eden again.'

'God,' I said.

'Hell's bells, you've taken it a step further than me. God,' muttered Francis. 'God. My God, we're not going to like it. Neither is He – the Other One, the Old Man.'

'Oh, He's out-dated,' I said, more confidently than I felt. He was using my lines. 'Don't worry, we'll build better next time. Any nonsense, and we'll put Him out of the Garden.'

'But what if He's the Garden?' I felt that slight but terrible shifting of the stomach.

'We've abolished God,' I said, feeling slightly silly. The room and his head were shrinking. Now his head detached and was floating away like a balloon, arms and legs drifting below like silly basket and ballast. It was as if a fantasy had come to life.

Behind the spectacles the eyes of Mr Francis glittered. 'Say we're building God in man's image – that right? – say we are, there'd be centuries of work in it. A big job and very attractive proposition for businessmen like us. Y'know, gives us what we've always wanted since the Victorian crack-up – an aim, a cause and a justification.'

'The man's a lunatic,' I thought.

'But what if it turned out to be a trap?'

'In what way?' I asked. I was sitting straight up, holding myself like a drunk, but from floating away, not falling. It was a very difficult exercise, and I was wishing my father was there, beside me, that rock of bigotry whom nothing could move.

'Well, perhaps we're not building God, perhaps we're only making Him a suit –'

'A what!'

'A new suit of clothes,' cried Francis. 'Maybe He's already measured Himself for it and maybe He's even tried it on. Then when the great day comes and we're in Eden again he'll just slip into it, and shuffle us out again. No, not that. We'll just up and out. I'll say one thing for man,' he concluded, 'he knows his place, and it isn't in the lap of God.'

He shook his head. It was a self-congratulatory movement. He was a boy, pleased with himself. 'Well,' he said. 'That was a jolly good discussion. I could do with more of that.'

Before he went he said, cryptically: 'I'll send for you when I'm ready.'

The encounter shook me. I know an act when I see one, and he wasn't acting. He really believed all this stuff. He'd that manic glitter my Uncle James' soap-box pals have in their eyes. The man was mad, and there was no one I could tell!

The Prinkstones invited me up to dinner. It was a good dinner – shoulder of mutton, oven-roasted, and rich mealy potatoes, a gravy against the world. There was a motherly woman who served. She was stout, clean, and had bleak, almost sinister, eyes. Waiting for dinner, Mr Prinkstone took me out into the solarium. There were midget palms and giant ferns, but no leopard. All London glowed fuzzily through the glass. I double-checked. There *was* no leopard. Mr Prinkstone took a bowl of corn and opened a door. A thousand starlings enveloped him. They swooped out of the night, perfectly timing the opening of the door. For a moment I thought it was an attack. They perched on his shoulders and clung all around his body. He stepped out into the garden on the roof and cast corn on the flower beds. The shy ones clustered on the ground; but a dozen or so stayed to feed out of his hands and from his lips. With glowing face he played with the mindless creatures. Some were as big as ravens. In the Bible a prophet was fed by birds such as these. It seemed more disturbing that Prinkstone should feed the birds. Their fixed alien eyes worried me, and I went back into the living room. I had also remembered the Chairman's tirade. I was sure I could trust Mrs Prinkstone.

She smiled as I told the story. When I'd finished she said: 'There are different kinds of madness.' She glanced towards the solarium.

'I don't deny that he's strange. But Mike Francis isn't – what would you say – well, madly mad. Every now and again he takes off the brakes. Wasn't Newton interested in finding a connection between the pyramids and the Book of Revelations? But Mike only takes it so far.'

'With Mr Prinkstone, too?' I asked.

She sighed. 'It can't do any harm. A harmless little conspiracy. A couple of people in the City know. So that they can disregard his instructions. Anyway, Mike has power of attorney. It keeps him happy.'

'He has his own brakes,' she said. 'It's when the brakes are gone –' She recovered herself. 'Mike's a poet. So are you. So let him find a new suit for God. You needn't be afraid. He'll turn the poetry into very businesslike propositions.'

Just before Mr Prinkstone came in from the solarium she said: 'I hope you have brakes as well. Don't go too far, dear boy.' In truth there was no need for the brakes. My fantasies had left me. Life itself was too full of something very like. So much so that I'd even stopped writing Messianic notes. Was I too in the heartland of a dream that had ruined Prinkstone – and was wearing down Francis? For I was not wholly convinced by her summing-up.

FOURTEEN

In the weeks that followed we observed a change in R. Walker Johnson. He walked vaguely along corridors and habitually collided with people. He would apologise and wander on his way to other collisions. The apologies were broken and unfinished and his words seemed to have travelled a very great distance. Visiting other offices he would leave a sentence unfinished and go visiting some unknown and secret place, in the spirit. In his own office he would sit, pretending to listen to you, tapping on the edge of his desk with his outspread fingers, eyes empty and upliftcd, as if playing a piano. A grand piano. But sending messages, not music, to a faraway destination.

At the beginning of the day he would sift through his post several times over with narrow, anxious eyes. Apparently he'd forgotten the formal language of business. Certainly he'd lost interest.

'Sometimes I sit for ages waiting for him to start dictating,' said Cathie. 'He looks so peculiar. Sometimes he looks at a letter and wrinkles his nose – as if it were a dirty piece of washing –'

'It's a new pose,' I said lightly. We were lovers and I resented even a mild concern for another.

'Last week I went in and found him sitting with his hands over his face. His eyes were shut. Then he opened them and looked at me, right between his fingers. Then he took his hands away . . .' She hesitated. 'I thought he was going to cry.'

'He's quite sensible?'

'There's no softening of the brain, if that's what you mean.' She hesitated. 'It's not his ability that's changed but his attitude.' Her voice dropped. 'His attitude is perfectly healthy. He's detached now. As you used to be, when you first came.'

'What do you mean?' I asked, offended.

'He's quite aware it's just a job, not a holy mission.'

'I haven't changed in that respect,' I said shortly.

She laughed. 'Listen to him! Strutting around like a little Napoleon!'

Picking up her bantering tone, I retorted: 'Not so dam' little!'

'Well, you strut. You go on like one of the elect. Like a man who knows he's going to win. As you are, but to what purpose –'

'I like my work,' I said.

'You like it all the time.'

'Not when I'm with you.'

'Oh yes,' she accused. 'You're never away from it. Once, you were detached and above it all. You laughed at the nonsense. Now you're part of it. And you never laugh. It would be blasphemy, wouldn't it?'

'I'll admit I'm more serious. We're doing an important job. People need food –'

'But not the kind of food you're feeding on. Why do you listen?'

'What do you mean – listen?' I said. But I knew what she meant. I'd an affection for the sounds of the building; lifts, telephones, typewriters – the ordinary noises which were apart but dictated by its needs. But beyond the trivial clatter was another noise. This was more than the infinitely small hum of power. It was the stirring of a presence. Of which I was part. And linked with Leviathan were people. Up above the prowling Prinkstone, kind and merciless, Francis with his touch of wildness – and Crumple, going down into the belly. So I listened. Sometimes I almost worshipped.

Crumple was given to ringing me at the end of the day when the building was clear. Hiding his face behind a telephone seemed to give him strength. Sometimes there would be long diatribes against Francis, or the rest of his colleagues. Sometimes he would talk about his life, as if at long last he was preparing an account.

'I was born in the Six Towns, y'know,' he would say. 'People say Five Towns but it's really Six. Bennett was to blame for that – you remember Bennett? Famous writer in his time. My father knew him. Father was society steward at the Big Chapel at Burslem, the one at the top of the hill, beside the conveniences –'

Not for a moment was I tempted to laugh.

'Father saw him. Little buck-toothed man, he said. Father worked at the sanitary fittings place. The big place. Lavatory pans and bowls. Funny when you think that I came to it in the end. I mean, the other end.

'I was ashamed. It's a long time ago but I remember being ashamed. The other kids used to hold their noses and pull an imaginary chain when I came along. The place was all soot and smoke in those days. Passed over it in a plane the other week. It's a big white city. They must have cleaned up when the smoke was gone. But you can still see the ashes and the pitheaps, some of them with trees growing . . .'

In the pause I attempted a small show of sympathy: 'You helped in all that.'

'I don't know. Sometimes I wish I'd gone into the works. Gone to chapel like my father, three times every Sabbath, joined the Freemasons. There's nothing to fall back on – here.'

'Oh, I wouldn't say that –'

'Nothing here. Nothing at all.'

But more often than not he would ask questions.

'Those people at Hartlepools still kicking up?'

'It seems to be dying.'

'I don't know. That sort of thing's a time-bomb. Mind you, I didn't realise . . . you know we discussed it?'

'Mr Small Summers told me about it.'

'Small Summers. What does he think?'

'He didn't like losing. But I wouldn't say there are any hard feelings.'

'It takes nerve to stand out one way or the other. I admire him for that. Takes equal nerve to say no.'

'Of course, sir.' The 'sir' indicated the birth of a little respect.

'The results are coming in. The computer investigation. Small plants, y'know. My father was a gardener. Great rose man. Pair of gloves and secateurs. Snip-snip-snip. It's the same with business. Or you're sunk. Too much dead wood. Not big bushes, healthy bushes, that's what we need.'

'It's a moot point, sir,' I said politely.

'Someone's got to do it. Bloody calculating machines they call us. Yet we give life.' I could think of nothing to say. 'Are you there? Have you seen Francis lately?'

'I spoke to him the other day.'

'Where – when?' I explained at length, with the feeling that I was being adjudged a liar. 'I suppose he made his impression. Bags of vitality. Bounces like a ball. The way he bounces his ideas. I'll bet he bounced some on you?'

'He did, as a matter of fact,' I said.

'And left you – flummoxed?'

'Well, a bit bewildered.'

'It's all a pose. Everything's a trick. Those silly paintings. Rubbing his hands. "What do you think about that?" What can you say if you don't know the lingo? Negative, he sneers. Positive, he gives you a haughty look. The kind that says you're putting on a front. And all this Biblical stuff. Texts from the Bible. He sits learning them off by heart, I'm sure, ready for a meeting. Doesn't mean anything. He looks and listens and reads, odd stuff, dredges it up. To enlighten? Not a chance. Just to fool . . . Are you still there?'

'Yes, Mr Crumple.'

'Did he drop any of that far-fetched stuff in your ears?'

'To be honest, I thought his ideas were a bit extraordinary. But he seemed to believe in them.'

Crumple snorted. 'You'll find out before you're much older.'

'I don't suppose he gives me a thought.'

'He does, he will. Give him his due –' In that last sentence there was the most intense loathing and disgust and, possibly, fear. 'Has he mentioned Sahara?'

'No,' I said, transferring the telephone from one ear to the other. 'We talked about anything but business.' I thought I was telling the truth.

'Did he mention me?'

'You, sir?' I asked, vaguely remembering some mention of Crumple and playing for time. 'I don't recall –'

'About a mistake – an error?' he asked.

'Well, we all make mistakes –'

'Not from where I am now you don't,' said Crumple. 'Not when

216

you've been riding high. Everybody makes mistakes in business. I've been more careful than most and I've still made a few in my time. I had an expensive training . . .'

'And this one's like all the rest.'

'You don't understand me,' said Crumple. '*He* made me make this mistake. That's the difference. That's the unforgivable thing. He got me down and I know he can do it again. That's worse than his disliking me and hounding me. If only you could see him as I see him! Yet the business needs me. He needs me. He needs me to hate . . .'

'I think you're exaggerating, sir,' I said, adding the 'sir' out of compassion.

'You think so? You think it's just play-acting? Perhaps you're right. I'll give him a fright one of these days, call his bluff . . .'

'Yes?' I asked.

His voice became suddenly cunning. 'No, I'll not tell you.' I thought that was the end, then suddenly he was off on another tack. 'I suppose you're wondering why I'm unburdening my soul? It's because I don't care any longer, and I've a little bit of a feeling for you. I want to warn you. Keep a little bit of life. Are you married?' I indicated not. 'When you are married, keep your vows. Don't give yourself up to business . . .'

'I'll try,' I said.

'My father used to say that you worked to live and not the other way round. He wasn't the sort of man to say much, but d'you know what – I never took a single thing he said to heart. The one about work, for instance. I'm just learning now. That's why I'm telling you.' His voice took on urgency. 'You could easily broadcast everything I've said –' He ignored my protests. 'You might at that. Well, I don't care. I'm weary with seeing it done. I've done it myself, it's quite easy. But in the end it sticks, comes back to you in the end, years after, when you'd think there was no reason to remember. Well, tell it around if you like, I don't care. For one thing –'

Wearily, I changed the telephone over to the other ear again. Now both my ears felt as if they had been hammered continually. So did my mind.

After the interval I heard Crumple's voice again. It was as if I'd never removed the telephone: ' . . . touched bottom, you start rising again. You could go on sinking, y'know. It's a relief to touch bottom and feel yourself moving up into daylight. And he's not a shark – can't literally eat you up.'

What *was* he talking about? His voice had suddenly become quite cheerful. 'You can tell him this, if you like . . . I don't mind. I'm actually looking forward to living again.'

'Mr Francis has nothing to do with that,' I said, quite firmly. For a moment only I was pleased with myself. It was like a return to my old form. Then I realised I was pitying Crumple because Crumple had given up the ghost and was almost gone. It was security, not form, that had led me to speak my mind. 'Well, thanks,' said Mr Crumple. The click was a token he'd hung up, but I continued holding the earpiece in position. I couldn't believe that it was all over. I was just a little stupefied. In the old days a man asked for a move from the blast, or the coalface, or put away his gun for ever, and thanked his lucky stars that loss of nerve hadn't been accompanied by lack of luck.

Although the line was dead it continued to talk, carrying the tick of my wrist-watch and also faint crackling noises that might have been a shifting of the tiny particles in the instrument. The line crept. I put the telephone into its cradle. It lay there, prone, which is to say face downwards. Like the fighting part of Crumple. I would sometimes think of Crumple when looking at telephones in days to come. A telephone and fear of defeat. My defeat.

Swearing, I picked it up again, and dialled Crumple's number. There was no ringing tone. The old devil had taken it off. He wasn't risking any after-wit. Game to the end. The last word.

'I think you're a bloody old fool,' I said loudly into the mouthpiece. 'Ever heard of staying power? Just last out and you'll turn the table without even trying.'

It was a Spring morning about six months after my arrival and one of the mighty was confiding to me the successive stages of his dissolution. It seemed like a dream. Perhaps it *was* a dream. One thing I know. That very morning Mr Crumple sat down and penned his resignation. His hand was small and neat, each letter perfectly formed, yet he wrote at great speed. His secretary took it over to the Chairman's office. Mr Crumple laughed as he handed it to her: 'You needn't wait for an answer,' he said. Now she was sure he was mad. Within minutes Mr Francis himself burst into Crumple's room. 'What on earth's all this about?' he roared.

'It's all in writing,' said Mr Crumple mildly.

'I'm not accepting it,' said Mr Francis.

'But you must accept,' said Mr Crumple with very great firmness. 'You mustn't look a gift horse in the mouth.'

Mr Francis was not to be drawn. Seating himself he waved the paper. 'You say here that you were responsible for a major mistake in policy. Let me tell you that you weren't. All of us were – or haven't you heard of the doctrine of collective responsibility?' He sat back triumphant.

'But I was the man that pushed it,' said Crumple, adding, 'not without some overt help.'

'Then all the more fools us, if we accepted it against our better judgement,' said Francis. 'As it was, we accepted the very good arguments you put up. Who were we to know that the Sahara deal would come off at last – or the Russian business?'

'You'd a good idea yourself,' said Crumple cuttingly.

'Had I?' said Mr Francis. 'On my heart, I'd no more idea than the rest of you. No, you're not resigning. What d'you think we'd do without your cold old antiseptic eye, eh?'

'Say what you like,' said Crumple, 'I'm going.' Francis walked over to his waste-paper basket and deliberately tore up the paper.

'I can always write another one,' said Crumple.

'Then I'll keep you busy writing them,' said Mr Francis, turning on all his considerable charm.

'You've kept me busy as it is,' said Mr Crumple.

'Ah, so that's it,' said Francis. He pondered.

'It's not often you're lost for a reply,' said Mr Crumple.

'You're right,' said Francis, smiling. 'But then, it's not often I'm in this position. Trying to convince a man who's determined not to be convinced. I suppose you're thinking of that unfortunate little mix-up when you suspected Marshall and me of having some fun at your expense –'

'I'm not,' said Crumple firmly. 'I'm referring to the mystery of your attitude to me. The thing with Marshall was only a symptom. You've changed your attitude to me. In simple human terms you dislike me almost to the point of hatred –'

'Good God!' said Mr Francis. 'You know my failings. I'm a bit of a jester I know, but hatred –'

'You don't like it when you see it face to face,' said Crumple. 'I thought it was over long ago.' Mr Francis looked at him. 'You rode me when you first came. No, don't deny it. Almost as if you resented my having been here since the beginning – since Prinkstone's day –'

'Ah, Prinkstone!' said Francis. Crumple waited expectantly, but Francis remained silent.

'Then it blew over,' said Mr Crumple. 'We were on good terms. Then you changed. Oh yes! I've been at the receiving end and I know it. You attack my dignity . . . I'm a man, Francis. I do have a sense of dignity and pride. I've invested a lot in this business and your treatment's a poor return . . .'

'And what of poor Prinkstone?' asked Mr Francis quietly.

'What had Prinkstone to do with it?' asked Crumple petulantly. Mr Francis shook his head.

'That's not the question,' he said. 'What had you to do with Mr Prinkstone? He had his dignity. He had his pride. They were taken from him. What had you to do with that?'

'Prinkstone has nothing to do with the point,' said Crumple. 'I worked with him, of course. What happened to Prinkstone was his own fault entirely. Indeed, had it not been for me he wouldn't have come out so nicely – he's sitting very comfortably up there, you know.'

'Without his dignity,' said Mr Francis.

'I have nothing to do with that,' said Mr Crumple, his voice rising. 'If you considered my behaviour at the time of the takeover less than honourable you should have had it out long before now. As it is, what happened so long ago shouldn't have any bearing on our relationship now. I mean your positive and active dislike of me – suddenly flaring up – pushed to the extreme – making me a butt among my colleagues . . .' His voice tailed away.

'You mean you can't stand my not liking you?' said Mr Francis, calmer now. His expression was worried. 'I wish you hadn't said all this. Puts a different complexion on everything. I mean . . . men can differ about policy and still manage to get along. But feelings of this nature . . .' He sighed.

'Your feelings!' said Crumple.

'My supposed feelings,' corrected Mr Francis. 'Out in the open. Made an issue. Puts a different complexion on things.' Bending down he picked up the pieces of Mr Crumple's resignation then let them slip one by one through his fingers. 'What do you want me to do, Crumple?'

'Tell me what's biting you. Tell me you were wrong – or tell me you were sorry. Then we can get back to the old easy way.'

Mr Francis exploded. 'My God! Now I know what you're after! You're not just attempting to call my bluff with a piece of paper. You're trying to get me down. It won't wash.' His face hardened. 'I tore that thing up because you're a good finance man and I need you – but only as a subordinate.'

Mr Crumple was quivering with passion. 'An equal. An equal. Not a subordinate. You're getting at me because of Prinkstone, I know. Because you're afraid –'

'Quiet, quiet,' said Francis. His voice was easy, good-humoured. He looked straight at Mr Crumple. 'If you still feel like resigning then write it out and I assure you it'll go straight to the Board. Otherwise we continue. As colleagues. Business colleagues. Understand?'

There was silence. It was only after a few minutes that Miss Cummings in the outer office realised that Mr Francis had gone. As she related the story to Mrs Arcot: 'That was the frightening bit. If he'd banged the door shut it would have been all right in the end. But he closed it. That's the time to watch the Chairman – when he's quiet.' But this came out much later, after Crumple had taken his pride to the irrevocable edge.

Elsewhere in the building reconciliation of one kind or another was in the air. I had won the respect of my staff. Small Summers liked me, or liked my advice. I was in and out of his office so much that it took all my skill to keep on good terms with jealous Mrs Arcot. Holinshed worked quietly away and seemed to live only for his weekends, when he spent at least one afternoon with his children. His mother-in-law was on his side and had told him that a reconciliation was only a matter of time. As for his affair with Cathie – having supplanted him I was content not to think of that.

I was in love and was almost content. I have to say 'almost' because of my feeling that our relationship was almost too good to last. But having it made me patient.

With R. Walker Johnson, for instance, who was considering his salvation and seeking advice. One day he told me: 'I'd a great-uncle who helped to found the ILP, you know.'

'ILP?' I asked. 'Ah, yes. Independent Labour Party.'

'You know all about the ILP,' said R. Walker Johnson reproachfully. 'I'll surprise you. Before that, he was in the Salvation Army. Helped to run a Land Settlement Scheme for General Booth. My father was more introspective. He joined the Christian Scientists. All hell was let loose when I had to have my appendix out. Considered it a slur on his spiritual progress. Wouldn't allow any of us to talk about Roman Catholics, thought it would expose us all to emanations.'

'My grandfather was one,' I said rapidly. 'I used to go to the Pentecostals. Speaking in tongues used to fascinate me. Did it myself after a long time and a lot of dithering. They didn't like it. I was 12 at the time. Chap with a wing collar carried me out. I remember his collar points scratched. I stood on the pavement and told him to go to hell. He was weeping with passion.'

'Religion should be taken seriously,' said R. Walker Johnson.

'Religion's all right until they all get together – the religious,' I said. 'Then it becomes comical.'

'I've been to the Friends, once or twice,' said R. Walker Johnson, shifting uncomfortably. 'But it's deadly dull. Like a hospital. Then I met this chap who teaches a new philosophy – it's a comprehensive sort of thing; dancing, praying, meditation, the lot.'

'Plenty of scope, eh?'

'It's exciting, exciting,' said R. Walker Johnson. 'This isn't power, y'know,' he continued with an expressive wave of hand and shirt-cuff. I stared. The shock was not in his words. His cuffs were filthy. 'I'm tempted to give up everything, every blessed thing. Marriage, career – I've given most of my records away, they're useless too. Time's too short as it is.'

'I agree,' I said. 'But only on the point of time.'

'I've chucked all my books out,' continued Walker Johnson

exultantly. 'So much lumber. Two or three volumes do me, now. Gurdjieff, Orage, Ouspensky; I can't eat for reading. I'm exploring every living moment.'

'You mentioned your marriage?'

'She went when I sold the records,' said Walker Johnson, staring blankly over my shoulder. 'Well, no use crying over spilt milk.'

'The records – she went because you sold your records?'

'Well, not really the records; the records were simply an excuse,' explained Walker Johnson. 'And, actually, she left the week before I sold them.'

'Oh, I see,' I said.

'Very practical woman,' continued Walker Johnson. 'Said it was all right selling them. But what about when we wanted them back . . . It would cost the earth. She was irritable all the week,' he said, still evidently trying to puzzle it out. 'I told her we wouldn't want them again. If anything that seemed to make her even more irritable. Then she exploded. I'd been talking about the meaning of colours, the *real* meaning, of course, and she said: "It's a lot of bosh, Josh. You've reverted to type, like that British Israelite father of yours." My father was really a Christian Scientist but she would insist on calling him a British Israelite,' he unnecessarily explained. 'A strict man. We quarrelled. I'm saying "was" – he's still alive. Haven't seen him for eight or nine years. Wasn't at my wedding. Kept mother away too.'

'I knew a chap whose father was a Plymouth Brethren member – no smoking, drinking, no television. Used to go six or seven times a week to the chapel,' I interjected with glazing eyes.

'Father's place was on top of a shop,' said Walker Johnson. 'Three times on Sunday. But he was satisfied if I went to one on Sunday and to one of the weekday meetings. That wasn't bad at all,' he explained. 'I mean, you could cheat in the meeting, day-dream, sleep or read the hymn book. But it was terrible at home. His friends used to come in. There was an ironmongery man called Stubbs and a schoolmaster, I've forgotten his name, was it Lancing? We had to sit and listen to all this nonsense, mother and me.'

'*That's* what your wife meant, then?'

'But this is quite different,' said Walker Johnson. He sighed. 'It

223

was the name that showed me she meant business . . . her using my first name.'

'Ah, yes,' I said, but I didn't. I'd been thinking of the volcanic stuff that lay beneath the ordinary-type skin of people. 'The name – Ah, I see. Your first name. Did you say Josh?'

I felt a stirring of excitement.

R. Walker Johnson leaned over his desk. 'Since my days here are numbered – and I've got over it now, anyway – I don't mind telling you. It's Joshua.'

'Ah, yes, Joshua,' said I. 'But wait a minute. Your initial's "R", surely?'

R. Walker Johnson smiled. 'It's a long story. It was always Joshua, at home and at school. There was a form-master, Routledge, who took a fiendish delight in calling me "Joshua". Mother called me "Joshua". Father, I can still hear his voice: "Are you ready, Joshua?" But Routledge was a swine. He'd a long Saxon nose and thin, bitter lips, and he'd say: "Joshua, your Latin's an insult to your school and your form. March against it, man, what you need is application, not trumpets" – he meant that the Latin was my walls of Jericho.

'I was sick and tired of the name by the time I left school. People used to sing that song . . . So I decided to get rid of the name. I suppose I could have left the initial letter, indeed, I did, for a time. But it stood there like a threat. I couldn't bear to write even the initial. So I changed it to R. Devious of me, wasn't it?'

'Extraordinary. I had trouble with mine. Especially when they gave it full value. And there used to be a thing they shouted after me – "Sam, Sam, the crazy man, washed his head in the frying pan" – but I got over it.'

'It was more than the name,' said R. Walker Johnson. 'It was the old man and those dreary meetings. Listening to all those lunacies. But I'm cured now.'

Looking me straight between the eyes, he said: 'And I'm not referring to the name business. Cured is a word that encompasses everything. You too can be cured.' Somehow it wouldn't have been so bad if he'd ranted like all the other fanatics. Instead, he spoke mildly, but with complete conviction, and the uncomfortable thing was that he seemed to be convinced that I was one who needed curing. 'I'm detached, now,' he said, in a matter-of-fact tone. 'And you're the one, you know. You started me. I used to envy you. Bluntness, courage, light-heartedness. But now I've got real detachment.'

'I always thought it was something really outrageous,' I said, referring to the hidden Christian name. 'Something like Rahab or Rastus or Revelation.'

'Revelation Walker Johnson?' said the Deputy Controller, shaking his head. 'No, give my father credit. There's a sort of lunatic rightness about Joshua Walker Johnson. He proudly flashed his filthy cuffs. 'But you're changing the subject. Now I'm really detached. I'd have died once rather than walk in wearing these.'

'It's all rather juvenile,' I said, angrily and for no apparent reason.

'I dare say it is from your side of the table,' said Walker Johnson mildly. 'You contract out a little bit at a time. It's fun.'

He had rocked me with his 'your side of the table'. It seemed to me that in the few months since our first interview in that room the tables had been completely turned. I didn't like it.

We talked about him that evening. 'He's quite a pet, now,' said Cathie. 'He's still trying, but this time he knows he's funny and pathetic. It's odd watching a man grow a sense of humour.'

'And watching another man lose it,' I said

'You said it, dear Sam,' she said.

'I wonder you bother with me.' I was still sore with that little bit of self-revelation in Walker Johnson's office. We had dined and were walking by the river. Soon I would see her on the train to Hammersmith and the friends I was never to meet. Perhaps that was my trouble.

'I can't help myself,' she said, drawing me into one of the riverside lookout points and putting her arms around my neck. 'You're my magnetic mountain. You're the rock I'm drawn to –' Kissing me lightly she walked away. 'Even although you haven't a harbour for me and I'll surely be wrecked.'

'You'll be wrecked real tenderly,' I jested.

'Be serious. I mean it. I can't marry you, that's the trouble.'

'Who said marry?'

She put a finger over my lips, smiled and said: 'You haven't asked me yet, but you will. And that's what I'm afraid of.'

'All right, then,' I recklessly said. 'I'm mad about you and this is the proof. Marry me. Or tell me what's to stop us.'

'Your religion.'

I was astonished. 'My religion – don't be silly. You're the religious member of the family, you're –' At her look I stopped.

'I mean you've sold out. In the last few weeks – I don't know when but between one day and the next you sold out to the business or the building, or both. You've suddenly meshed, like a busy little silkworm working away in the mulberry bush . . .'

'What's wrong with taking one's work seriously?' I asked.

She shrugged. I saw that her gaze was over my shoulder. 'You tell me. I don't know. Unless it's the old story of the man who sold his soul to the Devil – in modern dress, fifteen storeys high, with a computer in the basement and a lunatic on top.'

'I suppose you've been talking to your confessor,' I sneered.

She shook her head. 'This time I didn't need help. And I'm not enrolled. As always, I'm only on the sidelines.'

'I'm not all that bad,' I cried. I was perplexed. What else could I offer her? 'One doesn't need to be religious to be good.'

She stroked my cheek. 'That's what makes it so difficult. You're kind, gentle and detached. I couldn't trust my children to a detached sort of father.'

'Then we won't have children.'

'That's why I can't marry you. You can say that and mean it.'

I felt like a man lost in a maze. 'I'll withdraw what I said. About children. I couldn't refuse you anything.' She stroked my cheek. 'Oh, Sam, it's so difficult! You think you're all right. You say and do all the right things. But can't you see that I must have a whole man in my house? Not something that's left over from the mulberry bush . . . or will be, as time goes on.'

Thinking of my relationship with the building I said: 'I see what you mean. You're thinking I'm going to become a kind of zombie. I'll admit it's possible. I'll try not to be. And you could take me on trust.'

'Ah, but I know you,' she said

'Take me on trust.'

226

'Then I'll be wrecked again,' she said.

'Again?' I asked. I was shocked. I had managed to forget Holinshed.

She moved under my grip. 'Not Holinshed,' she murmured. 'That was – a kind of indulgence. I knew he'd go back to his wife. I knew I wasn't in any danger there. But I've been in love to the point of marrying before, you know.' She released herself again. I let her go. 'When you've seen obsession at work – it's worse than apathy. I'm not peculiar, Sam.' She came against me and laid her cheek against mine. But the salt was still alive in the wound. My besetting sin is that I want everything new. If that is impossible, the illusion. She had broken that. I saw her on the Tube. She waved as the train moved away. We both knew that the distance between us could be no greater than it was already.

I went home unfulfilled and unhappy. Esther was in the kitchen making coffee. I'd intended to make my own. 'I'll bring you a cup,' she said. I nodded and went back to my own room. I looked at a book, put on a record, threw off my jacket, then sat and worried about Cathie. I didn't know what I was doing until Esther came in with the coffee. 'Making sure you're really here?' she asked. Following her look I discovered that I was massaging my arms. 'Trouble?' she asked. My body turned to stone and my arms went like old putty.

'Tell me if it'll help,' she said. After a moment she turned away. 'Sorry I asked. I didn't realise it was so serious.'

'Bring your coffee,' I said.

Glancing at me, she said: 'Better not. We don't want trouble.'

'I don't know what the hell you're talking about.'

Smiling maliciously: 'You can't believe there's something you can't have.'

That hurt. Looking her up and down, I said: 'I'm sleeping with her.'

'You're mad about her, but she won't marry you. Is that it?'

'That's about half of it,' I said.

She shook her head mockingly: 'What an end for the great philanderer! When at last he's serious the woman turns him down.'

'You'd better go and get your coffee,' I said. 'In your own room.'

'Oh, to hell with you – and I hope she doesn't change her mind,' she said, sweeping past me. I remember she was wearing a red dressing-gown.

'Of course not. That'll leave the field clear for you,' I said. Without stopping she landed me on the side of the face, right down the jaw-line. It brought the tears to my eyes. I caught hold of the dressing-gown. I pulled it and it came away. There wasn't time to appreciate the low-cut night-gown. She came at me spitting fire, fortunately with fists, not nails. In the end I pinioned her on the floor. She began to cry. I was over her, kneeling. 'You shouldn't get rough,' I complained.

'I miss you,' she said. But I didn't see the tears for what they were. Her body was heaving below the thin stuff.

'Don't look at me like that,' she said. 'Sam – let me go.'

I released her wrists and took hold of the gown at her shoulders. The thin material shrieked. She beat me on the face. I took her where she lay, on the floor. After a while she stopped talking. It was the next best thing to murder. Yet she cradled my head when it was over.

So I slept that night. I had a dream. It was the last but one and it was the most vivid I ever had. In my dream I stood with a companion in a shabby old-fashioned bedroom. There was a brass bed with a mound in the middle. By the sound the man in the bed was dying. Shadowy figures watched around the bed, people passed in and out of the room, but we were ignored. At a distance from the dying man I talked with a young blade who was sometimes separate in identity and sometimes disturbingly myself. He raved.

'I said I'd bring him down. When I was a boy I used to tell them that I'd find a mighty arch, or a statue straddling the sea from Gibraltar to the African coast, and pull it down . . .'

'But you pulled down a man,' I said.

'I told my sister,' he said, ignoring me, 'I told her then. Look out, history, I said, for the whole wide world will resound with my name.' There was something familiar about his face. I questioned him. 'Surely you're the splendidly mounted horseman who sat his steed like a centaur as he careered down Pennsylvania Avenue?' My speech was thick. As I was saying them I thought how stilted the words were.

'The very man!'

228

'But the soft hat and gold-mounted riding whip – where are they?'

'Lost. But I still have my pistol and dagger. And the spurs, one of which caught on the curtain of the theatre and rended it apart.'

Now I knew the man and the deed. 'You must escape!'

'Time enough.' Walking over to the bed he looked down at the hollow, bearded face. The watchers ignored him. 'Death suits him. He was made for the assassin.'

'It's a good face.' I was standing beside him.

'Coarse – the face of a labouring man, or a man labouring in death.' He laughed.

'On such a night as this the lilac was created,' I said to him – to myself. He was gone. Leaving, he had murmured:

'See, the world's arch is pulled down!'

The breathing had stopped.

As I looked the face of Lincoln dissolved and became the face of my father. A small man with deep-set eyes said: 'Take this man.' About him was the smell of lilacs. Not to be too clever the actors were John Booth and myself, or Booth/me; Lincoln breathing his last and his Secretary of War, Edwin M. Stanton. At the time I made no attempt to interpret the dream. The sense of loss continued. Lincoln was dead, my own father was alive, yet I still felt a sense of loss. And guilt. Guilt for him. Guilt for Esther. Guilt for Cathie.

I should have known I was going to see my father. Not the morning after the dream, but the morning of the second day, I'd a letter. Short, as usual. He was coming to London for some kind of conference, and could he lunch or dine with me? Settling for lunch, the shortest of the two choices, would be much too obvious. I wrote and said dinner. Invisible gates closed around me; five minutes after throwing my answer into the out-tray I was sent for by Mr Francis.

I'll swear he'd just had a shower. There was a dewy freshness about his face. Leaning back in his chair: 'I won't beat about the bush. The time has come.'

'Ah, yes,' I murmured disinterestedly.

'Exultant underneath,' accused Mr Francis. 'Palpitating with excitement, swelling with pride, rosy with joy.'

'Of course I'm pleased,' I said, saying goodbye to freedom.

He grimaced. 'Don't rob me of *my* pleasure.'

'All right,' I said. 'I'm quietly and confidently warm inside. But I don't trust good fortune, and that's a fact. What's the move, Mr Francis?'

'You can take your pick.' He beamed. 'Walker Johnson's leaving. You can have his job. Or you can sit at my right hand.'

'I'll take the first,' I said in a flash.

'Oh – why?'

'Because I want to be as near boss of my own show as possible.'

'You'd get more experience with me,' he said.

'I have my own store,' I said.

'You don't want to take me as a carbon copy?'

'I'll take a hint. No more.'

'You'll have Small Summers to deal with, y'know.'

'Yes, sir. But I know what he wants.'

'What's that?'

'Someone to ease the horsework from his shoulders.'

'I suppose he told you this?'

'He didn't have to tell me. I know.'

He nodded approvingly. 'You have the gift all right.'

'Gift?' I knew, but I wanted to hear him say it aloud.

'Of perception. Knowing when to circumnavigate, when to set for a collision course, knowing when to wait. And knowing for sure.'

There was nothing to say to this.

'Well, that's fine, fine,' said Francis, rising.

'And thanks for giving me the choice.'

'There wasn't a choice,' he said flatly. 'Sitting on my right-hand was only a try-on. Any response in that direction and I'd have found an excuse to shunt you in another direction. But it was only to make sure.'

'You knew it would be otherwise?'

'I was pretty sure.' He shook hands. 'Now run along – oh wait a minute.' He pondered. Then he smiled. I didn't like the smile. 'Tell you what, pop into Crumple's office and tell him the good news. You are by way of being a protégé of his.'

'I'd rather not,' I said.

'Why?' The question came sharp.

'I don't know.'

'Ah! you don't trust me!' I smiled. He looked injured. 'I must say, I never suspected you were so cynical. Crumple, Small Summers and myself are at least alike in one respect; we like to know we can pick the winners. It's part of the fun in the job, looking out for the promising selling platers . . .' He smiled benignly. 'Once you've got them into your stable . . .' He paused to allow his smile to enrich. 'You can make sure they'll win all along the way.'

'Did you tell Mr Small Summers?' I pressed.

'Of course. And persuaded him to allow myself the joy of telling you. Big man, Small Summers – never stands on his dignity.'

He was steering me to the side door. 'All right, then. I'll tell Crumple. But you'll come with me. It'll be fun.' I held the two doors open and followed him into the corridor but somehow our positions were changed in the short distance from his to Crumple's door. I led the way in – after knocking, of course. It was obvious that this was what the strange man Francis wanted. It was difficult to escape his rule.

He boomed: 'Hope we're not interrupting, Crumple. You know Rowlands?'

'You leave me no choice, Chairman,' said Mr Crumple. With a cool look in my direction. 'Yes, I know Rowlands.' He turned to Miss Cummings. 'You may go, Sally.'

Something seemed wrong. First, I decided, it was that Mr Crumple had called his secretary by her Christian name. Later I learned he'd taken to this from the day his resignation had been offered and declined. But there was something else as well. His desk was piled high with documents. Francis didn't seem to notice a marked coldness in Crumple. 'Spring-cleaning, eh?' he said with a glance at the desk.

'You might call it that,' said Crumple.

'Well, here's another bit of it. You'll be glad to know that Rowlands is taking over as assistant to Small Summers.'

'Subject to ratification by the Board, of course,' said Crumple, showing his teeth.

'But of course,' said Francis. 'This is in advance of the red tape.

As you and I are in loco parentis – thought it'd be a good idea to celebrate a kind of coming-of-age.'

'Of course, congratulations,' said Mr Crumple. He didn't offer to shake my hand.

'You're not in good fettle this morning,' stated Francis genially. 'Well, we all get these feelings – all flesh is grass, etc.'

'Not in good fettle for Biblical quotations,' said Crumple, with a shudder. He opened an imitation Jacobean cocktail cabinet. 'We must have a drink on it, Chairman,' he said over his shoulder. Holding up a bottle of whisky he said: 'You see, Rowlands, I know what you like.'

'Not quite,' I croaked. Already I'd a feeling that the celebration wasn't going to work out quite as Francis had planned.

'Sorry about that,' he said. He seemed suddenly quite happy. Pouring with a steady hand he handed us our glasses. 'A toast seems in order,' he said. 'Something Biblical, eh, Chairman?'

'If you can manage it,' said Mr Francis, suddenly suspicious. I congratulated myself on having the sharper nose. Mr Crumple sauntered over to his desk. I'll swear he had it written down. 'Ah yes, bones, dry bones.' He raised his glass. 'To our young friend when he finds himself in the valley of dry bones – how does it go . . .'

Looking at Francis I held my breath. His face was expressionless, but I fancied he had it at the tip of his tongue. 'Ah, yes. "And, behold, there were very many in the open valley: and lo, they were very dry."' He looked at Mr Francis. 'Highly appropriate toast, eh? Dryness. Best way to deal with bones is to bury them I suppose.'

'Of course, in the end,' said the Chairman. His finger went to his lip.

'You haven't drunk to the toast,' said Crumple.

'In a minute when I've completed it for you,' said Francis. His face was beaming. 'Doesn't it go on to say: "Behold I will cause breath to enter into you, and ye shall live; And I will lay sinews upon you, and will bring up flesh upon you, and cover you with skin, and put breath in you, and ye shall live; and ye shall know that I am the Lord."'

There was a crash of glass. Fine splinters glittered at the foot of the window, bright against the peacock carpet, not far from where Mr Francis was standing. 'Pity there isn't a fireback,' said Crumple. 'Always wanted to do that, ever since I saw it in a film.'

'A fine dramatic finale for the toast,' said Mr Francis.

'Not quite,' said Mr Crumple, lifting his head. 'You quoted the text but you didn't hear what was said – "And ye shall know that *I* am the Lord."'

'Unmasked,' said Francis, dropping his arms in mock despair.

'As must we all in time, if only to ourselves,' said Crumple. Going behind his desk he started pulling drawers and sorting papers. Some he stacked to the left and some to the right.

'There's plenty of time for that,' said Francis mildly. 'Wouldn't it be better to discuss the practical arrangements?'

'I've drafted a note for the Secretary suggesting the final financial set-up. Naturally my shares will be on offer. I think you'll find everything in order.'

'I'm sure,' said Francis. 'What finally decided you?'

'What you said about Prinkstone,' said Mr Crumple. 'I knew there was a reason for this harrying. As you probably know, I've been up to see him – the man's obsessed. And you're infected as well. So I decided it was no use clinging. Incompatability's one thing. Madness is another. I'm clearing out.'

'God help us,' said Mr Francis. 'Don't tell me you mean it! Throwing everything up – all this?'

Mr Francis sat pensive by the window, the light glancing from his glasses and pink, bald head. Mr Crumple shrugged himself into his raincoat and picked off his bowler. He gave it a critical examination then put it firmly back on the stand. 'That's the end of that as well,' he said. 'I'll get one of those straw things when we reach Spain.'

'This is very sad,' said Mr Francis.

'Isn't it?' said Mr Crumple. 'But I expect we shall all recover. In God's good time. Goodbye.' He went out.

'A well-timed exit,' said Mr Francis a little later. 'You know, I suppose I was a little infected. Prinkstone had it in for him. I wish I knew what they said to each other. Now I shall never know.' I said that Mr Prinkstone would tell him. He gave me a whimsical glance, the kind I remembered from boyhood, but made no comment.

'Crumple was always rather an unpleasant kind of man,' he mused. 'I suppose I did go for him. But now I like him – I wonder why?' He was talking to himself and I thought it better not to try an answer. Later I was glad. There was no guarantee at all that I knew precisely the nature of the question he had asked himself.

FIFTEEN

The news of Crumple's walkout soon got around. As it generally does the story rose from the bottom upwards – Crumple told Henry, his driver, on the third leg of a rather complicated journey home to his wife and three unmarried daughters at Putney. His driver said he was so drunk as to be almost human. The big wave of joy in the letting of blood welled upwards and met the other wave coming down from the executive suite. No one was sorry. But all were grateful. It gave vent to pity at cost price. It was a reminder that success also has its hazards, and that failure at least gives a continuing peace of mind. Many, I know, felt suddenly glad to be small, dull, and working within the comfortable margin of an uninspired competence.

Going down in the lift a little late, because I was dining with my father, I'd an exchange with Herbert the lift boy.

'They tell me it was you that gave him the knock.'

'I wouldn't say that,' I said. 'I'm only very small fry, you know.'

'You were there, though.'

'I was in at the death,' I said, and it occurred to me that if Crumple had had any spirit he'd have shot Mr Francis dead and then cut his throat. We're a dull lot today.

'Henry – that's his driver as was – he's been telling the tale that you was a kind of secret agent, sorta spy . . .'

'That's a lie,' I calmly said.

'Reckons his old man told him.'

'It was a misunderstanding on his part.' For the first time in our acquaintance I was wishing myself out of his company. 'I was

235

simply a witness.'

'How did he take it?' asked Herbert. The lift had clicked to a standstill but he had his hand on the door and with no intention of opening it until he'd got what he wanted. And what he wanted was a little bit distasteful – to me.

'How did who take it?' I fenced.

'Mr Crumple, of course.'

'He was as happy as Larry,' I said, suddenly remembering Mr Francis' face as he sat by the window. 'But I hope I shall never see anything like it again.'

'But you said he was happy?' persisted Herbert. I kept quiet.

'It's a lot of crap about you latchin' on the poor old bastard,' said Herbert, and I felt suddenly grateful. 'I know them, I knows their ways. Bloody lunatics.' That dropped me, being one of them.

'You're a wise man, Herbert,' I said.

At my own level I was conscious of an uneasy feeling. Holinshed would fall silent. I would catch him studying my face. Wills was subdued; fear had sapped his natural vindictiveness. I was, after all, the hatchet man. The talk about Crumple's departure went on all around me. Only Cathie drew me into it. Over coffee when we were lunching out one day she said, with a hint of malice: 'Rampion's nicknamed you "the Finger".'

I told her the story of Crumple frozen in the act of rifling the Chairman's drawer. She laughed. She said it was incredible. 'You do tell a good story.'

'You're the first I've told.'

'Of course.' She looked me squarely in the eye, and I was comforted.

'Francis had known for years. He may even have used his failing – planting things, y'know. At the same time . . .'

'Go on,' she said.

'Francis cross-examined me. I didn't tell him anything, but he'd used my reactions. He's like a very clever barrister. And he has another knack. The kind those characters have on the stage who can tell all about you, blindfold. *They* have a code. His knack is something more subtle.'

'You're quite humble,' she said. 'In fact, you're learning.'

'You've got to learn quickly.'

'It's not worth learning,' she said. 'Chuck it while there's still time.' Her voice was low and hard, enough to cut through the chatter of the café all around us.

'It's a big job,' I said, dreamily.

'Then leave it to the big boys.'

'I can't opt out now.'

'Wouldn't you prefer to live?' she asked, breathlessly.

'I couldn't do that,' I said. 'I know it's killing for those who have to do it, but the end result's a chance of survival for people everywhere.'

'Chance of survival!' she flashed. 'The difference between a short happy life and a long, monotonous one.'

'I can't believe that,' I said. And it was true. Great-grandfather Joseph was a Primitive Methodist; a sense of service has survived in me. '*You* believe in life after death,' I accused. 'From then on it's easy to die. You can actually grow fond of the idea.'

'You're after another kind of death.'

'Someone's got to live in Leviathan,' I muttered.

'It isn't Leviathan at all,' she flashed. 'It's just a few old men, filing cabinets, machines and a load of mischief.'

'Will you marry me and walk into the mouth of Leviathan?' I asked, smiling stiffly, knowing the answer. Or thinking I did.

Opening her bag she took out a compact and started powdering her face. The waiter brought the bill.

Dabbing, she said: 'I'll make you a counter-offer. How much money do you have?'

I had to think a moment. 'Around a thousand, plus a couple of hundred I invested in the firm.'

'You *are* flush,' she said. 'I've six hundred, give or take a pound or two. Let's go and starve somewhere strange, in the sun.'

'Italy?' I asked, offended that I should be linked with that happy past to which she clung so faithfully.

'Or the South of France, or Spain, anywhere, so long as it's out of this smoke-free, water-filtered, antiseptic and completely filthy city,' she said, and shuddered. 'Clean as picked bones.'

'What have you got against the business – against the city?' I asked. She looked over the river.

'Francis got me with child,' she said, taking my breath away. 'It

237

was nothing. I went to the right kind of specialist, had an abortion, lost weight, and have never felt clean again. So every year I go abroad to be burned clean again.'

She laughed at my look of outrage. 'You'd fall for any story I chose to tell you, wouldn't you? You're really in love.' She sobered. 'And, if you must know, so am I. But not so much that I've lost my practical sense of affairs.'

'I'm a practical person myself,' I said, a little offended. It was *she* who was being romantic. Muddled – I began to wonder if there had really been something between her and Francis.

'All right, prove it. Marriage is a human relationship. Let's give it a chance. Let's get away from that dreadful building, like the man in the story who spent all his pension on some happy idle years, then had the courage to pay again with a pistol shot.'

'We shan't want to end it.'

'Of course not, my dear.' My world tilted at the endearment. But I couldn't accept the crazy idea of packing our bags and throwing ourselves away on a glorified holiday.

'Listen,' I said. 'I don't understand. If you love me – what's the difference? We'll make out anywhere.'

'You don't get the offer,' she said. 'For once I'm only prepared to do something on my terms. Not like the last time –' Her voice tailed off.

'It's a kind of revenge, then. For Holinshed?'

'For myself. Oh – I'm no fool. I know you're good, Sammy. You're well above average –'

'Well, thank you!' I muttered.

'– I know what'll happen in the end. We'll come to the end of the happy days and the money. We'll come back here –' she shuddered, '– you'll go right to the top. But then, you see, I'll be content, I'll have had my turn.'

I couldn't see it. My mind was in a whirl. The river was in full flow backwards. I could see the surge of salt from out there, from the immense open sea where a lightship rocked ever so gently over clean, shifting sands, the waste that Prinkstone had it in mind to tame. With myself and Mr Francis. A better prospect than idling away the time. I suddenly remembered that I detested the blazing sun, the dry heat, and torpor.

I told her the answer was no.

'Look,' she said. 'I love you, I love you, I love you. But see what I'm up against. Every time I look at you I see a century of days waiting in a nice house for you to come home. But I want my adventure first.' Her hand crept imploring over mine, under my sleeve, grasped my wrist. The hand continued to ask, long after the words.

Walking back to the office, she said: 'Anyway, I shan't give notice until Friday. It's Tuesday now. Thursday twelve midnight is your hour of decision.'

I looked at her. 'I shall ring you up.'

'You're pushing me,' I told her. 'You're after my blood.'

'I'm after your all,' she said, softly, taking my arm and coming in closely so that our bodies brushed as we walked along.

I was suddenly aflame. 'All right, I'll go! I'll walk out now!'

'You'll work to your contract,' she said firmly. 'We're an honest firm, remember?' I think I knew then that it couldn't happen. 'I'm so glad. You think you're losing, but you wait and see. You'll gain in the end.'

'You know, I think you're right.'

'Of course I am. We'll look at maps. Tonight.' She looked at me. 'I can borrow a flat.' I thought of Esther, but aloud said something else. 'I'm meeting my father for dinner.'

There must have been something in my voice.

'Are you sure it's just your father?'

'I've other things to settle,' I told her.

'Settle them,' she said. 'I won't ask questions.'

I'd arranged to meet my father outside the National Gallery. I walked up the Strand, through William IV Street, then looked for him. I was determined not to be there first. He wasn't there, so I walked up St Martin's Lane with the intention of cutting back through Cranbourne Street and so make my way back. But I found myself staring at the white, blank face of the building where the Coliseum used to be. That was the place where Danny Kaye had sat on the stage, dangling his long, lithe legs in the orchestra pits. I had seen the old films; I had certainly seen his best. I saluted his ghost.

My heart was thumping. Now he would be waiting. I cut through the street which is still miraculously lined with print and book shops. I crossed the road. He was standing motionless. As I approached the white blur of his face became familiar. Shadowed by the bowler it was mine. Same squashed nose, same deep-set eyes, but the hair under the hat would be greying. Yet he wasn't so old. And was he mellowing? He didn't glance at his watch. Nor did he say:

'You're late, Sam,' infuriatingly.

Instead he held out his hand, which I took in a daze, forgetting that we hadn't met for months and so were in the case of old acquaintances who seldom meet. His hand was bigger than mine. He is, indeed, a bigger man. My father is puny only in imagination. He has broad shoulders and stout legs, a ruddy complexion, and open eyes. You could take him for a farmer. He dresses very well. Nothing but the best for father.

'How are you?' I said I was fine.

'Your mother sends her love.'

There seemed to be nothing to say to that. It was as good as saying: 'Our spaniel bitch sends you a lick.'

'Where would you like to eat?' I asked.

'Well, you know, I passed a little place along Irving Street, just back there, it looked clean and peaceful.'

'Then let's go,' I said. We turned about. Going along I asked: 'What brings you to London, Dad?'

He took a deep breath. 'Well, it's a spot of promotion. So this is in the nature of a celebration – I'll tell you when we're inside.'

'That's funny,' I said. 'I'm celebrating too.'

'You've been promoted?' He seemed disappointed. No one likes to be capped, even by the child of his loins.

'It'll wait,' I said.

Funny how I noticed his clothes. The raincoat was check, and check-on. Surprisingly, he wore a tweed suit. His tie was a little bit rakish. Waistcoat, of course, and that sat well. He was in good condition. We looked at the very large menu.

'Do you know,' he said, 'I've never had venison.'

'Then let's have it,' I said.

'Have you?'

'Never. Or jugged hare. Or real turtle soup.'

We had real turtle soup to start with.

'What's your promotion, Dad?'

'You'll never believe it!' Coyness went badly with his stature. 'They've given me the Newcastle City Bank.' I must admit I was surprised.

'Well, that's real promotion, Dad. Congratulations!' I said, and meant every word. I knew enough to know that he'd picked up a plum job. 'You'll have an awful lot of people to rule.'

'More machines than people,' he said. 'Still, that's the way it goes. I started in the City you know. Would you believe it, I used to walk there from Percy Main, and back in the evening. I used to watch important people going into the manager's office. Ours was a cold draughty place. There was a big, nice coal fire in the manager's room . . .'

'Yes?' I asked, surprised that I was even faintly interested.

'Nothing, really. Just that your finger ends were really cold – the older clerks wore mittens y'know – and that was a glimpse of heaven . . .'

'And now it's central heating.'

'I daresay it is.' He paused with the full spoon halfway to his mouth. 'You haven't told me your news yet.'

'I'm being appointed deputy chief controller.'

'That sounds pretty important.' I didn't tell him it would bring me twice the amount that heaven with central heating would bring him.

'It's a good job,' I admitted. 'But I don't think I'll take it. In fact, I shall probably be going abroad in the Autumn . . . with a girl.'

'That's a pity. With all your faults, you've never played ducks and drakes with your work.'

'I shall probably get married as well.'

'You're old enough.'

'You didn't ask me who she was.'

'Is she in favour of this – this adventure?'

I nodded. I must say it didn't put him off his food. He methodically spooned and enjoyed his turtle soup. But I knew he was angry. At last – 'That tells me enough.'

I didn't want to walk out on him.

'Are you going to marry her?'

'I've just told you.'

'So you told that other girl – the one who kept ringing after you left.'

'She was a fool. I told her before –'

'Foolish enough to depend on you.' The venison arrived in time to prevent the battle.

'Have you enough money for this?'

'I've saved.'

'You'll need a lot, y'know.'

'I've got a good deal more than a thousand.'

He raised his eyebrows. 'In ready money?'

'I've a couple of hundred invested in the firm.'

Suddenly he cheered up. In fact, he almost beamed at me. 'Well, it's no use saying anything. We've had our battles. A fat lot of good they did. By the way, did you pay that bearded man his rent for the flat –'

'Did he call?'

'He certainly did. I told him vou'd pay.'

'You did?'

'Of course I did. You always do. I'd no reason to believe you'd finish up your Newcastle career with a bad debt – a money debt.' I ignored the inference about other than monetary debts.

'Well, thank you,' I said, and suddenly realised that I was sounding rather silly.

'Not at all. Let's enjoy our meal.'

We rambled around a string – and a very knotted string – of subjects, then suddenly struck something we had in common. He had made a study of office machinery, including computers. His interest was strictly figurative. A lot of what he said was quite beyond me. But he was really enthusiastic. He'd been on a couple of courses.

Suddenly, after a discussion of feed-back, he said: 'There was a man from the firm who told me that my name rang a bell. Asked me if I'd a son called Sam.'

'That must have rung a couple of bells.'

'That's what I told him.'

'And what did he tell you?'

He shrugged. 'To be honest, nothing. But it may link up with something he said in his talk . . . About a firm in London . . .

sounded like yours . . . conducting a computer investigation into staff capabilities.'

'Investigation of staff capabilities?' I echoed.

'He said the modern version of "Mirror, Mirror on the Wall, Am I the fairest of them all?" Or Herod calling the Wise Men into his presence. But for profit.'

'They wanted to nurse *their* infant, is that it?'

He glanced at me. 'Don't take this as gospel . . . But it did sound odd, knowing your name.'

'I don't think they can program a computer for that kind of work,' I said.

'Oh, but they can!' he said. 'Whether they ought to take any notice of the conclusion is quite another thing. But they can do it, Sam.'

I didn't enjoy my venison. It all fitted so nicely together. This powerful upsurge of interest in a rather callow provincial, Francis and his talk of 'picking winners'. I felt like the prize in a glorified bingo game. That the prize was myself to myself didn't help. Weighed in like a jockey. On weight alone. None of the mystical virtues. No account of presence, bearing, or a dozen other intangibles. Could a computer see the aura of power?

'You know, your imagination was always a bugbear,' remarked my father. 'I'm sorry I mentioned it.'

We went to a show. Then to his hotel. We had several drinks and I left him. On the whole it wasn't a bad night. Only in the early part had I detected that old trick of his, of holding me squirmingly up in his hand, so to speak, and putting me in the place he'd selected for me. I mean the file for bad risks. That had been turned off after – when? I re-ran the tape on my way home. The taxi was just turning left at the Zoo when it came to me. He'd stopped the treatment just about the time I mentioned investments. If that piece of information had given him an idea I was running true to *his* form, then he was very much mistaken. Those investments were expendable. I'd cash them in as soon as look at them.

Meg Surtees was waiting for me when I got home. I didn't like her face. Or what she said: 'Come into my parlour, Sam Rowlands, I've a bone to pick with you.' My God, had Esther told her about our peculiar situation? Me in love with Cathie, and Esther loving me – to the bitter limit? She didn't offer me a drink. That was bad as well. Guiding me into the room like a tug with a big ship in tow, she retreated, turned about dramatically: 'I'm asking you a straight question,' she said. 'Are you somebody's bad debt?' It took the wind out of my belly, and it must have shown. 'Not that I know of,' I said, relapsing into our native tongue.

'I thought not,' she said. 'That's cleared that one. Now for the next. Are you monkeying about with another man's wife?' I gulped relief, or suspended relief, and shook my head. 'No detectives on your heels?' I was growing tired of repeatedly shaking my head and probably going several shades of guilt deeper each time. 'Look,' I said. 'Hadn't you better tell me what it's all about?' She weighed me, gave me the benefit, and went to pour whisky for us both.

'I wouldn't have given it a minute's thought, but it seemed so funny when it was first one then another.'

'We'll sort that one out later,' I said.

'Well,' she said, 'it was like this – I was sitting in the window seat over there waiting for something to happen in this more dead-than-alive street, and for once it did. A taxi pulled up at the opposite side of the street and a big well-made feller wearing a bowler got out –'

'Wearing a checked raincoat, I'll bet,' I suggested.

'That's right – how did you know? Looked like the bank manager type to me,' she said, trying to read my face. I was enjoying this one. 'A respectable senior clerk or a manager of a bank,' she repeated.

I nodded, 'Just promoted,' I said. 'Go on.'

'It's a friend? Then why didn't he call? He studied the numbers at the other side of the road then walked over here, I lost sight of him, then he appeared again – outside this house, stopped a split second, then went over to the other side. There he planted himself. Seemed to be making a study. Couldn't see me behind the curtains. I'll shake him, I said to myself, and came to the door. He took one look at me and he took off!'

'He was a detective all right,' I told her. 'Very private and extremely paternal. My old man making a study so that he can go back and report to my Ma that I seem to be in a respectable enough place –'

'I should think so,' she bridled. 'But how funny of him not to call!'

244

'They've learned to give me a clean berth,' I said. 'The bowler and the check raincoat were a clean give-away. I've just had dinner with him.'

'God help us!' she exclaimed. 'All that expense and you could have brought him here, the poor man.' She didn't seem to have picked up my attitude to my parents. I let it go. But she wouldn't. 'Clean berth!' she suddenly said. 'Whatever do you mean?'

'I've just emerged from a life-long struggle with them,' I said gently. 'They're a couple of cannibals. Want to eat their cake and have it. Or their son, and still have him.'

'You're a funny lad.'

'You were a funny daughter, lass,' I reminded her. She flinched. 'Ask me another,' I said, leaning nonchalantly back and putting on a smile. The way one always does before the earthquake.

She'd had enough. 'Oh, I don't know that it means anything. Then again . . .' She gave me a look. 'A girl called – a girl getting on, in girth as well as age, if you know what I mean.' I was sincerely puzzled. None of my women fitted the description. Calling up my reserves I asked Meg – I dared her – to give me some details. 'Nothing to write home about. Dark and getting on as I said.' She gave me a look again. 'Older than you, but you wouldn't be the first to go after the older woman.'

My heart started beating again at the repetition of 'dark' and 'older'. It couldn't be Cathie. Who could it be? I was at a loss. Meg wasn't satisfied. Leaning forward she pointed her nose at me, the way my mother used to point, the way they all do, 'Perhaps this'll help. There was that look in her eyes, she was pinched about the face . . .' Making a motion with her hands around her hips. 'Big. Getting bigger. She was pregnant.'

'Not guilty,' I promptly told her.

'I'm relieved,' she said. 'Let's have another whisky. I'm more than relieved. I'm glad. I was thinking of Esther.' My heart gave a leap from its new position down near the guts. She took my glass. 'What about your friends?' Wracking my brains I pulled out Simon and the awful little bed that went bump in the night.

'There's a friend of mine, Simon, man called Simon. An artist –'

'Not so bloody simple and not so bloody artistic, if he's the one,' she shouted, and I shouted with her, realising that the noise came

245

from her immense relief. But I noted that she had been thinking of Esther.

'About Esther,' I said. 'There's nothing serious. I mean – we're very fond of each other but –'

'But me no buts, my lad,' she said. 'She's in and out of your bed and that's serious enough for me.' Her tone was gay but implacable. I silently toasted Esther. She had said nothing, then. But if and when she did I'd be in trouble. I felt truly thankful for Esther. As if echoing my thought the lady of the house remarked:

'I think the world of Esther.' That was all.

I went up to my room and lay on a comfortable settee. It was a large room. Every time I closed my eyes a film of the future flashed on. It was something of a horror story. I slipped into our common kitchenette and made myself hot chocolate. Then I put on some Grieg and read Carlyle's 'Letters of Cromwell'. The bedroom seemed much too big. I was listening for Esther.

At last I heard footsteps on the stairs, click of the key in the lock of the door that was always open for me, the vague little noises that said she was home. I had no rights in there. She hadn't said so, but sadness is better than a lock. As I lay and listened the room became really enormous. It was like lying in a bed on the narrow top of a mountain. All round was the same kind of space. I felt myself shrinking. The thumb of my hand between my thighs dwindled to the size of a matchstick and in time I was Tom Thumb myself. The vertigo passed. I lay and waited for the click of her light switch. It was a long time in coming. I'd a feeling she'd been in bed with the switch in her hand, waiting, like a miner holding the plunger for the explosives. I lay in my bed and mourned. I knew she was mourning as well. Two wakes with a wall between. And only a wall.

SIXTEEN

There are days which contain more than a year. Mondays are often full like this. The day I dined with my father was a Monday, and it was a full enough day. But the day after was a welter of events. If I'd known a tenth of what was to happen I daresay I couldn't have faced it. There's an idea. If we knew the future, time would have to stop. The following morning I left my door open. I saw Cathie pass. She gave me a smiling face. I liked it until I remembered that love meant changing my job as well as my ways. Then I thought of something. She might have been hurt. I rang Cathie.

'You must have thought it strange of me not to invite you to meet my father,' I told her.

There was a pause which buckled my heart. I was relieved to hear her voice, come at last, perfectly normal. 'I was waiting for Arcot to leave the room. It's all right now. Please don't worry about your father. I'd have liked to have met him, of course. But I was thinking of our adventure all the way home. And I've arranged to stay in Town on Thursday.' I wasn't worrying now. But I was kicking myself. Cathie could have been the perfect defence. Keeping the conversation on a neutral route. And it would have been interesting to watch their effect on each other.

At eleven in the morning a mystery was solved with a call from Dorothy Pennington. She sounded worried. Could I possibly slip out and have coffee with her. I said yes and was about to put the telephone down when I remembered the landlady's tale. 'You weren't looking for me last night?' I asked. Yes, she had. She would tell me why when we met. But now I knew what she would tell me, and had a fairly good idea of the advice she would be needing.

I allowed her to tell me and looked suitably surprised. I told her that Charlie was a lucky man. I told her twice that he wouldn't dream of thinking he'd been trapped. Now that I knew, it was plain. It was mostly in the eyes. I'd considered telling Charlie myself but one look at those eyes told me that this wouldn't do. I guided her to a telephone kiosk and rang our number. I asked for Charlie. Then I handed the telephone to her. I heard her telling Charlie she'd like to lunch with him. She put the telephone down. I said: ' And mind, I want to be best man,' and left her.

At three in the afternoon my friend Charlie asked me to be his best man, not knowing it was already arranged. I said I would be honoured, even to be a registry best man, and thought how easy it is to arrange other people's affairs.

I had lunched with Cathie and had told her about my father, but not about Sam being picked up by the machine downstairs. She said he sounded sweet. It was a startlingly new idea to me. We never mentioned the plan of escape. It wasn't necessary. She did say that Mrs Arcot had mentioned that Mr Small Summers wasn't too well this morning.

At three in the afternoon the Chief Controller complained of a tightness in the chest. This in the middle of dictating a letter. He was inclined to blame the fish he had at dinner the evening before. The fish was innocent. At three-thirty he called Mrs Arcot and asked in a tight little voice if she would pour him a glass of water. Reaching out for it like a very thirsty child he suddenly seemed to launch himself into a dive for the other side of the desk. In mid-air he collapsed and his face smacked the surface of the desk which had been his environment so long. His face was flat on the desk. He breathed heavily and seemed to shrink.

Mrs Arcot succeeded in turning his head and loosening his tie, but not his collar. She ran out and told Cathie, who telephoned our own MO and myself. By the time I arrived the two women had loosened his collar. We lifted him onto the carpet, and laid him gently down. That is perhaps why they give them so thick a pile for the executive's office. Cathie had removed his spectacles. There was a pathetic ridge, more naked than nudity, on the bridge of his nose.

Mrs Arcot was useless now. As useless as a loving wife. She stood with a handkerchief and stared unbelievingly at the figure on the floor. I was sure she loved him. The MO arrived with Walker Johnson – the latter had been out of his office and had met the MO in the lift. The MO moved quickly. By four-fifteen the Chief Controller was in St George's with his own specialist in attendance. So the thing had evidently been brewing for a while.

At four-thirty the MO, Walker Johnson and myself were talking in the Chief Controller's office when Mrs Arcot came in. 'There's a newspaper on the phone – they seem to know he's ill.' She began to weep.

'You'd better stay here,' the MO told her, and opened his case.

'One of you had better deal with the newspaper,' he said as he took out a couple of pills. Walker Johnson looked at me. The MO took the glass from the desk and flung the water out of the open window. It seemed an odd thing to do until I remembered that there was simply a well leading down to the underground car park. He refilled the glass. 'Now . . .' he said, holding it out.

'Not that glass!' said Mrs Arcot.

'You handle the call,' said Walker Johnson to me.

'Don't be silly, woman,' said the MO. He bullied her into submission, then looked at us. 'Well?'

'What shall I tell them?' I asked.

'Tell them he's had a slight seizure and he's in St George's. His own specialist has been called in. Consultation taking place.'

'Slight?'

'It's a handy term,' said the MO in a tone that chilled my blood. Walker Johnson's as well. As I left I heard him ask, childlike: 'Will he die, do you think?'

'Even chances,' said the doctor.

The newspaper man didn't press too hard. It eventually appeared as a stop-press note of about forty words, simply to justify the newsbills: 'Prominent City Man Seriously Ill'.

Immediately after returning to my own office there was a call from the Chairman, who had just returned from Moscow. 'What's this about Small Summers?' I told him. There followed a series of rapid-fire questions. Had his wife been told? His GP? What was the latest news. Ring up at once – no – I'll get Miss Plumb to do it. She won't take the usual guff.

Later I heard that he had also had the MO up in his office.

At five he rang me again. He told me what the specialist had said, and Small Summers' own doctor. 'It's been six months since he was warned. And never said anything.' He sounded indignant.

I said: 'I don't think he'd much apart from his work.'

'What a bloody epitaph!' I said yes, but I hoped no in this case.

'Hope so to. I like Small Summers. Now Walker Johnson – the man's off his nut . . .'

'He seemed all right when I left him.'

'I rang him before you, the other time. Couldn't get any sense out of him. Afraid of death? Probably the first time he's seen anyone on the point – practically wept over the phone.'

'We're all upset,' I said. 'We're very fond of him – all of us,' I added, remembering the tall, lean figure, the blue eyes, the detached voice lacking in warmth but also in vindictiveness.

'I'm sure, I'm sure,' said Mr Francis. 'And I'll tell you something else – he's not done for yet, not by a long shot – a bloody long shot. I'll lay ten bob he's back within the month.'

'I want him back,' I said.

'You'll need him, young feller-me-lad,' said Francis. 'We've got work to do.' His voice went on. It was like the prisoner sitting in his cell, listening to the merry noise of the carpenters in the yard outside. 'How long has Walker Johnson to go?' I said he'd given three months' notice. 'Oh, God, we've some hard graft to get through – tell you what, he's so much ballast – we'll get rid of him – generous severance payment – get him out of the road. That leaves you in charge. All right?'

I had been rehearsing. 'I must have time to think it over,' was out of the question. 'No thank you, I'm leaving as well,' was playing clever buggers. There was absolutely nothing negative I could say at that moment in time. And put my heart into it. In the event, I muttered: 'Yes.'

'Fine. Keep it under your hat until we get shot of him. Then we'll fix it. You'll be acting for the old man. Acting Chief Controller. Nice, eh? Oh, and get yourself up to my room in the morning. Assault conference. Expansion plans. Russia, Sahara. Plant and products. Operation Crab. Good night.'

'Good night,' I said. The last nail in the coffin of a love.

'And good luck. I'm going to work you into the ground.'

'Into the belly of Leviathan,' I said, as soon as it was safe.

I hadn't time to ponder my betrayal of Cathie. I had just signed the last letter of the day when Holinshed walked in. He seemed a little high. Rosalie Miffin lingered for more gossip about the event of the day.

'It's awful,' she said. 'I'm glad I wasn't there, Mr Rowlands.'

'He'll be all right,' said Holinshed, almost gaily.

'But it's a terrible thing – terrible –'

'I feel it in my bones he'll recover,' said Holinshed. I was beginning to feel resentful. As if I had a share, a lion's share, in Small Summers, at which they were biting.

'You'll miss the post,' I hinted. She took it.

'Light one of those little cigars of yours,' said Holinshed. He seemed delirious as well as drunk. 'You smoke a cigar and I'll light a subject. I've something to tell you.' We lit up. He leaned back. He said: 'My wife's coming back.' His face fell at my expression, and I was instantly sorry. I shook myself and said: 'I'm glad – I'm delighted.' I hoped it would pass muster. It did. He was living in his own moment and knew nothing of my condition.

'I've never been so happy,' said Holinshed. 'I've found my mark, stopped pushing. Now my woman's on the way back home.'

'You've just heard?' I said, a little enviously.

'Well, it's silly. I rang her this morning. Come to think of it – a lot of this happened over the phone, hasn't it? She wasn't very forthcoming. Never has been – on the phone, I mean. Doesn't like the thing. Well, anyway, don't know why, I said "If only I could see you," and you know what – she said she was coming to Town. Told me afterwards it was wholly to see me, not business or shopping. Said I'd meet her if she liked . . . and glory, she did!'

'That was good, eh?' I said with a certain degree of envy.

Waving his cigarette Holinshed said: 'It was very good. I've always hated Victoria Station, excepting once when I saw a steam locomotive. Otherwise, the very depths of hell, especially in summer, all those people going away . . . the wonderful suit-cases. Now I shall love it for ever. I thought it would cost the earth. In the end it only took a cup of coffee and a biscuit.'

'But you paid in advance.'

'I paid, and I'm lucky to get value for whatever it was that I paid with.' Solemnly he stood up and shook hands. 'Thanks for everything,' he said with a moist kind of eye.

'I don't think I helped much, but I'm glad for your sake,' I told him.

'Oh well,' he said, avoiding my eyes. 'You – you took up the slack, didn't you?' The impertinence of it took most of my breath away. Fortunately, the telephone intervened. Letting go of my hand. 'And, of course, teaching me not to care a rap about this – all this.' Beaming, he backed out of the room. Wondering what he meant I picked up the telephone.

'Are you alone?' It was Cathie.

'I was just having a chat with Holinshed – a very happy man –' I remembered she had been involved,'– for some reason.'

'About his wife? Everyone knows, of course. Congratulate him as well – for me.'

'He's gone,' I said

'Then I'll congratulate you. On your good luck.'

'News travels quickly,' I said. 'But you might have given me the benefit –'

'You haven't turned it down, then?'

'Well, no, but –'

'Then congratulations again. I hope you all live very happily together for ever and ever. You and Holinshed and Mr Francis.'

At that awkward moment the door opened and Pat Wills walked in. I waved him to a seat. I returned to the telephone. 'Are you still there?' I asked. At the other end of the line she said that she was. 'Then I'll be coming along to see you in a minute or two.' That was when I began to go wrong. I should have sorted each problem out in turn. I should have thought. No doubt the end result would have been the same. But at least it would have been tidier.

Wills was looking at me strangely. I re-focused and brought him into my field of vision at last. 'I just popped in to say good night,' he said. 'And to tell you how pleased I am at the news.'

I looked at him. He must have thought I was annoyed. 'I hope you don't think I'm fishing,' he said. 'Is it official?'

'Not yet,' I said

'Then at least it's true? Congratulations. You're the man for the job.' I murmured something. Ever watched a big dough-mixing machine in a bakery? Something like that, with big fists of steel, was pounding away at my insides. I said excuse me and picked up the internal. Miss Plumb answered. 'Rowlands speaking,' I said. 'Is there any chance of seeing Mr Francis for a minute or two?'

'He's out,' she said. 'I don't think he'll be back.'

'Is he in the building?'

She had to consider this. 'I wouldn't know,' she said.

'Listen, I want to see him, badly,' I said. 'Is there any way I can contact him?'

'I'm sorry. You'll have to wait until tomorrow.' I put the telephone in its cradle. Wills was watching my face. He was fascinated. Had it not been for him I daresay I'd have gone up to the penthouse. Even then I'd an idea that Francis was there. But I was embarrassed by Wills, and the way he watched me.

'A little bit of an upset?' he asked.

'A little bit of private business,' I snarled.

'Well, I'm pleased. Really pleased,' he rambled. 'You'll give this department just what it needs.' It was like sitting in a runaway plane with a neighbour telling you that the clouds are lovely. I said: 'Look, do you mind? I've a couple of things to do before I leave.' I brushed past him.

'We're all behind you,' he murmured.

'Thanks a lot,' I replied. He followed me into the corridor. 'All of us,' he continued. 'That's fine,' I said over my shoulder and speeding down the corridor. He must have known I was making for Cathie. I turned again. There was no riddle in the look on his face. Keen enjoyment. If he'd dared, he'd have followed. He waved. I waved back. I wasn't thinking. To put him off I turned into the room of the man who could read upside down, like myself. I walked over to the window and looked out. The sky was as red as hell. Osbourne had gone. I knew it. Wills knew it. After a decent interval I came out and went into Cathie's room. I might have spent a profitable five minutes' thinking. Instead I rushed on in a fever.

The keys were flowing and there was no recognition in the fleeting glance she gave me. 'Listen, Cathie,' I said. 'Don't jump to conclusions. It was done over the phone. Francis put me off my stride –'

'Good evening,' said Mrs Arcot. I hadn't noticed her. Perhaps she hadn't noticed me. She walked out like a sleep-walker. Ever since the collapse of Small Summers she had been in a daze.

'Put you off your stride!' said Cathie, still typing.

'He seemed to take it for granted. Didn't even ask me to consider. And I didn't like to embarrass –'

'Of course not. He's important, isn't he?' Her fingers flayed the keys. 'You wouldn't think that was a word of two letters.'

'I'm sorry you had to find out the wrong way.'

'Don't be sorry. I'm much more resilient than Mr Francis, thank you.'

'Will you stop typing?' I asked.

'That's my work,' she said. 'But only for another ten days. Then I'll be my own woman again. With or without you, it'll still be fun.' It was difficult to think let alone speak against the smooth noise and motion of the machine and her fingers. At last she stopped, resting both hands in her lap. Now there was a background noise in me. She looked at me. 'You know you're blackmailing me,' I said.

'Of course.' In the two words was her bad time. Holinshed abandoned her and that must have hurt. By my silence I in my turn had rejected her.

'It so happens that I intend to refuse the job – as soon as I can get hold of Francis.' She looked at me. 'Not that I quite know why –'

'As a sop to *my* pride and as a buttress for yours,' she said.

'Have faith in me,' I pleaded. I wanted her faith. I wanted to be back to where I was before the building and the business and Francis got hold of me. But at the same time I was fighting to keep the other things as well. She rose swiftly from the typewriter. I thought of the mess of deceit inside me. I thought it must be showing. Instead of slapping me, she cupped my face and kissed me.

'The fact that I bother proves I've faith in you,' she said. 'Not very much. But it's enough. Or should be.'

I became aware that Walker Johnson was standing in his doorway, dressed for the street. He said: 'I'm sorry. If I'd known I'd have used the other door – I just wanted a word with Cathie about something.'

Cathie laughed. 'We are only discussing our future,' she said. 'I'm sorry we embarrassed you. But I don't mind your knowing . . .' I wasn't exactly pleased.

'Ah well, I wouldn't stretch a friendship that far,' he said uneasily. He walked past us without looking at me. 'I hope you sort it out.' Again without looking at me. 'She's a wise girl and she's probably right.'

'That's very sweet of you,' said Cathie.

'Pat-a-cake, pat-a-cake,' I said. 'Fair enough. He tells *you* about me. Now he tells *me* about you. What have you told him about me?'

'God knows, not much, and nothing malicious, if that answers all three of your questions,' said Walker Johnson.

'You'd better apologise,' said Cathie to me.

'I'm sorry,' I said, woodenly. .

'Not to worry,' said R. Walker Johnson. 'A very pleasant evening to you both.' He seemed to be upset as he left the room. I don't know why. I thought he'd more than held his own.

'I didn't like that,' she said.

'Neither did I.'

'I meant your attitude,' she said.

'I'll admit it wasn't exactly wholesome,' I said.

'There's quite a lot that isn't wholesome about you.'

'Perhaps,' I said. 'Probably more than you imagine.'

'That girl on the night switchboard – Esther,' she said, a little sadly I thought.

'Sometimes,' I said, 'two love affairs can overlap.'

'I didn't know they had until this moment,' she said. I saw she was truly hurt. 'People saw you calling for her late at night. But that was some time ago –'

'It's all right,' I said. 'I wanted to tell you. It was wretched, painful. But that isn't what I was talking about. I was trying to tell you that I'm a very devious sort of person –'

'I know,' she said. She took a deep breath. 'I knew that you hadn't really placed your bet. You were hedging. You'd like to hang on until the very last minute. That means you'll keep me on a string until Friday at least – and the chances are that you'll choose this –' She encompassed the building with one swift motion of her hand. 'Then you'll tell me, probably on Thursday evening, that

255

you're staying. Just to give *me* time to change my mind. So that makes both of us blackmailers. But you're the ruthless one.'

'That was a good, good guess,' I said, conscious that the thing was getting out of control.

'It was an easy one,' she said. 'Your mind works in a perfectly normal way – selfishly. But you've lost. You won't get a chance to blackmail me now – like the others. You must choose now.'

'There goes your faith,' I said.

'There's still hope and charity,' she said.

'I'll take charity,' I said, not knowing what I was saying. 'Look at me, Cathie. I'm a divided man. I want to strive. But I can't strive in the sun. My place is here. But I'm also a coward. I'm afraid of dying alone. I want a son to walk the earth and remember me, not a stone with words on it. A coward needs protection – I need walls. Your flesh around mine as well as this building around my body. I need both of you to make something out of my life. Fame if you like, or at least the feeling that my work is going to mean something to people I'll never know . . .'

'Around and around the mulberry bush,' she said. 'But you've all the time in the world.'

'Time runs out,' I told her.

'It can't run out when you're right, when you're at home, Sam. Come away with me and give yourself a chance. Time can't run out –' I saw the look on her face. Her face was enrapt. *My* meaning hadn't reached her. I could never have eternity. She would never know the value of a little ordinary time to a man like myself who can never make obeisance before an altar. We were bound two ways. Both pilgrims. But I was walking through the hard, sharp world of matter. I told myself that the taint of the parents was there. She was after my soul. She would never have courage to go the full distance alone. She had to have me for that. That was the phantom in her. But I hadn't lost hope. There was still time for an appeal to the woman.

I touched her breasts.

'I want you to have my children.' She trembled. 'I want everything, but more than anything else I want you to bear my children for me.'

Without looking at me, she said: 'Then make me first.' Then I knew I'd lost her. But my momentum carried me on. 'Cathie, help me. All I have is a job. I'm the man in the middle of an iceberg, yelling to be out. Help me.'

She touched my hand. 'That makes two of us. And I need help as well . . . dearest, I'm sorry.' I think she was crying. I stroked her hair back from the forehead and down to the neck. I said goodbye to those delicious little tendrils. She averted her face. For the first time in my life I felt and saw the steel of a woman's will. She dried her eyes. I moved away and sat in Mrs Arcot's chair.

We sat and looked at each other. After a time she put on her coat. 'My train leaves at six-five,' she said.

'You've missed it,' I said. We both forced a laugh.

'Yes, of course I have. But I'll get the next one,' she said. I was thinking of father when I told him about the money I'd invested in the firm. He'd read me all right. She hesitated. For a moment I thought I'd won. Then she said: 'I'm sorry too. I mean, being so desperate. We're pretty much alike.'

I looked at her. Someone said:

'You in your iceberg and me in mine.'

The coat brushed against me as she left. My eyes were closed. They were more than closed. I was screwing the lids in against the eyes to stop hurt or tears. When I opened them I was alone. I sat and looked at her typewriter. It leered back like a deadly little monster. I can't remember noise but I recall the plug whipping out at the end of the flex. The next thing I knew the machine was twisted and broken and I was methodically dusting the pieces of chair. With my handkerchief. I sat down and waited until my breath was normal again. I felt a lot better when I was breathing evenly. There was nothing I could do about the loss. It was a necessary part of my life. It was a very necessary part of her life. Looking at the damage I was quietly and confidently satisfied. I was so completely caught up in it that I never thought of it as something which might interest, or amaze, or make contact with anyone else. Looking at the damage I felt quite happy.

The light was on in my office and Charlie was reading my *Times*. He looked up. 'Aya,' he said. 'I thought you might like a jar. So I waited.'

I was in no mood for friendship. 'No thanks, Charlie. You'd

better push off home.' I tried a light-hearted tack. 'You've your own responsibilities, you know.'

'I'm afraid you're one of them . . . Cancel the drink if you like. But we'd better tidy up.' I looked at him with honest surprise. Apologetically, he said: 'I couldn't help hearing the racket along there.' With his head on one side he was watching me. 'You could come home and have a meal with us. Afterwards, I mean.'

'There's no danger of suicide,' I said.

'It's straight hospitality,' he said.

'I couldn't stand the sight –' He knew what I meant. Of two ordinary, happy people in love with each other, and the knowledge that their love had made a child. 'Well, at least you can help me to get rid of the evidence,' he said. We carried the typewriter and the chair down into the basement storeroom. The chair was only fit for firewood and the typewriter was badly bent. It sat on the floor of the lift and leered at me with all the little eyes on its keys. We used the rear elevator. Charlie produced a key. We hid the damaged equipment in the darkest corner and selected another chair. 'You'll have to pay for repairs,' said Charlie. 'To the machine, I mean. At a rough guess, it'll cost forty quid. I'll come in early and get a replacement.'

We had our drink after all.

After the drink I said good night to Charlie and went the long way to UK House. The night porter knew me by now. I rang the bell and he let me in. He said: 'Everybody's working late tonight.' I didn't ask who. The whole world could work as far as I was concerned. I pressed the button to the fifteenth floor. I went up. I suddenly felt very tired and sat down. The paperback Herbert had left was *The Four Just Men*, that incredible relic of a time when men actually believed that you could kill them all, not realising that as quickly as you cut them down they grow again out of the parched brown soil.

I carried the book into that crazy lounge. I went into the palatial lavatories and gave myself a scrubbing. It was no good. I felt just as filthy as before. Then I returned to the lounge and selected a deep and handsome easy chair. It was like sinking back into the lap of a grateful woman bigger than you but not your mother. I read with my head between her breasts.

I read:

> If you leave the Plaza del Mina, go down the narrow street, where, from ten till four, the big flag of the United States Consulate hangs lazily; through the square on which the Hotel de la France fronts, round by the Church of Our Lady, and along the clean, narrow thoroughfare that is the High Street of Cadiz, you will come to the Café of the Nations.

A long time ago the wonderful first sentence of one of the great bad books of the language had held me entranced. Now I thought, fleetingly, that bad books had always been my undoing, and relaxed. I had been battered. I deserved this kind of bliss. I stopped reading.

When I awoke Francis had pulled a chair opposite mine. For a moment there was a feeling of being watched by one of the Four; Manfred, perhaps, sitting in the skin of a pink-skinned businessman. Then I realised that it was really Francis.

'I thought perhaps you wanted to see me,' he said.

'As a matter of fact I do,' I said.

'What seems to be the trouble?'

'Only me,' I said. He nodded.

'There's nothing we can do about that tonight.'

'I was just curious about the way you selected me.'

'God – I'd forgotten that,' he said. He seemed genuinely startled. 'Is that all?'

'It's just one thing,' I said. My heart was sinking because I knew I was going to be convinced.

'It seemed a lark at the time. It was Prinkstone who suggested it to me. Then I convinced the Board. We put a couple of hundred names through. Yours was the one that came up.'

'You weren't convinced by the computer, surely,' I said.

'Oh, you were a pretty good argument yourself,' he generously conceded.

'But you didn't need to push?'

'Normally, I suppose, we'd have waited for you to prove the machine – er – a good picker. But what struck me was the effect on Crumple. Uneasy as Herod the Great. Of course, it's only a machine. It gives you what you ask for.'

'Did you contrive that?'

'Good Lord, no! It wasn't necessary. But I laid it on thick about the way you'd rise. It crumpled him so much that he tried to get in first . . . to take you under *his* wing.'

'What if I want to make my own life?'

He shrugged. That hurt. 'You won't find me standing in your light. Do what you like, my boy. After all, there are two or three at your tail . . .'

'I thought you were looking forward to the idea . . .'

'I was. I am. In fact, I'm perfectly confident you'll stay. That's why I'm not fussing. Why fuss about something that's settled. By the way – how did you find out?'

'My father told me,' I said.

'It's a small world, isn't it?' he cryptically remarked. I'd an idea he'd worked it all out as quickly as that. He at least knew my old man wasn't a dustman or a roadsweeper. All on the card; the tape; eternally fixed in the whirring innards.

'Take Christ,' he said. 'A little bit of astrology started it all. A nova – new star – led the Magi. In business it only takes a trifle. With me – people look at my face. It's a deceivingly sympathetic face. A business bedside face. And of course,' he modestly added, 'the brains to go with it. Nothing was ever a trouble. Always time to think ahead. Now yours –' he gave it a long critical look '– not a sympathetic face at all. Serious handicap. Without the machine it might have taken you a very long time. So thank your lucky stars.'

I think he was putting me in my place. 'My face doesn't matter a dam',' I said.

'I wouldn't like to be dogmatic about that. It put Crumple off his stride, anyway,' he said with a ghost of a smile. He looked at me in silence for a moment. 'Well, are you going to stay?'

'I'm trying to make up my mind,' I said. 'That's why I'm sitting here.'

'And that's why I'm spending time telling you some home truths. You've been very lucky. Haven't you noticed? Snorry liked you, the computer liked you, I liked you – even Crumple liked you, after his fashion. But that doesn't say your luck'll continue indefinitely, that you're the Messiah. You have luck in your pocket. Don't throw it away.'

'I don't believe in luck,' I said sullenly.

'But you do believe in destiny. It's a tatty word, I know. But there *is* something that takes hold of a man and carries him, upward and onward as the poets used to say. Don't disown it!'

'I could walk out of this place and still have it – luck, destiny, whatever you call it,' I said.

'Not when you're bloody soft over a woman,' he said. 'Not when you'll sink everything and run off with a girl!'

'So you know about that!'

'It's my business to know,' he said. 'I don't have to try, you understand. Everything comes up here –'

'With a little encouragement,' I said bitterly. He gave a gesture and sank back in his chair.

'Look,' he said, 'go away for six months – or a year. Go off into the sun with the girl. We'll keep a job open for you.' I noticed, as he'd intended, that it was 'a job', not 'the job'. 'No, thank you,' I said. 'If I go, I go off my own bat.' He relaxed.

'I'm glad you said that. There are no fire-escapes for such as you and me. You could go away, but you wouldn't get out whole. You'd be crippled –'

'That's not to say I won't be crippled here,' I said. Over his shoulder I saw Prinkstone turn the corner carrying a briefcase. As he saw me he raised a finger to his lips. I suppose he wished to surprise Francis. He was beaming. Francis was so immersed in what he was saying that he didn't notice my change of expression; and I had no way of knowing that he might say something explosive. Spreading his hands he continued: 'There's no guarantee – this game tests to destruction. It got Crumple. It got Prinkstone too. You've seen Prinkstone. A good chemist, in a way; a fine mind. But no organising ability. Only a middle man. He was lost when he had to face the big stuff. Tested to destruction. A burned-out case. Just an old man wandering around in a dream – in his dreams . . . pathetic –'

Watching the change in Prinkstone's expression I had gradually risen to my feet. 'Don't run away,' said Francis, rising with me. Then at last it registered. 'What's the matter?' he asked, spinning round before I had time to answer. Prinkstone was standing motionless, hugging the briefcase to himself. 'Ah, you brought my briefcase – thanks, old chap!' said Francis merrily. He walked over to Prinkstone with his arm outstretched. Mr Prinkstone's face was collapsing. He clutched desperately at the briefcase, holding on to it as if it were a life-jacket. 'That's very kind of you!' said Francis.

Prinkstone was trying to say something: 'You-you-you said – an old man wandering in a dream.' His voice was vaguely reproachful. 'A burned-out case . . .'

'You *were* dreaming, old man,' said Francis heartily. 'Young Rowlands and I were just having a chat. Give me that briefcase and I'll see you back to the flat.' Prinkstone gave up the case. His face was beginning to clear. He even managed a confidential smile: 'You're a bit of a gaoler my lad, aren't you?' he said to Francis.

'I'm here to keep you in your place, if that's what you mean,' said Francis. There was brutal authority with the heartiness in his voice. They started to turn. 'Good evening, Mr Prinkstone,' I said.

'And good evening to you,' said the founder. I was certain he hadn't recognised me.

Francis was gone ten minutes. He returned mopping his brow. 'That was a near go,' he said. 'I think he's relapsing, don't you?'

'There's no fire-escape for him,' I said.

He shrugged. 'It's dam' pathetic, I agree,' he said.

'It's a hellish way to find out the truth.'

He stared at me. 'You think our little conversation hurt him? Prinkstone used to be an honest man. It was telling himself the things he overheard me telling you that brought him down. The truth wrecked him a long time before you came on the scene.' There seemed to be nothing to say. 'What's the truth about you?' he continued relentlessly. 'The truth about you is that you've made a bloody good show of indecision all day long. But you never intended to chuck the job and you know it.' I could have stamped the life out of him at that moment. He knew it, and sighed. 'It's being able to face up to truths of that nature that makes you a possible for this sort of work,' he said, glancing around with something like disgust. He waited but I had nothing to say.

'See you tomorrow, then,' he said and walked over to the lifts. I closed my weary eyes. The lift came and the doors opened. The doors closed and I heard it whistle away between the teeth of the building. I shouldn't have minded if the ropes had snapped. His absence didn't make any difference to my feeling about him. I knew it was unfair to hate him, but I went on hating. No argument could kill it. Only an act.

I left *The Four Just Men* in the chair, and went by the stairs to my own floor. The cleaners were busy. Every door was open. The polishing machines purred delightedly. Sacks of scrap-paper sagged like executed soldiers along the corridor. I was sitting in my revolving chair when one of the women looked in. In front of me was the file of dreams. I released the spring-catch and slid out the last thin sheaf of my youth.

'Sorry,' she said.

I told her to carry on.

'I'm just going round with the duster,' she said. I watched her. Whatever you do with the waste commodities there seems to be no escape from the waste that people carry round with them. She was a small woman with bleached hair, bleached eyes, a bleached soul. Her legs when she reached were knotted with varicose veins. Not so long ago they had been good legs. She caught me looking. I pretended to look through the pages I'd pulled from the file. It was like that ancient thriller. A good start, then a dribble of sick. My way of keeping in with Uncle James. She came over to the desk.

'If you'd just sit back a second or two.' I swung around in my chair, clutching the papers. The duster swept expertly over the surface while her other hand lifted and replaced the little furniture of work, blotting pad, calendar, ball-pen holder, telephone.

'There you are,' she said. 'Now I can see my face in you.'

She wasn't talking to me. It was the furniture.

'You don't get mucked up with cigarette ash. Only cigars. Three stubs today. But the dust comes through and lies like snow when the weather's as dry as it is.' She darted little glances at the desk. Hands on hips, duster hanging, reaching a verdict; 'Now you're lovely.'

She came back to me 'No, I'm not cracked. There's a big family at home. We talk all the time. Here it's lonely. I used to work myself into a panic until I learned to talk to it –'

'Talk to what?'

'Why, the office of course.'

'Does it ever answer back?'

'I suppose it does.'

'Your family must miss you.'

'They miss me. They're helpless. My man – poor man, he can't help it. He does his best. But the girls are helpless. I spoil them. Three boys and two girls. My husband took a disease – that arterio what's it –'

'Not arterio-sclerosis?'

'When I was younger I used to sing a lot,' she said. 'Hymns, all sorts of hymns. And pop songs. Learned them from the wireless. The supervisor won't allow us to have them here. He can move around and look after himself,' she suddenly resumed. 'He's not bad, really, but they say he'll get worse.'

She eyed me up and down. The reason for being in business, I wanted to tell her, is to make a lot of surplus time for the clever ones. Then they create things to fill the surplus time. But sometimes they find a way to kill the kind of thing that is eating your husband. There's a lot of loss, but there is gain as well. One step backward, two steps forward. But of course it was no good for her. No one could create surplus time for him, for her. She decided I didn't need dusting.

'Now don't get yourself upset,' she said. '*I'm* not cracked. Really I'm not. You get along with it. Only sometimes I get awful feelings in the night.'

I said good night and walked into the corridor. I ripped the sheets from my private note-book in half and dropped more material for the paper-chase into a sack. The sack didn't fall over. My eyes were smarting. I suppose it was the fine dust of business which the cleaner had stirred up as she talked against her loss. Soil ground small by the lift and fall of a mill made of fifteen million pairs of feet and a couple of million tyres, ordure of birds full of saltpetre, burning of fuel in which there is sulphur; the fine ash of office life: eraser parings, fragments of typewriter ribbon, particles of make-up powder, dried mucus, salty powder of fear, nail filings. Worth a guinea a box to witches.

Oh, Cathie where are you, goodbye. The building no longer talked. That woman's words bounced in my brain-box. The building was dead. I needed a renewal. A sacrifice was needed.

Cocking my snook at Francis. They were cleaning on the fifteenth floor as well. I looked at my watch. Almost nine o'clock. For the second time I entered the palatial lavatory, snatching up the copy of *The Four Just Men* on my way.

Locking myself in one of the posh little cubicles I settled down on the seat. I emptied my bowels. I finished the book. The ghost of the boy I had been responded to the letter written on a thin grey sheet of paper. I was cheered by the words:

> When you receive this, we who for want of a better title call ourselves 'The Four Just Men' will be scattered throughout Europe, and there is little likelihood of your ever tracing us. In no spirit of boastfulness we say: We have accomplished that which we set ourselves to accomplish . . .

I was reading the last page, in which a strong force of police raid the house in Carnaby Street and find only a half-smoked cigarette bearing the name of a London tobacconist and the counterfoil of passages for three first-class passengers to New York. The counterfoil was marked 'per R.M.S. *Lucania*', but although she was searched from stem to stern on arrival, The Four Just Men were not discovered. It was Gonsalez who had placed the 'clue' for the police to find.

I was Poiccart, I was Manfred, but I was most strongly Leon Gonsalez in that moment of enlightenment. To stay was to convince Mr Francis I was hooked and in his possession. That was the 'clue' I would plant.

At that very moment I heard the chatter of the cleaners as they left.

SEVENTEEN

I had no time to lose. I walked quickly to the Chairman's office and opened the outer door. Then came to a dead stop to listen. I almost convinced myself he'd returned and was in there waiting for me. I muttered to myself and threw open that inner door. The room was in darkness and companion crystal tombstones blazed away outside. Like the opening of a play. Any moment now one of those square-headed Gullivers would step forward and talk. That died on me. Now I saw only a great floodlit graveyard. I pressed the switch for lights. The tombstones faded. I pressed a second switch and rich red curtains swished to seal off my private stage. I had no wish for an audience, be it ever so dead. There was something wrong. I switched on the desk lamp then turned off the main lights. Then it was right.

The room was warm and sumptuous. Three paintings newly arrived from Rumania sparkled like medieval enamels and gave an impression of unfashionable tilted faces. You only saw them out of the corner of your eye. Most of them were smiling. I sat in the Chairman's chair. It was very comfortable. Outlines became sharper. There was a photograph of a woman and three boys. The boys were handsome. The woman was flat-chested and ineptly dressed. She looked learned enough to pass for a Professor of Gallic Law. Her smile told of patience but not as a game. My eye automatically travelled from the photograph in its silver frame to the historic drawer – poor Crumple! The itch was irresistible. I pulled it open, expecting to find a message. Such as 'Hello Sam!' But the drawer was clean empty. Or out of use. Some drawers one closes, some one shuts. This I shut. For a moment I considered putting a knife through those three expensive canvases. But I hadn't a knife. Laughing I went on to the fourth and final door, a door I had noticed but never remembered.

Inside was a small but luxurious bath-and-changing room. First came a cabin with a fitted wardrobe. I pressed a button and it snapped open. Inside were dinner-suits, dressing-gown, a pair of cord trousers and a very hairy pullover. In one of the drawers were shoes and a pair of carpet slippers, in another a selection of shirts. I lifted up a nice silk shirt. On top of the shirt I had exposed lay a phial of birth-control capsules. The bathroom had both shower and bath. The shower was enclosed in glass on which were engraved swans, pelicans and leaping salmon. There was no window on the world outside. But there was one outlet in the shape of a small fan to draw out the steam if the occupant so wished.

I'd a feeling the occupant coming up would so wish, not so much from a dislike of humidity as from a child's desire to use these toys to the limit. I pulled the cord and the little blades hummed. I turned on the water. The two taps and the fan made a merry noise. I pried into the cabinet beside the wash-basin. There was a wide range of pills, a safety razor with a real gold handle, and a cut-throat in a nice black case; the strop hung by the wash-basin. A well-equipped base of operations. There were even little piles of silver.

I almost missed the sketch of the nude woman on the inside of the cabinet door. She looked out of the bath, head thrust forward and hands on her knees. A wickedly mischievous piece of work. Not the face but the pose reminded me of someone. It had been done with a few economical strokes of a flo-pen, then abandoned. As though the artist as well as the man had spent himself. Was Francis by way of being an artist? The bath was now full. I turned off the taps and emptied in some red and purple crystals. Then I went out to his desk. The flat drawer ready to his hand contained enough odds and ends to fill the pockets of a dozen small boys. But there was no flo-pen.

I have always disliked washing my head and face while in the bath. Old habits die hard. I stripped to the buff and washed my tops. Then I dried myself and slipped into the bath. Along with the glow there is also less work and more time to enjoy what is really one of the most pleasurable of the minor physical experiences. I suppose Francis and myself are alike in our Roman blood. The water was hot to the edge of tolerance. I bore up to it then let myself slide back. After five mindless minutes of pure animal enjoyment I sat up and soaped myself, then sank back again. No scrubbing tonight. I wondered why Francis hadn't thought of a waterproof pillow. Some day I would see to it. But the water was good and hot. It baptized me free of contempt and betrayal; even momentarily of the shadow of original guilt. The fellow at the back of my mind took a running jump; that one who had shadowed me ever since the day they had pushed me on to the girl and I had closed her mouth with mine.

I thought of Charlie who still owed me three pounds from a fortnight ago. Now that he was getting married he would need a rise. I would have to promote him. Wills would move into my place and Holinshed would stay happily where he was. Which was as necessary to Holinshed's peace of mind as it was to my own comic sense of justice; let Iago, or Wills, in his turn inherit my room and the carpet with the hole in it. I put Cathie out of my mind before the sentimental orchestra took over and my eyes became damp.

Esther would return to me. I remembered her body and was glad. I remembered her love and was pleased. I remembered my landlady's intolerance and was secure. A large body of men followed the hearse to the cemetery. Speeches were delivered over the open grave and the coffin. The coffin remained tightly closed, for even in their heyday the comrades feared death more than counter-revolution; the worm more than the purge. Freely he wandered, freely he loved, until he remembered upon which side his bread was buttered. I would write to my father and mother and tell them I was now engaged to be married. I screwed my eyes and concentrated on the mirror brightness of the taps as I remembered that I might have slipped and taken her to dinner with my father. He would have known her. He would then have known of my failure to win her. Now all was well. I would also pen some lines to my Uncle James and tell him I had found the twentieth and the final one of my life. Let the other one wither in the blaze between the mountains and the sea.

I sat on the stool and slowly completed my drying while the water gurgled and the plumbing cleared its throat. I observed with a quiet glow of satisfaction the tide-mark of the dirt from my body. I sat on the stool and towelled vigorously away, worshipping my body in the act. I was feeling wonderfully relaxed and masterful. I opened the cabinet and took out shaving stick, brush and cut-throat, raising my eyebrows a second time at the sight of the little piles of silver – shillings and half-crowns. The captains wander the earth with silver to bestow on beggars. For some reason I thought it best not to look too long at the drawing.

Nothing could go wrong. I'd never used a naked razor before but no one would have guessed, as it moved with my hand to peel away the lather and hair and leave a sand-blasted smoothness. A glance at myself in the full length mirror was sufficient to tell me that I had never felt better; I looked it. Although still out of touch with the building I was whole.

I tried on the dressing-gown of pure silk and peacock blue with all the little feathered eyes, but decided it might be vulgar to be naked underneath. Snorry once met a woman in the garden of a tropical hotel and found her naked below her wrap. The affront took away his anticipation of pleasure as well as his breath. I put on my trousers and shirt, leaving the neck of the shirt open, then went into the office and opened the silver cigar box on the desk. A thin little tune came out before the long thin cigar. I remembered the words from Sunday mornings when I was a boy; my father still young, frying bacon and toasting bread for breakfast and singing as he worked:

> 'There they go, full of joy,
> Happy girl, lucky boy,
> And here am I . . . broken hearted.'

I lit the cigar and stretched myself out in his chair. The chairs were of a suitably austere design with red and gold seats but the divan against the facing wall was long and wide and blue. It occurred to me that Francis had a passion for blue. The Rumanian pictures were predominantly blue. I could not make a smoke-ring rise from my cigar but stopped myself from grieving. A hard-fought defeat is the next best thing to a bitterly-won victory.

The divan looked tempting. I stood up to see it better, and found my eye being led into the carpet. The carpet depicted a copper beech copse and a maze of paths; somewhere was a chestnut fox. But I could not find him. Was his tail up, all cheeky? Or was he lying in hiding with his mean little heart beating away at the ribs of its cage? My hand brushed the cigar box and the song was singing in my mind as I picked up the telephone. Like my father, Francis must have lived that song.

Her voice was low and cautious. 'Switchboard?' Wasn't there also a touch of fear or disgust as she breathed out the simple statement of location?

'I'm speaking from the Chairman's office. How's the darling of the switchboard?'

'Oh it's you, Sam – you fool!' There was relief in her voice.

'I'm looking over the throne of power – are you busy?'

'I'm on duty. Otherwise nothing seems to have happened since the last time I saw you.'

'Why not shut up shop and come up and see me?'

'Up there! Give me one good reason . . .' Her voice trailed away. Again there'd been that unlikely note of disgust or resentment. Was I really so much out of favour?

'I made a mistake,' I told her.

'You mean she turned you down?'

'It was mutual.'

'So you bounced back to me?' That was better! There was womanly bad temper in her voice now, not the thing which had been there before.

'Is that a fault?' I asked her, but the line had gone dead. I put it on the cradle and rocked it. There was no response. There was no vital juice. But I knew in my bones there was no chance at all of defeat. The whole world was under my feet. She had to come to me. That was the bargain. I padded out of the office and tried Miss Plumb's telephone. Absolutely no response. I pressed on, as my father is fond of saying, and lifted Crumple's telephone. The thing crackled and in my mind his thin, incisive voice whispered urgently that I too would have to fall like a star from heaven. I sneered mentally. The ghost-voice stopped and after a while Esther came through. 'I'm not coming, Sam,' she said.

'Not if I kneel at your feet?'

'Aren't you tired of kneeling?' she said. I had to wince. 'You've been hurt, I suppose. But as it happens, I love you. You shouldn't use my love, Sam.' I was truly ashamed of myself. There was nothing I could say. 'Are you there – are you hearing me?' she said. There was just a little panic in her voice.

'That's my trouble,' I said. 'I'm hearing you, and I agree.'

'I'm not coming. I'm sorry, Sam.'

'You could leave a line for the computer section,' I said, glancing at my wrist-watch. It was almost ten o'clock.

'You know it's not that,' she said.

I glanced at the view from Crumple's window. It consisted of the same kind of tombstones. 'It's a long way up to the fifteenth floor,' I said conversationally. 'My head's right up in the clouds and I daren't look down. Old Francis likes to say there's no fire-escape from this floor.' I waited for that to sink in. 'You'd better come here at once,' I said flatly. 'Otherwise I'll not be responsible for the consequences.' I heard her breath withdrawn and knew that I had her. Replacing the telephone I padded in my bare feet again, over the road, through the double doors, which I carelessly left open, and into the bathroom. By now I was beginning to be ashamed of my actions. I ran some water and cleansed away the tide-mark of filth. I tidied the place. That sly little fan was still running. I stopped him. I returned to the office and awaited her beside the door. Already I could hear her footsteps. She was running. I collected her. 'Sam – you fool – you made me think –' I kissed the tip of her upturned nose. She closed her eyes. I kissed her lips. 'Let me look at those lovely green eyes,' I said. She opened them. They were still anxious. I decided that the anxiety was good to see. I ran a finger along the edge of that full upper lip. She smiled.

And I smiled as well, as I noticed that she carried both coat and handbag. I took them to the nearest chair then guided her to the divan. I backed away from her. She was wearing something in gold. It went well with the blues in the room. She adjusted her skirt but that didn't hide the long beautiful line from ankle to knee and then on to the flank. Every little movement was a delight. 'I wanted to be reconciled,' I told her, talking desperately. 'I needed. I needed to be reconciled with you now . . .' She looked uneasy and childish in

271

that big beautiful divan. I sat in the boss's chair and told her of the way I had felt the night I'd waited for her to come in, and the way I had felt when at last she had. I told her of waiting for the click of the switch. I told her how frightening it was to be in bed with a wall between you and your love. As calmly as a boss interviewing a secretary I told her all this. I made it flat and unemotional. Cupping my face in hands and leaning on the desk I finally told her: 'I need you.' I remember she had turned to present her profile. I saw her lips tremble. I got up from the desk and walked over. She tilted her hand and said no, hadn't to be this way again: and again I noted something in her voice that couldn't be in reaction to myself. I was looking clean into those green eyes and also down into the warm comfortable cleft of her breasts. I leaned over and took the breasts as the beginning of my embrace.

After a time she murmured: 'I must make myself ready.' I watched her walk unhesitantly over to the fourth door of that room, the door I had noticed but never really observed until after a sequence of visits, and through the changing room into the bathroom. I heard the shower. But I already knew. A woman in a house of her own, or in a house of which she had once had the freedom. I remembered not only the unfamiliar note in her voice when I had invited her to the Chairman's office, but the odd little silences in past days when I had mentioned him.

Plumbing myself, I discovered that I was empty. The anticipation and well-being of a moment or two ago were as gone as the capacity for disgust or anger. I use the word 'gone' deliberately. I was cleaned out. Paid in my own coin. Somewhere inside me, I felt, there might be some life left. But it seemed a long way down. Something so far out you couldn't even begin to measure its distance in the light-years of the spirit.

I followed her into that place and took off the dressing-gown. A wonder she hadn't winced, seeing me in it. I held it over my arm. All the feathered little eyes winked in a way that hurt.

Make a portrait gallery of all the faces of all the women you have ever loved and feared and you will find that they are sisters. I didn't need to refresh my memory by looking at the sketch inside the cabinet door. I knew the posture. She had given me that look; she and Cathie and the rest. But not the girl in the ruinous bedroom of

272

the empty house.

I'd known, of course, that she'd given herself to another man, and perhaps another before. But it hadn't mattered then. Not when I was taking tribute. I could see the outline of her body through the glass frame and the engraved creatures. She looked as eager as the rest. You don't use love, she had said. Now I knew she was right. I went to the doors and made sure that we would be private. Closing them I said goodbye to Cathie. There was a catch for the door to Miss Plumb's office and a key for the inner door of the two that opened into the passage. Revenge is comic even when it works.

The shower stopped. I went into the place and was holding out the dressing-gown when she emerged. I suppose my smile was plastered on. It went away with the pang of seeing her naked and defenceless, fish-naked and vulnerable. But she must have seen that smile. Turning she began to confess. 'Sam – I must –'

'It can wait,' I said, silently adding for ever and hoping I could hold to it. I led her to the blue divan. She tried to tell me again. I stopped the words with a kiss. Only a moment before I'd dreaded this moment, thinking that instincts had blown with the rest. Now the life was struggling back with the instincts. A trace of care – that kind of love, at last. Knowing all the time that what she had to tell me was nothing to what I had locked away in my own small devious mind. She could tell me. But I could never tell her. So I was on the door-step, gentle, asking, taking no liberties.

So I came to her, and she came to me. The blue divan was our marriage bed and for the first time in my life I came humbly to the door-step of woman and lover. And for the first time since we had had knowledge of each other, she wept. I cut myself free from Cathie as I gave myself to Esther; Cathie – the enemy by whose very nature I might have been led to expose myself. If I had not indeed done that already, without knowing the day, the hour or the minute. Afterwards we made his dressing-gown into a cover as we lay in the dark and listened to our hearts. Leviathan was still. I lay and marvelled. The building had nothing to say to the outrage. The building was, after all, only the image of myself. I was captain; not the cabin boy deep in the belly. Leviathan took a sounding then rose with a rush. I and Leviathan coasted through the spume. It was time to go. I remember hearing the wind circling, searching, the building. It was only the wind. The building was only a building

We dressed in silence like successful conspirators. Then we cleared away every sign of our occupation. Sometimes we glanced at each other, and smiled, then had to look away, like well-behaved children on the edge of mirth. Then we left the room. Finger on switch I took a farewell glance, wondering what it would look like tomorrow. Then by great good luck I caught my fox. His head looked out from under the divan. He looked flat and foolish. He looked a little frightened. But he'd escaped and he looked all that tremendous relief as well, which is something to look. He was not Mr Francis. He was me. I was glad I had seen him.

Hand in hand we walked along the long corridor towards the lift. Just in time I remembered that romance of summary justice – and a world which went on just the same. I left it in the lift, cover upwards, for the lame man who was seeking revenge or justice for himself. We crossed the wide open spaces of the foyer together; instead of the roses there was a great scarlet orchid on the oval table. The man held the swing-door open for us to pass out under the canopy and into the street. He knew us of old. He must have been a romantic at heart. 'Together again, eh?' he said. 'Together indeed,' I replied, still holding her hand. 'You must come to the wedding.' He laughed.

We took a taxi to the bottom of Primrose Hill and walked the rest of the way, pausing for a while on the summit to look back again. The houses of the great merchandisers were sharp against the crystal Blue John of the Sky; the lights of those empty palaces outshone the tiny pulsing of the few scattered stars. It felt good to be going home, even though the home was by way of being an halfway house for both of us. It was good to be going together. Somewhere down there was Cathie who was not content with companionship. I said goodbye in the space of one heartbeat; the ghost inside me pronounced her name, and died.

We are very happy together. We miss each other during the trips abroad which are now an essential part of my work. Last week I flew back from Moscow with Ivan Sergei Koniev, who sat beside me, and Charlie, who sat over the aisle. We had talked ourselves tired as the vision took shape, and I fell into a fitful sleep. I was climbing from the computer room to the penthouse. But not the easy way, by lift. Not even by the curving stairway. I walked along every corridor of that building. It looks razor-tall in the sun outside; inside is a maze. Ahead of me in this maze was a figure. He was always vanishing around a corner and I never succeeded in really seeing him, but the set of his head and shoulders was disturbingly familiar, and I knew his walk.

I lost him in the Prinkstones' apartments and rushed through the solarium to find him – out on to the naked edge of the cliff. Those black devil starlings flew down at my eyes and I awoke with the sound of their wings in my ears. I have not dreamed since.

But I have a vague impression of walking down below in streets which are valleys. I travel the city, looking for a friend whose name I do not know. The streets are long and its buildings are as high as the sky. So high that you must not look up while you ring door-bells which bring no response and knock at doors that stay shut. It is the valley of dry bones. I never look up. Up there makes you and ruins you. It is a barren land where winners lose all as well as losers. Sometimes you doubt your own identity. Something is missing and it is still missing even when you reach out and touch a living woman in the dark. Something is always missing.

Sid Chaplin
THE DAY OF THE SARDINE
Foreword by Melvyn Bragg

'You'll roam afore you'll settle down.
You'll see strange sights, ports and people.
Might even end up on the moon . . .
you're no sardine.'

In *The Day of the Sardine,* Sid Chaplin explores the 'shadows
between boyhood and manhood'. His young hero, Arthur
Haggerston, tells his own story of growing up the tough way in a
northern industrial city surrounded by its shipyards, foundries
and factories.
Restlessly, Arthur goes through a rite of passage that includes gang
violence, a murder, the love of a lonely older woman and a romance
with a girl eager for his salvation. Throughout his troubles and
searches, he remains determined not to accept the values and
expectations of others, not to be another sardine blindly following
the shoal, but to navigate himself.

£4.95
available from
SCORPION PUBLISHING LTD

Sid Chaplin
THE WATCHERS AND THE WATCHED
Foreword by Stan Barstow

'With every word and movement of the terrible sacrament he was closing the door on the old wild ways. In swift seconds he was being imprisoned for life.'

Tiger Mason sees marriage as the end, but he discovers that it is also a beginning. Old ties are not cut, but are adjusted. Tiger finds himself thrust into a completely new intimacy with a woman; sharing a bed with a wife is different from loving in the woods. His childhood friends too enter into their own worlds of love and sex. Sid Chaplin's thoughtful novel traces the painful struggle within his independent masculine hero from an uncomplicated, popular youth to an acceptance of responsibility not just as husband and future father, but to himself and what he believes in. As Tiger adapts to his new role he is confronted by the realities of life and death. He begins to see himself, his friends and the tough, close community in which he was raised, with new, watchful eyes.

£4.95
available from
SCORPION PUBLISHING LTD